D0965210

Dear Reader,

I'm delighted to be a part of Silhou[...] celebration. The Silhouette Desire line has always been a particular favorite of mine; whether I was curling up with a book as a reader or laboring over one as a writer, I enjoyed the sexual tension and fast-paced stories.

So you can imagine my excitement when I was told that my first three Desire novels would be brought out in a 3-in-1 volume entitled *Maximum Marriage: Men on a Mission*, as part of the celebration.

Each book I have written has a permanent place in my heart. These three are no exception.

Hunter's Prey was my first Desire title. At the time I wrote it, I'd been away from Texas for many years and I missed it—the rugged men, the wide-open spaces and most important, I missed the sense of family. This book became a long love letter to my home state.

Bachelor Father reflected a different part of my life. I knew what it was like to raise a child on my own. In that respect, my second Desire novel was autobiographical and came from the deep feelings engendered by motherhood that I seldom expressed to those around me.

Hawk's Flight was sheer fantasy from start to finish. I created a hero I could love, then hunted for a heroine who would turn his world upside down.

My wish for you is that you might find a little of yourself in each of my books—your love for your homeland, your sense of yourself as a parent and your willingness to lose yourself in a fantasy that might actually come true.

Watch for my new Desire title, *Marriage Prey*, in November. I decided to have the daughter of Jason McAlister and Kristi Cole (from *Hunter's Prey*) unexpectedly meet the son of Tony Antonelli and Susan McCormick (from *Bachelor Father*).

In the meantime, I hope you enjoy getting to know the people in *Maximum Marriage: Men on a Mission* and that they become as real to you as they are to me.

Let the celebration begin.

Annette Broadrick

THE BOOKWORM
230-K E BETTERAVIA RD
SANTA MARIA CA 93455
BUY - SELL - TRADE

PRAISE FOR

ANNETTE BROADRICK

"I can think of a dozen adjectives that would equally apply to Annette Broadrick's books, such as exciting, passionate, and irresistible. But I can wrap it all up by saying simply that her books make you feel good when you read them. She's one terrific writer."

—International bestselling author Diana Palmer

"Whether she's writing romantic suspense or pure romance, Annette Broadrick always tells a great story! I love her tough but tender heroes!"

—Bestselling author Ann Major

"I *love* Annette Broadrick's books! They make me laugh and cry and then laugh again as she takes me on a whirlwind ride toward a wonderfully happy ending."

—Award-winning author Paula Detmer Riggs

"Annette Broadrick's glorious love stories always sparkle with irresistible joy and grace."

—Melinda Helfer, *Romantic Times Magazine*

"Any time I get an Annette Broadrick romance, I drop everything to read it. I always hate for her stories to end."

—Award-winning author Lauraine Snelling

ANNETTE BROADRICK

Maximum Marriage:

Men on a Mission

Silhouette Books

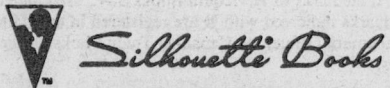

Published by Silhouette Books
America's Publisher of Contemporary Romance

If you purchased this book without a cover you should be aware that this book is stolen property. It was reported as "unsold and destroyed" to the publisher, and neither the author nor the publisher has received any payment for this "stripped book."

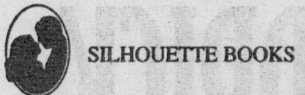

SILHOUETTE BOOKS

MAXIMUM MARRIAGE: MEN ON A MISSION

Copyright © 2000 by Harlequin Books S.A.

ISBN 0-373-48411-9

The publisher acknowledges the copyright holder of the individual works as follows:

HUNTER'S PREY
Copyright © 1985 by Annette Broadrick

BACHELOR FATHER
Copyright © 1985 by Annette Broadrick

HAWK'S FLIGHT
Copyright © 1985 by Annette Broadrick

All rights reserved. Except for use in any review, the reproduction or utilization of this work in whole or in part in any form by any electronic, mechanical or other means, now known or hereafter invented, including xerography, photocopying and recording, or in any information storage or retrieval system, is forbidden without the written permission of the editorial office, Silhouette Books, 300 East 42nd Street, New York, NY 10017 U.S.A.

All characters in this book have no existence outside the imagination of the author and have no relation whatsoever to anyone bearing the same name or names. They are not even distantly inspired by any individual known or unknown to the author, and all incidents are pure invention.

This edition published by arrangement with Harlequin Books S.A.

® and TM are trademarks of Harlequin Books S.A., used under license. Trademarks indicated with ® are registered in the United States Patent and Trademark Office, the Canadian Trade Marks Office and in other countries.

Visit Silhouette at www.eHarlequin.com

Printed in U.S.A.

CONTENTS

In celebration of our 20th anniversary, Silhouette Books proudly presents bestselling author

ANNETTE BROADRICK's

first three Silhouette Desire novels HUNTER'S PREY, BACHELOR FATHER and HAWK'S FLIGHT in one unforgettable collection:

Maximum Marriage:
Men on a Mission

Jason McAlister...Tony Antonelli...Hawk Cameron

Three charismatic, smolderingly sexy men who exude a power and passion guaranteed to intoxicate a woman's senses. Now these potently masculine heroes are on a collision course with temptation—and true love. Although they are steering clear of commitment, there's no denying that they are the maximum marriage catch! For fierce desire and irresistible romance unfold as these men on a mission boldly encounter the tantalizing beauties whom they are destined to have and to hold...forever!

And in November 2000, watch for MARRIAGE PREY in Silhouette Desire. In this captivating love story, Annette Broadrick brings together the families from HUNTER'S PREY and BACHELOR FATHER!

HUNTER'S PREY

To Pinkie,
with love...

Chapter 1

She saw him cross the hotel lobby, his boots clicking a staccato rhythm on the marble surface. From her vantage point near the dining area, she watched when he paused at the cavelike entrance to the lounge, removing his Stetson as he surveyed the room. Only after he had disappeared into the gloom did Kristine Cole discover she'd forgotten to breathe when she saw him. Jason McAlister had always had that effect on her.

His appearance miles from where she expected to find him temporarily banished all thoughts of food from her mind. With a start Kristi registered the weary patience on the hostess's face as she waited to show her to her table. Kristi smiled her apology and followed the elegant woman to a small table tucked between potted palms.

The hotel was Holiday Inn's contribution toward the growth of the small southwest Texas town near where Kristi grew up. It was built at the cloverleaf of the interstate highway that skirted Cielo, and neither the highway nor the hotel had been there when she left Texas five years before.

Jason McAlister was the reason she had not returned sooner. He was also responsible for her being there now.

What should I do? she wondered, chewing on her bottom lip. She'd driven her Triumph TR7 from New York, taking her time, enjoying the freedom of being on her own after years of restrictive schedules and demanding deadlines. She had stopped at the hotel on impulse. A night's rest before driving the final fifty miles to her brother's ranch had seemed like a good idea earlier in the evening. Now she wasn't so sure.

Of course, Kristi intended to contact Jason—she just hadn't counted on seeing him quite so soon. Why should she be nervous? She'd mingled with the rich and royalty, politicians and playboys. Why should one particular rancher in an obscure part of Texas cause butterflies to flutter up under her ribs? Why indeed?

What should I do? she asked herself once more. The dignified waiter standing with pencil poised implied that she could order her dinner as far as he was concerned.

Good idea. Without glancing at the menu, she said, "The dinner salad, please." His blank face almost registered an expression of surprise as his eyes scanned her slender figure.

Of course I'm thin, she thought with irritation. *That's because models go around half-starved most of the time.* She gave him her dazzling smile as an apology for her waspish thoughts.

"Will there be anything else?"

"A glass of chablis, please." *Hang the calories, I need a drink.* Her insides continued to quiver like jelly in an earthquake. Of course she didn't *have* to face him tonight. She could stick with her original plan to visit with Kyle and Francine for a few days, then call Jason and arrange to meet with him.

The waiter returned with her drink and it was only when she caught sight of her trembling hand as she reached for the glass that Kristi faced how unnerved she was. Lifting the glass to her lips, she managed to spill a drop or two on her muted green ultrasuede dress. She ineffectually dabbed at the spots with her napkin, her appearance the least of her concerns at that moment.

No one in her family could explain the genetic accident that gave Kristi her striking good looks. High cheekbones created mysterious shadows, and slanted eyes tantalized with the glitter of emeralds. Rioting waves of fiery hair held a shimmering life all their own, and when photographers discovered how her translucent skin glowed under their powerful lamps, her career was off and running. Her face now gazed from countless magazine covers in the States as well as in western Europe.

Kristi Cole was a celebrity but not in southwest Texas.

Would Jason find her changed? She bore scant resemblance to the teenaged tomboy who preferred Levi's and horses to satin and symphonies. However, inside she was the same person who'd spent her life in love with Jason McAlister.

Jason hadn't changed—physically at least. He still reminded Kristi of the mountain lion she once saw years ago while exploring the sand caves along the Rio Grande with Jason and her brother, Kyle. He moved with the same lazy grace, muscles rippling below the skin. Even his coloring was similar, his tawny hair sunstreaked a lighter shade than his skin, which was bronzed by the sun.

Kristi finished her salad. There was no reason to delay their meeting. He'd ignored her letters and refused to discuss the details of the divorce with her attorney, so she'd returned to Texas to face him.

Five years was long enough to overcome her feelings of loss and inadequacy. She had failed as his wife, but had become a success in her chosen career. She'd come to terms with the past, but needed to cut all ties to be entirely free.

With her chin slightly elevated, Kristi crossed the lobby to the darkened lounge. Following Jason's earlier example, she paused in the archway, her eyes adjusting to the lack of light. Candle-filled globes formed oases of light in the darkened room, silhouetting the occupants of the lounge. Cigarette smoke lent a mauve haze to the atmosphere. Near the door well-cushioned barstools held a half dozen men, and every man's eyes focused on Kristi as she stood there searching the room.

She was used to receiving stares and ignored them. The bartender paused in the midst of drying a glass and stared as though trying to place her. One of the men on the closest barstool smiled as Kristi hovered in the doorway.

"Lose somebody, honey? Or are you just looking for some company?"

A flash of green fire took in the man sitting there, his flabby stomach hanging over a polished silver belt buckle, his blue-and-white checked western shirt straining at the snaps. Her face composed, Kristi gazed at him without speaking until his smile faltered and his eyes dropped. She returned her attention to the room and took a graceful step forward. A slight turn of a tawny head in the back of the lounge caught the candlelight and glinted gold.

He was still there—alone.

Jason sipped his bourbon and water and watched the tall, slender woman make her cautious way through the crowded room. His jaw tightened. One of the soft lights briefly highlighted the red of the woman's hair and a familiar pain throbbed inside him. Why did every tall, redheaded woman he saw remind him of Kristi?

As she moved closer he studied her with cynical regard. Someone out looking for companionship. He certainly wasn't in the mood to provide it. When Alvarez called to arrange a meeting Jason had almost put him off, despite his urgent need to get the information Alvarez supposedly had for him. The call from Kristi's lawyer had been all he wanted to handle in one day.

How many times did he have to say it? He didn't want a divorce. He'd finally learned to live with the knowledge that Kristi preferred a career in New York to living with him. He'd finally given up hoping that she'd eventually return home. He shook his head and took another sip. He'd learned to live with the constant loneliness and the pain of knowing he'd been unable to offer what she wanted from life. There was no way he'd ever be able to give her up completely. She was too much a part of him.

Kristi moved toward Jason. As she approached him, Jason raised his head, glancing at her from below heavy brows. His topaz eyes took in the length of her and, without meeting her eyes for more than an instant, his gaze dropped to his glass once again.

Kristi paused, shocked at the icy glare from Jason. He didn't recognize her. Even though she was aware of the drastic changes in her appearance, his cold expression had caught her off guard. She sank into an empty leather bench seat at the table next to his, her knees refusing to support her any longer.

Her mind whirled with bewilderment. After she had

steeled herself for a confrontation, he hadn't even recognized her! She peered around the dimly lit room. Perhaps she might have had the same problem if she had not seen him earlier in the clear light of the lobby.

Now she faced the dilemma of whether to tell him who she was or to pretend she didn't know him. There was no reason for her not to stay and have a drink—she didn't have to speak to him. Tension eased from her at the thought.

From beneath thick lashes her eyes surreptitiously sought him as he sat there studying his drink, a bottle of bourbon near his elbow. Here was one change in his lifestyle—the Jason she remembered had an occasional cold beer on a hot day, no more.

A blond waitress paused at her table, her shapely legs revealed in fishnet stockings under a micro-mini black skirt. "What would you like?" She gave Kristi a haughty stare.

"A glass of chablis, please."

The woman flounced away. Kristi knew her thoughts as though they'd been spoken out loud. No one from around here drank wine— that was for Yankees and foreigners.

Kristi glanced up and caught Jason staring at her. Her heart leaped and began to pound in her chest like a herd of galloping horses.

Her voice had caught his attention. He hadn't talked to Kristi in years. He'd refused to torture himself by calling and listening to her soft voice. The woman at the next table had the same husky contralto, but there was no trace of a southern speech pattern in her words. Her voice was crisp and controlled. The flickering light cast shadows over her as his eyes settled on her hands, which were resting lightly on the table, the frosted pink polish on her nails glinting in the candlelight.

Kristi could feel Jason's gaze as he studied her. Her hard-earned poise helped her to stay composed. She refused to glance at him, determined to have her drink and leave.

"Would you like to dance, little lady?"

Kristi glanced up, startled. Silver belt buckle from the bar had decided to make his move. She gave him a polite smile. "No, thank you."

"Aw, c'mon, lady. No reason not to be friendly, is there?" His Coors courage seemed to convince him she could only find him irresistible.

"The lady said no, Herman. Just leave it." The sound of Jason's voice shot through Kristi as though she had touched a hot-wired fence. He stood there by her table, facing hefty Herman with a level stare.

"I didn't mean nothin', Mac, you know that," Herman muttered.

"Sure, I know that, but this young lady doesn't know you as well as I do." He watched Herman as he made his embarrassed way back to the bar, to the catcalls and comments of his drinking buddies.

Kristi gave Jason a tentative smile. "Thank you."

He stood there, an intent expression on his face. "At the risk of sounding like another Herman, would you mind if I joined you? I never did care to drink alone."

His lazy smile caused a problem with her breathing. *I can't sit here with him and not tell him who I am,* she thought with dismay.

Bemused, she nodded her head. He reached back and gathered his bottle, glass and money from the other table, then slid onto the bench across from her. Her uncertain gaze fell on his hands. A shiver ran through her at the memories evoked by those sensitive fingers. She noticed the wedding band with a pang.

Kristi was intrigued with the idea of meeting Jason as an equal after all these years. The ten-year difference in their ages had caused the eighteen-year-old Kristi to feel at a disadvantage during most of the months they'd lived together after their marriage. She took a deep breath and forced herself to relax. How long dared she continue the pretense?

"You don't live around here," he said before she had a chance to speak. The comment was more of a statement than a question.

"That's right. I'm just visiting."

Her voice kept striking chords within him. How could two women have the same voice, or similar enough to cause such a gut-wrenching reaction within him?

The waitress brought her drink but, before Kristi could remove the money from her clutch purse, Jason pulled a couple of singles from the stack of bills lying beside his glass. He shoved them toward the waitress.

Kristi dipped her head in mute thanks, raised her glass in a brief toast, then sipped from the tulip-shaped goblet.

"Do you come here often?" she asked, her head slightly tilted.

He looked at her with surprise. "Once in a while. Why?"

She smiled as she tipped her head toward the blond waitress who watched them covertly as she cleared a table nearby. "The barmaid has a rather possessive air where you're concerned."

He shrugged his unconcern. "Most everybody around here knows everybody else." He picked up his glass, drank half of its contents, then set it down.

Kristi studied the face before her. Sunlines fanned from his eyes, and the curves around his mouth had deepened. Strands of streaked gold fell across his forehead and teased Kristi's memory. She wanted to touch his face, to brush the hair from his forehead.

"Where're you from?" he asked, his tone polite. His eyes glowed in the soft light, the look of interest ensnaring Kristi as effectively as a rope. She wondered suspiciously if he were playing some kind of game with her.

"New York." Surely he'd respond to that information. How many tall redheads from New York showed up in Cielo these days, anyway?

In the same polite tone, he inquired, "What're you doing out here?"

Now was the time to tell him. I'm here to see you,

Jason. We need to agree to the terms that will dissolve our relationship. Instead, she heard herself say, "I'm on vacation, so I thought I'd come out this way." *The truth as far as it went,* she thought, dismayed by her cowardice.

"Are you trying to interview the natives or something? See how we survive in our primitive conditions out West?" His grin took away any sting in the words. He finished the contents of his glass and poured another, then reached into his pocket for a cigarette. He offered her one, and when she gave him a quick shake of her head, bent his head to the burning match and touched his cigarette to the flame.

The blonde materialized by his shoulder. "Jayson," she drawled, making his name into two words. "There's a Mr. Alvarez on the phone. Says he wants to talk to you."

Jason looked startled at the interruption, glancing at his watch in surprise. Excusing himself, he moved away from the table with catlike strides.

She remembered once accusing him of having Indian blood because of the silent way he moved. He'd laughed and ruffled her carrot-colored curls and admitted that most families who had spent years on the western plains of Texas had some Indian blood. The families never discussed it and certain strong features were ignored. Excited at the thought of such a romantic notion, Kristi had raced home to ask Kyle if they could have Indian blood as well. She still remembered his laughing at her gullibility.

Jason would not be amused when he discovered who she was. Then again, what if he already knew but was trying to figure out what she was hoping to accomplish by pretending not to know him? She herself wasn't sure.

If only she weren't so intrigued by the lazy masculinity that emanated from him. Her pulse rate hadn't slowed since she walked into the lounge. At this rate, Jason's presence would be as good for her as an hour of aerobics.

Kristi felt his anger when Jason returned to the table. He signaled the blonde to bring Kristi another drink, then poured himself one from the bottle, adding water.

"Is something wrong?" She'd always respected Jason's ability to control his emotions, almost envying him the skill at times, but it was obvious he was battling for that control at the moment.

"The man I was supposed to meet tonight can't make it. He left it a little late telling me." His drawl sounded more pronounced. He moved his hand until it rested against hers. "Care to dance?"

His question surprised her. She'd just about decided to leave. Kristi couldn't handle watching Jason drink so much.

He saw her surprise at his question. Actually, it surprised him as well. He wasn't interested in the woman except for her haunting resemblance to Kristi. Funny this woman should be from New York, too. Not that it mattered, he'd never see her again after tonight. So what was wrong with a dance? He'd like to forget Kristi, forget Alvarez, and forget the feeling of helplessness that threatened to engulf him.

Kristi rose from the table and started toward the center of the room. Two other couples swayed on the postage-stamp dance floor to the slow melody of Kenny Rogers's latest hit. She turned, ready for him to take her hand. Instead, Jason pulled her close against him, wrapping both arms around her. Kristi had no option but to place her hands on his shoulders. She felt the heavy muscles there flex as her hands slid around his neck. The years melted away as she caught the scent of his after-shave. The spicy fragrance teased at her as it evoked vivid memories. This man had always had a shattering effect on her.

When she'd left him, Kristi had buried her emotions deep inside herself. As time passed she eventually heard the name given to her by disgruntled males: the ice princess. It never bothered her because it was true. She didn't want to be touched. Yet as soon as Jason's arms slipped around her the ice began to melt. She relaxed against him.

The woman in his arms was too thin for his taste. His hands could almost reach around her tiny waist. When was the last time he'd danced? He couldn't remember, exactly. He'd taken Kristi somewhere.... Jason relaxed as the memories flowed around him. She'd always felt so good in his arms, whether they'd been on the dance floor or in bed. It was unfortunate this woman was so near the same height. He didn't need any more reminders. Not tonight.

Jason was light on his feet. He moved to the slow rhythm of the love song, his hands unconsciously caressing Kristi's back. They stayed on the dance floor until the musicians took a break, then returned to their table in silence.

Kristi took a large swallow of wine, almost choking. Her head spun from the intoxication of Jason's body pressed so intimately against her. Is this how he spends his time these days, she wondered? The sharp pain that shot through her at the thought shocked her with its intensity. Why should it matter to her? She'd made her decision months ago. They had no future together. She'd always wondered why he hadn't ended their marriage—he'd never made a secret of his dream of a large family. The familiar nagging sense of inadequacy niggled at the edges of her mind.

She'd had enough. Jason didn't recognize her or he would have said something by now. She looked at the bottle sitting there and shook her head slightly. Her memories had betrayed her. This man? This man wasn't the one she'd married. Her Jason would never have gone to a bar to drink and flirt with anyone who came in.

Kristi gave him a polite smile. "Thank you for the dance—and the drinks." She slid along the bench seat. "I think I'll go on to bed now—it's been a long day." As she started to get up, Jason pulled a cigarette from his mouth without lighting it, his eyes flicking over her with amused contempt.

"Is that an invitation?"

It took a moment for the sarcasm and sudden change of mood to penetrate Kristi's consciousness. She flushed a fiery red at the insult.

"I beg your pardon?" If the glittering green ice from her eyes hadn't warned him, the glacial tone of voice should have told Jason he'd made a serious mistake. He missed both.

"Maybe they do things differently in New York, but here in Texas a man likes to do his own running."

Grabbing her purse, Kristi rose with a smoothness that belied the tumult of rage threatening to overcome her. In a low, cool voice she let him have it. "Why, you supercilious, egotistical, drunken excuse for a west Texas cowboy, if I were looking for a companion, I could do a lot better than you!"

She spun on her heel and left through the outside door of the lounge. As soon as the door whispered closed behind her, Kristi stood on the walkway and took deep breaths, consciously calming her temper, glad to be away from the smoke and the smell of stale liquor.

Oh, how she wished she hadn't seen him tonight! She would have preferred her memories to the reality. The man she'd left just now bore little resemblance to the Jason McAlister she'd loved and married six years ago. Her decision to divorce him never seemed more right to her.

She followed the sidewalk as it wound its way through a miniature garden on the grounds of the large complex. Her fire-engine red Triumph sat in front of her motel door. She paused, fumbling in her bag for the room key, then inserted it into the door.

She turned the knob and started to push when a large hand reached past her and shoved on the door. Another hand gently propelled her through the opening.

Kristi gasped and spun around, then almost reeled with surprise. Jason stood there waiting for her reaction. Once again his silent approach had not warned her of his presence. Only now she was no longer impressed with his talent.

Her jaw hardened. "Get out of my room."

He glanced around, taking in the open suitcase at the end of the king-size bed, the few feminine items lying on the dresser and the sheer nightgown casually tossed across the pillows. The bright little car he'd seen outside was in keeping with her image of casual elegance.

Jason moved to the door, shut it, then turned to face her. He shoved his hat off his forehead and leaned lazily against the door. Kristi had left only the dressing area light on when she'd gone for dinner, and they stood in dusky shadows as they faced each other.

Jason pulled himself away from the door and approached Kristi, who stood by the bed. "I owe you an apology. I shouldn't have jumped to conclusions back there.'' He stopped when he came within arm's length of her.

Kristi looked him over from the tip of his boots to the top of his Stetson, then flicked her gaze to meet his. With something close to contempt, she said, ''You made a mistake, cowboy, but so did I. It was just a case of mistaken identity.'' She kept her chin high and her gaze steady.

He placed both of his hands around the curve of her neck in a gentle, caressing movement. His thumbs rested on each side of her jaw and massaged the area as he studied her face. ''Funny you should say that, because I've been feeling the same thing about you, Miss New York. What's your name?''

She knew he must feel the pounding of her pulse beneath his hands, a pounding that had started as soon as he touched her. Her breath fluttered in her throat like a trapped bird trying to fly free. She was surprised to hear her voice sound so unaffected. ''It doesn't matter.''

All she wanted was for him to get out of her room. She would deal with the legal termination of their relationship tomorrow. Tonight she had a dream to bury.

''You're right,'' he muttered, ''it doesn't matter.'' His mouth swooped down on hers. One arm moved behind her, effectively imprisoning her against his long, lean body, hard from years of physical labor. With his other hand he raked through her hair, which was pinned up, causing it to tumble down her back in a cascade of fiery flame.

His mouth surprised her with its soft, searching movement on hers. She'd expected a brutal assault that didn't materialize. Instead, his mouth caressed hers until his tongue began to outline the shape of her lips, coaxing its way through the barrier of her lips and teeth.

Damn him! How could he continue to have such an effect on her? She had thought she was over him; obviously, she wasn't. Her feelings for him were confused—but intense. She loved him—she hated him—she longed for him—she had to be free of him. But oh! It felt good to be in his arms again. Was it wrong to want to love him and hold him one last time? All of the locked-up feelings Kristi had carried for this man for so long were released.

With a groan she responded to his kiss. She wrapped her arms around his neck and ran her fingers through the golden strands that had tempted her earlier in the evening. She felt more than heard the muffled moan he made as her response registered.

Kristi felt the edge of the bed against the back of her legs. As she fell over, Jason followed her down without loosening his grip. His mouth continued to explore hers and his hands moved gently over her shoulders as though memorizing her. He found the hidden zipper at the V-neck of her dress and slid it down a few inches. His thigh moved between hers, pushing her skirt into folds around her hips, and his body pressed against her. He emphasized his possession as his mouth slipped from hers to explore her neck and the hollow between her breasts. He moved the zipper down until the lace from her bikini briefs was her only protection from his exploring hands.

A tremor shook her when his mouth eased over her breast. She reached for the buttons on his shirt and began unsnapping them, then tugged the shirt from his chest so she could feel his bare skin against hers.

He shuddered as he felt her warm flesh caress his. Her dress was in the way, and Jason slid it from her while he explored her body with work-roughened hands. She had never forgotten the touch of those hands as they taught her the intricacies of lovemaking.

He moved with controlled patience and subdued passion over her body, loving her with his mouth and hands. Her bones turned to liquid as his hand rubbed against her inner thigh, paused, then began a coaxing rhythm that caused her to quiver in response.

She was stunned when he moved away from her, slipping from the bed. He couldn't leave now! Her body ached for his possession. Then she realized that he was pulling off his boots and sliding out of the snug Levi's that clung to his muscular thighs. When he moved back to cover her with his body, she arched into him, wanting to feel his strength once more.

Kristi trembled as Jason's kisses slid down her breasts, then traced an invisible line to the top of her thighs. Only this man had the power to reduce her to a quivering mass of sensations. She needed him desperately. How had she ever survived without his tender strength and fierce passion?

The tension built within her and she moved her hips in an unconscious invitation as his hands readied her. He eased himself into her with a control that harnessed the powerful need building inside of him. She wrapped her legs around his hips in a possessive hold. For the moment, he belonged to her. For the moment, that was enough.

The stamina and endurance built up over years of long, grueling physical activity enabled Jason to take them both to the far reaches of the universe. Kristi felt the sudden release of her own body as it continued to cling to him, but he never slackened his rhythm and the driving force of his possession of her.

Time lost all meaning as they moved together in the choreographed moves of lovemaking, their bodies glistening with moisture. Jason's pace became more urgent and she heard his anguished cry as she felt him explode within her. At the same time her body responded once more with rapid contractions that drained him while fulfilling them both. As her arms convulsively squeezed him to her, he collapsed and his weight descended, holding her prisoner. ''Oh, Jase,'' she murmured, as he slid to one side, his arms and legs clamped securely around her.

Kristi floated in the afterglow of their tempestuous coming together and descended only when she realized what he'd said in his hoarse cry. Her name had echoed on his lips. Had it been a game with him and he'd known who she was all along? She pulled away and discovered that he was sound asleep. The combination of the whiskey and the exertion of their lovemaking had knocked him out. Was he even aware of having spoken her name? She had no way of knowing.

As Kristi contemplated the sleeping face next to her, she wasn't at all sure she hadn't received a metaphorical slap in the face. However, even in his sleep he hadn't let her go. She tried to shift away from him and his arms tightened. She relaxed. It was obvious she wasn't going anywhere. After traveling many miles and several years, Kristi was right back where she started—in Jason's arms.

A brilliant shaft of sunlight pierced Jason's heavy sleep. He woke with a start and looked around the empty room in bewilderment. What was he doing here? He peered at his watch and flinched at the time. It was after nine o'clock. He groaned.

He felt as though a hundred miniature soldiers were marching in his head, each of their tiny steps sending shooting pains through his brain, while his mouth felt as though someone had stuffed it full of dirty socks.

He had really done it this time. He should have been at the ranch hours ago with the day's assignments for the hands. Instead he had a thirty-five-mile drive to look forward to with the tiny soldiers marching on.

He knew better than to drink hard liquor. After a couple of drinks he saw Kristi everywhere. Getting that call from her lawyer hadn't helped, either, but he refused to excuse his behavior. After all these years without Kristi, he'd finally succumbed to the charms of another woman. She had had the same coloring and was the same height as Kristi, but otherwise she had borne little resemblance to the fun-loving, impetuous girl he remembered. Then again, maybe that Kristi existed only in his memories. He'd seen no sign of her in the cold letters requesting his cooperation in gaining her freedom which he'd been receiving from her these past several months.

There was no way in hell he was going to let her divorce him. If she thought differently, she was going to find herself with a Texas-size fight on her hands.

What had possessed him to follow the woman out of the bar? He vaguely remembered their conversation but couldn't recall what he'd said to make her jump up and leave. He must have followed her to apologize, but somehow he couldn't recollect why. Or how he came to spend the night. He had flashes of memory of her sleek body as he'd pulled her clothes away from her. She certainly hadn't put up a struggle!

Damn it! He wasn't some adolescent kid to be lured into a stranger's bed. He knew better than that! Jason pulled himself up and sat on the side of the bed, his painful head buried in his hands. "Serves you right, you stupid bastard," he muttered in disgust.

His pants lay in a crumpled heap beside the bed.

Jason leaned over very carefully in case his head should decide to tumble off his shoulders. He managed to stand and pull the pants up to his narrow waist and fasten them.

Within five minutes he let himself out the door, his hat in his hand, his wrinkled shirt pulled hastily over his broad chest. As he turned he noticed that the little sports car was gone. That suited him just fine. He sincerely hoped he'd never see the lady again. As a matter of fact, he couldn't really remember what she looked like. He hoped she'd have the same problem.

His pickup sat in the parking lot where he'd left it. With economical movements he got in and drove off. He planned to stop at the first restaurant he spotted for some much-needed coffee and aspirin.

Damn Alvarez, anyway! I ordered the bourbon for him. Why didn't he show up? He knows we're fighting time on this deal.

His mind skipped back to a picture of warm flesh glowing in the dim light; saucy breasts with pink tips luring him to touch, to taste, and to enjoy. He shook his head, stirring the tiny soldiers once more, and groaned.

A half hour later he pulled into a truck stop and carefully crawled out of the cab of his pickup, determined to forget the night.

Chapter 2

The warm Texas sun felt good on Kristi's neck and shoulders as she turned onto the farm road leading to her brother's ranch. By the time she'd finished breakfast, it had been warm enough so that she could put the top down on her car.

It was mild for April. Spring was already putting touches of lime green to many of the trees, and wild flowers were beginning to peek through the tall grass alongside the roadway. Winter had been left behind in New York.

The events of the night before continued to flash across her mind as they had done since she first awakened. She kept seeing Jason's eyes glinting in the candlelight, the flash of his smile in the darkened room, and she could feel his hard body pressing against hers.

She was having trouble reconciling her behavior last night with her carefully planned approaches to Jason. Everything had seemed so clear-cut in her mind before she actually saw him. After that…

At least the night had proved one thing to Kristi—her ice princess nickname was not appropriate. Because of her aversion to the groping and pawing most men felt to be their inalienable right, she'd convinced herself that she deserved her reputation. If it hadn't been for her memories of Jason she would have thought herself incapable of passion. After last night she knew better. Unfortunately, her responsiveness seemed to extend only to Jason McAlister.

Jason McAlister. Kristi couldn't remember the first time she saw him. He had always been a part of her life. Her mother once told her that the ten-year-old Jason had been completely captivated by his best friend's baby sister. At eleven, Kyle had had better things to do than waste time on a tiny baby with rosy wisps of hair framing her face, but Jason was fascinated by her. By the time she could walk, Kristi had become a tiny shadow following Kyle and Jason around. She remembered hearing her mother tease Jason that Kristi thought he was another brother, but Jason hadn't seemed to mind. Being an only child was lonely business and he spent more time at the Cole ranch than on his own, which adjoined theirs.

Kyle and Kristi lost their parents when she was nine. Kyle and Francine had only been married a few months when Jeremy and Carla Cole died in a multicar collision near Dallas. Kyle, Francine and Jason had tenderly enfolded the nine-year-old with their love and caring, actively seeking to fill the gap left in her life.

One particular day lingered in her memory of that time....

"I finished all my chores, Kyle! You promised I could go with you and Jase if I finished my chores." A boot-shod foot stamped the loose dirt of the barnyard as Kristi glared up at her brother. "You promised!"

An amused Jason watched the ten-year-old Kristi stand up to her brother. "C'mon, Kyle. A promise is a promise. If you told her she could go, let's get moving." Jase turned and vaulted onto his horse, impatient to be gone.

Kyle glanced back at the house as though hoping Francine would come to his rescue. He had promised and he knew it. "Hurry and get your hat, then, while I saddle Misty for you."

Kristi ran to the house but was back in moments, her hat on her head.

"Glad to be out of school for the summer?" Jason asked Kristi as she moved her horse alongside his.

"You bet. I hate being cooped up inside all day." She laughed up at him. "Wanna race?"

He grinned at her exuberance. "Not today, little one. Kyle and I stayed out late last night. I don't feel up to moving too fast today."

"I know." Kristi's curls bobbed as she nodded.

"Kyle really caught it from Francine over breakfast. She said you're a bad influence on him."

"Kristi, you don't have to repeat all the family secrets," Kyle interrupted with exasperation. Glancing at his friend with a sheepish grin, he added, "Jason already knows what kind of an influence he is."

It took several years for Kristi to appreciate the strain Kyle had been placed under when their parents had died, leaving him total responsibility for the ranch and his sister, as well as a new wife. She came to realize, also, how much Kyle had depended on Jason's encouragement and support.

"Look, Kyle. I see a stray over there," Kristi had yelled as she dug her heels into the sides of her horse. Her sharp eyes had spotted the first of several they found in the course of the day.

Perhaps her memories of that day remained so vivid because it was the last day the three of them spent together for six years. A few weeks later Jason had announced that he was going into the Army. She remembered that Kyle had tried to talk him out of it, pointing out how much he was needed at his own ranch. His dad was in poor health and Jason was his only son.

"You won't get drafted, Jase. You're needed at home...just as I am." Kristi heard the note of pleading in Kyle's voice. Jason, being Jason, refused to change his mind once it was made up. He'd gone off to fight a war in a country no one had heard of ten years before.

Kristi grew up while he was away. At sixteen she looked like a woman, but inside she was still the young girl who worshiped her brother and Jason.

Over the years she had let her hair grow instead of keeping it in short curls. Those curls became long waves cascading to her waist when she wore it down, which was seldom. Instead, Kristi wore braids, despite the ribbing she got from her classmates. Braids were not part of the "in" look, but she didn't care.

She had just finished bathing one evening and was trying to dry her hair when she heard Kyle's shout. "Jason! You ole son of a gun! How the hell are you, man?" She heard the laughing response as she dashed down the long hallway to the kitchen. She barely got a glimpse of the tall, too thin man standing there before she hurled herself into his arms.

"Oh, Jase— You're home! You've finally come home!"

She felt Jason stiffen. He pushed her away with a frown and stared into her face. She looked up at him with bewilderment, and his puzzled expression caused Kyle and Francine to burst out laughing.

"Don't you even recognize Kristi any more, Jase?" Kyle's lopsided grin failed to disguise his pride in his sister's beauty.

"Kristi?" Jason's hands framed her face as he stared down at her in amazement. She swallowed and nodded, embarrassed that he had not recognized her. "My God, Kristi, you've grown up." His tone was one of amazement and more than a little dismay.

She tried to cover her discomfiture. "Well, what did you expect?" She glanced over his face, noting the new lines, the haunted expression. "And you've grown old!" With her hands resting on his shoulders she leaned up and kissed him softly on the lips and murmured, "I still love you, though." She cocked her head, waiting for his reaction with wide-eyed innocence.

He carefully removed her hands from around his neck and stepped back. His face showed his shock at the changes in her. "Yeah, well, don't let your boyfriend hear you say that, love. We can't have him getting jealous of an old man like me." He moved away from her and sat down at the table where Francine had placed coffee and cinnamon rolls.

They sat around the table for hours that night, trying to catch up on six years. Jason had lost his father three years before, and the ranch had been run by the foreman who had been there when Jason was born. "Hell," he told Kyle, "Nate does a better job of running the place than I do, anyway. He and Molly have done a great job of keeping everything going for me."

Kristi noticed that he was reticent when their questions turned to the Orient and the war His stories centered around leaves he'd taken and the amusing incidents that occur when different cultures attempt to communicate. Kristi sat enthralled, watching the expressions on Jason's face, noticing how serious he looked when he wasn't talking, how thin he was.

The first time she rode over to see Jason his face

looked like a thundercloud as he approached her. "What the hell are you doing here?" His greeting certainly wasn't an auspicious start to the renewal of their friendship.

The sorrel she rode came close to matching the color of the braid tossed over her shoulder. She looked down at him from her position in the saddle, wondering why he looked so angry as he stood there, hands on his hips, waiting for her response.

"I came to visit you, Jase. Why? Is something wrong?"

"There certainly is, you little idiot. You have no business coming over here on your own. What's wrong with Kyle, anyway, letting you come over here?"

Kristi drew herself up to her full height in the saddle and in haughty tones replied, "For your information, Jason McAlister, I'm almost seventeen years old. Much too old to need Kyle's permission before I go anywhere."

Jason jerked the battered hat from his head and popped it against his leg. Tawny hair fell across his forehead as he rubbed his forearm across his face, wiping the moisture on the sleeve of his blue chambray workshirt.

"Let me tell you something, young lady. Your brother may find you all grown up and able to look after yourself, but I sure as hell don't and I don't want you riding over here by yourself again, is that clear?"

His eyes flashed as he took in her outraged expression.

He looked dangerous and she decided she didn't want to cross him. Changing tactics, she smiled with beguiling innocence. "I just wanted to come see you, Jase, what's wrong with that?"

He shook his head as he took her reins from her and led her horse to the barn. "All right, Kristi, you win for now. C'mon in the house, Molly's got lunch waiting for me or you'd never have found me." He watched her swing out of the saddle with no expression on his face. However, Kristi was relieved when he threw a companionable arm around her shoulders as they walked across the yard to the large, rambling house.

"Molly, hope you have plenty. We have company for lunch." Jason stopped just inside the doorway, his arm still around Kristi's shoulders. Molly, not much more than five feet tall, spun around from the stove with a smile.

"You know I always make enough to feed a crew of hungry men, Jase." She smiled politely at Kristi, then exclaimed, "Kristi! I almost didn't recognize you. How have you been, child?"

"Just fine, Molly."

Molly reached for another plate and began to arrange the table. Her weight did not keep her from moving lightly on her feet and she turned to Kristi with a hug. "My! Aren't you a beauty!" She glanced up. "Isn't she, Jase?"

His eyes narrowed as the two women waited for his comment. He shrugged with male nonchalance and moved toward the table. "Not nearly as beautiful as that table loaded with home cooking. Let's eat. I've got a lot of work to do before I can call it a day."

The two women looked at each other, puzzled at his response. Not that Kristi cared what she looked like or what Jason thought of her looks. She just couldn't get used to so many changes in him. It appeared that it would take them some time to regain their closeness.

The following months taught Kristi something about the unpredictability of human behavior. Jason made it clear that she would not be welcome over at his place unless accompanied by Kyle, Francine or both of them, yet he and Kyle seemed to have renewed their friendship and were closer than ever.

Jase had supper with them at least twice a week and it was those nights that convinced Kristi that not only was Jason no longer interested in having her as a friend, he didn't even like her. He would joke and kid with Kyle and Francine, but he maintained an aloof and polite distance from Kristi. She sometimes wondered if he even knew she was at the table.

Kristi remembered the night she had discovered just how aware of her he was. Jason had been home for almost a year and, as usual, had dinner with them. Also, as usual, he had ignored Kristi. After dinner, the men had gone out to the barn to look at a new foal while Kristi helped Francine with the kitchen.

They were unaware that Kristi had prepared the meal they had devoured with gusto. She had made Francine promise not to tell them.

"But why not, I'd like to know? You've turned into a great cook. It seems to me you'd be proud of it!"

"I just don't want them to know," Kristi insisted stubbornly.

"Have you ever given a thought to how I feel about accepting all their compliments?" Francine asked. "It's the same as telling a lie and you know it."

"No, it isn't. I can enjoy their compliments just as much as if they were being paid to me." Kristi walked over to the door and stared out into the night. "I don't want Jason to think I'm trying to impress him."

Francine's lack of response caused Kristi to glance around. Francine stood at the sink, her expression startled. Her eyes took in the casual picture Kristi made standing in the doorway. Her eyes met Kristi's. "You love him, don't you?" Francine asked softly.

"Haven't I always?"

Francine waved the thought away. "I don't mean your hero worship of him as a kid. I mean, you really are in love with him."

Kristi didn't like the look of concern creeping across Francine's face. She shrugged. "So what? He doesn't even know I exist. But that's all right with me, too! Who needs him, anyway?"

Francine sat down in one of the chairs by the table.

"Oh, Kristi, honey, I'm sorry. I should have realized."

"Oh, for God's sake, Francine. You're acting like I just contracted an incurable disease or something. I'm sure I'll survive." Her chin tilted slightly, daring Francine to disagree with her assessment of her condition.

Francine managed a faint grin. "Oh, I'm not worried about you surviving, honey. I'm more worried about Jase."

Kristi flew across the room and leaned against the table as she glared at Francine. "What's that supposed to mean?"

"Nothing insulting, so you can come off your high horse. I just have a feeling that if you really put your mind to bewitching a person, he wouldn't have a chance, and that includes Jason."

Kristi's frown grew deeper. "I still don't know what you're talking about."

"I'm talking about life, honey, and what you want to make of it." Francine got out of her chair and grabbed a cup from the cabinet. Pouring herself a cup of coffee, she continued, "My mother once told me that I should be very careful about what I wanted out of life, because I might get it." She saw the puzzled look on Kristi's face and smiled. "Like you, I didn't understand what she was talking about." She paused, gazing around the room, her eyes lingering on the colorful calendar hanging on the wall by the table. "Now I do."

She studied the young girl sitting across from her, and sighed. ''I suppose your one dream in life is to marry Jase, raise kids and help him on the ranch. Am I right?''

Kristi felt consumed with embarrassment. Had she been that obvious? Was that why Jason continued to ignore her? How humiliating. She would never be able to face him again! With her head down, Kristi muttered, ''How did you know?''

Francine reached over and took Kristi's hand. ''Because I had the very same dream the first time I laid eyes on Kyle, that's how I know.''

The tension in Kristi's shoulders eased. Maybe Jason didn't know, after all. Maybe it was just something women knew about each other that they didn't tell the menfolks.

''Does it show? My feelings for him, I mean?''

Francine patted her hand. ''No, Kristi, it doesn't show. In fact, I only guessed tonight, although I should have realized why you found his attitude toward you so upsetting.'' She smiled. ''I'm sorry it took me so long.''

Restless, Kristi jumped up and strode to the refrigerator. Opening the door, she took out a pitcher of iced tea and filled a large glass. ''I don't really think I expect him to be in love with me or anything, Francie. It's just that before he went away he at least seemed to like me and not mind when I tagged along.'' She took a large gulp of tea and almost choked. "Now, he acts like he can hardly stand to have me around."

"Have you taken a look at yourself in the mirror lately, Kristi?" Francine's question seemed to have nothing to do with the conversation.

"What does that have to do with anything?"

"Plenty. When Jase went away, you were a child. He returned to find a beautiful woman in the child's place. He hasn't had time to adjust to the change."

"How much time does he need?" Kristi wailed.

"As much time as he wants, honey. You can't rush things like that. In your case, I'm glad."

When she had finished her tea, Kristi rinsed out her glass and set it on the drain. "You seem to be talking in riddles tonight, Francie. I just don't understand you." She returned to her chair and sank into it as though giving up the effort to understand.

"My dream to marry Kyle was fine for me. It was all I could ever hope for. But you, Kristi, have so much more than most people. Don't you understand yet just what your stunning looks can do for you?" She paused when Kristi shook her head in disgust. "I mean it. You have a sexy innocence that advertising people would love to use to sell every product known to man. Would you want to waste that potential as a rancher's wife?"

Kristi shook her head as though weary of the conversation. "Francine, you've been reading too many romances. How would someone like me, living in the back of beyond, manage to interest anybody in my looks? I can't even interest Jase." She stood up and wandered to the door. "I think I'll go find the men—see what they're up to."

As her eyes adjusted to the dark Kristi saw the glow of a cigarette and headed toward it. "Kyle? Did Jase leave?" She stopped by the tall shadow of a man leaning against the wooden fence.

"No, Jase didn't leave," a husky voice answered.

"Oh, hi, Jase." She attempted a casual tone. "Where's Kyle?" She leaned against the fence. The moon was beginning to peek over the eastern ridge of hills, gradually shedding light over the landscape.

"He wanted to talk to some of the men about tomorrow's work. Said he'd be back in a bit." Jason dropped the butt of his cigarette and ground it out with the heel of his boot.

"You never used to smoke, Jase, before you went away." Her voice was hesitant, almost afraid of offending him.

She could hear the smile in his voice. "I know. I do a lot of things now I didn't do back then."

The warm tone reassured her. "Such as?" she asked.

He laughed. The sound sent chills down Kristi's spine. He had to have the sexiest laugh of any man she'd ever known. "They're not for the ears of innocent little girls like you."

His teasing nettled her. "I hardly think five feet eight inches makes me a 'little girl,' Jason. Try again."

His low voice drawled from the darkness. "Then how about an innocent young girl. Is that better?"

He was laughing at her. He never took her seriously and she resented it. She was surprised to hear herself murmur in a low tone, "What makes you think I'm so innocent, Jase?" Thank God it was too dark for him to see her flaming face. Whatever had possessed her to respond in such a manner? Good grief, she'd never even been on a date that wasn't part of a group get-together. At those times she'd shown no interest in experimenting with the opposite sex.

She realized that Jase had taken her remark seriously when he moved toward her and pulled her into his arms. Her gasp was muffled by his lips as they moved over her mouth. His kiss stunned her. It bore no relation to the loving kisses exchanged in her family. Then, suddenly, he lifted his head. "That's what makes me think you're an innocent, Kristi," he mocked. "You don't even know how to kiss."

Kristi's anger overcame her embarrassment, and before Jason could move away from her, she wrapped her arms about his neck, pulling herself up close to him, her small breasts pressed tightly against his hard chest. She could feel the beat of his heart as it marched double time. *Good,* she thought. *He won't have it all his own way.* "Why don't you teach me?" she asked as she touched her lips to his.

She could feel his body tense at her bold action. His firm mouth thinned under her lips and she could feel his arms moving to her wrists to remove them from around his neck. In an act of desperation, she ran her tongue over his lips, stroking them in quick, kittenlike licks. He froze at her audacious move, his mouth parting in surprise. Kristi's lips molded themselves hungrily to his.

Jason's arms came around her in a squeezing grip as he began to respond. She felt, more than heard, his amused chuckle as his kiss replied to her invitation. His mouth searched out all of her tender areas—he nibbled on her lobes, breathing softly in her ear. His lips traced a line over her cheek and returned to her mouth in a possession that made her forget where they were and why.

As her body reacted to his, Kristi began to imitate his moves, her tongue dueling with his, her hands stroking his back as she moved closer to him. She became aware of his arousal and her breath caught in her throat. *His body knows he's holding a woman in his arms, even if his brain refuses to admit it.*

Pleased with the thought, Kristi let her mind go blank and began to enjoy the new sensations taking over her body.

Jase shifted so that his legs carried both their weights as Kristi leaned against him, lost in the passion he'd so unexpectedly stirred within her. She could not get enough of him and wanted to learn all he could teach her. The slamming of the screen door startled them. Jason jerked his head away from her. Kristi stood there with her eyes closed, feeling suddenly cold without his warm lips possessing hers.

He whispered, "I'm sorry, Kristi. I don't know what I was thinking of." She could feel the moonlight touching them, surrounding them with a magic silver cloak. Her eyelids slowly fluttered open and she gazed into his face, which was half in shadow.

"Jase?" she asked in a wondering voice. She had just received her first taste of the sensual pleasure she had pretended to know already. She'd had no idea her body was capable of such feelings.

"You'd better get on into the house, Kristi. I need to get home myself." His voice was cool, as though he was unaffected by what had just happened. Kristi knew better. She was still close enough to hear his uneven breathing. Her hand was resting on his chest and she could feel his heart racing. Why was he trying to deny what had happened between them?

"What's wrong, Jason? Didn't you want to kiss me?" She was puzzled and hurt by his reaction.

"I'm too old to be playing kissing games in the dark, Kristi." His voice sounded harsh. "Why don't you do your experimenting with someone your own age?"

She stepped back as though he had slapped her. She'd made a complete fool of herself, throwing herself at him like that. Pride came to her rescue. "Now why didn't I think of that? Maybe I will." She spun away from him and stomped toward the house.

It was a long time before Kristi slept that night.

Kristi graduated from high school two weeks after her eighteenth birthday. As far as she was concerned, she was through with school forever. She'd enjoyed parts of it—the English, history, speech and art classes, and she'd hated parts of it—the math and science classes and phys. ed. She'd made good grades, but she was glad to have school behind her.

When she tried to talk to Kyle about taking on more responsibility around the ranch, he was vague in his responses, but he allowed her to spend most of her days with him as she had during the past summers.

Francine felt that Kristi could have a career as a model. She decided to have pictures of Kristi made and insisted on driving all the way to Dallas to a professional photographer. She explained to Kristi that she wanted pictures of her at that age, but Kristi thought the whole trip a waste of time. The photographer spent hours with her, having her change from casual wear to formal, all of which Francine just happened to have with them, but Kristi balked at donning her two-piece swimsuit.

"No way, Francine. You can remember me with clothes on, or not at all." The photographer and Francine exchanged looks, and Francine shrugged, knowing that was one battle she wouldn't win.

Kristi had her own plans. Ever since that night in the spring when Jason had kissed her, she had considered what she should do about him. He was not indifferent to her—she had discovered that, but she was uncertain how to use the information. One thing was certain, by the end of the summer Jason McAlister would see her as a woman!

First of all, she knew she had to convince him that she wasn't too young for him. What was ten years' difference, anyway? Especially if they both were adults. She knew she wouldn't convince him of her maturity if she made calf eyes at him every time he saw her. So she began a subtle campaign to convince Jason that she saw him only as a friend, nothing more.

After months of observing his wariness around her, she was heartened to notice that he was beginning to relax and treat her in much the same way he treated Francine.

Kristi had been out of school a couple of months when she made her next move.

"Kyle, could I borrow the station wagon to go into Cielo? There's a movie I've wanted to see for ages and tonight's the last night." Her eyes held all the starry-eyed innocence of youth as she looked first at her brother, then at Francine, and glanced quickly at Jason before she looked down at her plate. Dinner was almost over.

Kyle frowned. "Kristi, I've never known you to want to drive into town this late at night. It would be after midnight by the time you got out, then you'd have that long drive home." He looked to Francine for support.

"Kristi, if you want to see a show tonight, I could take you, if you'd like." Jason's voice sounded casual and friendly, nothing more.

Kristi looked up, surprised. "Oh, thanks, Jase, but that's okay. If Kyle doesn't mind my using the old car, I'll be fine." She finished the remaining food on her plate, then looked back at Kyle. "I'll be all right, you know."

Kyle frowned, then cleared his throat. "Uh, Kristi, I don't want to sound hard-nosed about this, but I'd be much happier if you'd let Jase take you into town. You could have car trouble or something and I'd really worry about you." His eyes begged for her understanding of his position.

Oh, how she loved her brother! She was almost sorry she'd put him through all of this. Glancing down at her empty plate, then ruefully at Jason, she smiled. "I'm sorry, Jase. I didn't mean to be rude. If you're willing to take me, that will be fine." Kyle's sigh of relief echoed around the kitchen.

As it happened, the movie turned out to be a double feature. The first one, a western, kept them both entertained. The second movie, a love story that reduced Kristi to tears at the end, moved Jason as well.

By the time they left the theater, the town was closed. They returned to Jason's truck, in silence and drove toward home. To comfort her, Jason pulled Kristi over to his side and drove with one arm, keeping the other one firmly around her shoulders. Kristi let her head drop onto Jason's shoulder, her mind still on the movie. Only gradually did she become aware of the musky smell of his after-shave, of the muscles of his thigh bunched beneath her hand. She hadn't realized how natural it was for her hand to rest there. His fingers drew soft designs on her arm and she shifted a little closer to him and spoke softly into his ear.

"Do you realize this is the first time we've been alone together in months?" Her breath brushed softly against his ear. She noticed his shiver.

Removing his arm from around her, he reached into his pocket for a cigarette. She punched the lighter on the dash and waited, then held it to his cigarette.

After it was lit, he moved both hands back to the wheel. "I know."

She waited, but he said nothing more. "Are you still angry about that night?"

"What night?"

"The night I kissed you."

"I thought we both did a pretty good job of kissing each other," he replied, a hint of humor in his voice.

She laughed. "Yes, I guess we did at that. Anyway, I'm sorry my behavior caused you to steer clear of me after that." She watched his profile, mentally tracing the strong nose and jawline, wishing she were an artist who could portray the strength in him.

"That isn't the reason I've been avoiding you," he said in a low tone.

Her heart did a flip. He'd admitted that it had been intentional. "Oh?" She tried to sound uncaring. "What was your reason, then?"

His eyes cut quickly to her face, barely discernible in the light from the dash. "I knew I wouldn't be able to keep my hands off you, so I stayed away." He dragged deeply on his cigarette, then leaned over and put it out.

"But now you've discovered you can?"

"What do you think? Didn't I behave myself at the movie?" His grin slanted across his face, causing Kristi's breathing to do strange things.

"Did you find my crush very embarrassing, Jase?"

"Your crush? I don't know what you're talking about."

"Of course you do. All my fantasies have been about you. Surely you knew that?" She watched his face for a reaction but saw none.

"That's okay, honey. Because all my fantasies since I got back home have sure as hell been about you!" He reached out and pulled her back to his side. He leaned over and whispered as he watched the road, "I would have been thrown out of the movie tonight if they had known some of the fantasies I was having about you."

Kristi started laughing. "Oh, Jase. This is crazy. If that's the way you feel, why haven't you said anything?"

"I've been waiting for you to grow up, Kristi, as patiently as I know how."

"Don't look now, Jason, but you done missed it." She leaned over and kissed him on the ear. "Not only am I now eighteen years old, but I'm a high school graduate—ready to meet the world."

He slowed the truck as he turned off the highway

and took the farm road that led to their respective homes. "What do you want to do now that you're out of school?"

"Love you."

Her quiet reply startled him so much that his foot slipped from the accelerator and the truck suddenly slowed. After a moment, Jase put his foot on the gas pedal again. Kristi laid her head back on his shoulder, content to let him decide what to do with her statement. They rode along in silence for several miles, and Kristi was almost asleep when Jason spoke.

"What do you want to do, Kristi?"

Her head jerked up. For a minute she was uncertain whether she was dreaming or he'd actually spoken. They pulled into the drive of the ranch and he flipped off the lights and engine.

"About what, Jase?"

He turned so that he was leaning against the door and facing her. "About us."

She had never heard him more serious and Kristi's heart lurched at his acknowledgment that there was an "us."

She grinned, feeling more sure of herself with Jason than she ever had. "What do you have in mind?" Her teasing tone caught him on the quick.

"I want to take you somewhere and love you until you cry for help." His tone sounded almost grim.

She tilted her head. "Fine. How about next weekend?"

He jerked upright. "Are you serious?"

"Sure. Aren't you? I can tell Francine I'm spending the weekend in town with a friend...only I'll spend it with you."

Jason couldn't see the panicky expression in her eyes as she heard herself blithely plan a stolen weekend with him. All he heard was her light, casual tone.

"You see nothing wrong in going off with me for a weekend?" His tone was carefully neutral.

Kristi was glad he was no longer touching her because her whole body shook with every heartbeat. She loved this man too much and had loved him too long to turn back now. "No, not if you want me."

"Oh, I want you, Kristi, never doubt that." He pulled her into his arms, ignoring the steering wheel that suddenly poked Kristi in the ribs. His kiss made no allowance for her youth or lack of experience as he proceeded to show her how much he wanted her. Only her gasp of pain as the steering wheel continued to gouge her side caused him to ease his grip on her. "This is obviously not the place for this," he muttered with disgust.

Kristi sat back, trying to get her breath, hoping the panicky feeling would go away. This was Jason, and she loved him. That was all that mattered.

It was easy to get away for the weekend. When she told Francine she was spending the weekend in town with a friend, Francine commented that she must be getting bored with ranch life already. Kristi ignored the comment, knowing better but unable to explain.

Kristi had never lied to her family and they trusted

her completely. Not even Kyle was suspicious when Jason arrived to give her a lift into town.

"Where are we going?" They had been driving for miles and Jase had said nothing; he had just stared down the road, frowning.

"Nuevo Laredo."

"Mexico?"

He heard the shock in her voice and glanced at her for a moment before returning his eyes to the road. "What's wrong with Mexico?"

"Oh, I don't know. I guess I was just surprised."

"Where did you think I'd take you? To my place, for Molly to look after us?" He sounded angry, which wasn't a good sign for the weekend.

"I wasn't thinking, Jase. Anywhere is fine."

They continued to travel in silence. This wasn't how Kristi had imagined their time together. Not that she had any intention of changing her mind, but she thought Jase would be more relaxed so she could be. After all, he probably did this sort of thing all the time. A pain shot through her at the thought. She tried to shrug it off. He was twenty-eight years old; she couldn't expect him to have reached that age without experience. She just preferred not to think about it.

Kristi's surprised turned to alarm when, after crossing into Mexico, instead of looking for a hotel, Jason stopped in front of an official-looking building. "Where are we?"

Jason turned to her, a determined expression on his face. "Kristi, I'm not going to sneak off with you for a weekend in a motel, then casually return you to Kyle. I thought I could do it, since it was obviously what you want, but I can't."

Kristi's heart plummeted to her toes. She should have known that he didn't find her attractive enough, that he'd been amusing himself at her expense. So why had he stopped here?

In the same determined voice, Jason continued. "We're going inside, Kristi, and we're getting married." He held up a hand as she started to speak. "I don't want to hear any arguments, dammit. I love you, and there's no way in hell I'm going to be able to make love to you and then walk away. We're getting married, and when we get back I'll tell Kyle and Francine what we've done. They're going to be upset, and I'm sorry we're doing it this way—" he paused, reaching out to her cheek as though unable to resist touching her "—but I've waited too long for you now to wait until we can plan a big wedding."

"Oh, Jase!" Kristi threw herself into his arms, oblivious to the passersby and their curious stares. She began to kiss him—quick kisses across his cheeks, eyes and nose—laughing at his startled expression. "I never dreamed you'd want to marry me, Jase. I was willing to accept whatever you offered. Of course I want to marry you, you crazy idiot. That's all I've ever wanted out of life."

As they walked into the building hand in hand, he muttered, "I still feel like a sneak."

"That's because you are," she admitted as she

hugged his arm to her. "And a thief, stealing your best friend's little sister." She laughed, happiness radiating from her.

His indulgent smile made her want to weep. "I'm not stealing, just borrowing."

They spent the weekend in a luxurious Mexican hotel.

Nothing in Kristi's experience prepared her for Jason's lovemaking. He recognized her nervousness and didn't rush her. If he had any doubts because she was so young she quickly disabused him of them. She was ready to learn more about the sensual side of her nature and he was the one she wanted to teach her. Her love for him grew as he took the time and patience to show her how beautiful lovemaking could be.

During the daytime they enjoyed touring the shops and marketplace, and they eagerly embraced the custom of siesta time, although they got very little rest.

They intended to leave early on Sunday so they would have plenty of time to talk with Kyle and Francine, but even with the best intentions, they continued to be distracted during the process of showering, dressing and packing, and it was midafternoon before they pulled up at the ranch.

Kristi was nervous. With her marriage a fact, she began to worry that perhaps she wasn't prepared for marriage and all it entailed. Although she eagerly looked forward to moving in with Jason, she was unsure about what he might expect of her as his wife.

Jason and Kristi walked into the living room and

paused inside the door. Kyle was stretched out on the couch watching television while Francine, in her third month of pregnancy, busily crocheted something tiny and intricate.

Kristi was the first to speak. "Kyle, Francine... we've got something to tell you." She paused as Kyle rolled to a sitting position, then, seeing Jason, stood up and stretched.

He grinned at his friend. "H'lo, Jason. Didn't know you were here. What did you do, go all the way into town to pick up Kristi?"

"Not exactly," Jason drawled. "I never dropped her off, Kyle. Kristi and I were married on Friday."

Kyle froze in his position as though caught in the frame of a moving picture, his arm raised to push his reddish brown hair from his forehead, a half-formed smile stranded on his face.

"Oh, no!" Francine jumped up, yarn, pattern and needle falling unheeded to the floor. "Oh, Kristi, you didn't!" She looked stricken and Kristi felt a pang of remorse as she quickly moved to Francine's side.

"Oh, Francie, I'm sorry we didn't tell you, but we didn't really decide to do it until Friday, and then it was done." She put her arms around the smaller woman. "Please don't cry, Francie. You know this is what I've always wanted."

Kyle suddenly regained movement and straightened to his full height, a couple of inches taller than Jason. He shifted toward the younger man, anger warring with pain on his face.

"Is there some particular reason you had to be in such an all-fired hurry, Jase?" His penetrating blue eyes speared his friend, as he waited for an explanation.

Kristi watched the color wash over Jason's cheeks. He wasn't the kind of man to explain himself to anyone, but Kyle was different. No two men had ever been closer. "No, Kyle, there wasn't the kind of reason you're implying. You know me better than that."

"I thought I knew you better than that, but the Jason McAlister I knew wouldn't have snuck off with my sister without a word, either." Kristi had never seen her brother so upset, not since they had lost their parents.

She left Francine and threw herself into Kyle's arms. "Please don't be upset, Kyle. I couldn't stand that. I love Jason, you've always known that. Our getting married was an impulsive decision, that's true, but it would have happened, anyway. Jason is all I've ever wanted out of life. I was marking time until he decided to see me as an adult."

"From the sound of things, he managed to do that," Kyle responded with an attempt at humor. He held out his hand to Jason. "I guess at this point all I need to do is welcome you to the family, which seems a little strange. You've always been that." He gripped his friend's hand, and they stood there looking at each other, neither one willing to be the first to end eye contact.

"Oh, Kristi, I had such great plans for you, too," Francine wailed as she picked up the items she'd dropped. "I've sent all those pictures to a New York agent in hopes of getting you into a modeling school."

Both Jason and Kristi turned to her in surprise. Jason was the first to speak. "What are you talking about, Francie?"

"I took Kristi to Dallas and had a portfolio of pictures taken several weeks ago. Everyone who knows anything about the business says she's a natural with her unusual coloring and skin tones, not to mention those eyes. I've just been waiting to hear from the agent before I said anything to Kristi."

Jason's eyes hardened as he turned and stared at Kristi. "I didn't know you wanted to be a model, Kristi. You never mentioned it."

Kristi was appalled to see the cold, aloof Jason where her warm and passionate husband had been just a few minutes before. She moved over to him and slid her arms around his waist. Gazing up at him, she tried to make him understand. "I don't, Jason. This is the first time I knew anything about such plans."

"You posed for the pictures."

"Francie said she wanted some pictures of me. I had no idea she intended to use them for anything but to have here at home."

Francine spoke up. "That's true, Jason. It was my idea. I felt that Kristi has too much potential to waste on a ranch." She faced her new brother-in-law with spirit, determined not to back down.

Kristi broke the tension in the room by leaning into Jason and kissing him in the V of his shirt. "You're all I want, Jason. Haven't I made that plain enough this weekend?"

She could feel his body's response to her closeness and gloried in her ability to affect him. Her power over this man was new and fascinating. When she glanced up at him she recognized the desire that darkened his topaz eyes. "It's just as well, Kristi, because it's too late to change your mind now. You're my wife. You said that was what you wanted and I believed you." His arms encircled her in a possessive hug as he spoke to her, both of them absorbed in each other and unaware of the other two in the room. "You'd better go pack your things. I need to get home."

Kristi saw very little of Kyle and Francine during the next few weeks—she was too engrossed in settling into her new position as Jason's wife. Although she was an accomplished cook, she begged Molly to stay on as Jason's housekeeper, insisting she still had a lot to learn about home management. Amused, Molly consented and gently guided Kristi through the steps of running a large household.

Kristi had been living with Jason for a little over a week when the phone rang one day. "Is this Kristi Cole?"

Momentarily forgetting her new married name, she answered, "Yes."

"Kristi, this is Jonathan Segal. I've just been chatting with your sister-in-law, Francine. She was kind enough to give me your phone number."

Who in the world was Jonathan Segal? "I'm afraid I don't understand, Mr. Segal. Why did you want to contact me?"

She heard a chuckle over what sounded like a long-distance line. "Mrs. Cole explained to me that she was the one who sent me your pictures. It doesn't matter to me who sent them. I wanted to let you know that if you'd come to New York, I think I can help you get your pretty puss on the cover of every national magazine published." He laughed. "Except, perhaps, *Field & Stream.*"

He must be the agent Francine had mentioned. "I'm sorry you had to waste the call, Mr. Segal. Surely Francine told you I'm married and not interested in a career in modeling."

There was a moment of silence as her comment was weighed and evaluated. "I see." A longer pause. "That's really too bad. You're one of the most photogenic young women to come along in a long while. You don't seem to have a bad side or angle. With your looks and my contacts, you could very easily become the highest-paid model around in a few short years."

For a moment, glamorous pictures of exotic locales and glittering showrooms flitted through Kristi's mind. Could the man be for real? Then Jason's face superimposed itself over the other imaginings and she smiled. "I appreciate your interest in me, but I'm afraid I have other commitments now."

She heard his sigh winging across the wires. "All right. But, Kristi, if you should ever change your mind, please give me a call."

She laughed. "I'll do that, Mr. Segal. If I ever decide to become rich and famous, you'll be the first person I notify."

"You think it's a joke at the moment, my friend, but that's exactly what I can do for you. Just keep it in mind."

As the months passed, Kristi forgot the call. She became too caught up in the problems that seemed to be appearing in her marriage. Jason began to spend time away from the ranch, but would give no explanations to Kristi as to why.

She was still awake late one night when he carefully climbed into bed beside her. It was almost two o'clock and her imagination had been torturing her with pictures of Jason with another woman, or in a car wreck, or out drinking with his buddies while she waited for him at home. Was he bored with her already?

"Where have you been?" She'd been determined not to let him know she was awake. Where was her self-discipline?

He pulled her into his arms, his hands roving leisurely over her body, seeming to enjoy the curves his palms outlined so faithfully. "At a meeting. It ran a little later than I expected. I would have called, but I was afraid I would wake you." He began to kiss her just below her ear, an action that he'd discovered guaranteed her full attention.

"You didn't mention having anything planned at supper," she murmured, recognizing that, as usual, his hands and mouth were seducing her to forget her tension and unease.

"I didn't know about it then. The call came later."

"What kind of meeting, Jase? What's so important that you drop everything every time you receive a phone call and go rushing off?" She moved her mouth slightly to avoid his and heard him sigh.

"I'm sorry, Kristi, but I can't talk about it. Don't let it come between us." She heard the tenderness in his voice and melted against him, knowing she could never resist him for long.

His secret meetings did come between them. As the months passed he began to stay away for a night or two at a time. He was always careful to let her know when he'd be gone, and he made sure that Nate and Molly were around to look after her. Kristi grew more frustrated as time went on. Why did he have to be so secretive? Why did he continue to treat her like a child? Maybe not exactly a child—more like a pampered plaything, waiting to fall into his arms every time he returned. She had a disgusting habit of doing just that.

Perhaps in time Kristi would have overcome her

insecurities as a new bride and continued her life with Jason if she hadn't lost their baby. She'd been so excited when she found out she was pregnant. Francine had given birth to Kevin only a few weeks before and she was delighted to think they would both have babies near the same age. Jason treated her as though she were suddenly made of priceless porcelain, and life began to seem much more worthwhile to Kristi. However, he continued to disappear periodically with little warning and still refused to tell her why.

Kristi was in her twelfth week of pregnancy when, during one of the nights Jason was gone, she woke up suddenly, realizing that something was drastically wrong. Panicked, she flipped on the lamp by the bed, reached for the phone and called her brother. He and Francine arrived within minutes.

Kristi remembered very little about that night, but clearly recalled the details of the next morning when the compassionate, white-haired doctor took her hand and explained that she had lost the baby she and Jason had been awaiting so eagerly. The doctor patted her hand as he made his explanations.

"There were complications during the surgery we had to do, Kristi. It's hard to predict the outcome of some of these things, you know." His eyes had the sad look of one who had seen too much to believe that everything always worked out for the best. "There's a strong possibility that you won't be able to have children, Kristi. Only time will tell."

She heard his voice and saw his lips form the

words, but her mind rejected what he was trying to tell her.

"No! That isn't so. Jase and I plan to have a big family. He hated being an only child. We're going to have lots of children, Doctor. I've already told you." She grabbed his hand and squeezed it as though to force him to acknowledge that he was wrong.

He nodded his head. "I know, Kristi. There's still a chance. I just thought it better to prepare you in case things don't turn out quite as you planned."

He sat there with her as she broke down and cried—for her lost baby, and for the ones who might never come—then cried again because it was the doctor who sat by her side comforting her, when all she wanted in the world was Jason.

Only Jason wasn't there.

It was long after visiting hours that night before he tiptoed into her room. Kristi had been lying there staring at the reflection of the night-light. The cover was fluted, causing a flowerlike silhouette on the wall. She turned her head at the slight sound of the door closing and watched him come toward the bed. He knelt down beside her, his arms going around her as he placed his head on her chest and held her in silence. Her hand moved up to his tawny hair and her fingers gently combed through it.

When he raised his head, she saw the wet sheen of his golden eyes as he leaned down and kissed her gently on her lips. "I'm so sorry, Kristi," he whispered.

"I know," she murmured, glad to have him back even while she wondered how long he'd stay before disappearing once again.

"Has the doctor said how long you have to stay?"

"I can leave in the morning. He wanted to make sure I didn't start hemorrhaging again."

He started to speak and his voice broke. He tried again. "I should have been there with you." There was nothing she could say to that.

In the weeks that followed, Kristi found less and less to say as she began to retreat from the pain of her loss and her bewilderment about Jason. He appeared to love her and his desire for her was evident every time he was within touching distance, but she could no longer cope with the complexities of her new adult world.

It was during one of Jason's absences that Kristi remembered Jonathan Segal. For whatever his reasons, Jason no longer seemed to need a wife, especially one who might never have the family he wanted so badly. If she left him he could divorce her and remarry. In her depressed frame of mind Kristi felt she no longer had anything to offer him.

Jonathan Segal made it clear that she had plenty to offer the modeling business and assured her he would make all the necessary arrangements to get her into a highly prestigious school. All she needed to do was to let him know when she would be arriving.

Jason made no argument when she announced her decision to leave, but she remembered that his tan suddenly stood out on his face as though painted on. Perhaps she had hoped he would beg her to stay—she wasn't sure what she had expected—but he didn't. So she left.

Still locked in her cocoon of grief, Kristi moved to New York and began training to be a model. She met the challenge of a strict diet, stringent schedules and constant demands on her time and energy, glad to be distracted from her memories.

The sadness lurking in her eyes gave a haunting quality to her photographs. Jonathan pointed out that every man who looked at them wanted to be the one to make her eyes glow with happiness. It wasn't long before she found herself in constant demand, which was fine with her. As long as she stayed busy, she didn't have time to think.

Superficially, her social life was full. She learned to be at ease in the sophisticated circles that included many of the wealthy and the famous. She was immune to the propositions and proposals that came her way—all of her emotions had been left behind in Texas.

As the years passed she emerged from her self-imposed emotional prison and took a more active part in the direction of her life. Kristi wasn't sure exactly when she decided to cut her ties and ask Jason for a divorce. She could not bring herself to return to Texas, despite Francine's many letters importuning her to get acquainted with the rapidly growing Kevin and his younger sister, Kari. However, when her lawyer told her that Jason was proving to be most uncooperative and suggested that she might wish to discuss the divorce with him in person, Kristi knew it was time for her to face him.

There was no reason for Jason to balk—she'd made it clear that she wanted nothing from him. She just wanted to be free to live her life.

As she drove toward her brother's ranch that fresh, spring morning, remembering her night with Jason, she began to wonder if she would ever be free.

Chapter 3

Kristi had an opportunity to note the changes in the ranch as she followed the long, winding private road from the highway to the ranch buildings and the home of her childhood. She had waited a long time to return. She hoped it was long enough. Last night had shown her that Jason had a stronger hold on her than one person should have over another. Her only protection was in not letting him know.

Her car had no sooner stopped than the screen door of the house flew open and twin tornadoes burst into view. For a quick spasm of time, Kristi's heart felt squeezed by a giant hand, then the pain was gone. She was back in the present once more.

The children tore across the front porch and down the steps, then came to a screeching halt—their shyness of strangers overcoming their anticipation of meeting, at long last, their aunt.

Kristi recognized the family resemblance. Kevin, tall for almost six, was slender like his dad. He stood watching her as though hoping she'd have something for him to do. Kari, at four, showed signs of beauty. Both had their father's reddish brown hair—Francine's black curls didn't show up on either child.

They watched as Kristi stepped nimbly from the car. She smiled and asked, "Would you like to help me with some of my luggage?"

That was the invitation they needed to send them darting toward the car. Kevin took Kristi's keys and went to the trunk while Kari proudly lifted the overnight case from the front seat.

Francine joined them, hugging her sister-in-law. "Oh, Kristi, I'm so glad you came home." She hung on for a moment, struggling to keep back the tears. "It's so good to see you."

Kristi laughed, the abandoned, joyous laugh that used to echo in the old homestead. "I'm delighted to *be* home, little sister." She hugged the smaller woman back. "I'm glad to see your tribe in the flesh. They're definitely livelier than their pictures indicated."

"That's for sure. Now you can understand how difficult it was for me to get them still long enough to snap a photo."

As they walked toward the house, the children bringing up the rear, Kristi asked with a chuckle,

"Are you sorry you followed Mom's idea of naming the children with a *K?*"

"I have to admit it's been confusing. Kevin is incensed when I slip and call him Kari, so I've learned to be careful."

"At least Kyle and I never had that problem. I guess Mom had gotten used to saying his name before I came along."

They walked through the side door that opened into the kitchen.

"Oh, Francie, this is beautiful. When did you have it done?"

Francine blushed with pride. "Actually, I just finished hanging the curtains when I heard your car in the drive."

Kristine remembered the kitchen, the room where most of the family congregated, as being cozy, but not particularly stylish. Now one wall was covered in red-and-white wallpaper and matching curtains hung at the windows. The cabinets were stained pecan, and the counter top echoed the bright colors of the curtains and wall.

"You're a magician," Kristi added as she smiled at her sister-in-law. She wandered over to the window that looked out on the yard. "I suppose Kyle is out somewhere on the ranch."

"Yes, but he'll be home for dinner as usual. He'll be surprised to see you. You were so vague about your plans on the phone that we had no idea when to expect you."

"I know. I didn't want a tight time schedule. One of the purposes of this trip is to rest and relax, something I've almost forgotten how to do. So I didn't push myself at all." She walked over to the large refrigerator and opened it, found the pitcher of iced tea she knew would be in there, and poured herself a glass. "What did Kyle think about my coming home?"

Francine placed some homemade cookies on a plate and motioned for Kristi to sit down at the table as she replied, "I believe his exact words were something like—" she dropped her voice to mimic her husband's husky drawl "—'it's about damn time.'" They both started laughing.

Kristi sank into one of the kitchen chairs and reached for one of Francine's fantastic cookies. She hadn't realized how much she'd missed them until now. Francine's next words suddenly jerked her back from her nostalgia. "Jason's coming over for supper tonight, Kristi." She paused, watching the expression on Kristi's face before she continued. "Unless you want me to suggest he not come."

Why did her pulse rate have to increase at the mere mention of his name? Kristi struggled to overcome her sudden nervousness. She was almost twenty-five years old, not eighteen, and had learned to handle herself with poise in the most difficult situations. Forcing herself to relax, she smiled and answered, "Oh, I don't mind his coming over, Francie. We're bound to see each other sooner or later." She pushed the thought of the night before out of her mind. "Of course, I'm not sure how he's going to feel about seeing me again."

Francine studied Kristi, searching for the young girl she used to know in this self-contained, beautiful, young woman. She had an almost otherworld loveliness, an ethereal beauty—definitely not the stuff a rancher's wife was made of.

"Jason told us you'd had divorce papers sent to him."

"Did he?" Kristi replied in a neutral tone.

"Yes." Francine hesitated, unsure of herself with this new Kristi and conscious of past mistakes. "You know, Kristi—" she paused and licked her dry lips before continuing "—I made a vow when you left that I was going to stay out of your business. I did enough damage when I took it upon myself to contact Jonathan Segal—"

Kristi interrupted. "And you were right, you see. You were proven right, and I've never even thanked you for helping me get where I am."

"Right or wrong, I had no business butting into your life like I did. During these past few years I've kept my mouth shut—" her gaze pierced Kristi as she continued "—until now. I think there's something you need to know, and you sure won't hear it from Kyle or Jason."

Kristi stiffened but there wasn't a thing she could do. She knew she wasn't going to like what Francine had to say. "Go on." She nodded, waiting.

"I don't know why you decided to leave Jason, Kristi, and I don't want to know. You were hurtin' pretty bad when you left Texas and maybe it was the best thing for you to do—to get away, learn something about the world, discover your own potential. Obviously it helped to heal your hurts." She leaned closer to Kristi. "Did you ever think of Jason and his pain?"

Kristi clutched the glass in her hand, staring down at the floating ice cubes as though searching for an answer written on one of them. She took a long swallow, then set the glass down on the table. "I'm sure he was hurt that I left, Francie, although he never suggested I stay."

For a moment anger flared in Francine's eyes, then it was gone as she shook her head in weary acceptance. "You just don't have a clue yet to Jason, do you, Kristi?"

"What do you mean?"

"Jason McAlister has never been able to deny you anything you ever wanted in your entire life. Why would you expect him to stop you if you decided you wanted to become a model in New York?"

"He could have said something, but he didn't. As a matter of fact he didn't have much to say about anything after we lost the baby." She moved her glass in absent circles, watching the liquid swirling.

"Kristi—I know you suffered when you lost the baby, but don't you see? Jason suffered right along with you. And he felt guilty for not being there that night, as though in some way he could have prevented it, just by being there.'' Francine paused, searching for words. ''Then, as if that wasn't enough, he lost the wife he adored, as well. He had to stand there and watch you walk out of his life, because if that was what you wanted, he wouldn't stop you.''

Kristi stood up suddenly, needing to release some of the nervous tension building within her. She moved toward the window and gazed out at the familiar view. ''Then why doesn't he give me the divorce I want?'' She spoke with her back to Francine, refusing to face her.

''Maybe he thought you should ask for it in person.''

Kristi spun around. ''That's exactly what I intend to do. That's the other reason I'm here, as I'm sure you've guessed.''

Francine stood up slowly, as though all of her joints were resisting each move, almost as if she were an old woman. ''Yes, I guessed as much.'' She watched the fey creature at the window, then decided to finish what she'd started. ''I don't want you to give me the answer to this question, Kristi. It's one I think you need to answer only to yourself. Do you think you've been fair with Jase? Have you ever looked at what's happened from his point of view? Because if you haven't, I think you should.''

She carried their glasses to the sink, her tone lightening. ''That's all the mother-henning I intend to do, so you can relax. I want you to enjoy your stay here for however long you can be with us. You don't owe me any explanations. I don't think I'd even want to hear them." She walked over to Kristi and hugged her again. "C'mon. Let me show you your room."

Francine led the way into the hall. "I turned the spare room into a guest room so that when you decided to visit you'd have a comfortable place to stay." She paused and allowed Kristi to enter the room first.

The room at the end of the hall had always been a "catchall" room when Kristi lived there. The sewing machine, ironing board and half-completed projects of one nature or another had been stored in the room. The change in the room took her breath away.

The walls had been tinted with a soft yellow that reminded Kristi of the sky on clear mornings as it was first touched by the sun. Lace curtains covered the windows that looked out over the colorful flower garden Francine had so carefully nurtured. French provincial furniture with its touches of gold on white gave the room a feminine look. Kristi walked over to the four-poster bed and smoothed the light blue, patterned spread that was draped gracefully across it.

"Francine, you could have made a fortune as a decorator. This room is really special." She glanced around and saw Francine's cheeks turn pink with pleasure at the compliment.

"Thank you, even if you are prejudiced. Unfortunately, I can only seem to decorate in down-home, country style, which I'm sure wouldn't impress any of your New York friends. Anyway, I'm glad you like it. I guess you can tell that I had you in mind, especially when I picked the carpet."

Kristi had already kicked off her shoes, and her bare toes curled into the thick nap of the plush, navy blue rug. "I don't suppose I can get too much blue. Thank you for thinking of me." She hadn't realized until now, when her muscles were beginning to relax, how tense she'd been. "If you don't mind, I think I'll stretch out for a few minutes."

"Sure. Kyle should be here some time within the next hour."

"If I doze off, be sure to wake me when he gets here."

Francine laughed. "Don't worry. You'll think there's a stampede let loose in the house when Kyle sees your car out front and knows you're here." She glanced out the window as she spoke. "By the way, that's a mighty fancy car you're driving, lady."

Kristi stretched out on the bed, reveling in the luxurious feel of the springy mattress. "I know. I had to have something to get away in on weekends. That car used to be my magic carpet, whisking me to upstate New York whenever I had the chance to escape."

Francine stopped by the side of the bed and touched Kristi's shoulder. "It's certainly done that for you now. It's almost as good as Dorothy's red shoes." She started out of the room, then paused and looked back. "Remember what Dorothy learned, Kristi. There's no place like home."

* * *

"Do you suppose this is Goldilocks sleeping in my bed?" Kyle's voice brought Kristi from a sound sleep. As her eyes opened she saw her brother standing by the bed, flanked by Kevin and Kari.

Kari giggled. "She's not Goldilocks, Daddy. Goldilocks has yellow hair!" Kari's blue eyes flashed up at her father.

"Hmm." Kyle rubbed his cheek as though in serious thought. "I think you're right, Kari. So who could this be?" His solemn expression was belied by the dancing eyes peering down at Kristi.

In his most adult voice Kevin explained, "It's Aunt Kristi, Daddy. Mom told you she was here."

Kristi struggled to a sitting position and smiled. "You're right, Kevin. I think your dad is trying to be funny."

"*Trying* to be funny," Kyle repeated in a wounded tone. "Boy, I thought I'd get a little more respect from you after all these years." He sat down next to Kristi and pulled her into his arms. He studied her face as he added in a suspiciously gruff voice, "Welcome home, baby sister. It's about time."

Kristi's head dropped on his shoulder. "It's good to be home, Kyle, and you're right. It's long overdue."

"You see, you and I have always agreed on the important things." He pulled her with him as he stood up. "C'mon, lunch is ready and I'm starving." The two children bounded down the hallway ahead of them. Kristi stood there for a moment, taking in the changes in Kyle. If anything, he looked more handsome. He'd put on some weight that he carried well. The laugh lines around his blue eyes and the lines around his mouth gave mute evidence that the years in between had been happy ones for him. She hugged him to her.

"You're looking great, Kyle. Sexier than ever. I bet Francine has to beat all your admirers off with a stick whenever you leave the place."

He grinned as he tucked his arm around her waist and headed her down the hallway to the kitchen. "Not so you'd notice," he drawled. "If you don't mind my saying so, you're looking awfully thin, seems to me."

"This isn't considered thin, I want you to know." She paused for a moment and posed. "This is all the rage in New York—willowy and winsome." She blinked up at him with an exaggerated pout. "Surely you've noticed."

"You might look great by New York standards, honey, but I'd say you look like you're sickening over something. I've got newborn calves that look healthier than you do." He burst out laughing at her offended expression. She gave up trying to look wounded and joined him.

"It's been years since I heard you two trading insults, but you sound like you've had daily practice," Francine commented as they sat down at the table. "Nothing changes, regardless of the time passing."

But Kristi was aware that there had been changes.

During the meal she enjoyed watching Francine and Kyle with their children. Pride and love for their offspring glowed in both faces. Kyle answered Kevin's perpetual stream of questions with no sign of impatience. Francine made sporadic conversation with Kristi while taking time to see that Kari got enough food on her plate.

Kyle glanced over and spoke to Francine. "Did you call Jase and tell him Kristi was here?"

Kristi's heart thudded to a halt. As it slowly picked up its rhythm once more, she waited for Francine's answer.

"No, as a matter of fact, I didn't think about it." She frowned slightly as she looked at her husband. "Do you think I should?"

Kristi realized that they were worried about Jason. Had she been so wrapped up in her own grief that she'd never given thought to his? She kept her eyes on her plate as she waited for Kyle's answer.

"It may not be necessary. He sent word earlier he might not make it. Said something about running late and if he wasn't here by six-thirty or so, not to expect him." Kristi glanced up to see her brother watching her. Silently she pleaded with him not to discuss Jason at the moment.

The conversation veered to other subjects, for which Kristi was thankful. She wondered if her brother knew how much Jason drank these days. She could hardly mention it to him, under the circumstances. Could his drinking habits have anything to do with her? Suddenly, she felt the need for reassurance that her absence in his life hadn't had such a debilitating effect on him. Jason was so strong. She had never pictured him as having any weaknesses. Could it be possible that he was vulnerable where she was concerned? She had a lot to think about before she would be ready to talk with Jason.

Kyle saddled one of the horses for Kristi after lunch and they spent the afternoon together. He showed her the many changes and improvements he had made, was making, or intended to make. It was obvious that he was content with his life and his family. He had all kinds of questions regarding her work, her life, and whether she was happy. The subject of Jason was conspicuous by its absence from the conversation. Whatever his feelings regarding their split, Kyle obviously intended to stay out of it.

Kyle halted his horse at the edge of a small creek and stepped down from the saddle; then he helped Kristi down.

Although she'd kept up with her riding as often as possible while back East, she could already feel the sore muscles that complained she'd gone far enough today. *How quickly they forget,* she thought ruefully as she rubbed her tender bottom.

"How long are you going to be able to stay?" Kyle asked as he watched Kristi wander over to a grassy spot and gingerly lower herself to the ground.

"I don't have an assignment until the first of June, but I doubt I'll stay here that long."

"Why not?"

Nothing like being direct, dear brother, she thought with a twinge of exasperation. "That's rather a long time to visit anyone, don't you think? We're talking about two months or more."

Kyle threw himself down beside her in a lazy sprawl. "That depends. Do you think you'll be too bored to stay that long?"

"Of course not. I'm more afraid you'll be tired of having me around."

Kyle watched her for a few moments, enjoying having her home, wishing he could solve whatever her problems might be, but knowing that wasn't possible. It was her life—she needed to be in charge of her decisions. They were quiet for a while, savoring the peace of the afternoon, before Kyle sat up, peering at the hills in front of them. "Guess we'd better head back toward home. You're going to be feeling this little trip for a few days, I'm afraid."

"And here all the time I thought you were just being too polite to mention it." She groaned as she got up. "I should have known better than to think you'd ever be polite to me."

They mounted and started home at a slow pace, to help ease the strain on Kristi's unused muscles. All she could think about was soaking in a hot bath for hours. *Welcome home, Kristi,* she thought with wry humor. *We're going to have to get you toughened up, it seems.*

* * *

An exhausted Jason pulled into Kyle's yard late that afternoon. Everything that could possibly have gone wrong that day had managed to do so. They'd found a fence down, which meant unplanned hours of chasing cattle back through the break, and one of his men had received a nasty tear on his arm when some barbed wire suddenly snapped and wrapped around it. Plus, he'd been fighting the granddaddy of all hangovers most of the day.

And, worst of all, he'd been remembering the months after Kristi had left. He couldn't sleep then; he would lie awake night after night trying to come to terms with what had happened to their marriage. He'd made some really stupid mistakes with her. In his need to protect her from all unpleasantness he'd refused to explain what he was doing on the nights he was away from home. Once she left, it was too late.

He had discovered that he could sleep when he drank himself into oblivion, which he proceeded to do every night until Kyle finally stormed over one night and lit into Jason for trying to destroy himself. He had managed to pierce the apathy surrounding Jason and had made him so mad that he had taken a swing at Kyle, much to Kyle's delight. He'd provoked a reaction—as he had hoped to do.

Jason had stopped drinking and slowly learned to live with his ghosts. Until last night. What had happened to him last night?

He shook his head in disgust as he swung his truck

around the house and came to an abrupt stop behind a fire-engine-red Triumph with New York license plates.

"Oh, my God!" He sat there staring at the car. Kristi. Of course it was Kristi. Somewhere deep inside he must have known it was her. How else could he explain his responses?

His thoughts flew back to the night before. Where earlier he'd ruthlessly shoved the upsetting memories away, now he searched for them frantically, wanting to relive each one.

It had worked! He'd lured her to Texas after he'd almost given up hope. A slow smile crept across his weary face. So she wanted a divorce, did she? No woman could respond to a man as Kristi had last night without having strong feelings for him.

Had she intended to go to bed with him? Somehow he didn't think so. She'd been too aloof until they danced together. Once again he felt her body pressed against his, moving languorously to the music.

Now that she was home, he'd move on to the next phase of his plan. Discovering that she hadn't been able to overcome her attraction to him gave him an edge he hadn't counted on. He certainly intended to use every advantage he could get. Kristi had belonged to him from the day her mother had first placed the tiny infant in his arms. He wasn't about to lose her now that he had her in his territory again.

A very subdued Kristi sat soaking in hot water. Although her muscles felt better, her conscience still smarted. She'd been looking at her actions of five years ago through the eyes of her family and Jason and didn't much like what she saw. Had she really been that selfish? Or had she just been immature? She'd discovered that several notions she'd hugged to herself for years needed to be tossed out the window.

Where did that leave her? The only thing she knew for certain was that, regardless of what she felt for Jason—and admittedly she was very confused about that—there was no way their marriage could work. She was another person now and they had nothing in common. Somehow she needed to convince him of that. If only he didn't have such a stronghold on her emotions.

Getting ready for supper, Kristi slipped into a cinnamon-colored caftan; its slim lines clung to her long legs. She tied her hair loosely in a topknot. She was stepping into heelless slippers when she heard Jason's voice. Surprised, she paused and unabashedly listened.

"Whose car is that outside, Francie? Looks a little out of place with the pickups and station wagons around here, don't you think?" His voice sounded pleasant, almost cheerful.

"Oh, hi, Jase." Francine's voice revealed her nervousness.

So Jason had come for supper after all, and no one had bothered to warn him that she was home. Feeling sorry for Francine, Kristi left her room. After all, she had the advantage. He had no idea she was around, nor did he know she was the woman he'd spent the night with. The thought amused her, at the same time she mentally acknowledged the butterflies that had suddenly taken up residence somewhere in her middle. She paused at the doorway of the kitchen, drinking in the sight of the man standing by the table. There were tired lines in his face, dark circles under his eyes. He looked like hell. But then, he didn't get much sleep last night.

That thought brought a slight smile to her face. "Hello, Jay-son."

He spun on his heel, taking her in at a glance. The look in his eyes caused Kristi to panic. He knew! Somehow he'd known that she was here and that he'd spent the night with her. His elevated brow even acknowledged the slight mimicry in her pronunciation of his name. Then she had no more time to think.

Jason moved with swift strides across the room and pulled her into his arms. Without a word he lowered his lips to hers. The kiss was a continuation of the ones they'd shared the previous evening. It spoke of wanting, of loving, of never-ending need, and effectively wiped out every coherent thought in Kristi's head. She clung to him, knowing that if he were to release her she'd fall in a heap at his feet. His kiss was leisurely and very thorough. Finally, he eased his hold and withdrew his lips enough to whisper, "Welcome home, Mrs. McAlister."

"Jase?"

He laughed, and his laughter was an unrestrained, joyous sound. Pulling her tightly against him once again, he murmured, "Good. At least you still recognize me. That's a start." He swung her around so they faced an astonished Francie. She was no more surprised than Kristi. Of all the ways Kristi might have envisioned their meeting, this one hadn't come to mind. Jason's eyes sparkled as he spoke to Francine. "I take it you intended to surprise me. You couldn't have given me a nicer one." He kept his arm securely wrapped around Kristi's waist, making it plain that he had no intention of releasing her any time soon.

"Well, not exactly, Jason," Francine stuttered, trying to get a grip on her thoughts. She'd never seen him like this before. Did he think Kristi had come home to him? Surely not. He was the one who'd told them about the divorce. Then what was going on? She hurried to explain. "I mean, we knew she was coming for a visit but she didn't say when, just some time in the next few weeks. Kyle said you might not make it over tonight, so I didn't think to call and tell you."

Kristi thought she knew Jason in all of his moods, but, like Francine, she couldn't decipher this one. She could feel the tenseness in his body, pressed so intimately against her side. She also knew that he'd been as affected by their kiss as she, but she couldn't understand why there wasn't some animosity or resentment toward her. After all, she had played a rather underhanded trick the night before by not identifying herself. Or had he known who she was all along?

Kyle bounded into the room from outside. "Glad you could make it, Jason. Sorry I'm late. I'll get washed up and we can sit down." He glanced at Jason's arm possessively wrapped around Kristi and smiled. Then he turned to Francine. "Where are the kids?"

"Oh, I fed them earlier. There was a special on television they wanted to watch, and I thought we could visit better without them."

Kristi took the respite and attempted to move away from Jason, a little surprised when he allowed it. She'd made a mistake in underestimating this man. She'd been feeling sorry for him and what she'd inadvertently done to him. She would need all of her wits about her to deal with this frankly sensual male whose eyes openly stripped her of everything she had painstakingly placed on her body. That was definitely an X-rated look he was giving her, and she wasn't unaffected by it.

The meal turned out to be much more pleasant than Kristi had imagined. She began to relax slightly as the four of them shared years of memories. It was as though each of them had made a pact to recall only the good times, and there had been many of them.

When Kyle started reminding them of some of the things that had happened because of Kristi's impulsiveness, and her red-hot temper, laughter rang out, including Kristi's. Yes, she could certainly understand what a handful she'd been for all of them.

Laughing as she raised her glass, Kristi looked at Jason's face and froze. For a moment he allowed her to see the overpowering love and need he felt for her, then he dropped his eyes, leaving her shaken.

Jason sat there soaking up Kristi's nearness as she visited with her family. Had she laughed last night, he would have known immediately who she was. He had always enjoyed her laughter. She hadn't had much to laugh about after they were married. If she gave him the chance, he would make sure their life together was happier. She *had* to give them another chance.

After the children were in bed, the four adults sat around in the living room. The men talked about ranching and the women listened. Feeling comfortably drowsy, Kristi was unprepared for Jason to stand up and say, "Why don't you come home with me tonight, Kristi? We have some catching up to do." Her face flamed crimson. Then he added, "We have quite a lot to talk about that really isn't of interest to Kyle and Francine."

He'd done it on purpose! Her flush went even darker when she recognized that Kyle hadn't missed any of the byplay and was amused.

Kristi stood up and said coolly, "No, thank you. I don't think that's a very good idea under the circumstances, Jason. Besides, I've got a lot of *catching up* to do—'' he smiled at her emphasis ''—with Kyle and Francine as well.''

He stalked catlike toward the door and paused. ''Then how about walking me to my truck?'' She caught the look Kyle and Francine exchanged and could have kicked him. Why did he have to sound as though he could hardly wait to get his hands on her?

''All right,'' she agreed, determined to let him know exactly what she thought of his behavior. Neither one of them said anything until they reached his truck. The faint light from the porch bathed Jason's face in a golden glow as he looked at her car, then back at her.

''What was last night all about, Kristi? Is that the way divorces are taken care of in New York?''

She'd known it was coming and had decided that he wouldn't have it all his own way. ''I didn't think you'd remember much about last night, Jason.''

The hat Jason had put on as he stepped out of the house was shoved to the back of his head. ''Very funny. The only thing I'm hazy about is why I woke up in your bed.''

Dancing lights began to fill her eyes as a mischievous grin appeared on her face. ''Probably because that's where you fell asleep—or passed out, whichever best describes your condition.''

''Never mind my condition, what the hell were you trying to accomplish?''

''Would you believe nothing? I saw you go into the lounge and decided to let you know I was in town.'' She leaned against the truck in a deceptive pose of relaxation. Her nerves sang at his closeness. ''I didn't know what to say when you didn't recognize me, so I decided not to say anything.'' She was glad he couldn't hear her heart beating a frantic rhythm in her breast.

He touched her cheek lightly with his palm, causing alarms to go off throughout her body. ''What were you doing there, anyway?'' His voice was husky, and he seemed to be more aware of her than of their conversation. She was having a little trouble concentrating herself.

''I'd decided to wait and get a good night's sleep before coming on to the ranch. I was on my way to dinner when I spotted you.''

He leaned down and feathered light kisses along her jawline. ''I didn't see you.''

''No. You walked across the lobby like a man with a purpose which was one of the reasons I was surprised to find you alone.''

''You had other reasons to be surprised?'' His arms were now around her waist, forcing her against his body so there was no way she could ignore the effect she was having on him.

''The Jason McAlister I knew wouldn't have sat in a bar for hours drinking alone. That surprised me.'' She forced her eyes to meet his, knowing that he could see her expression by the porch light.

His hands roved caressingly along her sides, stroking her. ''Would you be interested in sticking around to rehabilitate me?'' He paused, but she refused to answer. ''People change, Kristi. You have...I have...that's part of life. But one thing has never changed....''

Her hands lay against his chest where she felt the heavy thump of his heart. She was drowning in the sensations he caused within her. ''What's that?'' she managed to mumble.

''The way we react to each other.'' His mouth came down on hers in a searing possession that robbed her of thought. Her mouth parted, inviting his invasion, and his tongue took advantage by slipping between her lips. She felt the sigh he gave deep within his chest and her body warmed to the nearness of him as he pressed her back against the cab of the truck. One of his hands found the zipper at her throat and slid it down to her waist, giving him access to her breasts.

Kristi's arms slid around his lean torso, her hands insinuating themselves into his tight jeans and pulling the shirttail away so she could feel the hard muscles of his back as they rippled under her touch. How many times had she fantasized about holding him like this? She knew his body as well as her own and she quickly refamiliarized herself with the muscular feel of his shoulders, then the ridge of his spine.

His lips were making their own discoveries as they slid down her neck and explored the valley between her pink-tipped breasts. He could smell her light perfume—the perfume that had haunted him the night before—the teasing fragrance that had lingered with him all day.

Suddenly, Jason jerked away from Kristi and, with trembling hands, pulled her zipper up to its position under her chin. He buried his head in her neck, holding her achingly close to his aroused body. "Come home with me, Kristi," he murmured. "Let me love you."

Kristi clung to him, trying to regulate her breathing. She felt as though she'd been on a carnival ride too long, her head whirling. How could he continue to have this effect on her? She couldn't give in to her purely physical reaction to him, she just couldn't.

She shook her head. "I can't, Jase. Don't you see? It would solve nothing."

He grinned as he took long breaths like a runner after crossing the finish line. "I can think of one or two problems it would solve."

She moved away from him, needing the distance to get her emotions under control. Then she glanced back at him as he leaned against the truck, watching her. "I don't belong in Texas, Jase, surely you recognize that. My career is in New York. That's where I live—where I want to live. We should have ended our marriage years ago." He became very still, studying her like a hunter stalking his prey. "Why won't you sign the divorce papers?"

He jerked open the door and stepped into the cab of his truck. "I refuse to discuss it with you here. We can go home and go into it if you wish."

"Not tonight, Jason." She moved closer to the truck, and he suddenly reached out and caught her, pulling her to him. She didn't resist, feeling the power in his arm as it drew her closer to the window of the cab.

He nodded. "All right, not tonight," he agreed. "I'll give you some time with your family, then I'm coming to get you. You might as well accept it." He cupped his hand around the back of her head and brought her mouth down to his, touching her lips in a surprisingly soft kiss that ignored the passion pulling them together. "I'll never let you go, Kristi, you may as well understand that right now," he muttered as he released her.

She stood watching as he backed out and drove away, her fingertips pressed against her mouth, swollen from his possession. What had she done by coming back? She had been sure she could resist him, only to be proven wrong the first time she saw him again.

A very thoughtful Kristi returned to the house and her family.

Chapter 4

The next few days drifted through Kristi's life like a soft breeze whispering in the cottonwood trees. She got acquainted with her niece and nephew, and reacquainted with Kyle and Francine. Unconsciously she waited for Jason to reappear.

One midafternoon found Kristi in the porch swing, reading one of the books she'd brought to catch up on. The wind rattled the leaves of the large cottonwoods planted nearby, blocking out the sound of a truck pulling into the yard. Engrossed in her book, she was startled to hear an unforgettable voice.

"Must be interesting reading."

Jason stood on the bottom step, one foot propped on the next step. Dusty Levi's gave evidence to his busy day. The color of his shirt came close to matching the sherry of his eyes as they stared at her through narrowed lids.

Kristi's gaze moved over him eagerly, and she realized how much she'd been looking forward to seeing him again. Not a good sign for her original plans. As his eyes lazily studied her, she nervously fingered the top button of her jade green shirt. She watched him as he sauntered toward her with his silent stride.

Several different swings had decorated the porch over the years, but none had seemed so small as this one when Jason settled into the space beside her. The spicy fragrance of his after-shave mingled with the scent of his warm body, and Kristi had to struggle to control her own body's reaction to him.

He dropped his arm along the back of the swing. "Where is everyone?"

Kristi reached for her single braid nervously, needing to keep her hands occupied as she absently pulled on it. "Francine took the kids into town. I decided to stay home and read." She twisted the braid around her hand. "I'm not sure where Kyle is."

Jason gently removed the plait from her twisting fingers and stroked it. Trying to ignore her response to his presence, she unwisely burst into speech. "What do you want?" The minute the words left her mouth she knew she'd said the wrong thing. She watched the smile appear on his face with fatalistic calm, but he surprised her by letting the provocative question pass.

"I wondered if you'd like to go with me this afternoon. You used to enjoy riding with me and I need to check out the river section.'' He continued to play with her braid as he talked. The message in Jason's eyes was about another subject. Her mind flashed to their night together and how good they had been with each other. His eyes registered similar thoughts. He lightly brushed the soft curls that clung to her neck as he waited for her answer.

A light shiver ran through her at his touch. Was he aware of the effect he had on her?

When she didn't answer him, he continued. ''One of the men reported seeing smoke in the south part of my property a few days ago. I need to take a ride and check it out; we've found people camping there in the past.'' He grinned as his hand slid around the nape of her neck. ''My property is a little too easy to reach from the other side of the river.''

Kristi knew of the narrowness of the Rio Grande along this area. During the dry summer months there were times when it dried up enough so that people could walk across without difficulty.

''Are you having trouble with illegal aliens?'' she asked in an attempt to show him how little effect he had on her. She wasn't sure whether she succeeded. Jason knew her too well.

He began to massage the taut muscles in her neck. ''You could say that.'' He nodded, a little amused at her serious expression.

''Kyle mentioned something the other night, but said there hasn't been much publicity in order not to discourage the tourists from visiting Mexico." She shifted slightly, hoping to move away from his body, but there wasn't enough room in the swing.

"I know, but I don't agree with the theory. I don't think the tourists have any business going into the interior right now."

"What's happening?"

"Mexico's poor economy has created an internal turmoil that's become explosive. The peso's been devalued twice in the past five years. Those who can, sneak across the river to find work." His face settled into grim lines. "Not that I blame them, but the Naturalization authorities watch all of us here on the border, trying to insure that we don't hire any of them. I can't afford to have them camping on my land." He grinned. "I don't expect to find anyone today, though." He tilted her chin so she was looking up at him. "Do you want to come?"

When he looked at her like that, she found him impossible to resist. "I might as well." She glanced down at the forgotten book in her hand. She had no idea what it was about. "I'll need to change shoes," she said as she stood up, more to get away from Jason's seductive presence than because she was in a hurry to leave.

He followed her into the house, which did nothing for Kristi's peace of mind. Hoping to deter him, she murmured, "I'll be right back." She discovered when she came out of her closet with an old pair of riding boots that she hadn't stopped him. He stood in the middle of the bedroom, looking around at the furnishings and at her personal belongings scattered around the room. "I never said I was neat," she muttered as she sat down on the bed to pull off her sandals.

"That's true, you never did," he agreed with a grin. His gaze traveled leisurely across her body, causing it to tingle as though he'd actually touched her. "However, you do have other redeeming virtues."

She refused to allow him to see how his teasing affected her. With admirable nonchalance she stood up, stamping her feet into the boots. "That's true. Just consider me the drinking cowboy's gift, come to console you in your time of need." She glanced at him from beneath thick lashes. "You never did tell me why you needed consoling the other night."

"Can't remember. Your consoling did the trick." They stood there in the bedroom, both conscious of the bed a couple of feet away. She would give a great deal to know what he remembered of that night. Was he aware how much she gave of herself, or that she'd never been with anyone else?

"Will I need a jacket?"

"It wouldn't hurt. I'm not sure how long we'll be. You might want to leave a message for the Coles."

Kristi left a note on the kitchen table, propped against the squat sugar bowl. She had a strong hunch that neither Kyle nor Francine would be surprised to learn she'd gone with Jason.

* * *

Kristi noticed the changes Jason had made to the property as they drove up to the ranch headquarters. The most noticeable was the blacktop on the formerly graveled road, an improvement which greatly reduced the dust in the area. The large two-story frame house had a fresh coat of white paint with a bright blue trim that lent a pleasing decorative touch. The familiar giant live oak trees continued to cast their generous shade around the house, framing it protectively.

Jason parked the truck and started for the barn. Kristi followed more slowly as she silently registered the well-kept appearance of the place. She glanced toward the house and wondered if Molly still worked for him.

As she watched Jason saddle two of his horses, she asked about Nate and Molly.

"Oh, yes. I doubt that I could function around here without those two. Molly still tries to fatten me up and Nate makes sure I don't get too complacent by pointing out the mistakes I make." His warm tones, more than his words, expressed his feelings for the couple.

Jason led the horses toward the house. "I need to pick up something—come in and say hello to Molly." His arm came around her in a familiar gesture and rested on her shoulders. He gave a gentle tug and settled her against his lean body as they followed the path to the house.

Molly greeted Kristi with a hug and beaming smile.

"With that pigtail hanging over your shoulder, you barely look sixteen." She paused, taking in Kristi's slim build. "Actually, you were more curvy back then than you are now."

Jason burst out laughing at the expression on Kristi's face. When she glared at him he spread his hands in a gesture of innocence. "What can I say, Kristi? Molly's always been one to tell it like it is." He paused, his gaze touching her body like a caress as he drawled, "What did you do with those curves, anyway?"

He prevented Kristi's swing from connecting with his shoulder by grasping her wrist. His maneuver didn't improve her temper, nor did her obvious irritation prevent his laughter.

Turning to Molly, Jason mentioned that he was taking Kristi with him. He reached into the refrigerator and took out a large container which he slipped into a sack.

"Oh, before I forget, Jase. Mr. Alvarez called."

Jason looked up sharply. "When?"

"Must have been about half an hour ago. He left a number." She handed him a slip of paper.

Jason stood there for a moment, his head down, then he seemed to come to a decision. "Excuse me." He smiled at Kristi. "I'd better get back to him." He walked through the door leading to the hall and his office.

Kristi looked around the room. Changes had been made inside as well. "The place looks great, Molly.

Jason's made quite a few improvements.'' Her gaze fell on the microwave.

Molly smiled. ''That he has. Something set him off a few months ago. He had a crew in doing some remodeling inside and refurbishing out.''

''What sort of remodeling?''

''Oh, he knocked out a wall upstairs and enlarged the master bedroom, added a nice large bathroom off of it, all fancy and modern. Kinda surprised me—he's in the house so seldom.''

A few months ago, Kristi thought. She'd first contacted him about the divorce a few months ago. Why would that have anything to do with his making changes in the house? Did he remember her once mentioning how nice it would be to have another bathroom? If he'd signed the papers she would have assumed that he was planning to remarry, but he'd been adamantly against the divorce.

They needed to discuss their relationship. Their lives had gone in different directions over the past five years. They could no longer ignore the situation.

Jason's voice exploded from his office, interrupting her reverie. ''Come off it, Alvarez. I waited in town for hours the other night and you canceled on me. Dammit, man, you know I've got to have your help. We can't waste any more time.''

Molly and Kristi glanced at each other, then away, embarrassed to have heard his private conversation. When Jason rejoined them, he looked dangerous.

Kristi decided she wouldn't want to be the one who crossed him.

He picked up the package he had taken from the refrigerator and started toward the door. "I'll see you later, Molly." When he reached the horses, he began to fill a saddlebag with the contents of his sack. It looked like food. Surely they weren't going to be gone long enough to eat, although she knew from experience that Jason never left the ranch headquarters without some supplies, including water and his battered coffeepot.

As they rode toward the southern rolling hills, Kristi enjoyed the day's promise of springtime. It was her favorite time of year in Texas. In another couple of months it would be so hot that going without a hat would guarantee sunstroke. Now she let her hat sit on the back of her head as she renewed her acquaintance with Jason's heritage.

"Do you ever think about living somewhere else, Jase?"

He'd been deep in thought and her question pulled him away from whatever caused his brow to crease so deeply. He, too, scanned the wide open area before them. He shook his head. "My time in the service convinced me that I wouldn't be happy anywhere else. Why?"

"I just wondered. I can't even picture you in any other surroundings."

They rode along in silence, Kristi concentrating on the scenery around them as she remembered her first days and nights in New York, miserably homesick, yet refusing to consider returning home.

The rolling hills were deceptive, looking smooth until they moved closer to view the rough ground, scraggly mesquite trees and occasional cactus. Clumps of grass grew in sparse oases of green and Kristi noticed several dry creek beds. The weather had not been kind to the area in recent months.

Jason eventually reined in and stepped out of the saddle, checking the ground. Kristi put gentle pressure on the bit as her horse also came to a stop. Remains of a large campfire were in evidence, but whoever had built it had taken into consideration the dry conditions. Large stones had been placed in a tight ring around the blackened dirt, which sat in an open clearing. As she signaled her horse forward, Kristi noted that the creek bed here was larger, fed by an underground spring that bubbled nearby. The area was peaceful and she had trouble seeing it as a possible spot for conflict.

Kristi eased from the saddle with care and ambled over to the side of the creek. A couple of weeping willow trees leaned close to the side, as though embracing the life-giving liquid rippling by. Glancing south, she wondered how far they were from the Rio Grande and how many people had gathered around a warm fire at this spot on the first night of what they hoped would be a new life.

She glanced over her shoulder then spun around and demanded, "What are you doing?"

"What's it look like I'm doing?" Jason replied as he continued his task.

"It looks like you're unsaddling our horses," she responded in a testy tone.

Jason solemnly acknowledged her comment. "Give the little lady a prize for being observant." Without looking in her direction he pulled off bedrolls from the saddles and unrolled them near the stone-ringed fire pit. "Why don't you look around for some wood—we might as well have a hot meal."

"Jason! We can't spend the night out here!"

"Why not?" he asked, stopping what he was doing and gazing at her with a steady look, his hands resting lightly on his hips.

"You know very well why not. Francine and Kyle will wonder what happened to me."

"Why should they? You left them a note saying you'd be with me." He began to pull packages out of the saddlebags and place them on the stones.

"They won't be expecting me to spend the night and you know it." Impatiently she watched him settling in. "What's this all about, anyway?"

"I wondered when you might think to ask that question." He reached into his pocket and pulled out a battered pack of cigarettes. Then he took one and stuck it between his lips. Cupping a lit match, he touched it to the end of the cigarette, inhaled, then blew out the match.

Kristi was no longer the wide-eyed eighteen-year-old who accepted each pearl of wisdom from his lips without question. Unfortunately, at twenty-four she still had to fight her strong feelings for him, despite his arrogance.

"If I'd known we were playing games I'd have asked for the rule book," she commented sweetly.

Her answer was not what he expected. In fact, her attitude was different from anything he'd seen in her, and he knew her well, or so he thought. His eyes narrowed as he took in her belligerent stance, then he began to smile. He may have married a girl, but he had a full-size woman on his hands now. He needed to remember that. "Relax, Kristi. I thought it would be a good idea for us to get away and give ourselves a chance to get reacquainted. You used to enjoy camping out—I thought you might like it now." He paused, drawing on his cigarette. "Do you really think Kyle and Francine are going to expect me to return you to them tonight?"

The blaze of desire that lit his eyes scorched Kristi across the space between them. The slanting sun cast shadows across the campsite and Kristi dropped her eyes, no longer able to meet his gaze.

Unable to find an answer for him, she remembered his earlier comment. "I'll look for firewood," she muttered as she looked around. Since the same thought must have been in the minds of the previous visitors, the immediate vicinity was bare of anything burnable.

Glancing across the creek, she decided to start hunting over there.

Jason watched her graceful movements as she crossed the creek, stepping on the stones uncovered by the gurgling water. He wondered if he would get his fill of just looking at her. After enduring the past few years, he rather doubted it.

He started after her.

They found several low-growing bushes and a few dead branches broken off mesquite trees. The companionable search relaxed Kristi as it brought back memories of earlier times. Jason had been right. She'd always enjoyed camping, and he and Kyle and Francine had often spent as long as a week out together when she was growing up. Had those times meant as much to Jason as they had to her?

By the time they returned to camp and got the fire going, it was dark. The smell of the burning mesquite erased the years as they cooked their meal. Jason's mysterious packages had contained ground beef hash, reheated pinto beans and cornbread ready to be baked in an iron skillet. After eating a heaping plate of the familiar fare, Kristi felt that she was truly back in Texas.

The bedrolls were placed end to end by the fire and Kristi leaned back on hers and studied the night sky. She'd forgotten how bright the stars looked away from the night glow of the city. She could feel the tension seep from her as she gave herself up to the night and her surroundings. For this time, at least, she could pretend there'd been no years in between. She moved her head lazily to watch Jason as he stirred the campfire, adding more wood. He placed the coffeepot over the fire and the aroma of fresh coffee wafted to her, teasing her senses. Coffee always seemed to taste better when made over an open fire, as though it absorbed the wood smoke as well.

Jason settled back on his bedroll with a contented sigh and admired the long length of Kristi stretched out so relaxed nearby.

"I've missed you, Kristi."

His husky voice reverberated through her body. Warm green eyes reflected the firelight as she watched him.

"I've missed you, too, Jase."

"Then why didn't you come home?"

"I couldn't."

He made an impatient move, then stopped abruptly. Slowly lighting another cigarette, he asked, "Why not?"

She gazed into the fire for a long moment before attempting an answer. "I couldn't face you, knowing I'd failed as a wife. I had to gather strength by looking forward until I was strong enough to look back."

The night sounds around them were a muted background to their low voices. The fire crackled occasionally, sending its sparks toward the bright stars flickering overhead. The faint call of a coyote drifted toward them and Kristi shivered at the lonely sound.

Jason's voice was low when he finally spoke. "I never realized you felt that you'd failed as my wife." She could hear pain in his voice, which surprised her.

"I wish I'd known, so I could have reassured you." He'd been staring into the fire but with his last remark he turned his head, and his pain was reflected on his face. "I'm sorry I didn't understand before. Why did you feel you had failed?"

His question brought painful memories flooding through her and she slid her arms around her bent knees and squeezed, trying to control her feelings. "Because I couldn't have the family you wanted... because you were gone so much...because you had a life away from me that you wouldn't share." She forced herself to meet his gaze as she attempted a smile. "I was such a child in so many ways. I didn't know what you expected of me, and I failed at the only thing I could do to make you want me."

Her obvious pain thrust into him like a knife blade and without thinking he moved over toward her. His shadow blanketed her for a moment, as he stood between her and the fire. For the first time she felt the chill of the night air. Then he settled beside her and pulled her into his arms as though he could erase the anguish she was feeling.

"Hush, Kristi, love. You don't know what you're talking about. You're all I've ever wanted... everything that I could possibly want, and you've always been that for me. I thought you knew."

She shook her head mutely against his shoulder as he held her against him.

"You must understand that you were more than a baby machine to me. Besides, you never gave us a chance to be parents after that. The doctor said we should wait a few months before even attempting another pregnancy." He paused. He shook her gently. "Remember?"

She nodded her head, but refused to look at him. He lowered them both so they were stretched full-length on her bedroll. It felt so good to have her back in his arms. For a while Jason was content to lie there with her snuggled against him. The conversation brought back many painful memories for him. How differently he might have handled her if he'd understood her insecurities.

"I wish I'd been more open with you about what I was doing back then."

His remark caused Kristi to pull away and stare up at him in surprise. Although those mysterious trips played a major part in her nightmares during that time in her life, she never expected to receive an explanation. She wondered why he mentioned them now.

"I had some cockeyed idea that I was protecting you from the harsh realities of life. Instead, I caused you to face different ones that weren't even necessary." His eyes full of love, he traced an invisible line along her jaw with his forefinger.

Kristi watched the shadows cast by the flickering firelight with fascination as they highlighted Jason's serious face. *How can I possibly cut this man out of my life,* she thought with quiet despair, *when he's part of me.*

Jason stared into the fire as he began to talk. "I was with the Army intelligence unit when I was in the service. When I got out, I did my best to forget that part of my life, but things don't always work out the way you want them to." His hand moved down her neck in a gentle stroking movement. Kristi caught her breath at the immediate response of her body to his touch. She forced herself to concentrate on his words. "A couple of years after I returned home I was contacted by the government to help with a covert investigation along the border. Both governments were trying to put a stop to heroin smuggling between the two nations."

Kristi relaxed as Jason's hands worked their magic. His gaze had dropped to her once more and he leaned over and kissed her lightly on the lips. With a rueful shrug, he acknowledged, "Since my ranch is located on the border, it made sense that I could move back and forth without arousing suspicion."

Unexplained happenings took on new meaning as Kristi recalled the early days of her marriage. Would it have made a difference if she'd been aware of his activities at that time? She would never know now.

"Are you still involved with them?" Her tone reflected her relaxed state.

"No, I'm not." Jason's hand paused at the top button of her shirt, toyed with it for a moment, then slipped it loose. "We were able to get enough evidence against the ringleaders to bring them in about six months after you left." His hand moved to the next button. "By then it was too late for me to explain to you what I'd been doing." With the last button undone, Jason slid his hand back to the front opening of her bra and undid the hasp. "You seemed to be happy with your new life."

"What gave you that idea?" Her heart was beating so rapidly it shook her body.

"That's the impression you gave Francine whenever she talked with you."

"Why didn't you ever call me, Jase?" she asked in a breathless whisper.

"Because I knew better. If I'd heard your voice, I would've been on the next plane to New York to drag you back home." His ragged tone did nothing for her peace of mind.

Her hand caressed the nape of his neck, feeling the springy hair that grew there, lost in the feeling of his lean strength pressed against her. "If that's the way you felt, why did you let me leave?"

His head bent toward her. "I had to face the fact that when I married you, you were too young to decide what you wanted in life." His hand cupped her breast, his fingers rubbing lightly over the peak until Kristi could no longer lie still. She shifted restlessly as his fingers edged to her other breast. "I'm not man enough to let you leave me like that again, Kristi, I'm sorry." Jason placed his lips with gentle care on hers, moving them in a silken glide that sent quivers rocketing down her body. As her lips softened in response, he moved his arms around her, drawing her closer to his hard frame.

Kristi responded to his possession, her tongue darting to meet his. He shifted his weight, lifted her and removed her blouse. Then he began to explore the soft contours of her body, the smooth silkiness of her back. He unsnapped her jeans and his hands followed the rounded contours of her hips as he slipped the rest of her clothes from her trembling body.

Had Jason said anything, whether imploring or demanding, perhaps Kristi could have resisted him. Instead, his silent seeking into her most secret places caused her to lose all desire to resist. She would enjoy this for just a while longer, then she must put a stop to it. She needed to explain to him there was no going back to their old relationship—they were two different people now—yet the feelings she was experiencing were familiar and very powerful.

Kristi wasn't aware when the lazy, exploring strokes changed to determined movements with definite goals. All she knew was that her body had burst into glorious flame wherever he touched. She moved closer to him, her hands searching his body. Her trembling fingers fumbled at the snaps of his shirt, hastily pulling until his chest was bared. Her hands explored the broad expanse of hard muscle and soft curls, relearning a once-familiar terrain. As her hands crept around his back, he shrugged off his shirt, then pulled her back to him. Her breasts pressed against him and she felt the quick catch of his breath at the touch.

Kristi's hands paused at his waist, frustrated in their attempts to renew her acquaintance with his body. She felt cool air play across her hot skin and realized that Jason had pulled away. Her eyelids fluttered open and she watched as he pulled off his boots and Levi's. She'd forgotten the strength in his hard muscled buttocks and thighs, the powerful body kept in whipcord condition.

He lay back down beside her, his legs tangling with hers, his arousal hard against her bare thigh. Kristi trembled with the force of her emotions. His hands drew a pattern on her inner thighs that sought to drive her out of her mind. Just as she thought he would stroke the most sensitive area, his hand would dance lightly away, only to begin the pattern once again.

"Oh, Jase," she moaned, wanting him to take her so badly she ached.

"I'm right here, honey."

"Love me, Jase. Oh, please, love me."

His uneven breathing tickled her ear and she knew how badly he wanted her, but he seemed intent on teasing them both by postponing their joining.

Her hand reached out and touched him as he nestled along her thigh. His whole body jerked at her touch. She stroked him, the full, strong length of him, and heard his groan. He raised himself, slipped his hands under her hips and pulled her up to him. Then he eased himself into the loving warmth of her body.

For long moments they lay there, held tightly in the closest embrace possible, his warmth filling her, her warmth surrounding him. When he began to move she wrapped her legs around him in an effort to absorb all of him. Her movement spurred him into a faster rhythm that caused Kristi to explode inside. He paused, holding her close until her body slowed the trembling from within, then he began to move once more.

Kristi was unfamiliar with the pleasure of reaching the peak of sexual gratification, then continuing. Her body seemed to be so much more sensitive to the sensations he created within her and it reacted to the stimulus with added fervency.

As Jason's rhythm increased once more, Kristi gripped him with such intensity that Jason had trouble breathing. Her pulsing body was more than he could withstand and he gave one final lunge into the deep softness that surrounded him. He was positive he'd felt the earth shake. Their ardent lovemaking served to sedate them and both fell asleep as they lay, in a tangle of arms, and legs on top of Kristi's bedroll.

As the night breeze grew more brisk, Jason stirred, moving carefully so he wouldn't wake the sleeping woman by his side. Stepping cautiously around the fire he grabbed his bedroll and unzipped it, moving it next to hers. He shifted Kristi into the opened bedroll, holding her close for a moment. Then, taking hers, he zipped the two together and pulled it over them. He pulled Kristi back into his arms, and she shifted until her head curved into the hollow of his shoulder.

He lay there for a long time, holding her in his arms as he stared at the silent stars blinking in the black night, before drifting off to sleep once more.

Chapter 5

Jason watched as morning light silhouetted the eastern hills. Kristi still slept soundly in the circle of his arms. How many nights had he dreamed that he held her in his arms, only to wake up alone? She had listened to him last night, but he wasn't sure how she felt. Her lovemaking had been spontaneous and fervent and he knew he still had the ability to arouse her, but did she still love him? Was she willing to make something of their marriage? He had loved her enough to let her go once before, but he knew he didn't have the strength to do it again. This was one contest he had to win in order to survive.

Kristi dreamed that Jason held her in his arms, his hands molding her to his body. She shifted closer to him, wanting to feel the power of his love once more, when she realized that she wasn't dreaming. Just as her eyes struggled open, his mouth found hers in a hotly passionate kiss and she melted into the arms already holding her.

His lovemaking that morning was aggressive and demanding—as though he couldn't get enough of her. The raging storm within him quickly ignited Kristi and she responded almost savagely. Tenderness had given way to raw passion and Kristi matched Jason's demands with equal fervor. She stayed with him this time and waited until she heard his cry as he went over the edge before she gave in to the sensations she'd fought to delay.

They lay gasping for air, damp from their exertions, their down-filled cover long since discarded. As she lay limply against him, Kristi felt Jason's chuckle start deep in his chest.

"You're something of a tiger when aroused, aren't you, lady?"

She thought about that for a moment, trying to equate the picture with her ice princess image. She began to smile as she reached up and smoothed the damp hair from his forehead. "Would you have preferred me to cringe and pull away?"

This time his laugh rumbled into the open. "You would have had a hell of a time trying to pull away this morning, that's for sure."

"That's what I decided," she answered demurely.

He shook his head in bewilderment. He didn't know this bewitching creature with the ability to tease when he least expected it. His love for Kristi had been with him for so long it was as essential to him as the air he breathed, but discovering the mature personality kept him slightly off-balance. He had a hunch she preferred him that way.

Kristi rested against him, admitted to herself that she felt as though she'd come home. All of her calm, rational plans to return to Texas and get Jason's signature on the divorce papers seemed to have drifted away in the smoke of their campfire the night before.

She sat up, ignoring the morning chill and her bareness. "Jason, we need to talk."

He watched the morning light touch the dainty curve of her breasts. He leaned over and kissed one of them lingeringly. "What about?"

"The divorce."

He stiffened, then slowly straightened to look at her. In a low, firm voice, he stated, "There will be no divorce, Kristi."

The chill Kristi felt was not entirely due to the morning breeze. He had misunderstood her. She tried to explain. "What I mean is—"

"I know what you mean, Kristi, and I'm telling you right now I don't intend to agree to it."

Frustrated that he wouldn't let her finish, she jumped up and looked around for her clothes. They lay near the bedroll on a clump of grass, for which she gave thanks. Sand would not improve them at all. She tried once more. "Would you just listen to me for a moment? I know how you feel—you've made that clear enough. It's just that my job is in New York and—"

"I know where your job is, damn it. I've known for five lousy years." Jason had grabbed his clothes and was dressed by the time he finished speaking. He filled the coffeepot with water and set it to the side as he began to rebuild the fire. "I thought from your response to me you were willing to consider staying here. Obviously, I was wrong."

Determined not to lose her temper, she waited until her voice sounded calm. "It isn't quite that simple, Jason. I have certain commitments—"

"You sure as hell do. You made a commitment to me before you decided modeling was your lifelong dream. That's a commitment you've been willing to overlook until now."

"That's not true, Jason, and you know it. I didn't think you wanted me. You didn't ask me to stay—you never called or wrote and asked me to come home. How was I to know you still wanted me?" She slid her hands in her back pockets as she glared at him.

The fire caught and Jason added the small twigs needed, then slowly stood up. "You should have known I still wanted you because I stand behind my commitments."

"To the bitter end. Yes, I know. Well, I didn't want to continue as your wife just because you were stuck with me. You wanted children—we both knew that—"

"Not that again. Yes, I wanted children, Kristi, but if you can't have them, then we won't have them. You're too important to me to give you up over an issue like that!" He stood a few feet away, glaring right back at her.

"I am?" Her voice faltered.

If anything, his frown deepened. "You're damned right."

"So why didn't you ever tell me?" she asked wistfully.

He threw up his hands in disgust. "I give up." He spun around and stalked away from the campsite.

Kristi wandered toward the stream, then crossed it as she sought some privacy among the brushy hills. She needed time to think.

Had she expected too much of Jason? He'd never been one to talk about his feelings, but she had always known he was there when she needed him. Maybe that was it. She had relied on him all her life without question, until they lost the baby, when she'd begun to question everything. Because he hadn't supplied the answers, she'd felt that he let her down.

What had she done to him?

When she returned to the campsite, Kristi caught the strong aroma of coffee brewing over the campfire. Jason sat near the fire and, when he saw her, grabbed the pot and poured two steaming cups full, setting one down beside him and blowing on the other. She murmured a soft "thanks" and picked up the cup, wrapping her fingers around it. She could feel his tension but was unsure what she could say that would ease it. Everything had seemed so clear before she arrived. Now their situation seemed like a tangled mass of thread, and she wasn't sure how to start unraveling the misunderstandings. In her youthful exuberance Kristi had thought that loving each other was all that was necessary to make a relationship work. She had learned painfully that, although vital, love wasn't enough. No relationship could survive unless the individuals involved communicated with each other and unless each had a basic understanding of the other's feelings.

She vented her frustration with a sigh.

"I want to ride down to the river," Jason announced. He stood up, reached for the saddlebags and brought out a wrapped package of cinnamon rolls. "You'd better eat something. Molly made these yesterday."

Kristi's mouth watered, remembering the taste from years past. She took one from him and bit into it, savoring the sharp bite of cinnamon and the creamy texture of icing. Glancing up, she noticed a slight smile curve the corner of Jason's mouth. Swallowing the bite, she asked, "What's so funny?"

He continued to take in the picture she made—her clothes wrinkled, her long braid matted and unkempt, her face shiny—then explained. "If your New York friends could only see you now."

She shrugged, unconcerned, and took another bite.

New York seemed light-years away—an alien planet that had little allure.

After filling both cups with the remaining coffee, Jason packed the remaining items with sure, deft movements. He had both horses saddled and ready by the time Kristi finished her roll and coffee.

The day promised to be another warm one, with only a slight breeze. Jason seemed preoccupied as he followed a trail indiscernible to Kristi. They came over a rise and halted, and she was surprised to discover the river so close to their camping site. The Rio Grande flowed sluggishly by, looking muddy and ugly, hardly what would be expected of a major boundary between two nations. Kristi compared the two sides of the river and saw no difference. It was hard to believe that another government, another language, another way of life took over once the river was crossed.

Jason signaled his mount to move down the incline until he reached the banks of the river, then he rode along studying the ground. Eventually he angled away from the river once more and turned north. Kristi moved up alongside of him and glanced at his grim expression. Whatever he'd discovered, he didn't like it.

They rode for miles in silence, Kristi soon losing herself in thought. Jason had made his position clear. Where did that leave them? Her career required that she live in New York. Did she want to return to that busy world and continue as she had been during these last few years? Married, but not married? Is that what Jason wanted? What *did* he want?

The memory of his recent lovemaking brought a flush to her cheeks. He'd made it quite clear what he wanted! Could the magnetic force that pulled them together in such heated response to each other be a strong enough foundation for their relationship? Kristi glanced at Jason from the corner of her eye. His eyes searched the underbrush. He seemed unaware of her presence.

Kristi smiled as memories of other overnight camping trips came to mind—especially the ones they'd taken after their marriage. Had he always looked at her with such possession, as though branding her with every look? If Jason had his way, she would stay right there on the ranch with him, as he had intended when he married her.

I wonder what Jonathan would do if I were suddenly to call and tell him I want to retire? Would she miss the frenetic atmosphere, the excitement, the clothes, the money, the recognition?

She didn't know. She'd never considered it before.

They were little more than a mile away from the house when a horse and rider raced toward them, raising a cloud of dust that trailed behind like exhaust. It was one of Jason's ranch hands. He began to shout as he pulled up in front of them.

"Nate's been hurt, Mac," he panted. "We're afraid it's bad. No one knew where you were." He stopped to get his breath. "Molly had us bring him into the house and we called the doc, but he isn't here yet."

"How bad is he, Pete? What happened?" Jason's questions flew over his shoulder as he leaned over the long neck of his horse and took the lead. As they galloped, Kristi heard Pete answer.

"That new horse you bought started bounding around and threw him. Before we could get to him, the damned fool thing stepped on his leg. We heard the bone pop clear across the corral." They reached the yard and Jason leaped from his horse. "He may have some busted ribs, too. Molly's afraid he's got a concussion." Pete ran to keep up with Jason. "He don't look too good."

The string of expletives coming from Jason painted the air blue as he took the porch steps three at a time and disappeared into the house. Kristi had grabbed his horse's reins and led it down to the barn, knowing both animals needed cooling off.

Pete took the reins from her as she climbed down from the saddle. "I'll see to the horses, ma'am. You might want to go in to comfort Molly."

Of course. Nate and Molly were inseparable. Kristi thought of them more as an institution than as a couple. She trotted back to the house.

As she passed Jason's office she heard him on the phone giving directions. He slammed down the receiver and strode past her down the hall. His voice sounded calm, as though he hadn't been giving orders and directions like a machine gun spitting out bullets.

"A helicopter will be here within fifteen minutes. They'll fly you to San Antone, Nate. You're going to be fine."

Kristi paused at the door of one of the bedrooms and took in the tableau before her. Nate lay stretched out on top of the multicolored quilt covering the four-poster bed, his face as gray as his grizzled hair. Molly sat in a straight-backed chair by the bed, holding Nate's hand, appearing composed; but the panic in her eyes told of her real state. Jason stood at the end of the bed, legs braced, his hat still grasped in one hand, forgotten.

Nate had taken the place of Jason's father in his life. Jason fought to hang on to his control. Why the hell did these things have to happen?

Jason's glance fell on Molly. "You better get a bag packed, Molly. No tellin' how long you'll be in San Antone."

Molly looked up, startled. "I can't go with him, Jase. You've got those extra men coming in tomorrow to help with the inoculations and branding." Her eyes fell to the pasty face on the pillow, then looked up at Jason, trying to hide the welling tears.

Without glancing at Kristi, Jason replied brusquely, "Your place is with Nate, Molly. Don't worry. Kristi's here. She can handle this end."

Nate was the only one who didn't react to his statement. Molly's face broke into a trembling smile that would have lit a dark room, and Kristi's astonishment at being volunteered so casually would have been comical if the occasion hadn't been so serious.

"Oh, Kristi, could you?" Molly's voice quavered and she paused. "They'll only be here three days—but that's twelve hungry men to cook for."

The sardonic smile on Jason's face spurred Kristi's response. "Molly, there's no way I could ever take your place, but I'll do my best to see that none of them starve." She met Jason's amused gaze with a level one of her own.

The whumping sound of giant blades cutting through air grew louder and Molly jumped up. "Oh, the helicopter's coming. I'll be ready in just a moment." She dashed out of the room faster than Kristi had ever seen her move before.

Jason stepped over to Nate's side and checked his pulse. Kristi heard a commotion on the porch and stepped back into the hallway. She saw two paramedics with a stretcher and bag push through the front door, and she motioned to them.

A flurry of activity accompanied Nate's removal from the house. Molly stayed as close to Nate as possible as they carried him through the kitchen and out to the waiting copter. Kristi admired the well-planned procedure that enabled the men to respond so quickly to emergencies. As she followed them out the door she saw Jason talking to the pilot.

A car slammed to a stop and the local doctor leapt out of it. Jason met him before he got halfway to the house, but the noise from the helicopter drowned out his explanations. Both men stopped talking and watched as the large chopper lifted off and rapidly disappeared from sight. The strain on Jason's face was more evident now that his stoic attitude wasn't necessary.

"Hello, Dr. Johnson. It's good to see you, even if your trip out here was wasted." Kristi joined the two men, her memory relentlessly returning to the morning that this man had sat by the side of her bed attempting to comfort her.

"Kristi! I hadn't heard you were back, child. It's good to see you." He grabbed her hand and squeezed it affectionately while Jason watched them in silence.

"Do you have time for something to drink, Doctor?" she asked, pleased to see him again.

"I think I'll take time, Kristi. I'm just sorry I didn't get here sooner." He turned to the younger man. "What do you think, Jason? How bad was he?"

Jason rotated his shoulders in a weary gesture and turned toward the house, motioning Kristi and Dr. Johnson to go in front. "It's hard to tell, doc. The paramedics seemed to think he was in pretty good shape, from all his vital signs. We'll have to wait until Molly calls to find out what the X-rays show."

Kristi was astonished to discover that it was after one o'clock when they reached the kitchen. *Jason must be hungry by now.* She checked the contents of the large refrigerator and smiled. They certainly wouldn't starve to death, that was certain. A large bowl of crisp vegetables waited, as well as slices of ham and roast beef. Potato salad nestled among pickled beets. Kristi began to set the food on the table, grabbing a pitcher of iced tea as she swung the refrigerator door shut.

It didn't take much convincing to get the doctor to stay and eat with them. After lunch Jason saw him off and returned to the kitchen, where he poured himself another cup of coffee. Kristi watched him, reminded again how seldom he showed what he was feeling. She wished he wouldn't try so hard to hide his concern for Nate.

Kristi cleared the dishes from the table. "I'll need to go get my clothes and explain to Kyle and Francine what happened, if I'm going to stay here."

Jason's eyes followed her movements between the table and sink. His voice was low. "Was there ever any doubt?"

She leaned on the back of her chair, watching him. "I'm going to stay here, Jason, because *I* want to, not because *you* decided I should."

"Oh." He leaned back in his chair, amused at her tone. "Is that the way it is?"

"That's exactly the way it is. When I'm ready to leave, I'll leave."

His eyes darkened to amber as he continued to watch her. "Did you think I had some intention of locking you up?"

She flushed at his tone of voice. "No, I just wanted to make it clear why I'm staying." She hated the amused look on his face and was determined to erase it. "I intend to stay in one of the spare bedrooms." She watched one of his brows arch slightly, but he made no comment as she glared at him.

The silence thickened in the room as they stared at each other. Jason's expression didn't change, although a twinkle danced in his eyes. Finally, he nodded. "Fine with me. Take your pick," He shoved away from the table. "I've got some work to catch up on. Go ahead and take my truck." He paused in the doorway. "You might want to have Kyle and Francine over for dinner, if you're up to it. I know they want to spend as much time with you as they can."

His tone almost dared her to have them over. What was the matter? Didn't he think she could handle the task of cooking for everyone? "Good idea," she responded with a smile.

She heard his quiet chuckle as he crossed the porch and headed for the barn.

Infuriating man!

Kristi crawled into bed with a sigh. It had been a full day since she'd awakened in a sleeping bag with Jason. Dinner had been fun, though. The atmosphere was much more relaxed, as though Kyle and Francine fully approved of her being back with Jason. He'd been his teasing, provocative self, his amusement at her aloof attitude apparent. She didn't care. She was not going to fall into his arms every time he held them open. He was a stubborn, opinionated, arrogant man.

Her reason for staying was to prevent Molly from worrying. Jason needn't think she was staying for his sake.

He'd made no comment when she unpacked all her clothes in the front guest room upstairs. When she'd announced that she was going to bed he'd just nodded and continued to read a report Kyle had brought over.

The bed felt marvelous. Kristi couldn't understand why she couldn't fall asleep. She turned over, restless. Then she heard Jason's soft tread on the stairs and knew that she'd been waiting to hear it. She held her breath as he walked past her door and into his room across the hallway. She sighed, reluctant to admit that she thought he might try to coax her into his bed. He knew better.

Kristi was drifting off to sleep when she heard the slight creak of her door opening. Her eyes half opened and she watched the shadow glide silently toward the bed, reach down and lift the covers, then slide in beside her.

"What are you doing in here?" she mumbled.

Jason pulled her against his body, curling around her so she was cupped by his warmth. He whispered in her ear, "Thought I'd find out what it's like to be a commuting husband."

Kristi began to stir.

"Go to sleep, darlin'. Five o'clock's going to come awfully early for you, now that you're back to keeping ranching hours."

She settled into his warmth, drowsily aware of his hand cupping her breast. Then she was asleep.

Chapter 6

The spicy scent of masculine cologne teased Kristi as she slept. She stirred. Firm lips touched hers in a soft caress. Her eyes blinked open. The bright gleam of tawny cat eyes filled her vision. She focused on Jason, dressed in a blue chambray work shirt and multiwashed Levi's. He leaned over the bed, watching her indulgently.

"Time to get up, love," he murmured as he continued to drink in her fresh beauty. Rioting curls fell around her face and shoulders, framing her radiant face. She smiled up at him, still influenced by her delicious dream. Lifting her arms languidly she draped them around his neck, then slowly kissed him. They celebrated their being together again with a kiss that began to get out of hand. Jason pulled back, a little breathless.

"Honey, I can't handle that kind of greeting this early in the day and expect to get any work done." He straightened, pulling her from the bed until she stood on the floor beside him. "You've got a busy day ahead of you, yourself."

His hands slid down her slender curves and he jerked them away as though scorched, then backed toward the door. "We'll be in to eat in about half an hour." She watched him grab his hat and heard his heels tapping a rapid retreat downstairs. Stretching lazily, Kristi caught sight of her reflection in the large dresser mirror. Her diaphanous seafoam nightgown hid nothing from view and she grinned, remembering Jason's reaction when he pulled her from bed.

He wants a rancher's wife? Well, he's going to get one, she decided as she grabbed her underthings and walked into the hall. There was a bathroom shared by the upstairs bedrooms and she started toward it, then remembered what Molly had told her. She turned and strolled into Jason's bedroom, instead. It was twice as large as the room they had once shared. She noted that it was more lavishly furnished than the rest of the house and couldn't help wondering why. The plush chocolate-brown carpeting made a dramatic contrast to the blue-and-white of the walls, window coverings, and upholstery. She was surprised to discover that he hadn't insisted on masculine decor for the room. A chaise longue by the window definitely called for a languishing female.

Kristi wandered into the bathroom, took one look

and burst out laughing. This was too much. The tub was at least four by eight feet, and one wall was made up entirely of mirrors. Even the shower stall was built for two! All right, Jason, I get your message!

After a quick shower, she dashed back across the hallway, slipped on jeans and a pullover navy blue knit top that clung. She pulled her hair into a rubber band at the top of her head, the long waves falling down her neck and shoulders. It was time to show Jason that she hadn't forgotten any of her skills....

Breakfast was fun. She didn't know any of the new men helping Jason during their spring break from Texas A & M College. Jason's voice had rung with quiet pride when he introduced her to them as his wife. She enjoyed listening to Jason's chuckle during the teasing and talking over breakfast, and she laughed with him when he threw his head back in a hearty bellow at one of the jokes currently crossing the campus.

Was it possible that her presence made such a difference to him? She found herself hoping so. Jason had always been so special in her life—he'd always been there to rely on when she was growing up. She hoped she could learn to give a little of that love and concern back to him. Why couldn't she have understood years ago that it wasn't enough to take his love and support—he needed much the same thing from her.

The hands noisily trooped out to a chorus of compliments on her cooking. Their youthful exuberance made her feel old enough to be their mother. Jason paused beside her and placed his hand on the soft curve of her derriere. Smoothing the curve with his hand, he leaned over and spoke softly in her ear. "We're going to have to fatten you up. A few more meals like that one should do it."

When she turned from the sink to look at him, his kiss was waiting. The gentle salute affected her as strongly as his most passionate lovemaking. He stepped back and grinned. "That should hold me until lunch."

Her first day set the pattern for the several that followed. The news from San Antonio was good: Nate was recovering rapidly. Although the concussion was mild, the break needed traction. It would be several weeks before he and Molly returned home.

The house seemed different to Kristi than it had five years before. With Molly gone, she was in charge. She no longer felt overwhelmed but accepted the challenge and began a campaign of spring cleaning and meal planning with zest.

Jason seemed to find a suspicious number of chores to do in and around the house, so she really didn't have time to miss him before he was there, coming up silently behind her to steal a kiss or tenderly pat a part of her anatomy. No one seeing him could doubt his joy at having Kristi home with him once more.

The house was finally ready to greet Nate and Molly when they returned. Francine had been helping

Kristi with the preparations for their arrival. It was early evening and everyone had gone home. Kristi finished putting everything away in the kitchen and wandered down the hallway to the office where Jason was working. She paused in the doorway, enjoying the sight of him. She glanced past him and absently noted her flower bed touched by the setting sun. She'd planted seedlings of marigolds, zinnias, and pansies, and they were covered with buds, ready to blossom any day. She'd forgotten how much she enjoyed gardening and wondered how she could have been content away from the soil for so long.

Her mind flashed back to her apartment in New York. She had given it surprisingly little thought since she'd gotten so involved here. She rarely spent time in the apartment, other than to sleep. Looking back on her life in New York, she realized how hectic it had been. She'd enjoyed it—how could she not? It had been exciting. Her job had brought her money and fame. She had met many glamorous and renowned people.

She missed Jonathan and his dry wit, as well as several models who'd become friends over the years, but none of them could take the place of Jason in her life.

Jason glanced up from his ledger and saw Kristi standing there, her gaze focused out the window behind him. His eyes roamed over her with possessive pleasure. The snug fit of her jeans reminded him of those she'd worn as a teenager when he'd tried so hard to ignore the voluptuous temptation she presented. She'd definitely filled out since arriving at the ranch. The golden blouse strained at the snaps and he grinned, thinking of her grumbling comments as she dressed that morning. The tips of his fingers tingled at the memory of how much enjoyment he found exploring those curves.

Kristi realized that Jason was looking at her and she wandered into the room and leaned her hip against his desk. She tilted her head and looked at her husband, whose tawny hair was highlighted by the slanting rays from the window. His lazy grin clutched at her heart. She reminded herself that she had come in for a specific reason.

"Who is Alvarez?"

Jason took his time answering as he leaned back in his large leather chair, dropping his pen. He'd been on the phone earlier with Alvarez and wasn't too surprised by her curiosity.

"He's a contact I need in Mexico. Why do you ask?"

"I'm not sure," she admitted slowly. "I guess I want to know why he causes such a reaction in you whenever you talk to him."

Jason's smile faded and he sat up a little straighter. Genuinely puzzled, he asked, "I don't follow you."

Kristi's frown deepened as she searched for words. "Whenever you speak to Alvarez your voice goes icy and aloof—very businesslike. To me it's obvious that you don't like him. But if that's true, why do you talk to him so often?"

Her slightly tilted green eyes searched his, their earnestness triggering a slight alarm within him. *Careful, Jason, here's a test for your new relationship,* he warned himself. *Don't blow it this time.*

Jason stood up and moved over to the corner of the desk where Kristi half leaned, half stood. He ran a callused finger down the softness of her cheek, aware of how vulnerable this one particular human could make him feel. The word *love* was inadequate to describe the tumultuous feelings she stirred within him.

He strolled toward a large leather-covered chair on one side of the stone fireplace, gently tugging Kristi by the hand. When he sat down he pulled her into his lap, cradling her in his arms as though she were a small child.

No one else has the power to reduce me to a quivering mass of sensations, Kristi thought with wry amusement. *I've already forgotten what I asked him.*

For a moment she thought he must have forgotten as well. He began to talk about someone else.

"I've never told you about my friend, Joe, have I?" he asked as he ran his hand along the curls clustered on her neck.

She shook her head.

"Joe Guerrero and I met during Army basic training. He's from El Paso—a couple of years younger than me." He smiled at some thought as he absently stroked the back of her neck. "Joe rushes out to meet life—he's too impatient to wait for it. He's gregarious, exuberant and the best friend a man could possibly want.'' His hand slipped to her arm.

''Joe and I ended up in the Orient together and were picked for several special missions. It didn't take me long to discover I couldn't have a better man guarding my back than Joe.'' Jason smiled. ''We used to joke about who had saved the other last, but it wasn't a joke—not really.'' The smile disappeared as memories unrolled in his mind. ''You never forget that kind of relationship. Looking back, I realize now it was a miracle neither of us were killed.''

Silence lay in the room like a silken net. Kristi could think of nothing to say, and so waited to see what Jason's story had to do with Alvarez.

''Joe returned to the States several months before I did and by the time I returned, I'd lost track of him.'' Jason paused, as though caught up in a private memory, unrelated to his story. Then his gaze returned to Kristi. ''He was one of the men involved in the smuggling investigation. I had no idea he was a part of it until I discovered him working undercover for the Mexican government. Part of Joe's family still lives in Mexico. His cousin got involved with the smugglers and, when he tried to break away from them, they killed him. After that, Joe offered to help the Mexican government stop them.'' Jason's stroking caused Kristi to want to purr with contentment. ''We were careful not to let the drug dealers know that we knew each other, and as far as I know, no connection was ever drawn between us. The arrests made as a result of our work were done when we were 'conveniently' away."

Jason glanced at Kristi and touched his lips lightly to hers.

"Alvarez was one of the men involved in that job. He was supposedly a friend of Joe's, although I doubt that Alvarez understands the meaning of the word." He dropped his head on the back of the chair and sighed. "Anyway, Alvarez contacted me just before you arrived to say that Joe was in trouble down in Mexico and had sent Alvarez to let me know." His eyes studied her from half-closed lids. "Joe is being held prisoner down there, Kristi. I'm going to get him out."

Horrible memories from her early married life came running back to engulf her—nights when Jason was gone, when she didn't know where he was. She forced the word from her stiff lips. "When?"

He pulled her closer, nuzzling her neck. He had to be honest with her. Their relationship had to be based on truth and trust. "As soon as Alvarez can finish making the arrangements. We're hoping he can find a guard in need of a little ready cash. It would make things a lot simpler."

"Why is Joe being held?"

"Joe must have gotten on the wrong side of one of the officials down there. According to Alvarez, some parts of the smuggling operation have started functioning again." He frowned. "Alvarez thinks a minor official wants in on the take and plans to hold Joe as a hostage until he gets what he wants.'' Jason shook his head. ''Mexican jails aren't known for their pleasant accommodations.''

''Couldn't he explain he's a United States citizen?''

''Do you think anyone in some sleepy little village cares? Charges were brought against him—trumped-up charges according to Alvarez—and they can keep him indefinitely without ever bringing him to trial.''

Kristi could feel the anger building within her. ''That's awful!''

Jason felt her body quiver with indignation. ''I know. That's why I intend to do something about it.''

''But what if bribing a guard doesn't do it?'' she asked with suspicion. ''What will you do then?''

His tone was nonchalant. ''Break him out.''

''By force?''

''I certainly hope not, but it may be necessary. Joe and I know a few tricks that might get him out without alerting the entire village. Once I get down there, I'll have a better grasp of the layout.''

They sat there in silence as Kristi began to put the bits and pieces of her previous knowledge together with what he'd just told her.

''Was Alvarez the reason you were drinking the first night I was home?''

He looked at her, surprised at the question. ''He was supposed to have been there to meet me, which was why I'd ordered a bottle for him.'' His face expressionless, he commented, "I thought you'd decided that I have a drinking problem."

"I did. You gave an excellent performance of a drunken cowboy looking for a little action that night." Her mocking tone brought a faint trace of red across his high cheekbones. "But you've allowed me to spend too much time with you to buy it." She held up her hand and started to tick off points on her fingers. "For one thing, you've never had anything stronger than coffee to drink since I've been here, even when Nate had his accident." A mischievous grin flitted across her face. "Of course, the way you like your coffee, that's plenty strong enough." She paused, her eyes skimming his broad shoulders. "Second, I don't think you could stay in such good physical shape and drink as much as I first thought you did."

"Darn, and here I was hoping that you were working at rehabilitating me." He slid her off his lap and stood up.

She looked at him, puzzled. "You *wanted* me to think you had a drinking problem?"

"Not necessarily, but I rather enjoyed your watching over me so nicely." He grinned as he suddenly swung her up in his arms.

"What are you doing? Jason, you idiot, put me down!"

"Huh-uh. I have to maintain my strength and stamina." His chuckle echoed deep in his chest where Kristi's head rested. He took the stairs two at a time.

He pushed the bedroom door open with a booted foot, then shoved it closed with the same foot once they were inside the room. He laid her gently on the bed, his hands quickly unsnapping her shirt, leaving her upper torso bare to his view. Her jeans were unbuckled, unsnapped and lowered over her hips in less than a minute. If there were ever contests for undressing a woman in the shortest amount of time, Jason would win a championship award!

Kristi lay there watching him as he jerked off his boots, quickly discarded the rest of his clothes and climbed into bed beside her. She could make no pretense of protest—she loved this man too much. All she ever seemed to want to do was hold him in her arms.

He seemed to have other ideas. Kneeling beside her, Jason started to kiss her, starting at her ankles and working his way up. She groaned at the sensations he aroused. She heard him mutter something.

"What is it, Jase?"

His hands stroked her inner thighs with such a light touch it felt like a downy feather caressing her. He raised his head and looked at her.

"Whenever I'm out on the ranch during the day, all I can think about is you. I fantasize about all the things I intend to do with you when I return." His head dropped as his tongue drew designs on her inner thigh.

Kristi could feel the desire building within her. As his hands and mouth continued to caress her, her body convulsed in response. "Oh, Jase!" His harsh breathing assured her he was not unaffected by what he was doing. She gripped him with both hands, then let go as the sensations of bursting fireworks took over within her. "Oh...God...Jase!"

Jason moved his body up over hers as he stretched out between her legs, taking in the dreamy expression on her face. "Aren't you used to that?" His voice rasped husky with emotion.

Her voice trembled. "You should know—you've never done that before."

She felt his body stiffen, then go very still. She opened her eyes. He was looking at her with infinite tenderness. "Kristi?" he said with soft amazement. "Are you trying to tell me something?"

She blinked. What had she said?

"Haven't your New York lovers worshiped your body as I have?" Her bewilderment must have shown in her eyes. As he lowered himself so their bodies fit together, he asked, "Hasn't anyone else ever made love to you?"

Caught by the fervent expression on his face, she shook her head. "Of course not, Jase. I thought you knew."

"Oh, Kristi." He sighed as he gathered her to him in a rib-cracking hug. "I didn't want to know—I was determined never to ask—but I couldn't help myself." He leaned down and captured her lips in a kiss so loving that her heart seemed to forget to beat. As he slowly pulled away, he brushed the soft curls clustered around her forehead away from her face. "It wouldn't have mattered, you know, but I'm still glad I've been the only man in your life."

"Jase?"

"Hmm."

"Did you know who I was that night we met in the hotel lounge?" Her eyes were luminous in the soft light touching the room with silver.

"What do you think?"

"I don't know what to think. Are you in the habit of going to bed with women you meet like that?"

"Kristi, I have not made love to another woman since the night you decided to practice your feminine wiles on me and kissed me out by the barn." Gentle amusement laced his words.

"That's a long time, Jason."

"Yes."

"You must really have loved me back then. I wish you'd told me."

"Honey, I thought you knew. Why would I marry you, otherwise? You had me out of my head wanting you, loving you, and I thought you felt the same way."

"I did, Jason.... I still do. I could never love anyone else."

Her comment seemed to cause Jason to lose whatever control he had and he kissed her again with passionate abandon that brought a quick response from her. His provocative position caused her to shift enticingly under him. He reacted predictably by suddenly possessing her with a strong, driving movement. As he filled her she recognized that her body was already sensitivé from her previous response to his lovemaking and each thrust caused rippling sensations that made her gasp her pleasure.

His touch drove her to imitate his rhythm, struggling to possess him in the same way. She lost track of everything but Jason and how he made her feel. Eventually he took control, slowing them down to delay their inevitable climax, his hands causing as much pleasure as his mouth and body.

Oh, how she loved this man! His sensitivity to her needs continued to amaze her as he brought her with him to a shuddering conclusion. Kristi was lost in a world of sensation and satisfaction, barely having the strength to grip him to her as they began their long, slow descent.

Jason rolled to his side, taking her with him. Kristi lay in his arms, a peaceful expression on her face. He listened to her soft, even breathing and smiled. Giving her a gentle kiss, he continued to hold her possessively in his arms as he joined her in sleep.

Chapter 7

Molly and Nate's arrival home was a cause for celebration, or so Jason decided after Nate had settled in. He was using a walking cast to help him to get around once more. Jason got on the phone and called everyone he knew for an impromptu party to welcome the couple home.

Kristi stood near the porch railing on the evening of the party, her hand resting on the support post, as she surveyed the crowd of people gathered on the lawn. Everyone he'd called must have come. Kristi saw friends from school—now married and with families.

Multicolored lanterns hung in a large circle, swaying in the soft, warm breeze. A large barbecue pit gave off the delicious aroma of charcoaled fajitas, steaks and ribs. Heaping dishes of salads and vegetables filled the long trestle table set up nearby. No one would go away hungry unless their willpower was stronger than hers.

Laughter drifted from the pit, where several men stood around with beer cans clutched in their fists as they watched Jason turn the meat on a mammoth grill. The signs of strain had disappeared from his face. Molly had commented on the change in him. He seemed more like the young, carefree man she'd watched grow into the responsible, quiet adult. She didn't hide her pleasure at finding that Kristi was once again sharing Jason's bedroom.

Francine hugged Kristi soon after she and Kyle arrived. "Are you sure that's the way a model dresses?" she inquired as she raised one eyebrow. Kristi glanced down at the western-cut, turquoise satin blouse tucked neatly into the small waist of her designer jeans.

Kristi chuckled at Francine's remark. "As a matter of fact, I look more like an Easterner's idea of a Texan than anyone here." They both glanced around, then smiled at each other.

Francine wore a flowing dress that enhanced her petite figure. She nodded. "You're right. None of us would be caught dressed in such a ridiculous outfit." Her eyes danced with mischief as she waited for Kristi's response.

"For some reason, Jason wanted me to dress this

way and I'm discovering how much I enjoy dressing to please him.'' She grinned at her sister-in-law.

Jason's yell caught everyone's attention. ''Food's ready, folks. Grab a plate and dig in.''

Almost everyone had full plates by the time Kristi appeared at the pit. Jason's eyes lit up when he saw her.

''I wondered what happened to you. Aren't you hungry?''

''Starved. I thought if I waited long enough, maybe you could take time to eat with me.'' She took in the smile that played across his mouth, a sudden desire to kiss him taking hold.

Jason glanced around, noting what Kristi had already seen—everyone seemed to be busy eating. ''I think you're right. Anyone wanting seconds can serve themselves.'' After heaping two plates with the succulent meat, they helped themselves to the other dishes, found a small clearing under one of the towering oaks and sat down.

When they had eaten most of their food, Jason paused and gave Kristi a sideways glance. ''Enjoying yourself?''

Surprised at the question, she responded, ''Sure. Didn't you expect me to?''

''I wasn't sure if you'd feel you had much in common with these people anymore.'' He waved a half-eaten rib in the direction of the crowd around them.

Kristi's voice was scarcely audible when she spoke. ''That bothers you, doesn't it, Jase?''

"You're damn right it does. I have no intention of letting you leave me, you know, but it'd be nice to know you're happy here." The half smile didn't cover the serious expression in his eyes.

"Jason, it isn't going to be possible for me to give up my career overnight. I thought you understood that."

Jason's hand paused in midair, holding a beer can halfway to his mouth. With careful deliberation he brought the can down to rest on his knee. "What does that mean?"

"I have commitments in New York that I can't get out of. Things that have been scheduled for months." Her heart sank as she saw his face grow grim.

"Such as?"

"Well, I have to be back in New York by the first of June."

"That's only a few weeks away."

"I know."

Jason took a long drink, then smiled, although the smile never reached his eyes. His voice sounded gruff as he asked, "Do you intend to go ahead with the divorce?"

"No! You knew after the first week that I'd never be able to divorce you."

"Did I, Kristi? You must see me as some kind of mindreader, then. So. We're going to stay married." Jason's gaze took in the milling guests, some of whom were beginning to dance to the taped music coming from the large speakers he had set up on the porch. "I suppose that's a victory of sorts." He pushed himself up. "Looks like we'd better get back to our party. You ready?" He stretched out his hand for her and she placed hers in it, the strength and warmth a comfort after the sudden chill caused by their discussion.

Kristi went into the house and returned with a multilayered chocolate cake and two cherry pies. She set them on one of the picnic tables. Her eyes unconsciously searched for Jason and, when she saw him, her heart seemed to lodge in her throat. She spotted Francine nearby and sauntered over to her, her tone casual. "Who is the woman dancing with Jase?"

"That's Lucinda Reyes. She lives with her brother, Ramon, who bought the old Stoddard place a couple of years ago. They moved up here from Monterey. Probably just got here or Jason would have introduced you." Francine watched her sister-in-law as she studied the couple dancing. "Rumor has it that Luci has been eager to console Jason for his lack of companionship these past few years."

Unfamiliar butterflies lodged themselves in Kristi's midsection. The mutual smiles and warm looks passing between Jason and Lucinda made their friendship obvious, even if the hastily smothered comments around them hadn't given Kristi a clue. What did she expect? Jason was unusually attractive. Just because the locals had always paired them was no reason to expect a new person to understand.

She found it strange that no one had thought to tell

her about Lucinda, but from various remarks overheard during the evening, Kristi recognized the curiosity of many of the guests. How would she react to meeting Lucinda?

Lucinda's obvious attraction to Jason was hard to ignore. Kristi had never felt quite so vulnerable as she watched them circle the area designated for dancing, Jason bending close to Lucinda to hear what she was saying. When he threw his head back with unrestrained laughter, a spasm of jealousy shot through Kristi.

They looked so good together. Jason's blondness was accented by Lucinda's olive skin and the midnight hair that fell like an ebony waterfall down her back. Jason's hand came close to encompassing Lucinda's tiny waist and Kristi forced her eyes away from the couple, refusing to punish herself by watching them any longer.

"I don't believe we've met." A low voice at her side caused her to jump. She turned around and saw a slender, dark man with a beautiful white smile. "I'm Ramon Reyes. That's my sister dancing with your husband." His grin was contagious and she found herself returning it ruefully.

"So I've been told." Her eyes drifted back to Jason in time to see him pull Lucinda close against him as he made a swinging turn.

"Don't look so pained, Mrs. McAlister. Lucinda has always known that Jason is in love with his wife.'' He shrugged, his smile flashing against his dark face. ''She understands.''

''She cares for him a great deal. It shows.''

''Yes. Jason has been a good friend to us both. He has never encouraged her in her feelings.'' He paused, his dark eyes filled with compassion. ''I wanted you to know that.''

She could feel the tenseness of her earlier conversation with Jason coming back, along with the beginnings of a headache. ''Thank you for telling me. You're very kind.''

''And you're very beautiful. Would you like to dance?''

Glancing at the others, Kristi decided to quit lurking in the shadows. ''Yes, thank you.''

Kristi and Ramon danced, then various other men came to claim Jason's missus. A glass of punch was placed in Kristi's hand and, thirsty from the exertion, she drank it, unaware of the potent additions to the innocuous-looking drink.

Her headache seemed to disappear as she relaxed and drifted to the music. As the last strains of Waylon Jennings's upbeat number about being used, but not used up, died away and a slow number by Willie Nelson began, a strong arm slid around her waist, turning her into a hard, lean body.

She knew the feel of Jason and was already smiling as her head lifted, her green eyes glowing. His clenched jaw barely moved as he muttered, ''I believe it's my turn, isn't it?''

She laughed, her earlier fears forgotten. With her head tilted in a provocative pose, she murmured, "Were you waiting for me to ask you to dance?"

He pulled her closer to his body. "Fat chance," he grumbled. They danced as Willie lamented that the last thing he needed the first thing that morning was to have his woman walk out on him. Jason increased the pressure of his arms around her, edging his muscled thigh between hers, causing riotous sensations within her.

"Jason. Behave." She felt her face flush, more with desire than embarrassment, but he needn't know that.

"I'm behaving, love. I've behaved all night. But if these people don't start thinking about going home soon, their host and hostess are going to disappear upstairs."

Her earlier pangs of jealousy seemed ridiculous to her now. She was about to snuggle her head into Jason's shoulder when a movement near the house caught her attention. A slim man who appeared to be in his mid-forties stood just inside the light of the yard. As Kristi watched, he lifted a thin cigar to his mouth, causing it to glow a brilliant red in the shadows. Dressed in black and with dark skin, he was not noticeable to the others.

"Who is that, Jase?"

Jason turned his head, then came to a sudden halt. "Alvarez. Wonder what he's doing here."

As soon as Jason saw him, Alvarez made some sort

of signal and stepped back into the shadows. Jason began dancing again.

"What's he doing here?"

"I'm not sure, honey. I'll find out later."

The music ended and several couples headed for the punch bowl. Kristi and Jason followed. Jason had been drinking beer all evening so when he tasted the punch he burst out laughing.

"What's wrong?" Kristi had already drained her cup and was busy refilling it. "Don't you think the punch tastes great?"

"I'm sure it does," he agreed with a wry grin. "Someone's been having some fun—didn't you notice the extra ingredients?"

Feeling a little sheepish, and more than a little dizzy now that she'd quit moving, Kristi shook her head—a big mistake. She put a hand to her face. "I have a feeling that last cup may be the one to do me in."

Jason laughed, his good humor restored as he slipped his arm around her waist once more. "Now I have a good excuse for putting you to bed." He started walking her to the house. Alvarez materialized at his shoulder as he started to climb the steps.

"I need to talk to you as soon as possible." Alvarez's tone was so low that Kristi barely heard him.

Jason nodded. "Let me get my wife upstairs and I'll be back with you."

Neither of them said anything as they went up the stairway. Kristi's headache had suddenly reappeared and she went into the bathroom for some aspirin. Jason followed her to the doorway, concern written across his face. "You all right?"

Without turning her head, she muttered, "As well as can be expected. The only thing to do at this point is to sleep it off, I understand." After carefully swallowing the tablets she managed a grin. "Don't worry about me. I'm going to bed. Sorry I couldn't outwait our guests."

The sound of his warm chuckle wrapped around her heart. "Don't worry about it. I'll probably be up shortly—after I see what news Alvarez has for me."

Only he wasn't.

Surprisingly, Kristi couldn't fall asleep. She had so much to think about. Jason's reaction to her plans to return to New York. Lucinda. Alvarez. She dozed off, her restless sleep filled with bits and pieces of the evening—Lucinda crushed in Jason's arms while he was saying, "I'll never let you go—" Alvarez explaining why Jason had to spend time in a Mexican jail.

She reached for him in her sleep, but Jason wasn't there.

Chapter 8

Kristi reluctantly opened her eyes. The aspirin she had taken the night before hadn't helped much, and her head felt swollen twice its normal size. She turned carefully on the pillow and peered at the other side of the bed. Jason's pillow was undisturbed. He hadn't come to bed at all.

The shower helped. She let the warm water pour over her until she felt a little more like facing the day. Why hadn't Jason come to bed? What news had Alvarez brought?

It was almost eleven o'clock by the time Kristi managed to make her way downstairs, where a cheerful Molly exclaimed over the success of the party.

"Too bad Jason had to leave so early this morning. I doubt he managed to get any sleep."

After a reviving mouthful of coffee, Kristi asked, "What do you mean?"

Molly bustled between the stove and table, leaving ham and biscuits in front of Kristi. "He left one of the men in charge—said he'd be away for a few days." She sat down with another cup of coffee and brushed a white fluff of hair from her face.

Kristi frowned, trying to follow the conversation. "He never mentioned anything to me about leaving. Did he say something to you or Nate?"

"Jason quit reporting to us years ago. He must figure he doesn't need to answer to anybody."

Kristi flushed. "He doesn't have to answer to me, either, but it would have been polite if he'd at least told me."

"Maybe he left a note or something."

Remembering how little she had actually seen when she got up, Kristi nodded. "That's a distinct possibility. I'll go up and check right now."

She heard Molly protesting that she hadn't finished eating as she hurried up the stairs and into their bedroom. There, propped up on the dresser, was an envelope with "Kristi" in large letters. *Guess you feel a little foolish now, huh?* she asked herself as she tore open the envelope. The note read:

Kristi,

It looks as though things are falling into place

down south. I'll be back as soon as possible. I love you.

Jase

She stared at the note, written in bold, slashing strokes, and realized that this was the first written communication she'd ever received from him. She sank down on the bed, still staring at the paper in her hand. "I love you, Jase." She wondered if she could have that blown up to a gigantic poster.

Her mind wandered back to the young, insecure bride who could have used just this type of encouragement when Jason suddenly disappeared, as it was obvious he'd done again.

Jason had told her that he was no longer involved in government activities. Yet once again he'd taken off on what could be a dangerous assignment. She had a strong hunch that what he planned to do was not legal in any country.

Kristi wandered downstairs to find that Molly had placed her breakfast in the microwave and warmed it for her.

"You were right. He left a note—said he'd be back in a few days." She ate the food without tasting it, thinking of the day stretching ahead of her. She finished her coffee and stood up. "I think I'll see what Francine is doing today."

Kristi made her call and agreed to go over to the Coles'. She needed to get her mind off what Jason was doing—and why he insisted on getting involved in that way of life once more.

* * *

Jason was gone for five days. And nights.

The nights were worse. Kristi discovered that no matter how hard she worked during the day, no matter how many hours of physical labor she put in, she couldn't rest peacefully. Either she lay awake or she fell into a nightmare-haunted sleep.

She began to understand how Jason must have felt after she left. It had been different for her. She'd become involved in another way of life. Nothing was similar to her previous lifestyle so she wasn't constantly reminded of him.

Everywhere she turned in this house, she saw him or heard him—and she missed Jason with an ache that left her trembling. Is this how he had felt? If so, how had he coped? And why hadn't he let her know how he felt?

Would she have believed him? She shuddered at the memory of the young girl she'd been, wrapped in her own misery, shut away from anyone's pain but her own.

Life had taught her so much while she was away. She'd learned to appreciate the values that were such a basic part of Jason. The treachery and ruthlessness of the advertising world made Kristi understand how fortunate she had been to have Kyle and Jason, and later Francine, play such important roles in her early life. Their training had given her a sense of self that kept her going during the confusing time when she first became a success. Her love for Jason had kept her innocent of relationships that might have destroyed her.

Although she felt better equipped now to handle a relationship with Jason, she knew she would find it impossible if he chose to continue working for the government or getting involved in their activities. She could only pray that he was sincere when he told her he was through with such involvement.

Kristi went to bed determined to face Jason with her feelings when he returned.

A slight noise downstairs brought her awake and she sat up, listening. She heard nothing more. The room was so dark that she couldn't even see shadows. Kristi slipped out of bed, grabbed her short robe and slid into her slippers. Opening the bedroom door, she peered into the hallway. Soft moonlight from the window at the end of the hall allowed her to see that the corridor was empty. Feeling ridiculous for the heavy pounding of her heart, Kristi tiptoed into the hallway and looked over the rail. A thin slit of pale light came from Jason's office. He was home!

She ran down the stairs, pushing the office door open as she entered. Her breath caught in her throat. He stood there with a torn shirt pulled half off his shoulders, a bloodied bandage wrapped around his upper torso. Her sudden entrance caused him to spin and grab a pistol lying on the desk. She stood there petrified.

"You startled me, Kristi. I thought you'd be

asleep." An unshaven Jason stood there, weariness in his voice as he replaced the pistol on the desk.

"What's happened? You're hurt!" She moved toward him, her arm outstretched.

He waved her away. "It isn't as bad as it looks. Just a flesh wound that bled all over the place. I'll get cleaned up in a minute." He looked at the gauzy material of her short robe with lazy approval. "Get back in bed, love—I'll be there before long." He started toward the door.

She waited until he reached her side, then turned and went back upstairs. Jason followed her into their room and stepped over to the boot jack where he pulled off his boots. He peeled off his grimy clothes and left them in a dusty heap.

He didn't look as though he'd eaten since she saw him last. His ribs stood out prominently and there were long creases around his nose and mouth. He started toward the bathroom.

"Were you able to rescue Joe?" Her voice sounded breathless in the quiet of the night.

Jason paused, glancing around at her. "Yes." His face grew even grimmer, if possible. "He's downstairs...we'll talk about it tomorrow." The door closed behind him with a firm click, leaving her standing in the empty room.

She spun around and ran down the stairs once more, going to the first aid supplies kept in the kitchen. After gathering up all she needed, she dashed back upstairs and began to lay them out on the table by the bed.

Jason came out of the bathroom freshly shaven, a towel loosely draped around his hips. Kristi was ready for him. "Lie down, Jason, so I can see what you've done to yourself," she ordered in firm tones. His expression of surprise was almost comical, but Kristi wasn't in a laughing mood. There was more than a slight graze. A jagged wound gaped along his side, looking fierce and angry. Since it was directly below his right arm, she wondered how he'd managed to bandage it.

"Joe knew a family who helped us," he explained in answer to her question. He flinched as she began to place antibiotic ointment along the edges of the wound. Whoever had cleaned it originally had done a good job. There was no sign of infection. He was lucky.

"I take it you put Joe in the downstairs bedroom." She kept her voice low, afraid he'd hear the fear that still held her in its grip, knowing how close he'd come to permanent injury or death.

"Yes. He's in no condition to negotiate the stairs for a while."

"What's wrong with him? Was he shot, too?" She could hear the strain in her voice and hoped he'd ignore it.

"No. He's been locked up for over six months with no exercise and poor food. The conditions were a little tough." He groaned as she began to wind the gauze to hold the new dressing in place. Then he grinned. "You're enjoying being in charge, aren't you?" The tired lines seemed to be easing away as he sprawled on the bed, his towel forgotten.

"Not especially," she grumbled as she tied the bandage. "I suppose you guys enjoyed this little stunt." She began to stroke his chest, glad to have him within touching distance once more.

"It wasn't that bad, actually. Everything went according to plan. I have to admit I'd underestimated Alvarez—he had everything worked out with precision. He works for the Mexican government. Joe was one of his best people. He couldn't afford to leave him in jail. Joe had gotten word to him that he and I had worked out some effective escape techniques years ago. That's why Alvarez needed me. I knew what Joe had in mind." He shifted slightly, then pulled her down to his uninjured side. "Do you think we could continue this discussion in the morning? I haven't slept much since I saw you last." He kissed her on the forehead. "It's good to be home, honey."

Kristi leaned over and clicked off the light. "It's good to have you home, but I haven't forgiven you for leaving without telling me."

He pulled her closer. "I know I took the coward's way out. I discovered that I couldn't tell you goodbye. You and I have done enough of that, love. It was easier to leave a note." He nuzzled her neck and murmured, "You knew I'd be back."

"When, was the question."

"As soon as possible. I don't want to spend any more time away from you than I have to." His words were softer and slower and Kristi felt his breathing even out into soft sighs. She fell into a peaceful sleep for the first time since he'd gone.

Jason was up, dressed and outside by the time Kristi got to the kitchen the next morning. She looked at the clock. It wasn't quite six and the men didn't come into eat until six-thirty. She had told Molly to keep Nate company this week while she did the cooking. She'd needed something to keep her busy and Molly had understood. Nate wasn't the most patient of convalescents and Molly's presence kept him in better spirits.

Kristi's breakfasts were routine; she mixed biscuits and orange juice and made a large pot of coffee while still thinking about Jason and Joe. She wondered how much he intended to tell her about what had happened. Probably no more than it took to get her to drop the subject.

Kristi heard the men clomping up the steps and across the back porch. As they filed into the room and headed for the table she knew there'd be no conversation until after breakfast. Unfortunately for her peace of mind, Jason started out the door with the men after breakfast.

"Jase?" She stood by the table, fighting to keep her voice calm.

He glanced around with impatience. "Not now,

Kristi. I've got to get the men started on some projects that got dropped last week." He pushed open the screen door. "I'll get back to the house as soon as I can." His eyes darted to the hallway, then back. "Try to stay out of mischief, until I get back," he added with a grin. He left, causing Kristi to gnash her teeth in a most unladylike way.

By the time she'd vacuumed the downstairs and put a large roast in the oven, Kristi was ready for another cup of coffee. She'd just poured herself a cup when she heard a noise in the hallway. Glancing up, she saw a man leaning weakly against the doorjamb between the hall and kitchen.

His pitch black hair hung limply across his forehead and around his ears and his clothes looked like something beggars would scorn to wear. They hung on him, making his shrunken body seem even smaller. His olive complexion appeared yellow and only his eyes showed any life. They glowed like black coals set deep in their sockets.

She had to strain to hear him when he spoke. "Where's Jase?" Even the effort of speaking appeared to be too much for him. Kristi realized that he barely had the strength to stand. How had they ever managed to get him this far? Moving quickly toward him, she offered her arm and, in a calm voice, replied, "He's out with the men right now, but should be back soon. Why don't you come have some coffee with me?" While she talked, she guided him over to the table and let him sit down. They were about the same height, but he seemed to be more of a walking skeleton than a grown man. As he rested his face in his hands, Kristi asked in a matter-of-fact tone, "Would you like some breakfast? There are some biscuits left over, and it won't take much to fry some eggs and bacon." She cocked her head and watched him, wondering if he should even be out of bed.

His head came up from his hands and he stared at her as though he didn't understand. Didn't he remember English? She'd forgotten the little bit of Spanish she had learned. Where was Jason, anyway?

When he spoke, she heard only a slight trace of an accent, more of a careful enunciation of words than the slow drawl spoken in Texas. "Breakfast sounds like a dream. Yes, I would like that, very much."

Glad to have something to do so she wouldn't sit and stare at him, Kristi managed to pour another cup of coffee and set it down in front of him, then busied herself once more at the stove.

He had eaten most of what she'd placed on his plate and was sipping his third cup of coffee when Jason arrived.

"Joe! What the hell are you doing out of bed, man? I didn't go to all that trouble to get you back over here just to lose you now." Jason's concern overrode the exasperation in his voice. Kristi heard the warm note of caring.

"Say, amigo, I'm not in that bad a shape. It'll take more than a stinking Mexican jail to put me out for the count." He grin was pitiful, stretching his already taut skin until it looked as though it would split. Kristi noticed that for all his bravado, Joe was shaking so hard he could barely hold the cup.

Without a word, Jason took the cup from Joe's hands, placed it on the table, then scooped him up as though he were a rag doll. He strode down the hall with him and Kristi could hear him all the way.

"Damn it, Joe. You don't have anything to prove to me, you witless wonder. Now, you're going back to bed and this time you're going to stay there. Kristi can make your meals and I can bring them to you for a few days. Just give yourself some time, that's all I'm asking."

She followed them out into the hallway, but hesitated to go into the bedroom. She heard Joe's weak voice. "Kristi? That was Kristi? You never told me she was back, amigo. Afraid I'd try to cut you out, huh?"

The rumble of Jason's laugh echoed down the hall. "You got it. I never could trust you out of my sight. This last little escapade certainly proves that." His voice dropped and Kristi couldn't hear more than a murmur. She started back into the kitchen when Jason called, "Kristi, would you come in here a minute? I want you to meet this character in a proper manner."

She stepped into the bedroom and realized why Jason had chosen it for his friend. With windows on two sides, he could see for miles. The view was very peaceful and tranquil, and if a Mexican jail had reduced Joe to his present condition, he needed all the peace and tranquility he could find.

Jason held out his hand to Kristi in a natural gesture. As she took his hand, he drew her closer to the bed where Joe lay propped up on several pillows. She noted that Jason had slipped a pajama top on him in place of the tattered shirt he'd worn to the kitchen.

"Kristi, this is Joe Guerrero, a friend who goes back many years." He paused, his eyes sparkling like topaz stones in the sun. "Joe, I want you to meet Kristi."

Joe took in the couple before him with evident satisfaction. "I am very pleased to meet you, Mrs. McAlister. You are even more beautiful than my friend here said you were, which was intentional, I'm sure." He fell back against the pillows. His eyes rolled in disgust. "I don't even have the energy to kiss the bride."

"That's just as well," Jason answered laconically. "In the meantime, the best thing you can do is chow down on her fantastic home-cooked meals and get some meat back on your bones." He strode toward the door, his arm wrapped possessively around Kristi's waist. "Get some rest, now. We'll talk later."

Kristi ran her hand from Jason's waist up to his side. "Should I check your dressing?"

The sun lines around his eyes crinkled as he smiled down at her. "By all means. I'm in need of all kinds of tender, loving care." He turned them up the stairs.

Jason surprised Kristi by taking off his boots before

sitting on the side of the bed. She stepped over to him and he pulled her between his muscled thighs. Trying to appear unconcerned, she unsnapped his shirt, only to discover he was offering her the same service.

"What are you doing?" She pulled away from him in surprise.

"Helping you take off your shirt." His face remained expressionless but dancing lights appeared in his eyes.

"I don't need my shirt off to change your dressing."

"I know, but it affords me a distraction while you tend my wounds." His hands smoothed the shirt off her shoulders and lingered on her back. She felt the hook give on her lacy bra.

"Jase!"

"Hmm?" He pulled the scrap of material away and ran his hands along her ribs and upward, cupping her breasts. His touch on her skin set off a quivering inside her.

Kristi tried to ignore him as she removed the gauze holding his dressing in place. His wound was healing nicely, and she quickly placed new pads over it, this time taping them in place.

Jason's hands had been busy while she worked. He had unsnapped her jeans and eased them over the soft curve of her hips so that they fell to the floor. His fingers began an insinuating foray along the lace of her bikini panties, darting underneath to stroke the softness hidden beneath them.

Kristi's breath caught in her throat. She attempted to step back from him only to lose her balance from the hobbling effect of her jeans around her ankles. Jason laughed and pulled her toward him, rolling to his side as he caused her to fall forward onto the bed next to him. "Jason! Your wound," she exclaimed, trying to pull herself up.

Jason's hands continued to be heavily occupied as he slipped her jeans and shoes off, then began exploring once more along her inner thighs. Somewhere in his investigation Kristi forgot to struggle. She wrapped her arms around his neck and kissed him—long, searching kisses to which he responded with eagerness.

Her last scrap of underwear was discarded and Jason's warm hands continued to explore her, causing quickened breathing for both of them. Kristi's hands fumbled at his belt buckle, suddenly urgent to feel his body unclothed against her. Jason seemed unaware of her movements as his mouth slid down her neck and came to rest along the swell of her breast. She tugged on his jeans, but his weight prevented her from removing them. Kristi sat up and yanked at them once more, this time receiving Jason's wholehearted cooperation.

As she pulled his jeans from his long, strong legs, Kristi kissed the exposed portion of his lower body, starting with the inside of his knees and moving upward. She reached up and found his briefs, which she quickly removed. As she continued her explorations she heard Jason's groan.

"C'mere, honey. Let me love you," he muttered as he reached for her. His hand found her breast as her tongue made darting contact with him. She felt him stiffen and he hauled her above him, lifting her astride him. His swollen manhood slipped inside her as she lowered her body over him with a sigh.

Jason pulled her down to him so that his lips touched the soft mound so conveniently presented. His mouth surrounded the peak of her breast and began a pulsing rhythm that matched the strokes of his body. Once again Jason's brand of magic transported Kristi into another plane of existence. Her last coherent thought for long moments was that she loved Jason beyond bearing.

Jason had spent hard days and rough nights away from Kristi, hating the thought of leaving her, even temporarily, hoping she understood the necessity of his sudden disappearance. He had fantasized how it would feel to have her in his arms once again, but none of his fantasies could compare to the reality.

As he held Kristi in his arms while they both calmed down, he knew he would have to continue to fight the compulsion to beg her to stay with him. He loved her too much to force her to stay if she wanted to go but he was very much afraid he wouldn't be strong enough to stand by and let her walk away from him again.

Chapter 9

Although the calendar suggested late spring, summer had arrived in southwest Texas. The days burned their bright way through the morning haze and Kristi began to pamper her flower garden with extra care and water.

Joe also responded to the nurturing he received at the hands of his friends. Kristi soon recognized why Jason enjoyed his friend's company. Outgoing and full of energy, Joe had an indomitable spirit. He kept Kristi entertained with his outrageous stories, most of which were true, according to an amused Jason. Kristi knew she'd miss him once he recovered and continued his travels. She overheard him laughingly point out to Jason that he never held a grudge—he just got even, and Kristi wondered if the person responsible for his recent enforced visit in Mexico might live to regret it. She had a feeling his treks across the border would not cease because of his recent setback.

Jason intended to drive Joe home to El Paso and before he did Kristi invited the Coles for dinner as a farewell celebration. As usual, Kevin and Kari kept everyone laughing with their remarks and antics.

It was Joe who made the casual remark that found its way to Kristi's hidden pain. "I'm surprised you haven't started your family by now, Jase. When we were in the Army, that's all you talked about." He laughed as he finished off his drink, then noticed that the room had fallen silent. He glanced at each face, then back at Jason. "Say, I'm sorry for popping off, my friend. That's none of my business—I know that." Kristi couldn't stand to see him uncomfortable. He was right. Everyone who knew Jason knew how much he longed for a family. Her family needed to understand that she'd come to terms with the past.

"That's all right, Joe. There's no way you would know," Kristi hastened to reassure him. She reached for Jason's hand and squeezed it. "I had some bad luck with a pregnancy a few years ago." Her eyes turned to Jason's and she saw the pain in his. Was he still carrying around the guilt for something over which he had no control? She added casually, "The doctor assures me there's no reason why another pregnancy wouldn't be normal."

Her comment caught everyone as unaware as Joe's had. She caught Kyle's "No kidding?" as she heard

Francine's exuberant "That's great news." She waited for Jason's response.

Those tawny eyes glowed as a slow smile crept across his face. "When did he tell you that, Kristi? You never mentioned it."

"That's because he only told me today. I didn't mean to blurt it out in front of everyone." She looked around the room at the pleased expressions. "I'd planned to announce the fact a little later when I had Jason's undivided attention." Her flushed face caused them all to laugh with understanding.

It was much later that night when Jason growled in her ear. "You little tease. You certainly can pick your moments to pass on good news." They lay together in a tangle of sheets, a silent reminder of their earlier activity.

Her smile reflected her complete relaxation and amusement. "At the time, all I wanted to do was to rescue Joe. He looked so unhappy when he realized he'd brought up a touchy subject." She nuzzled her face into his neck, the feel of the corded muscles reminding her of his strength.

Jason's hand slid along her spine, feeling the slight dampness from her recent exertion. He grinned at the memory of her response.

"Kristi, what about your career?"

Her drifting mind came back to earth with a thud. Of course, her career. "Well, I'll just have to call Jonathan and explain that I'm needed here."

"You're certainly needed here, love, but then you

always were.'' His hand cupped her shoulder, turning her so that his lips could find hers. A satisfying silence ensued. ''Then you don't intend to go back to New York?''

''I'll have to go back and get Jonathan to release me from my contracts; then I'll have to sublease my apartment and pack my things, but there's no rush about that.'' She snuggled back down into his arms. ''I'm afraid you're stuck with me,'' she murmured in a drowsy tone.

''I'll see if I can take better care of you this time,'' he said, but he doubted that she heard him as she drifted off to sleep.

Kristi was on her way out the door the next morning when the phone rang. Jason and Joe had left early that morning for El Paso; Jason intended to spend the night there and return home the next day. Kristi and Francine had made plans to shop for some refurbishing Kristi had in mind.

She ran back and grabbed the phone. ''H'lo?''

''Kristi?''

Jonathan's voice came as a shock—she had pushed him so completely from her mind.

''Yes, Jonathan. How are you?''

''Damn it, Kristi. I'm fine, now that I've managed to find you. I've been calling all over the Lone Star State trying to track you down.''

''Sorry, Jonathan. Only Texans are entitled to tell tall tales.''

"My, my, aren't we impertinent these days. Your vacation must have done you some good."

"Uh, yes, it has. About that vacation, Jonathan—"

"That's exactly why I'm calling. The schedules have been revised and they're going to be shooting your sequences in the morning. I've been trying to reach you for the past several days. I finally came across your brother's name in my card index." He chuckled. "Couldn't remember your married name."

Kristi appreciated Jonathan's garrulous nature at the moment. She could not have responded to him immediately—she found it hard to catch her breath. When he finally paused, she managed to respond. "Jonathan, there's no way I can be there in the morning."

"There's no way you cannot be here, old girl. It's too late to find a substitute. Besides, you signed the contract several months ago."

"But not for tomorrow."

"Don't be silly. You know the contract states that you're to be available when they're ready to shoot. Well, tomorrow's the day and you'd better damn well be here."

Her brain ceased to function. All she could think about was Jason. What was she going to tell him? Then it hit her. She wouldn't be able to "tell" him anything. He wouldn't be home before tomorrow. She glanced at her watch. She needed to leave within the hour in order to make any connections to get to New York before midnight.

"All right, Jonathan, I'll be there. But you and I are going to have a talk."

"Great. I've missed you. We can catch up on all the news when you get here. Call me back with your flight time and I'll pick you up."

Dispiritedly she muttered, "I'll do that. Goodbye, Jonathan."

Kristi meticulously placed the phone in its cradle as though it were imperative that it be placed exactly. She felt as though all of her carefully made plans were coming apart.

She wandered into the bedroom and looked at her clothes. Most of them would be useless in New York. Gathering her toiletries, she tried to collect her thoughts as well. She'd have to leave a note for Jason, but couldn't even tell him how long she'd be gone. Jonathan was right. The contract guaranteed her availability until the advertising firm was through with scheduled shots as well as any additional retakes needed.

Francine was waiting when Kristi pulled into the driveway. One look at her tear-streaked face and Francine was by her side. "What's happened?"

"Nothing tragic, really. I'm just terribly disappointed. I got word this morning that I have to return to New York two weeks early." She sat down at the table while Francine poured the cure for all ills, a cup of coffee.

"Oh, my. That isn't going to make Jase very happy." She dropped into the chair opposite Kristi.

"I know. What's worse, I don't have time to tell him. I've got to leave now, and he won't be home until tomorrow."

"Now? You mean this minute?" Francine frowned as she glanced at the clock.

"Well, we do have time to finish our coffee, but I'm relying on you to get me to the airport." She paused as she glanced toward the door. "Also, I guess you'll have to get my car back over to the house."

"That's no problem." She was silent for a moment. "Poor Jason."

"How about poor Kristi? I feel every bit as bad about this, you know."

"Except that Jason is going to feel like it's happening to him all over again." She stood up and carried their emptied cups to the drain. "It can't be helped, I suppose. Let me get the kids cleaned up and we'll get you on your way."

Tears filled her eyes as Kristi looked at her practical sister-in-law. "What would I do without you, Francie?"

"Darned if I know. I don't intend to let you find out." They both laughed and Francine went in search of her offspring.

It was after eleven o'clock when Kristi's plane touched down. She felt as though she hadn't slept in days, and her head pounded with every step she took. Even seeing Jonathan's tall, elegantly clad figure waiting for her didn't relieve her depression. The noise bombarded her. She'd forgotten the sounds—the confusion of many voices stridently echoing around her. Had she ever felt comfortable here?

"You're looking marvelous, darling. Such a healthy bloom on your cheeks," Jonathan enthused as he took her overnight bag, the only luggage she had brought with her. "My, you certainly travel light these days," he offered when she explained that there was no checked luggage. "I've got a limo waiting. Nothing but the best for our ice princess, you know." Kristi cringed at the teasing tag. How much of her thinking had changed during these past several weeks? After all these years, why did Jonathan's breezy self-assurance grate?

"I'm surprised I have any color. I've got the grandmother of all headaches," she muttered as she sank back into the luxury of the limousine and sighed.

"We'll get you right home and into bed then. Remember you have to be ready for the all-seeing eye of the camera in the morning."

"Yes, Jonathan. I'm aware of that. Otherwise I wouldn't be here."

"Testy, aren't we? Ah, well, you were never one who liked to travel. I remember the summer we did all those fabulous scenes along the Mediterranean. You actually made the whole trip seem like a chore."

"It was. I felt totally out of place."

"The trouble with you, my love," Jonathan expounded, "is that you're a contradiction. On the outside, you're a beautiful, sophisticated, cosmopolitan woman.'' He paused, his eyes flashing over the chic golden jumpsuit she wore. ''While inside, you're the young girl from Texas who still prefers horses and the wide open spaces to the adulation of the world.''

She blinked, then slowly turned her gaze on him. ''Of course you're right, Jonathan, but I'd never thought of it.'' She was amazed at his insight.

''I'm not clairvoyant, Kristi. I helped to manufacture that glossy exterior you exhibit with so much panache. I'm aware how little of it is you.''

The rest of the trip was made in silence, as though both of them had their own thoughts to put in order.

Jonathan insisted on going with Kristi into her apartment. Even when she reminded him of the modern security systems in her building, the fact remained, he was quick to admonish, that she'd been away for some time. It didn't hurt to be too careful.

The apartment looked just the same. Even her plants were doing well, thanks to her next-door neighbor. Kristi had forgotten how small the apartment was, she'd grown so used to the sprawling ranch house.

After checking every possible hiding spot for who knew what, Jonathan proclaimed the place safe for occupancy. Kristi managed to get rid of him by solemnly swearing to go directly to bed as soon as he left. She was more than ready.

Her alarm went off too soon the next morning. Her body was still on Texas time. She groaned, knowing that she had no choice but to start her day.

* * *

Over lunch—a small salad—Kristi explained to Jonathan why she couldn't stay in New York.

"So what's a few pounds, Kristi? You can take them off in no time." Jonathan waved his hand as though dispersing unwanted weight.

"I don't want to lose pounds, Jonathan. That's my point. I feel much better at this weight. It's probably my normal weight, anyway. I don't want to go around hungry all the time." She looked down at her salad with disgust. Had there been a time when she was content to eat like an underfed rabbit?

"But, my dear, these people call the shots. If they say the camera makes you look too heavy, you have no choice." His earnest expression irritated her. Why did he have to sound so damned reasonable when she felt so contrary?

"All right, I know that, but what I'm trying to say is I don't want to model anymore." There. It was out. She stared at him defiantly.

Jonathan straightened in his chair, his dignity settling about him. In the three-piece pearl gray suit that matched the frosting of silver in his dark hair, he looked every bit the hardheaded businessman he was. "So that's what all this temper tantrum is about, is it?"

"I'm not having a tantrum, Jonathan, and you know it. You've often told me that I'm one of your least temperamental models."

"I must have lied through my teeth, then. Just

when did you decide in your wisdom that you don't want to be a model?"

He was taking this every bit as badly as Kristi had imagined he would. She had never attempted to defy him before.

"I'm not sure I ever really wanted to be one, Jonathan."

"I should have known. It was those nasty white slavers who captured you, forced you on the plane, and caused you to seek my help." His long, slender fingers drummed an irritated tattoo on the table.

"Please don't be sarcastic, Jonathan. It doesn't solve a thing." She glanced around the fashionable restaurant, wishing she'd never brought up the subject. She had to return to the studios in little over an hour. Why had she decided to meet him for lunch and explain why she couldn't stay in New York?

His smile was without humor. "Of course it does, darling. It vents just enough steam to allow me to sit across the table from you and converse in a civilized manner, even though I'd much prefer to jerk you out of that chair and shake some sense into you." He picked up his glass with commendable control and sipped his wine.

"You knew I was married, Jonathan."

"That I did, although I quite distinctly remember your explaining that the marriage was over, done with, forgotten, and it has never been a subject for discussion since. What's changed?"

She could feel the heat burn its way into her

cheeks. He was right, of course. She forced her eyes to meet his and cringed at the anger in their onyx depths. "I discovered I'm still in love with Jason."

"How touching."

"Don't!"

"What the hell am I supposed to say, Kristi? I've spent a great deal of time, not to mention enormous sums of money, in building the image that is dazzling every male in this room. Now you tell me you don't want to continue with the career you were so willing—" he stopped, then continued "—even eager to have. What do you want from me?" His hand clenched as he continued to stare at her; a muscle pulsed in his cheek.

His reaction was worse than she'd anticipated. "Perhaps we should discuss this later." Kristi took a large sip from her ice water, the only drink she could allow herself at the moment. She'd had no idea until this morning that she'd managed to gain twelve pounds during the past two months. There'd been a delay in shooting while the wardrobe lady readjusted the waistline of her dress and she'd received a royal lecture on the sins of gaining weight.

"Perhaps we should. I do want to remind you, my dear, that I have been hard at work while you've been playing at home on the range, getting you bookings for the next several months." He leaned toward her, his glance cutting through her like a laser. "Don't you dare try to get out of them, do you hear me?"

In all the years she'd known Jonathan, she'd never

seen this side of him—perhaps because he'd never needed to show it to her before. She'd always been biddable, almost passive, in her dealings with him. She never really cared what she did or how hard she worked. Until now. Now she felt she was fighting for her life. She was—her life with Jason.

Jonathan punctiliously escorted her back to the studio, his anger carefully masked as he wished her "good day." A familiar refrain began to run through her mind as the hours passed.

"What am I going to do?"

Chapter 10

The bright headlights from Jason's pickup illuminated the drive as he pulled in. He noticed that the house was dark. Not that he expected Kristi to wait up for him—he hadn't given her a time to expect him. He had a feeling she wouldn't stay asleep long once she knew he'd returned.

He swung the truck in a wide arc and pulled into the covered shed used for parking. Kristi's car wasn't in its usual place. He glanced down at the illuminated dial of his watch—it was close to midnight.

Puzzled, he crawled out of the truck and headed toward the house. He ran up the stairs and flipped on the hall light. He had made no effort to muffle his steps. They echoed through the house, but he heard no other sound. A sudden fear clutched at him, the kind of irrational emotion felt in nightmares.

The bedroom door stood open and he knew before he turned on the light that he would find no one there. She was gone. He saw the envelope propped up on the dresser, exactly where he'd left one for her, and his mind played back their earlier conversation.

"I haven't forgiven you for leaving without telling me."

"I know I took the coward's way out. I discovered I couldn't tell you goodbye. You and I have done enough of that, love. It was easier to leave a note...."

It was easier to leave a note. It was easier to leave a note. The sentence kept pace with his slow footsteps as he crossed the room. He stood there staring down at the envelope; his name was written across the face in Kristi's dainty handwriting.

He saw images—Kristi when he used to perch her in the saddle in front of him before she'd even learned to walk; Kristi as he sat her in the saddle of her first pony, her pride of possession shining from her bright face; Kristi as she looked the first night after he'd returned home from overseas, her glorious hair gleaming in the light, her eyes warm as she threw herself into his arms; Kristi, lying deathly still and white in the bare hospital room.

"Dear God, I can't go through this again. Kristi!"

His shout echoed through the empty rooms. He picked up her message, then sank down on the edge of the bed. His hands shook so much that he had trouble pulling the single sheet from the envelope, and he flinched as he read the opening endearment.

Jason, my love,

Jonathan called to say my schedule has been revised. I have to be available in the morning.

His eyes sought the top of the page. It was dated the day before. She'd already been gone a day. She was already in New York, back into her other life. His eyes returned to the note.

I hated to leave without seeing you, but Jonathan reminded me I have no choice—I signed the contract.

He could no longer read the graceful script as it began to blur before him. An excruciating pain filled his chest and doubled him over.

Jason felt that he was in the grips of a chill as the years without Kristi flashed through his mind. He managed to strip and crawl under a hot shower, where he stood and let the water beat on him while his mind tried to accept the unacceptable.

Kristi was gone. Whether she wanted to or not, the fact remained that she had left. The world of glamour and dazzling lights had a stronger hold on her than he ever could.

When the water began to cool, Jason turned off the taps and stepped out of the shower. He dried himself carefully, then drifted back into the bedroom. His eyes averted from the bed, he picked up the note, then walked out of the room and downstairs. There was no way he could sleep in that bed. Not tonight, anyway. He found himself standing in his office, a bottle of bourbon in his hand. He poured a small amount in a glass. Why not: A little anesthesia never hurt anyone.

He sank into the large leather chair and opened her note once more.

> Darling, I'll be home as soon as I can. I already miss you so much. I'll write every day and call whenever I can. You'll probably be so busy you won't even notice I'm gone.

A groan of pain escaped him.

> (Hopefully you'll discover something missing when you go to bed at night!) Don't ever forget how much I love you.
>
> Your Kristi

He let his head fall on the back of the chair. It was going to be a long night.

Kristi's schedule had been grueling and she returned to her apartment limp. How had she ever kept up the pace before? She hadn't realized how keyed up she'd been for so many years until she'd completely relaxed at home.

Home. Home is where the heart is, and her heart had been left behind with Jason. As she got ready for bed she called him. The phone rang and rang, but there was no answer. She looked at her watch. It was a little after eight back there—barely dark. If she weren't so sleepy she'd stay up and try to call later, but she was so tired.

Kristi curled up into a ball, clutching her spare pillow in both arms, and dreamed of Jason.

She dreamed she was calling him but he wouldn't answer the phone. It kept ringing and ringing and—She sat up. It was her phone ringing. She fumbled in the dark to find it.

"H'lo?" she murmured, still more than half-asleep.

"Ms. Cole?" a strange male voice asked.

A little more awake, she answered, "Yes?"

"This is Malcolm Metcalf, Ms. Cole. I'm one of the security people here in the building."

"Yes?" responded a puzzled Kristi.

"Uh, I'm sorry to bother you so late, Ms. Cole, but you see, there's a man down here demanding that we let him come up to your apartment." He cleared his throat nervously. "He says he's your husband." His last statement almost sounded like a question.

"Jase?" Kristi rolled out of bed, her tone echoing her astonishment.

"Well, his I.D. says he's Jason McAlister, but he insists he's married to you, Ms. Cole."

Kristi started laughing in shocked amazement. Jason here? In New York?

"I guess it's all right to let him come up, then?" the guard questioned.

"Oh! Oh, yes, of course. Thank you so much. I mean, that will be fine." The phone fell from her numbed fingers as she jumped out of bed. She found the light switch, then reached for her robe. It was the old cotton duster she wore when she cleaned the apartment.

Jason was in New York. He was on his way to see her. She raced to the door and, after shaking fingers unlocked the deadbolts and chains, she threw open the door and stared at the elevator. It remained frustratingly closed. How long did it take to ride the elevator upstairs, anyway? She'd never paid any attention. Now she knew. It took forever.

The elevator doors slid open with silent ease and Jason stepped out. He looked around and saw her standing by the open doorway to her apartment. With angry, catlike strides he advanced on her.

"Jason," she cried as she launched herself into his arms. She almost knocked him over. He paused, but only long enough to scoop her up in his arms. Then he stalked through the doorway, kicking the door closed behind him.

He looked so good to Kristi. He was in a tan, western-cut suit, the style and cut emphasizing his broad shoulders and slim hips. The trousers faithfully molded his muscular thighs and flared below the knee to fall gracefully to highly polished boots. Never had his resemblance to a mountain lion been more noticeable. A very angry mountain lion.

"Why in hell didn't that guard downstairs know

you were married? Is it some deep, dark secret you can't share with anyone back East?'' he demanded to know.

Jason stood in the middle of her apartment, making it seem even smaller than it was as he glared down at her. At least he tried to glare, but she was too busy kissing him on every exposed part of his neck and face to notice. He stomped over to a stuffed chair and sank into its depths, still holding her. ''Answer me, damn it!'' He even roared like a mountain lion.

Kristi pulled back to look at him, her eyes brilliant green in the light filtering from her bedroom, her smile gleaming with delight. ''I'm sorry, I missed the question.'' Before he had a chance to say any more she leaned over and kissed him on the mouth, her lips moving in a soft caressing movement. Her tongue probed his firm lips, seeking entrance. When he started to speak she took advantage of the chance and darted her tongue to meet his. He could no longer ignore her warm touch and the feel of her soft body against him. It was several minutes before they paused, breathless.

''What did you ask, love?'' she murmured as she kissed him along his jawline in front of his ear.

''Why didn't the guard know you're married?''

''Because nobody in New York either knows or cares about anyone else's business, Jase. I don't know the man—he doesn't know me.'' Her hand found the buttons of his shirt and slipped them from the buttonholes. ''What are you doing here?''

"I came to find my wife, that's what I'm doing here." Belligerence punctuated each word.

"Well, cowboy, you done found her. What do you intend to do about it?" she asked, her hands parting his shirt and running over the thick fur of his chest.

"You and I have some talking to do," he stated firmly.

"Talk! If you can hold me in your arms and let me kiss you and rub all over you, and the only thing you can think to do is *talk*, you're older than I thought!" She sat up and attempted to look indignant.

He picked her up once more and strode toward the bedroom light. "You looking for a little action, are you? Well, if you don't want talk, let's try something else!"

Jason paused in the doorway of her bedroom, analyzing the room. He moved closer to the bed and zeroed in on a large picture on Kristi's bedside table. Taken several years ago, it showed him and Kyle laughing into the camera as they leaned against a fence. He vaguely remembered Francine taking it one day, with a joking comment about labeling it "cowboys at work." He was surprised to find it in New York with Kristi.

Placing her on the bed, he leaned over to concentrate all his attention on her. He ran his hand through the fiery waves of hair as they cascaded around her shoulders. She was so beautiful and he loved her so much he ached from it.

She lay there in the soft lamplight, her eyes shining

with the joy of his presence when she'd thought him thousands of miles away. Her hand touched the lean smoothness of his cheek, then drifted downward until she felt the roughness of his beginning beard.

"I need a shave."

"Uh-uh. You're just right." Her other hand reached up and cupped his face, slowly pulling him down to her waiting mouth. Their kiss was an expression of their love for each other. It was as though their spirits could only commune through the physical medium of touching. They each found the answer they were seeking—the need for reassurance was past.

"Why are you here?" she whispered as he pulled himself back a few inches, his eyes glowing with love.

He started to answer, and his voice broke. He cleared his throat and tried again. "Because this is where you are, love. I discovered I can't function with a long-distance marriage." He shrugged slightly. "So if you live in New York, I guess I'll be here, too." His voice was husky, as though he found it painful to express the emotions he felt.

"Jason? You can't possibly mean to stay here. You'd go out of your mind cooped up in an apartment in New York City." Kristi struggled to sit up.

His eyes narrowed. "I'll go out of my mind if I stay in Texas, Kristi. I've already tried it your way—I can't go that route again." He took her hand and kissed the palm, gently folding the fingers around it. "I'd rather stay here with you."

"What about the ranch?"

"Nate's almost totally recovered, even if he won't be showing off on any new horses for a while. I'm not worth much back there at the moment, anyway." He gave her a wry smile, "So I might as well learn to like city life." He watched the expressions flit across her face. He could almost follow her thoughts.

"Oh, Jason. I don't know what to say. I can't think of anything more wonderful than to have you here with me, but it would never work. You'd end up hating me." She leaned up on her elbow and gave him a fierce kiss. "I can't deal with that, you know."

"But you were ready to divorce me."

"Yes. I felt the only way I was ever going to find peace of mind was to cut you completely out of my life."

"Which is why you keep a picture of me by your bed, I guess." His eyes danced with amusement.

"But don't you see? That's been the whole problem all along. You aren't just my husband. You're my childhood, my growing up years, my first love, my last love. There was no way to cut you out of my life—you're too much a part of it."

"When did you make that profound discovery?" he asked as he removed the cotton robe and tossed it on a nearby chair.

"When you followed me to my room at the motel."

He slipped the tiny straps of her nightgown from her shoulders. His gaze caught hers in surprise at her words. "That soon?" His tone echoed his astonishment. "I wish I'd known," he muttered.

Their conversation didn't slow his systematic stripping of Kristi, then himself.

"What do you mean?"

"I wish I'd known my plan had worked so quickly."

"What plan?"

"The plan to get you back to Texas." He jerked his boots off, then stood up and quickly pulled off his slacks and shorts, leaving him bare.

"You didn't bring me back to Texas. I returned on my own."

He crawled into bed and pulled her into his arms, making sure each part of her body touched his. "To get me to sign divorce papers."

"Oh, that."

"Yes, that. I figured if I refused to cooperate, sooner or later you'd have to come to me." He grinned when he saw the expression on her face. "That's an old hunter's trick, you know. Stand still and let the intended prey come to you. It took you long enough to fall for it."

"I really thought I could do it, you know," she whispered, "until I saw you that night. I began to have doubts then, but refused to acknowledge them. I even refused to face them when I left you the next morning." She ran her hand lightly across his chest, causing him to quiver. "Oh, Jase, I love you so much." Her kiss promised him her total commitment.

"How long will we have to stay here?" he murmured, refusing to be distracted.

"I don't know. Jonathan is furious with me. Not that I blame him, exactly, after all he's done for me."

"Don't buy into that one, honey. You've done just as much for dear old Jonathan; don't let him kid you."

"He says he's got several commitments lined up through the rest of the year, and he expects me to fulfill them." She pressed her head against his chest. It would never work for Jason to stay here, but she couldn't bear to be without him.

Kristi felt his chest quiver and knew he was as upset as she was. She could see no way out for them. Then his chest shook harder as he began to laugh.

"Jase? There isn't anything funny about what I just said."

"I know, honey, I was just thinking about good ole Jonathan's reaction when you explain to him that you can't possibly fulfill those commitments for him."

Kristi sat up, ignoring her unclothed condition. "But, Jase, that's what I've been trying to tell you. I have to fulfill them. I have no choice." She looked down at him, amazed that he could be so lighthearted. She'd never seen him so relaxed and happy, not for years. Maybe the strain had been too much for him. She began to stroke his brow and croon softly, which caused him to laugh even harder.

"I forgot to mention a message I have for you," he finally said, his grin still very much in evidence. "I, uh, fell asleep in the den the night I found you gone." He winced at the memory of that bleak night. "I overslept. The phone woke me about midmorning." He paused, wondering how to phrase what he had to tell her. "You didn't mention that you'd had some tests run while you were at the doctor's."

Her eyes widened. "They called? What did they say?"

His grin spread. "They said that in a little over six months you're going to have a hell of a time modeling anything but tents, love." He watched the dawning comprehension on her face, glad he was there to enjoy her reaction. With a poor attempt at a frown, he asked, "How come you didn't tell me about having the tests run?"

"I was afraid to tell anyone, afraid I'd imagined the symptoms, and the doctor would tell me I was wrong." She threw her arms around his neck. "We did it. Oh, Jase, we're going to have that family we wanted." Her voice choked to a stop and she buried her head in his neck.

"I know, honey. You can imagine my reaction. It was all I needed to come get you." He pulled her back to him, running his hand down the long length of her spine. "I don't think even your agent can do much about impending motherhood."

"Just let him try," she muttered fiercely. They lay there for several moments, then Kristi leaned back far enough to see Jason's face. "You know, when I first thought about going to Texas I fantasized about getting pregnant, and then having you decide you wanted me as your wife after all." Her eyes sparkled as she met his gaze. "So I guess *my* plan worked as well as yours."

Jason had been patient long enough. His next kiss let her know he was through with light courtin'; he was ready to get on with it. His last coherent thought drifted across his passion-filled mind:

Who exactly had been the hunter?

* * * * *

BACHELOR FATHER

To Dave, Rick, Randy and Kevin,
who taught me all I know about ten-year-old boys.

Chapter 1

The phone rang for a second time before Susan paused from reviewing the contract in front of her and absently reached for the jangling instrument.

"Susan McCormick." Her voice was carefully modulated to sound confident and professional, as befitted a competent corporate attorney.

"Mom! You'll never guess who was at school today!"

A warm smile appeared on her face and she glanced at the walnut-framed photograph on her desk. The smiling face of her exuberant ten-year-old son stared back at her, his black eyes filled with mischief, his curly dark brown hair falling over his forehead.

"Probably not, Steve," she responded with a chuckle. "So why don't you tell me?"

"Tony Antonelli! Can you believe it? The star left fielder for the Atlanta Aces came to our school and spoke to us!"

For a moment Susan thought she was going to faint. Blood rushed from her head and dizziness overcame her. Tony was back in Santa Barbara. Her thoughts flew back to her childhood and she remembered black eyes sparkling in a tanned, laughing face, a white, dimpled smile flashing, unruly black curls tumbling over a forehead. Her thoughts flitted to her teen years and the bronzed male that could have been the inspiration of the Renaissance artists, his muscled arms and shoulders developed from years of playing sports of all kinds—especially baseball.

Tony—who had taught the young Susan to enjoy being young and alive, who'd given her her first taste of freedom and companionship and friendship, and later was responsible for her first lesson in how to survive the loss of a love.

"I bet that was really exciting, Steve," she heard herself saying faintly, her voice betraying her with a slight quiver.

"Yeah," her son responded with enthusiasm. "I had PE right after he spoke and we were playing baseball and I saw him talking to the coach and—Mom?"

"Yes, Steve?"

"How come you never told me you knew Tony Antonelli?" His tone bordered on accusation.

"How did you find out I did?"

"He told me."

Susan leaned back in her chair, helpless to combat the whirling sensation she was feeling. "You talked to him," she stated in a calm voice while she watched her hand tremble against the arm of her chair. She wasn't ready for this. She should have been given some warning. Some small voice should have told her when she got up that morning that this was not going to be a good day.

"How did you happen to be talking to him, Steve?" She didn't have to fake her interest. His answer was of vital importance to her.

"The coach called me over." His voice suddenly went up several notes. "I hit a triple and I guess Tony was watching or something. So when I crossed home plate he called me over."

"Sounds like you've licked your batting slump, doesn't it?"

"Yeah." He tried for nonchalance but couldn't quite carry it off. "The coach introduced me to Tony and when he heard my name was McCormick he told me he'd grown up with a Michael McCormick. I told him that was my dad's name and he said he grew up with you, too." His tone hardened. "Is that true, Mom?"

"Yes."

"Then why didn't you ever tell me? I didn't even know Tony was from Santa Barbara. You've never once mentioned his name!"

What could she say? She could hardly lie to him and say she hadn't thought he'd be interested. She knew him too well for that. Sports seemed to be his whole life. It had been hard for her to accept, but she'd slowly forced herself to face the fact that Steve didn't take after her as far as his interests were concerned. She didn't care for sports and Tony Antonelli had a great deal to do with her feelings on the subject.

Steve said something, but she didn't catch it—something about dinner. "What did you say?"

He groaned, impatient with her lack of attention. "I said that I invited him to have dinner with us tonight, since you guys are old friends and everything."

"Stephen Spencer McCormick! You did no such thing!" Never had Steve taken it upon himself to invite anyone to their home without checking with her first. And Tony, of all people!

Steve knew he was in trouble. His mother never used his full name. Never. He wasn't sure what its use portended, but he had a bad feeling about it.

"What's wrong, Mom?"

Susan no longer had to worry about dizziness. All of her blood had rushed back to her head, where it pounded in heavy waves of anger and fear. She did not ever want to see Tony Antonelli. He was part of her past and she wanted him to stay there.

She had to say something to Steve. She knew her reaction had alarmed him—it was so much out of character for her. Normally Susan remained calm and rational, her emotions carefully controlled.

"You don't invite someone to dinner without

checking with me first, Steve, and you know it. How could you?''

Puzzled, Steve wasn't sure what to say. ''But, Mom, he's a friend of yours.''

''Hardly a friend. We just happened to live next door to each other while we were growing up.'' *Why was she denying their shared past? As some sort of protection?* She attempted to salvage the truth. ''We haven't seen each other in years.''

''I know. That's why I thought you'd want to see him now.'' Thinking to appease her, he added, ''I've already told Hannah there'd be company for dinner. She didn't seem to mind.''

''That's hardly the point.'' She paused, trying to calm down and to get a grip on her emotions. ''I take it he accepted?'' *What was she going to do?*

''Oh, yeah, he said he'd be here at seven.''

Susan glanced at the large calendar hanging on the wall by her desk. ''Steve, you *are* aware that today is the first Wednesday of the month, aren't you?''

Silence. Then a groan. ''Oh, Mom, I forgot.''

''Yes.''

More silence. ''Couldn't we call Grandmother and explain that something came up? I mean, we go over there all the time,'' he muttered with some exaggeration. ''Would it really matter if we missed just this once?''

''What do you think?''

''Aw, Mom. I didn't do it on purpose. Honest. But

Tony Antonelli, Mom! Maybe Grandmother would understand if we just explained—''

''No, your grandmother would not understand, believe me.''

What were her choices, after all? Did she want Tony aware of how little desire she had to see him? Did she want him to feel he had that much importance in her life? Of course not. On the other hand, was she ready to face her mother with yet another example of her shortcomings as a loving, dutiful daughter?

Her silence was more than a ten-year-old could handle. ''What can we do?''

She could hear the hurt and dejection in his voice. Why should he be faced with a dilemma he couldn't understand?

''I'll call your grandmother and ask if we can visit her tomorrow night instead.'' Approaching the guillotine appealed to her more.

''Would you, Mom, would you really? Oh, that would be super. So you'll be home at the usual time, then?''

Wondering if she'd get any more work done during the rest of the afternoon, she nodded absently. ''Yes, I'll be home by six.''

Susan stared at the phone in its cradle long after she'd hung up. The most important thing for her to remember was not to let Steve know how upset she was. Somehow she would get through the evening. She would just have to concentrate on keeping her composure.

She pictured Tony the way he'd looked the last time she'd seen him. At twenty-one he'd been breathtaking, and the seventeen-year-old she'd been had been mesmerized by him. Unfortunately.

Susan shook her head in an effort to dispel the memories that had arrived with Steve's call. Determined to face her next unpleasant task with composure, she picked up the phone once again. She dialed briskly and listened to the ring. Then a voice answered.

"Hello, Claudine, is Mother around?"

"Just a moment, Susan."

Susan stared at Steve's picture, at the compelling grin that caused everyone he met to smile back. Meeting Tony was probably the most exciting thing he could imagine happening to him. She refused to allow her feelings to interfere with his enjoyment of the evening.

"Susan?"

"Hello, Mother."

"Why are you calling?"

Why don't you give me a chance to tell you, Mother? Pushing her resentment of her mother's attitude to the back of her mind, Susan answered, "I'm calling to let you know that Steve and I won't be over for dinner this evening."

"Why must you shorten Stephen's distinguished name with that slangy expression, Susan? If the name is good enough for your father, it is certainly good enough for your son."

"Yes, Mother."

"What do you mean, you aren't coming over tonight? You know we expect you on the first Wednesday of each month."

"I know, Mother. That's why I called. Could we make it tomorrow night instead?"

"You know very well my bridge club meets on Thursday afternoons, Susan. I am absolutely exhausted by evening."

"Of course, Mother. It just slipped my mind."

"Why can't you come tonight?"

"Stephen—" Susan emphasized the name slightly, the only sign she gave that she'd been holding on to her temper with a firm grip "—invited a friend over for dinner tonight. He'd forgotten what day it is."

"Which friend is that?"

"Why do you ask?"

"Well, I certainly hope you've met all of Stephen's friends, Susan. When you refused to allow him to go to private school, I warned you how little control you'd have over the type of person he meets."

Please, dear Lord, give me strength. "I'll be sure to have his friend bring his pedigree, Mother, which I will check over very carefully before allowing him to enter our home."

"Is that supposed to be funny?"

"Not really, Mother."

"Good, because I do not find it amusing. And I think you are being most inconsiderate to cancel this late in the day. Claudine will undoubtedly be most upset.''

I doubt that very much, Mother. ''Please give her our apologies.'' Noting the time, she asked, ''Then we'll see you next month?'' Her tone betrayed her impatience.

''No, wait a moment, Susan. I'll make a trade with you. I'll forgive you for not showing up tonight if you'll come to dinner on Friday instead.''

Suspicious as to why her mother was so willing to concede the issue, she asked, ''What's happening this Friday night?''

''Oh, Edwin and Lorraine are back from Europe and we're having them over for dinner.''

Edwin and Lorraine were the biggest bores Susan had ever had the misfortune of meeting. Her mother found them fascinating and, as usual, no one seemed to know how her father felt about them. Stephen Spencer was always unfailingly polite, but gave nothing of his thoughts away. She wished she knew how he did it. One of these days, if she were ever able to get him alone, Susan was determined to ask him how he put up with her mother and her mother's friends.

''Mother, I'd rather not, if you don't mind. I have a heavy schedule in the office that day and—''

''It is rare that I ask anything of you, Susan, and you know it. I wouldn't ask now if Lorraine's nephew weren't coming with them. I really do need the extra person at the table to even out the numbers.''

''You could always have Claudine eat with you,

when she wasn't serving, of course." Silence. *Oh, dear. I've gone too far.* With a sigh of unwilling acceptance, Susan asked, "What time should I be there on Friday, Mother?"

More silence. *Ah, yes, I remember this treatment well. For years you managed to intimidate me, Mother, but now I've discovered that silence works just as well for me.*

The wire hummed in the background as the two strong-willed women waited each other out. Susan began to read the contract before her. She was tempted to put the call on the speaker phone while she waited but decided she'd done enough for one day.

A long-suffering sigh eventually drifted along the wire. "Dinner will be at eight o'clock, Susan. If you think you can be polite and not insult anyone, you might wish to come at seven-thirty, to meet Harry."

"To meet who?"

"Harry Brulanger, Lorraine's nephew."

"Oh. Fine, then. I'll see you Friday."

Replacing the phone, Susan picked up the contract once more, eager to bury her thoughts in the familiar legal terms, hoping to blot out the recent conversation from her mind.

Tony Antonelli looked around the hotel suite with disgust. He was sick of staying in hotels. After his mother's death five years before, he'd sold the home he'd bought for her. He'd moved around so much, he hadn't known where he wanted to settle, so he'd rented apartments for years.

No more. He was back home now. The season was over and he was tired. He'd come back to Santa Barbara to look around for property. He might buy a condo on the beach. He didn't know what he wanted anymore.

He stood before the bathroom mirror knotting his tie. He hated the damn things. However, he was determined to show Susan and her son that he, too, could look and act like a gentleman. He gave an unamused laugh. Not that it would matter. Susan had long ago made it clear how she felt about him. He wondered how she'd react to the discovery that her son looked at him as though he expected him to take off in the air any moment to fight crime and preserve truth, justice and the American way.

Tony grabbed his hairbrush and once again tried to force his black curls into some semblance of order. As soon as he brushed them back they immediately fell forward across his forehead. *What the hell.* He threw the brush down. He caught the glitter in his eyes and looked away with disgust. *You're excited about seeing her again, you stupid fool. You'll never learn.*

Susan Spencer was the only woman he'd ever wanted to marry. He couldn't remember when he first fell in love with her. It seemed as though he'd always loved her, and like a fool he'd believed she felt the same way. He could still feel the terrible pain of discovering that even at seventeen she had known what she wanted, and it hadn't been he.

She'd taught him a valuable lesson. In the eleven years since he'd faced the fact that all of her protestations of love had been lies, he'd never been tempted to risk being played for a fool again. He'd never lacked for female companions, but he never intended to marry any of them.

He was glad his mother never discovered his feelings. She had often talked of the day when he would settle down, marry and have a family. He felt another twinge of pain. Yes, he'd wanted children. He and Susan had talked about what kind of family they would have. They had decided to have four children, he remembered with a slight smile, as though they could make plans and they would all materialize just as they wished. Only it hadn't worked out that way. He'd been someone for her to tease and torment until Michael decided to marry her. He just wished he'd understood before he'd gotten so involved with her.

He wondered what she looked like now. Her son said she was an attorney. He had trouble picturing her in a law office counseling clients. How did she wear her hair these days? He could remember the fine blond hair, bleached by the hot southern California sun, hanging in rippling waves down the straight column of her spine. Of course that was only when she managed to escape from her dragon of a mother. Otherwise she had worn it in prim braids wrapped around her head.

He wondered if her eyes were still the color of turquoise, so clear he had always felt he was looking into the depths of her soul when he looked into them. Her skin had always glowed, golden with the perpetual touch of the sun. She'd been beautiful, even as a child. By sixteen she'd taken his breath away. Fat lot of good that had done him. He'd been the son of the next door neighbor's housekeeper.

He admitted to himself that she and Michael had never seemed to care about his background when they were growing up together. Because he'd been three years older than Michael and four years older than Susan, they had looked up to him and followed his lead. He grinned at some of his memories. He'd thought up some great adventures over the years and they'd gamely followed him, taking their scoldings from their respective parents courageously, but always willing to follow him again.

He'd been sorry to hear about Michael's death four years ago. What a waste. Michael had been a musical genius, a child prodigy. Perhaps that was one of the reasons the two of them had been so close. Everybody else had treated Michael like a freak. He'd loved Michael like a brother and had been ripped apart by the news of his sudden death. Leukemia had taken him at twenty-four. Tony glared into the mirror. How ironic that Michael should be the one to go, with all of his musical talent, while a jock like himself was as healthy as a horse.

He picked up his suit coat from the bed and

shrugged into it, trying to halt his unchecked memories. Even now, he still had feelings of inadequacy that assailed him whenever he recalled his past. Because of his careful investments over the years, he was confident he was the financial equal of the McCormicks and the Spencers, but whenever he returned to Santa Barbara he once again became the son of the McCormicks' housekeeper.

He tugged the hotel room door closed behind him and strode toward the elevators. He didn't know why he'd agreed to this dinner anyway. There was something in the boy's eyes that had pleaded with him and he couldn't say no. Tonight would be his final visit to the past. He wanted no reminders.

Susan McCormick never dithered. She was a calm, resolute woman who made a decision after carefully considering all known factors, then refused to waste a moment worrying over the correctness of her decision—which was why she was unnerved to discover she couldn't decide what to wear for dinner.

She first thought she should appear tailored and businesslike. After all, this dinner was for Steve's sake anyway. She had put on her gray suit and was coiling her hair on the nape of her neck when Steve paused by her door.

"Mom! You aren't going to dress like a lawyer for dinner, are you?" He stood in the doorway of her room, his hands on his hips, his face wearing an expression of disgust. ''Why can't you put on something pretty for a change?''

The disappointment in his eyes convicted her.

However, when she put on her sheer pink dress with the swirling skirt and full sleeves, she wasn't at all certain her choice had been the right one. Would he think she was dressing up to impress him? Then again, what was wrong with looking feminine and desirable? She glanced into the mirror, undecided. Perhaps it would be better to put her hair in a coil, as she had earlier planned, rather than having it fall to her shoulders.

Susan heard the doorbell and knew she didn't have time to redo her hair. He had arrived. She stepped into her matching pink sandals with the three-inch heels. At five feet four inches, Susan wanted desperately to look tall and slender tonight. She would have to settle for slender, she supposed with a sigh. After one last glance in the mirror, she walked down the hall.

Tony almost didn't recognize her. Where was the sparkling young girl with the flashing eyes and golden skin? This woman was too thin and pale. Was she ill? The thought caused a shock of pain to shoot through him, making a mockery of his earlier thoughts about her. His feelings for Susan had always been too intense for either of them to handle. Nothing seemed to have changed for him in that respect.

He held out his hand. ''Good to see you again, Susan.''

She stared at him in confusion. This wasn't the Tony Antonelli Susan remembered—in jeans, sneakers and a sweatshirt. He bore no resemblance to the ballplayer she'd seen pictures of, either. Instead he looked like one of the many businessmen she dealt with daily. He also loomed broader, larger than she remembered him. There was no trace of the boy of her memories. Susan wasn't at all certain she could treat the man with the necessary aloof politeness she'd planned. She could feel her heart beating erratically as she tried to adjust her mental picture to the reality.

She placed her hand in his, and immediately recognized her mistake. The warm, callused hand sent a tingling through her and she resigned herself to the knowledge that Tony would always have an effect on her that she wouldn't be able to control.

"It's good to see you, too, Tony," she responded. "May I get you something to drink?"

"Yes, please. Bourbon and water would be fine."

She moved away from him gratefully and walked over to the bar, keeping her back to him as she tried to steady the trembling in her hands. He mustn't see how he affected her.

Steve, unaware of the undercurrents, took over. "I saw you in the World Series, Tony. You were really great."

Tony turned to look at the boy and smiled. "Thank you, Steve."

Steve dropped his head for a moment, then looked

up at the man with a shy smile. ''I guess you hear that a lot, huh?''

Tony grinned. ''Some. But that's okay. It's always nice to hear.''

Susan handed Tony his drink and motioned to one of the sofas arranged before the large fireplace. Tony sat down and Susan sat across from him, while Steve, too excited to sit, paced around the room.

Tony gestured toward the large picture sitting on the mantel. ''When was that taken?''

Susan glanced at the portrait of her, Michael, and Steve. In a low tone she answered, ''Five years ago.'' She knew without looking what Tony saw—Michael smiling serenely into the camera, his light brown hair combed to the side, his gray eyes filled with good humor, while Susan sat in the curve of his arm, her smile radiant, as though she were amused by something the photographer said. Steve, at five, stared into the camera with a mischievous grin, his curly hair tumbling over his forehead. Susan had chosen that particular proof because of the expression on Steve's face. His eyes had sparkled, as though he knew something the rest of them didn't. As it turned out, that was correct. Just as the picture was snapped the photographer stepped back solidly on a cat's tail, creating quite a commotion. Only Steve had noticed the cat wake up earlier and descend from its perch on a chair to begin licking its paws, directly behind the photographer.

She loved that particular expression of his; it epitomized how much he enjoyed life and everything around him.

"I was sorry to hear about Michael, Susan. By the time I got the news it was too late to get back for the funeral."

Susan stared into his glittering black eyes and wondered if that were true. Would he have come? It was no longer important.

"It was a shock to all of us. We had no warning he was that ill." She took a sip of her drink. "He'd been playing with the Los Angeles Symphony for two years and was doing very well. He'd also been working on some compositions of his own."

Hannah, a solidly built woman of indeterminate age, appeared at the arched entryway between the living room and dining area. "Dinner is ready whenever you are, Susan," she announced.

Susan glanced up. "Thanks, Hannah. I want you to meet Tony." Starting toward the dining area, Susan paused at her housekeeper's side. Glancing over at Tony, she said, "Hannah Stilling, Tony Antonelli."

Hannah smiled. "I knew who you were, of course. Your coming to dinner has been all Steve could talk about since he got home from school."

She radiated good humor. Tony was amused at Susan's attitude. She treated Hannah more as family than as hired help. He wondered what her mother thought of that. "I'm very glad to meet you, Hannah. Have you been with Susan long?"

She nodded. "Ever since Steve was born. I was hired to keep him while Susan went to school."

Tony glanced at Susan. Why was she looking at him with such apprehension? Did she think he might snub the woman? That was a laugh, considering his background.

"You've set only three places, Hannah. Which one of us isn't supposed to eat tonight?" Susan asked with a grin.

"Me," Hannah responded. "I ate earlier because I wanted to watch a program on PBS that starts in a few minutes. I thought you might be able to look after yourselves just this once."

Susan laughed. "We'll try to manage without you, but it won't be easy."

Tony could never remember later what they'd eaten that evening. He found himself joining into the conversation, telling stories to Steve about some of the antics he and his mother and father used to pull, while Susan laughingly protested that he didn't need any more ideas—Steve came up with plenty on his own.

Steve began to lose his awe of Tony and started asking him pertinent questions about baseball, some of the players and batting techniques. Tony soon realized the boy was highly intelligent and well-versed in the sport. The intelligence didn't surprise him, but the love of baseball did. Although Michael and Susan had willingly tagged along after him, neither one of them had shown much interest or aptitude in sports.

Tony watched as Steve explained something to his

mother he'd recently seen on television. It was obvious to the most casual observer that Susan and her son were very close. He wondered if Steve had spent much time with his father.

"Were you ever in Boy Scouts, Tony?" Steve asked.

"As a matter of fact, I was. Why?"

In a careful, offhand manner, Steve answered, "Because I'm a Boy Scout and we have an all-day hiking trip planned in a couple of weeks." Steve darted a glance at his mother, then quickly looked back at Tony. "You could come along as my guest, if you want. All the other guys are bringing their dads."

"Stephen!" Susan's shocked tone echoed around the room. He looked at her with a mixture of apology and defiance.

"He can always say no, Mom. It's no big deal."

Here was one young man who wasn't being browbeaten by a possibly overprotective mother, Tony decided. "Exactly when is this all-day hiking trip planned, Steve?"

"Saturday, the eighteenth. We're going to meet at Mr. Spangler's house at seven in the morning." He was unable to meet Tony's gaze.

"I'm sure Tony has better things to do than go hiking, Steve," Susan managed to interject.

"On the contrary," Tony drawled. "I think it sounds like fun. You've got yourself a date."

Steve sat there for a moment, stunned. Never in his wildest dreams had he considered that Tony would actually go with him. He wasn't even sure why he'd asked him. Now that he had an acceptance, he didn't know what to say. He managed to choke out, "That's swell," and then took a large drink of milk.

"I thought you had to be ten to be in Scouts. Or are you a Cub Scout?" Tony asked.

Steve looked up in surprise. "No, I'm a Boy Scout, and I'm ten."

Tony sat staring at Steve. "You're ten?" he asked, his muscles tensing as a suspicion suddenly gripped him.

"Yes, sir. I was ten on February seventh."

Tony sat there as though a bomb had exploded on the table before him. *February? Exactly nine months after he left Santa Barbara?*

Steve couldn't understand it. Why did Tony look so upset? His face had darkened and his eyes seemed to be shooting sparks.

Tony's gaze clashed with Susan's. "How very interesting. Imagine my not knowing that."

Susan refused to look away. "It never occurred to us you'd be interested, Tony."

He sat there, stunned by the information he'd just received, stunned by the implications, then caught the bewildered expression on Steve's face. Forcing himself to relax, he attempted a smile at the puzzled boy. "I didn't even know you existed, Steve, until I read about your father's death."

It was Susan's turn to look bewildered. "You mean Mama Angelina never told you about Steve?"

His look barely concealed the contempt he felt. "I doubt very much Mama ever knew about his existence."

"That's not true! Steve and I used to visit your mother often when he was little. She was lonesome in that big house you bought her—never felt very comfortable with the neighbors. Steve loved to go visit her."

Steve blurted out, "You mean Mama Angelina was your mother, Tony?" Never had he found an adult conversation more confusing.

Tony's head was whirling, his thoughts zooming around his head in a kaleidoscopic display of confused images. His mother had known about Steve and had never told him? He stared at the boy before him, taking in the darkness of his eyes and hair, the same unruly mop of curls that caused him so much trouble. How could he have missed it? How could anyone who knew him? Was that why his mother had never told him?

When Tony didn't answer Steve's question, Susan responded. "That's right, Steve. I guess I never mentioned that to you."

Steve looked at the two adults with dismay. "It seems to me there's a lot you haven't told me."

Tony looked at her with an identical expression. "So it would seem." Two pairs of black eyes filled with accusation stared at her. She was definitely not ready for this.

Susan hastily shoved her chair back and stood. "If

everyone is finished, how does ice cream sound for dessert?'' She gave Tony a look that pleaded for understanding. Couldn't he see they couldn't discuss it now?

Apparently he recognized her concern and agreed. She watched as he unclenched his fists and visibly relaxed his shoulders. ''That sounds fine. How about you?'' he asked Steve.

The adults seemed to be changing the subject, which was all right with him. He shrugged. ''Sure, sounds great.''

When she returned with the ice cream Susan was forced to keep the conversation going. Tony had withdrawn and made no effort to contribute more than an occasional answer to her questions. Only with Steve did he come out of his self-imposed silence. She was relieved when dinner was over and she excused herself to clear the table.

When she returned to the living room, Tony immediately stood. ''I'm going to have to be going.'' He saw Steve's expression fall and frowned. ''I'm sorry, Steve, but I promised to meet a friend later.''

Steve tried for nonchalance. ''Sure, I understand. I know you're busy.''

''Not too busy to forget that hike, though.''

Steve's expression wavered. ''You mean you'll still go with me?''

Tony rested his hand on the boy's shoulder. ''I wouldn't miss it, champ. I'm hoping you and I can get much better acquainted.'' He caught Susan's gaze with a level one of his own. "I intend to settle in Santa Barbara. There's no reason why I can't spend time with you and Steve, is there?"

A sharp pain caught Susan in the chest, as though his words were stilettos piercing her skin. The look he gave her challenged her and she wasn't ready to face that challenge at the moment. "We'll see," she murmured in as noncommittal a fashion as possible.

"That we will, old friend." He turned and grinned down at Steve. "You were right. Hannah's a great cook. You're very lucky."

That was all the encouragement Steve needed. "You'll have to come over again some time," he offered with the expansive graciousness of a good host.

Susan fought to hide her negative reaction to Steve's suggestion. She didn't want to discourage the hospitable part of his nature, but found herself wishing he'd practice on someone else.

"I'd like to see you tomorrow, Susan. How about lunch?"

His request caught her off guard. "Uh, I don't think so, Tony. I have a rather full day scheduled."

He smiled, but the smile never reached his eyes. "We really need to get together and catch up on old times, you know."

Had there been an implied threat in his remark? There was nothing he could do to her, absolutely nothing, *except hurt Steve. He's already aware of my vulnerability where my son is concerned.*

She raised her chin slightly. "We don't have anything to discuss. Eleven years is a long time."

He stared at her, incredulous. "On the contrary. I believe we have a great deal to catch up on." He stopped, noting the bewilderment on Steve's face at his harsh tone. He reached over and ruffled the dark, unruly curls on Steve's head, a sudden sharp pain constricting his chest. *Susan has a great deal to answer for. One point I intend to find out—why I've had to wait all these years for some explanation.*

Tony opened the door, then paused, catching Susan's attention with a long, intent stare. "I'll call you."

Her small nod signaled Susan's reluctant acceptance of the inevitable.

She watched him walk down the long, curving walkway from her condominium to his low-slung sports car parked by the curb. She'd had a reprieve, but she knew she would have to be prepared to answer his questions. Why should she feel guilty? He was the one who'd left, not her. He was the one who'd never cared enough to find out if there had been any repercussions to their last evening together.

She closed the door and slowly walked down the hall to her bedroom. She owed him no explanation. She owed him nothing.

Then why had she felt like wrapping her arms around his lean waist and holding him close when she saw the first flash of pain on his face as the truth had hit him?

Susan's deeply buried feelings for Tony Antonelli had suddenly appeared from nowhere after all these years. She had honestly thought she was over him. It had taken only a few short hours in his presence to bring all of them tumbling back.

Chapter 2

Susan lay in the darkness of her bedroom, staring at the shadows on the wall caused by the security lamp outside her condominium.

She reviewed the events of the evening and recognized a certain sense of inevitability about what had happened. Now that Tony was back, she realized it had been only a question of time anyway. The older Steve grew, the more he looked like Tony.

Tony had been Steve's age the first time she ever saw him.

She and Michael had been playing in the gazebo in the elaborate gardens Marsha Spencer took such pride in displaying. They'd both been told to go out and play but not to get dirty, an admonition that greatly limited their choice of entertainment. She would never forget the moment when she looked up from watching Michael building a skyscraper out of his construction set and saw Tony watching them, a slight frown on his face. At that moment Susan was convinced she'd never seen a more beautiful person. The smooth bronzed complexion caused a spurt of envy as she glanced down at her pale arms and legs. His black curls glistened with a vitality sadly lacking in her fine straight hair.

When Michael saw him, he stood up and walked over to him.

"Hi. I'm Michael. This is Susan. Do you want to help us build a city?"

Tony's startlingly black eyes looked first at Michael, then shifted to Susan. "Is that all there is to do around here?"

Michael shrugged. "I dunno. What do *you* want to do?"

Tony glanced around at the elaborate gardens. "Doesn't anyone play ball in this neighborhood?"

Susan remained silent as she waited for Michael to answer. "What kind of ball?"

"Any kind. Baseball, football, soccer."

"We don't have anything to play with."

Tony had slumped against the door frame, but straightened at Michael's remark. "I have a bat, ball, and a couple of gloves. How about some batting practice?"

Michael glanced over at Susan, hesitation plain on

his face. Susan stood up, smoothing the wrinkles from her playsuit.

"That sounds like fun," she said. "Where can we play?"

Tony glanced over the hedge into the neatly clipped lawn next door. "How about over there?"

That had been the beginning of their friendship. Tony explained he was the son of Angelina Antonelli, who'd just been hired as housekeeper for the McCormicks. He and his mother had moved into the apartment located over the three-car garage.

He didn't seem to mind spending his time with the younger children, which endeared him to them. He found games to play that stretched and taxed them, but were never beyond their ability. Unfortunately, they quickly discovered it was impossible to spend time with Tony and stay clean.

Their first day together set the pattern of their relationship. Susan took her turn chasing batted balls and tried desperately to catch a ball coming toward her. Running backward and leaping high to catch it, she lost her balance and fell into the goldfish pond. The water wasn't deep, but it was brackish and she climbed out with slimy water and mud all over her. Her neat pigtails had degenerated into a wild tangle of dripping hair.

It was unfortunate that Susan attempted to sneak into the house just as Marsha Spencer was showing her garden club members the flower beds. Susan would never forget the look of horror on her mother's face, nor the amusement on the faces of her mother's guests. She'd been banished to her room without supper and without regard to the scraped knee that needed attention.

Susan couldn't remember the name of the housekeeper at the time, but she remembered her gentle scolding and compassion as she helped Susan to strip and get into the tub, and her gentle ministrations later. She'd even smuggled some dinner up to her that night in rebellion against Marsha's edict, which was probably why she hadn't lasted very long.

Even at six Susan knew better than to tell her mother about Tony. It was at that point in her life that she became quite protective of him where her mother was concerned. She never spoke his name, nor made any reference to him.

It wasn't long until Marsha discovered for herself who was luring the two quiet children into disobeying their parents, and she began to wage a battle to keep Susan away from Tony, even suggesting to the McCormicks that they dismiss Angelina. Susan was always grateful to the McCormicks for refusing to bow down to Marsha, which caused a distinct cooling of the friendship between the two families. The ensuing lack of communication further assisted the three children to spend time together without Marsha discovering what they were doing. As long as Susan would announce she was going to see Michael, she had her mother's full permission and approval. It didn't occur to Marsha that the two children were disregarding her rules by spending all their free time with Tony.

Whenever Susan read stories about the perfect male, she always pictured Tony. His body was a well-honed instrument trained to do what he wanted it to do. What he wanted it to do was to play baseball and he did that very well, indeed.

When he graduated from high school, Tony received a baseball scholarship to attend the University of California at Los Angeles. He seldom came home because he was also working part-time to help with the finances.

Mama Angelina was very proud of him.

She'd always been Mama Angelina to Michael and Susan—she was the mother Susan had secretly wished she'd had, though she refused to acknowledge the sacrilegious thought aloud. It was with Mama Angelina that Susan shared her small triumphs and tears, her first boyfriend, her first formal. It was Mama Angelina who could talk with her about Tony to Susan's heart's content.

Susan was fifteen when Tony first asked her for a date. It was the first time Susan couldn't ask Mama Angelina's advice. He'd invited her to a movie. It was summer and he was working full-time at a service station not far from their home. She'd missed him so much during the year and wanted to spend time with him, yet she knew her mother would never allow it.

It was then Susan began the deception that was to trap her later. She told her mother she had a date with

Michael. Her mother lectured her on how young both of them were, but in the end didn't refuse to let her go. Susan, being her usual direct self, immediately found Michael and told him what she had done. He thought it was funny. He also agreed not to give her away.

Susan spent as much time with Tony as he chose to give her that summer. He was casual, but seemed to like being with her. While Michael was involved with special lessons at the conservatory, Susan went with Tony to local ballgames, watching as he played on the city league. It was a very beautiful, very innocent summer for them.

By the time another year rolled around, there had been several changes for both of them. Susan had been slow in developing, but that year her slender body began to show the soft curves of ripening womanhood. Her face had lost the roundness of childhood and her eyes, with their slight slant at the corners, had become mysterious pools of blue staring out at the world.

Susan would never forget the morning she discovered Tony was back home for the summer. She'd burst into the garage apartment to show Mama Angelina something now long since forgotten. Tony was in the kitchen with nothing on but a skin-tight pair of cutoff jeans, his hair rumpled from sleep.

"Tony!"

He glanced around from pouring a cup of coffee,

then stared in surprise, absently setting the pot down. "Susan?"

She laughed, delighted to see him. "I didn't know you were home. When did you get here?"

He continued to stare at her in the shorts and halter she used as a summer uniform. "Late last night."

"It must have been. I didn't think I could sleep through the sound of your car. You must have gotten a new muffler on it."

He grinned. "As a matter of fact, I did, brat. You should show that car a little more respect, you know. It's older than you are." He turned back to the counter and without looking at her asked, "Do you want a cup of coffee?"

"Sure, but I came over to see if Mama Angelina was here."

Still with his back to her, Tony replied, "No, she took the car and went shopping. I don't know when she'll be back."

Susan had known Tony for ten years by that time and during those years had seen him in various states of undress. She couldn't understand why the sight of his bare back should affect her so. She only knew it did. His shoulders were broad and heavily muscled, and his spine was indented, forming a slender valley down his back to disappear into the low-hanging cut-offs. She had a strong urge to run her hand down that slight indentation, to feel the muscles that seemed to ripple just below the skin.

She was still staring when he turned around with

her cup of coffee. They were a few feet apart and she looked at him as though mesmerized. She saw a flame suddenly spark in his dark eyes and he closed the distance between them. His gaze fell on her soft lips, and she self-consciously licked them, remembering she had dashed over before bothering with any makeup. Suddenly shy, she dropped her gaze and took the offered cup.

"So how did you do in school this year? Are you going to be a senior in the fall?" Tony's voice sounded relaxed, although she wondered at the slight drawl, as though he were teasing her. She nodded, still watching her coffee.

"Me, too, although I'm not sure I'm going back."

She glanced up, startled. "What do you mean?"

He grinned. "I think I may get an offer to play professionally. If I do, I'm not going to wait to graduate. I'm going for it now."

"But, Tony, you'll need your degree to get a job."

"If I become a pro, Susan my sweet, I'll have the job I want for several years to come."

"That isn't a career, Tony. That's just a hobby."

"Maybe so, but it's helped to pay for my college education, and if I'm good enough, it may pay my way for several years."

She stared at him, amazed. She'd never thought about being able to make money by playing ball. Every man she knew worked in some type of business. Her father ran the family firm and, being an only child, Susan had begun to think about learning how to take over when he retired. She'd already begun to map out her college curriculum, and was interested in the possibility of a pre-law course. A good businessman needed to know the ins and outs of the law, or so she decided.

"Don't you have any ambition to become successful?"

Tony stared at her for a moment, then raised his cup to his lips. After a moment he shrugged. "I suppose we need to define the word *success*. We probably have different ideas as to the meaning." He glanced out the window. "But it's too nice a morning to waste on a philosophical discussion. Why don't we go play some tennis?"

Tony and Susan spent their free time together that summer, but there was a difference in the relationship she could never quite understand. Tony didn't seem as relaxed around her as before. It seemed to Susan he went out of his way not to touch her. Before he had always taken her hand to guide her, or draped an arm around her shoulder. Now he was very polite about opening doors, but he never came close to her. And she missed his touch. She found that many of her dreams were about him, and in all of them just as he would start to put his arms around her, she'd wake up.

What was wrong? She'd never had the nerve to ask him for fear she wouldn't like the answer. She would have been more upset if he'd been seeing someone else, but she knew he wasn't. He still seemed to want her around, but only at a slight distance.

They didn't see much of Michael that summer. A couple of times he joined them for a hamburger and once went to the movies with them. He seemed to be involved in his music and content to live in his own world. Susan hadn't realized how far they'd drifted apart, and she felt a sharp jab at the loss. She loved Michael, but she didn't miss him as she did Tony when he was at school. All of her dreams and desires seemed to revolve around Tony, but she knew Michael was there if she ever needed him.

Tony ended up returning to school his final year after all, and their last evening together that summer forever changed their relationship.

Susan stirred restlessly, her thoughts a torment. She had pushed them to a corner of her mind, where they had been content to stay until Tony stepped into her life once more. She didn't know how she was going to be able to cope with his presence now. She closed her eyes, willing herself to sleep. Instead, her thoughts drifted once again to the last summer she and Tony had spent together.

She remembered she'd gone to a ballgame in which he was playing, and several of his teammates and their girlfriends had decided to go to the beach afterward. They had all piled into various cars and driven to Piedmont Park. There was a full moon, which brightened the beach so that they needed no artificial light. The fire that was built gave off a cheery glow and they all enjoyed the quiet of the moonlight and the soft sighs of the waves.

They sat around the fire, laughing and talking, and Susan was surprised when Tony suddenly stood up and pulled her up with him. "Let's go for a walk."

She was pleased to have a few minutes alone with him. It had been hard for her to ignore the fact that he was leaving the next day. He seemed to think nothing of it. He'd left to return to school each fall and she'd never seemed to care before. Susan admitted to herself she didn't understand why she was upset now. However, she knew there would be an empty place in her life and she wasn't at all sure how to fill the void.

Tony surprised her once again by pulling her close to his side and leaning over to whisper into her ear. "I'm going to miss you, Susan my sweet. I've been thinking about bundling you in with my clothes and taking you with me."

His arm felt warm around her shoulders, so why should his words cause a slight shiver to run down her spine? She looked up at him uncertainly. "I'm going to miss you, too."

He stopped and turned her to face him. "Is that why you've had such a long face tonight? I thought you must be bored with the game."

She grinned. "How could I be bored when you hit two home runs and a triple? Surely you heard me screaming."

"Oh, was that you? I thought it was a siren going off somewhere."

She doubled her fist and poked him in the ribs. "Very funny, Antonelli. You trying to make it as a comedian in case you don't get picked up as a ballplayer?"

He pulled her closer to him, looping his arms behind her. "Something like that," he murmured.

He stood with his back to the light, so that Susan couldn't make out the expression on his face, but his husky tone caused a tingling feeling inside her. She glanced up at him. He lowered his head until his mouth brushed hers, but stopped when she stiffened in his arms.

"Hey, what's the matter, haven't you ever been kissed before?"

She attempted a nonchalant shrug. "Sure," she lied. "Lots of times."

He brushed his lips across hers once again. "Do you have something against my kissing you?" he whispered.

She shook her head, her voice suddenly gone.

Even now, Susan recalled her initiation into the sensual world with quickened breathing. He'd been so gentle with her, coaxing her to respond to him. As she relaxed against him, he began to explore her mouth with tender persistence until her lips parted slightly in a soft sigh. He slipped his tongue between them, playfully pursuing her tongue until she pulled away from him, trying to get her breath.

"Are you certain you've been kissed before?" he asked in a teasing whisper.

"Not like that!" She felt as though she'd been running and couldn't catch her breath. All her fantasies about Tony seemed to be coming true, and she wasn't sure she was ready for the reality.

He caught her to him, softly stroking her back. "I'm sorry, honey. I didn't mean to frighten you."

Susan buried her head in his shoulder. "You didn't frighten me," she admitted.

He laughed. "Good. Then you won't mind repeating the lesson. We might as well practice until we get it right."

Eventually they returned to the fire, where no one seemed to have missed them. Susan knew that those few minutes on the beach had changed her, awakening her to her own body and its needs. Nothing would ever be the same.

Tony came home for Thanksgiving. Normally he stayed in Los Angeles and worked through the holidays. Their first evening together took up where their last evening left off—in each other's arms.

"I want you to marry me, Susan," Tony managed to say as he forced himself to put some distance between them.

Susan stared up at him with shining eyes. "Oh, Tony, I never dreamed you really wanted to marry me. I love you so much." She sighed. "But I have to finish school, and I still have college ahead of me."

"Marriage won't stop you from getting your education. I'll see to that. There's been enough interest shown in me that I know I'll be picked up next spring. We'll have enough money to do anything we want!"

They sat curled up together in the front seat of his car, the waves on the nearby beach playing a background symphony to their conversation.

"Mother will never agree to my getting married so young."

"That isn't it at all, and you know it. You'll never be old enough to marry me."

"Well, you have to admit it's going to be a shock to her. She doesn't even know we've been seeing each other."

"She can't be that much of an ostrich, Susan. Do you mean to tell me she still thinks you're seeing Michael?"

"Yes."

"When are you going to tell her the truth?"

"I'm not sure."

"Well, it might be a good idea to mention who the groom's going to be so she won't faint at the wedding, don't you think?"

"Do we have to think about it now, Tony?" she asked as she curled her arms tighter around his neck. His soft moan as he found her lips was a very satisfactory answer.

During Christmas break Tony insisted on giving her an engagement ring. She reluctantly took it, but explained she would wear it on her finger only when she was with him. The rest of the time she wore it on a chain around her neck.

Not that he blamed her. She was only seventeen, after all, still in high school, and had never shown the least amount of rebellion toward her mother's rules, except for seeing him. He knew she loved him, just as he loved her, but it was going to take her time to break the strings her mother had so carefully tied to her.

It took all of his willpower not to initiate her more deeply into the loving side of her nature. She was so spontaneous with him and so very trusting, but he refused to take advantage of her innocence.

An unusually warm May evening found Susan arriving home about eleven. She'd spent the day with a couple of girlfriends at the beach, working on her tan. The evening was spent sharing their plans for the summer.

Susan hadn't told anyone how serious she was about Tony. Perhaps it was because it didn't seem quite real to her. She knew she loved him, but she could never picture her mother giving in to her marrying before college. However, she knew that when Tony got home in a few weeks he would insist on their setting a wedding date.

The thought of being married to him, actually married, set off tiny explosions of feeling within her every time she thought about it. If she could just keep that thought in mind, she was sure she could face her mother with calm determination.

Her friends let her off at the end of her driveway, and she had almost reached the sidewalk when she heard a voice.

"Susan?" A low-voiced shadow moved toward her. She recognized Tony's broad shoulders and lithe stride.

"Tony! You're home!" She ran to him, throwing her arms around him. "When did you get here? What are you doing here so soon? I thought you had another two weeks!" Her words tumbled over themselves as she kissed him repeatedly on his chin and jawline.

"Where have you been?" His voice sounded harsh. He took her hand in a firm grip.

A faint light from the streetlamp cast shadows across his face. She strained to see his eyes, but had no trouble recognizing the frown that furrowed his brow. "The beach, why?"

Tony took her past the flagstones that led to her front door. Instead, they continued down the driveway and toward the gazebo. "Who were you with?"

Susan's amazement became tinged with irritation. "What difference does it make? I already have a father, Tony." She planted her heels, refusing to enter the gazebo.

Tony faced her, moonlight etching his features. His wry smile echoed the sheepish tone as he responded, "You're right, honey. It's just that I've been waiting around to see you for hours."

Bewildered by the underlying excitement in his voice, Susan turned and went into the darkened shelter of the gazebo. "Why?"

"I wanted to let you know that I'm leaving tomorrow."

"Leaving? To go where?"

He laughed, his excitement pouring over. "I was notified today that the Atlanta Aces want me for their farm team. I'm to report to Florida tomorrow, which means catching the first flight out of here."

Susan sat down with a thump, her legs no longer capable of bearing her weight. "You really mean it, don't you? You're going to play professional ball?"

Tony sat down beside her, grabbing both her hands. "Yes. Now we can get married, honey, just as we planned. I'll have to find out when I can get some time off to come back to get you, but we're going to get married as soon as I can arrange it." His determined tone made her realize how serious he was.

"Oh, Tony, everything's happening so fast!" She could no longer see him, but she could feel the heat from his body radiating the male scent of aftershave that would always make her think of Tony whenever she smelled it. Unaware of her actions Susan reached for him, clutching his warm muscular body to her. "I don't want you to go," she whispered.

His arms slid around her in a possessive grip. Her hair brushed against his face and he touched his lips to her forehead. His hand slid gently under her chin and lifted it, so that his lips found hers.

It had been months since she'd seen him, lonely months of wondering how they were going to make their dreams come true. Now that she was in his arms, anything seemed possible.

His first kiss was warm and seeking, and she felt as though she were exploding in a million different pieces with the pleasure of being in his arms. He seemed to sense her total surrender and drew back for a moment, giving them both a chance to breathe. Then he began to kiss her once more.

His second kiss became more possessive and the intimate exploration of his tongue created a tremor within her she couldn't control.

By the time Tony relaxed his hold on her, Susan refused to allow him to pull completely away. Instead, her hands crept under the pullover shirt he wore and stroked across his broad chest. Her lips found the corded strength of his neck and began a trail of warm, moist kisses.

"Susan, baby, you've got to stop that," he growled into her ear. She ignored him. Her inquisitive fingers roamed to his back, where the indented spine continued to lure her into exploring. Her head fell against his shoulder, her long hair falling loose from its casual topknot and snaking down along his shoulder and arm. His mouth unerringly found hers once again.

Susan never remembered how they came to the point where they were both nude and stretched out on the cushioned bench. She could still recall her panicky feeling when she recognized what was happening. Tony's hard body pressed down against her, his leg heavy across her thighs as his hands explored her quivering body. Susan knew she had no business being there with him like that—knew she had to leave right away, but a treacherous feeling of languor and longing to enjoy for a few minutes more the strong feelings he evoked within her lured her to imitate Tony's movements. Her hands continued to stroke the muscular contours that gave mute evidence to Tony's athletic way of life.

Once his hand reached her inner thighs and began a pulsating rhythm she lost all reasoning powers. He gently nudged her legs apart with his knee as he continued to kiss her with slow mind-drugging movements of his lips and tongue. She was scarcely aware when he moved between her legs, then paused.

"Oh, honey, I'm sorry, I can't wait. I love you so much. And we'll be married in a few weeks. Let me show you my love," he whispered, his voice husky with controlled passion. "I don't want to hurt you," he murmured. She stiffened at his words, but she was too late. With strong, steady pressure he possessed her, his mouth moving on hers at the same time, absorbing any sound she might have made.

After the first sharp pain Susan discovered a very pleasurable sensation. Her body took over and responded to his lovemaking as though instinctively aware of how to please him. It was too late for second thoughts. Besides, this was Tony. Whatever Tony did was all right.

Susan felt a tension, a continuing tightening deep within her as Tony's pace quickened. He continued to plunge deep within her and she gasped as a sudden shower of stars fell around them. Her body made a convulsive contraction that overcame Tony's control and he made one last plunge, then collapsed in her arms.

They must have slept as they lay, Tony's weight partially resting on the side of the bench. Susan felt dazed when she became aware of where she was, her arms draped around Tony, his body partially covering hers. When she attempted to move he stirred.

She heard him mutter something, his tone disgusted. She felt a frisson of fear as she realized what they had done.

"You okay?" he asked as he pulled away from her.

She nodded, then realized he couldn't see her. "Yes," she answered hesitantly.

She heard him moving, a rustle of clothes, then he placed something across her. "Here are your clothes," he whispered.

Susan automatically pulled them on, wondering what to do or say. Tony sank down beside her, pulling her back into his arms.

"I didn't mean this to happen, baby, you know that, don't you?"

Fear of rejection caused Susan to stiffen. "Do you think I did?"

He began to stroke her back, trying to remove the

sudden stiffness he felt. "Oh, no, honey, that isn't what I meant. I didn't do anything to protect you."

"Oh."

They sat there in silence as Tony continued to stroke her. "I've got to leave tomorrow—I have no choice."

"Yes."

"As soon as I know where I'll be staying I'll call you, okay?"

"Okay."

"Dammit, Susan, don't make this harder for me. If I could, I'd take you with me. As it is, I'll be back to get you before you even realize I've been gone."

Although the warmth of Tony's body still protected her from the cool night air, Susan suddenly felt alone. Tony was leaving. There'd be an entire continent between them.

"I need to go inside, Tony," she murmured softly.

"I know, love, I know. I'm so sorry for losing control tonight. You don't need the extra worry."

"What do you mean?"

"Oh, Susan, don't you understand you could be pregnant? I didn't want to start our marriage out on that note."

"If I'm pregnant, I'll have to face the consequences."

"No. If you're pregnant, *we'll* face the consequences...together."

"It may not happen."

"I know."

"I don't want you to marry me because you have to."

She could feel his chest shake just as she heard his chuckle. "Believe me, Susan, I wouldn't be marrying you because I have to. You've been all I've wanted for a wife since I first met you. But six was a little young to propose." He kissed her softly on the forehead. "Why do you think I want to play professional ball? I've got to make enough money that even your mother will consider me worthy of you." He kissed her cheek softly. "Go on inside, love. Just don't forget I love you, and I'll be back to get you in just a few weeks."

Susan went back to the house that night and dreamed of Tony, confident in their love for each other. She waited for him to call, she waited for him to write, and she waited for him to come back for her, but she never heard from him again.

It was a long time before Susan finally fell asleep that night.

Chapter 3

Late the next afternoon Donna, Susan's secretary, burst through her office doorway, her eyes wide with excitement. "Susan! Tony Antonelli is here to see you. Omigosh, he's even better looking in person. I didn't know you knew him. Why didn't you tell me?"

Susan had been dictating when she was interrupted and she stared at Donna in surprise. Her unflappable, experienced secretary generally had a professional air about her that could not be shaken regardless of the crisis, yet there she was blithering like a teenager over a rock star. She eyed the woman thoughtfully.

The expression on Susan's face stopped Donna in her tracks. What had she done? She'd just burst into Susan's office, that's what she'd done. Susan generally kept her door open, so that when she shut it, the closed door was a signal that she didn't want to be disturbed. Donna could feel the heat of embarrassment surge through her.

"I'm sorry for bursting in like that, Susan. You can imagine my surprise when I looked up and saw Tony Antonelli standing there, smiling at me." She noted that Susan had not changed her expression, but continued to watch her impassively.

"Did he say why he was here?" Susan asked.

"Oh, of course he did. He said he wanted to talk with you if you had a few minutes." She took in the stack of files Susan was methodically reviewing. "I didn't bother to ask if he had an appointment because I knew I would have remembered it."

Susan glanced at her watch. It was after four o'clock. She, too, studied the files on her desk, then sighed with resignation. Whatever it was he wanted to discuss with her must be very important, for she had told him how busy she would be today. The Tony she remembered would never have come to the office without very good reason. She was afraid he found Steve good reason, so she might as well get it over with.

She carefully laid the microphone down on the transcriber and stood up. "Of course I'll see him," she said with a smile that successfully hid her trepidation. She walked to the open door and paused. Tony stood in front of Donna's desk, his head bowed as though his thoughts had taken him far away from the quiet luxury of the law office. Donna slipped past Susan and returned to her desk.

"Hello, Tony."

His head snapped up and he stared at her in disbelief. The woman in the severely tailored navy suit, with her hair pulled into a knot low on her neck, bore little resemblance to the woman he'd seen the night before.

"Susan?"

She smiled. "Come in," she said, motioning him to enter.

He tried to regain lost ground, tried to remember his anger and bitter feelings toward this woman who had hidden from him for ten long years the fact that he had a son. Instead, all he could think about was the tremendous change in the woman he had known as a child. The change was not for the better. It was almost as if all her joy and excitement had been removed, leaving this calm, unemotional person instead. What had happened to her to have caused such a tremendous change? Was she still grieving for Michael?

None of his thoughts were apparent as Tony stepped past her into her office. "Very nice," he murmured, unsure of how to broach the subject now that he was here.

"Thank you."

She motioned to one of the chairs, then sat down in another one a few feet away. She wondered why Tony was so insistent on talking with her. It was obvious from the set of his jaw that he was determined to discuss something. Didn't he understand that he was eleven years late with an apology, if that was what he intended? Somehow a simple "Oops, sorry" seemed singularly inappropriate.

Her training helped Susan to control her emotional reaction to his presence, and she appeared relaxed and courteous. Her restless night showed in the slight mauve shadows under her eyes, intensifying her look of vulnerability. She wished she'd gotten more sleep the night before rather than spending so many hours reliving the painful memories that Tony's visit had evoked.

"I'm sure you won't be surprised to learn I didn't get much sleep last night." Tony's gruff words almost made her jump, they were so similar to her own thoughts. "I had to sift through some strong emotions before I could begin to deal with them." He leaned forward, resting his elbows on his knees.

"I can imagine," she said quietly.

"Can you?" He glanced up under his thick brows. "I wonder. Do you have any idea how it feels to think you know someone, and then have them act in such a way that you realize you never knew them at all?" His tone was almost meditative as he turned his head and stared out the window.

"Of course I do. That's exactly the way I felt when I realized all your talk about calling me, and arranging to marry me, were all lies. You've just described the feelings I had at that time."

"What are you talking about?" He was staring at her with a puzzled expression. "I never lied to you in my life. But how do you think I felt when I thought you felt the same way about me, while all the time you were making plans to marry Michael?"

Suddenly too agitated to sit still, Susan stood up and went over to the window. With her back to him she finally spoke. "You know better than anyone, Tony, that I never had any plans to marry Michael."

"Oh, c'mon, Susan. That's all your mother talked about for years, and you know it."

She turned and looked at him. "If you'll remember correctly, you, Michael and I spent years laughing at most of Mother's plans regarding Michael and me."

Tony stood up and walked slowly toward her. "When did the two of you stop laughing, Susan?"

She stared up at him in disbelief. Was he trying to place the blame of not knowing about Steve on her? She could feel the cold anger begin to build within her as she remembered the scared seventeen-year-old he'd so blithely forgotten on his way to becoming a star.

"I quit laughing the day I faced the fact that I was pregnant by a man who professed to love me but who disappeared out of my life when I most needed him!"

"You know, that righteous anger is a good touch, and that story may have impressed your sympathetic friends, but you seem to forget it's me who's your audience this time. And we both know I did everything *but* disappear." He watched her eyes snap. "I *am* curious, though. Did Michael ever realize Steve wasn't his?''

Her hand swung before Susan consciously recognized her reaction to his insult, but Tony's legendary quick reflexes caused him to grab her by the wrist, swaying with his whole body as he stopped her swing. ''Sorry, sweetheart. I don't allow anyone to slap me, not even an illustrious Spencer-McCormick.''

Susan could not remember ever having been so angry. For the first time in her life she experienced what she'd always thought was merely an expression—she glared at him through a red haze.

Her breathing, as she took several deep, steadying breaths, was the only sound in the office. When she felt she had herself under control, she said, ''I don't know why you've come back, Tony, or the reason that you are in this office, but I don't intend to listen to your guilt-based accusations and insults. All right. So you didn't handle things as well eleven years ago as you would now. I can accept that.'' She felt her knees starting to tremble in reaction to her emotional state, and she casually seated herself in a chair by the window. ''Why don't we consider your apology has been made and accepted, and leave it at that.''

''My *apology!* What in the hell do I have to apologize for? Not only did you disregard everything we had planned together, not only did you decide that a McCormick was a much better risk in the marriage stakes than the housekeeper's son, but rather than let me know you were pregnant you jump at the chance to use the pregnancy to consolidate your position, and you think *I owe you* an apology?'' His voice had risen with each phrase, and Susan found herself on her feet once more.

Her voice shaking with intensity, she started toward him. ''You really are a bastard, aren't you? But don't worry, that isn't anything I just learned about you. You want to know why you never heard about Steve? Well, I'll tell you. Because I didn't know how to get in touch with you, that's why. I waited and waited and waited for you to write. I watched the mail every day for weeks until it began to dawn on me that you had never had any intention of writing me. All those loving endearments had rolled off your tongue, and like a fool I believed you. But I paid for it. Oh, God, did I pay for it. I don't know what I would have done if Michael hadn't been there. He was the only person I trusted enough to tell. And he stuck by me. He was the one who suggested we get married and let the family think the baby was his. He knew that as far as Mother knew, he was the only one I ever dated. He didn't push me. In fact, he even offered to try to contact you himself, if that was what I wanted. But it wasn't. I had no desire to see you forced to return home and marry me. My dreams died hard, Tony, but they did die. I don't owe you any apologies for anything. You did your very best to make my life a disaster, but thank God I had Michael. He was worth ten of you!''

It was only when she stopped talking that Susan

realized she was crying, the tears pouring down her cheeks in an unchecked flow. She couldn't remember the last time she had cried, but it had been years—probably not since Michael's death. Tony had managed to unleash all of her emotions and if he didn't like being the brunt of them, that was too damned bad!

Tony stood there, an arm's length from her, his face gradually softening as he continued to watch her. He reached out tentatively and brushed one of her cheeks. "You never got any of my letters, did you?"

Her laugh was a half-sob. "You never give up, do you? Does it somehow absolve you of your guilt feelings to pretend?"

He placed his hands on her shoulders and gently rocked her until she was forced to rest her hands on his chest for balance. "Oh, Susan, what have we done to each other?"

She tried to push him away, but he held on, steadily tightening the pressure until she was standing in the circle of his arms. She dropped her head wearily against his shoulder, the outburst of rage leaving her perilously weak. "It doesn't matter anymore. It was all so long ago. It could have happened to two other people."

"But it didn't. It happened to us and there is a young boy out there that shares everything we are or ever hoped to become." He tilted her chin slightly with his forefinger. "I think we need to sit down and try to work out the misunderstandings. It's important to all of us."

Susan had forgotten how it felt to be held in a man's arms. Most particularly, in Tony's arms. The strange familiarity of being back within the protection of his quiet strength was curiously peaceful, considering the storm that had recently filled the room.

"Why do you insist there was some misunderstanding? The only misunderstanding I can see is that for some reason you think I chose to marry Michael rather than to marry you."

"Are you telling me that isn't true?"

"Are you going to believe me if I tell you?"

He studied her soft features, so dear to him. "Yes, love, I'll believe you."

"The only reason Michael and I married was because I was pregnant and didn't know which way to turn. I wanted the baby—" she felt his arms tighten with her words "—and Michael understood my fear of telling Mother and giving her control over us."

"Then your mother didn't know about the pregnancy?"

"No. She has always explained to everyone that he was premature."

"How can she look at him and believe he isn't mine?"

"She never had any reason to think otherwise. Remember, she never knew I was seeing you."

"Then how did she explain away all my phone calls to you?"

She jerked back in his arms, and stared up at him. "What phone calls?"

"The ones I made when you didn't answer any of my letters."

"You really did write to me?"

"I really did."

"And you called?"

"Many times. Sometimes I talked to your housekeeper...Dora, was it?"

"Yes, I think Dora was working for Mother then."

"Your mother always said she had given you my message but that you had been with Michael and no doubt hadn't found the time to return my call."

"Mother said that?"

"Oh, yes. She was very civil."

"Mother? Did she know who it was?"

"Of course. I always left my name and phone number."

"Didn't you find it strange that she wasn't cold to you?"

"Your mother has always treated me with aloof politeness."

Susan was quiet for a long while. Then she spoke in a faraway voice. "Mother knew you were calling me. She must have also known you were writing, but she never mentioned it to me. Not ever."

"The last time I called, your mother informed me of your engagement to Michael and suggested it would be better if I didn't call again."

"Tony, Michael and I were never engaged. We

went to Mexico and got married and came back and told everyone. We knew they would never agree to our getting married that young. I was seventeen, he was eighteen. We figured if we presented them with the accomplished fact, they would have to accept it."

"Obviously, they accepted it."

"After Mother read us her sensible, sane approach to life sermon and the sins of impetuous behavior. She insisted on a church wedding, so that no one would be cheated out of the spectacle, and Michael and I agreed to go along with it."

"When did you get married?"

"July."

"You didn't wait very long after I left, did you?" There was still a hint of bitterness in his voice.

"I knew three weeks after you left there was a very good chance I might be pregnant. I waited another month, hoping I was wrong before I talked to Michael about it. He saw no point in our wasting any time, once we decided."

"Why didn't you try to contact me through Mama?"

"For the same reason I decided against tracking you down and confronting you with what had happened. If you didn't care enough to contact me on your own, I knew we had nothing upon which to build any kind of relationship."

"You still don't believe I tried to contact you, do you?"

"Yes, as a matter of fact, I do. But you have to

understand that I can't change the thinking of eleven years in a few short minutes. I can see Mother doing exactly what she did. She assumed that eventually you would get tired of writing and phoning when you never received a response. When that didn't work, she made up a phony engagement."

"The question is, what do we do about it now?"

Startled, Susan asked, "It's a little late to do anything, don't you think? It certainly wouldn't accomplish much to confront Mother after all this time."

"Susan, I was raised without a father. I can't stand by and watch my son in the same situation without trying to do something about it."

Susan could feel the heat flow through her at his low-voiced comment. What could he be suggesting? Trying to sound as noncommittal as possible, Susan said, "Yes, I can understand your feelings."

"Let me get acquainted with him, spend some time with him. Let's give you and me a chance to catch up on the last few years."

"There's no reason to include me in your plans, you know. I have no objection to your seeing Steve and spending time with him. I don't believe any child can receive too much love. And you'll find him very easy to love." *He's like you in so many ways,* she thought, unaware of what she was admitting.

Tony stared at her, wondering if she had any idea how he felt. She had lived with the knowledge for years. He was just now coming to grips with the idea.

She sounded so calm. Didn't she have any deep-seated feelings at all anymore?

"You're telling me you don't mind my getting to know Steve, but that's as far as it goes?" he asked.

She nodded. "Yes. Whatever you and I once shared is no longer there and I see no reason to pretend."

Tony stared at her for a long moment. "I see," he said finally. "All right. If that's the way you want it." He started for the door, then paused. "It's all right, then, if I go ahead and call Steve?"

She nodded, unable to say anything else. If he would only get out of her office before she broke down! He smiled, the flashing smile that had always made her knees weak. Obviously, that was one thing that would never change.

"Thanks for your time, counselor. I promise to stay out of your way." The door closed softly behind him.

She wondered how long it would take her to find the concentration necessary to focus once again on her work.

Susan slowly came awake, relaxed in the knowledge that it was Saturday and she didn't need to hurry. It had been a hard week, although the dinner party the night before had gone much better than she expected.

Harry Brulanger had been quiet but amusing in a rather droll way. If he were kin to anyone besides Lorraine she might have accepted his invitation for dinner, but she knew better. Any sign of encouragement and Lorraine and her mother would be off, eagerly making wedding plans.

Her thoughts turned to her mother and how she had manipulated events eleven years ago. Susan knew she had to talk to someone about what she'd learned from Tony. She had arrived early enough at her parents' home to find her father alone for a few minutes. He'd been in his study, reading, when she peeked in the door. She stood there watching him for a moment, then tapped on the open door. He glanced up over his reading glasses and smiled. "Come in, baby. I didn't hear you come in."

She stepped inside, carefully closing the door behind her. "That's because I snuck in, Daddy. I was hoping to get a chance to talk with you."

He placed the book and his glasses down on the table next to his favorite chair. Motioning to the chair next to him, he said, "Fine. What shall we talk about?"

Her father was a slim man of medium height. His unobtrusive style of dress once caused a younger Susan to accuse him of being able to lose himself in a crowd of two. She'd gotten her clear blue eyes and slender build from him; often she wished she could have inherited his wisdom as well.

She sat down, relaxing for the first time that day. "I need your advice, Daddy."

A slight smile lifted the corners of his mouth. "I've never been very good at giving advice, you know."

"Actually, you've always given excellent advice.

The trouble has been trying to corner you so you would."

"So you think you've cornered me tonight?"

"I hope so." She hesitated, unsure of how to begin. Finally, she looked up and met his calm gaze. "Tony Antonelli is back in town." She watched for a reaction, but got none. Her father would make an excellent poker player. "You know who he is, don't you?"

His clear blue eyes held a wicked gleam. "Yes, dear, I believe as old and decrepit as I am, I still know who Tony Antonelli is, and the fact he won Most Valuable Player this year in the World Series."

"You know very well that's not what I meant!" She tried hard to mask her agitation, willing herself to sit quietly in the chair.

Stephen Spencer studied her for a moment, the gleam disappearing from his eyes. "Are you afraid he'll make trouble over Steve?" her father asked in a quiet voice.

Susan's head jerked up, her body jolted by his unexpected statement. "You know about Steve?"

His eyes narrowed as he studied the confusion in her face. "Susan, anyone looking at Steve has to be reminded of Tony at that age. He's an exact replica of him."

"Does Mother know?"

He paused. "I believe your mother has chosen not to see the resemblance."

"What am I going to do?"

"What do you want to do?"

Once again he surprised her. She hadn't thought about it that way. She had wondered what she could do, perhaps, but never what she *wanted* to do. "I don't want to see Steve hurt."

"Do you think Tony will hurt him?"

"Not intentionally, perhaps, but yes, I think having Tony in his life will be the worst thing possible for Steve. He's content now. Once he's spent time with Tony, he'll always yearn for more."

"Are you thinking of Steve...or yourself?"

"Me? Of course not. Anything I might have felt for Tony was over years ago."

"I wonder. You were his shadow for so many years, and you were such a loyal little thing. It's hard to believe those emotions would ever disappear."

"Well, they did." Stephen made no response and for a while they sat there together in companionable silence. Susan eventually spoke. "Did you ever know of Tony calling me, Daddy?"

"When?"

"Oh, back when he first went with the farm team."

"You mean, just before you married Michael?"

She refused to meet his gaze. "Yes."

"I really don't remember, why?"

"He said he did."

"Was it important?"

"Of course it was important! I needed to talk to him then. Desperately. Only I couldn't reach him, and I never got any calls from him. He told me yesterday that he *had* called, several times in fact, and left messages, but that I never called him back."

"Would you have married him, Susan?"

Without realizing the implications of her answer, she replied instantly, "Oh, yes!"

His eyes grew sad as her father continued to study her. At last he sighed. "Poor Michael."

Susan got up from her chair and knelt by her father. "Oh, Daddy, not you, too. Tony assumed I hadn't told Michael the truth, too." Tears welled in her eyes and she brushed them away impatiently.

"That wasn't what I meant, dear. Of course Michael knew Tony was the father. I was just remembering how often he lied to help you and Tony, even to accepting Tony's baby as his own. He was quite a man."

Susan rested her head on her father's knee and nodded. "Yes, he was," she responded in a muffled voice. "I really did love him, and I tried my best to make him happy."

Her father stroked her hair as she knelt there. "I'm glad to know that. He deserved your love."

He continued to stroke her head until she finally raised it. "What should I do about Tony, Daddy?"

He shook his head. "I can't tell you that, I'm afraid. You're the only one who can make that decision."

As she got up from her kneeling position, she tried for flippancy. "Too bad I can't be more like Mother.

She has no trouble making all kinds of decisions for other people.''

Her father reached for her hand and patted it. ''Don't be too hard on your mother, Susan,'' he said, and stood up. ''She has had a difficult time with life. It's unfortunate that none of the people she loved ever measured up to her expectations. It's been her affliction that she's been unable to accept us as we are. Instead, she's tried to make us what she wants us to be.''

''How can you bear it, Daddy? I've often wondered how you've managed to live with her all these years.''

He pulled her close to his side, hugging her. ''I love your mother very much, Susan. I always have, and I always will. I've been able to accept her as she is. Maybe someday you'll be able to do the same.''

''Oh, Daddy, I don't know. How can I ever forgive her for interfering in my life? I would have married Tony years ago and none of this would be facing me now.''

''True. Are you wishing away those years you had with Michael, making a mockery of what he did for you and Steve?''

She looked at him in horror. ''No!''

''Since you can't change the past, Susan, it might be a good idea for you to accept it and put it behind you.'' He opened the door and went into the hallway. ''We'd better let your mother know you're here. You know how she frets about things.''

* * *

The doorbell interrupted Susan's thoughts and she glanced at the clock with dismay. It was only eight o'clock. Hannah was gone for the weekend and Steve had spent the night with one of his friends rather than have Susan pick him up after last night's dinner party. She would have to go to the door herself.

It rang again as she dashed down the hall, pulling on her robe as she ran. Breathless, she called, "Who is it?" and quickly tied the sash.

"Tony."

No, it couldn't be. She wasn't ready for him, not first thing in the morning. She opened the door.

"Good morning." He stood there grinning, looking incredibly virile in a crimson pullover shirt and fleece-lined denim jacket, his jeans outlining his well-developed thighs.

She stepped back with a sigh. "Good morning, Tony. You might as well come in."

"Such an enthusiastic greeting. I'm overcome."

"Steve isn't here."

One brow rose as he took in her attire. "And you were sleeping in?"

"Something like that."

"I'm sorry I woke you."

"Oh, I was awake, just not out of bed." She turned and started back down the hall. "Come on back and I'll put on some coffee." She measured the coffee, filled the pot with water and carefully poured it into the machine, then flipped on the switch. When she turned around, she saw Tony leaning against the counter watching her with amused interest.

"Aren't your feet cold?" he asked. She glanced down at her bare toes peeking from beneath her robe.

"As a matter of fact, they are. I'll get some clothes on and be back in a moment." She indicated the coffee machine. "Help yourself when it's done."

She tried to keep her mind free of all thought while she dressed. She had agreed that Tony could get to know Steve, but she wasn't at all sure how she was going to handle seeing him on a regular basis.

When she returned to the kitchen in jeans and a long-sleeved plaid shirt, her feet shod warmly in socks and sneakers, she found Tony sitting at the table, calmly reading the paper and sipping a cup of coffee.

He glanced up. "I happened to see your paper outside when I came up. Hope you don't mind my getting it."

She shrugged. "Not at all." She poured herself a cup of coffee and sat down across from him. He laid the paper aside and once again watched her, which made her nervous.

"Are you having second thoughts about letting me spend time with Steve?" His voice showed little inflection and his face gave nothing of his thoughts away.

She sighed, recalling her conversation with her father. "No, not really."

He grinned. "Good."

"But I have wondered what sort of relationship you're hoping to build with him."

"How about friendship?"

"How many ten-year-old friends do you have?"

"Several, why?"

She was certain her surprise registered on her face. Of course, he was a famous ballplayer. They would naturally flock around him. "How long do you intend to stay in Santa Barbara?"

"Permanently."

"You mean you've quit baseball?"

"Not necessarily, but during the off season I intend to stay here. I'm looking for a place to buy now, which is one of the reasons I'm here. I thought maybe you and Steve would like to come with me today. I'm going to be looking at some property along the coast. Hopefully, I'll find something I like. I'm sick of hotel rooms."

She'd just started to say, "I'm not sure when Steve—" when she heard the front door slam.

"Mom! There's the neatest car parked out front," he hollered as he trotted down the hallway. "It's silver and—" He came to an abrupt halt. "Tony! Is that your car?"

"Sure is. I take it you like it."

"Wow, do I ever! Is there a chance I could maybe go for a ride in it?"

"Funny you should ask. I was just asking your mother if you two might want to take a drive along the coast with me today while I look at some property."

Steve's eyes widened and his infectious grin appeared. "Hey, that would be great, wouldn't it, Mom?" He bounced over to the table. "You wanna go?" There was no doubt in Susan's mind about Steve's preference.

"Sure. Sounds like fun," she lied. She was rewarded by an exuberant hug.

"I've gotta call Scotty and tell him I can't meet him to play ball this morning," he said as he dashed out of the kitchen once more.

"Such enthusiasm," Susan muttered.

"Such energy," Tony added.

"That, too. You may not be aware of what you're getting yourself into." For the first time since he'd seen her last Wednesday, Tony received a relaxed, natural smile from Susan. His heart lurched in his chest. It was so much like the young girl he'd once known. Was there any other trace of her in this composed woman? He was going to do his damnedest to find out.

Susan offered to sit in the back seat, which was truly a sacrifice of the highest order, since there was no room in the back area for such things as knees and legs. Tony explained that Steve could sit in the smaller space more comfortably, a fact neither of them could argue, and Susan resigned herself to spending the day next to Tony.

With Steve's enthusiasm for the venture, and the

hundred and one questions he had for Tony, Susan didn't have to worry about making conversation. She was literally along for the ride. It was just as well. Spending the day with Tony wasn't the smartest decision she'd ever made. It gave her too much time to compare her past to her present. Although maturity had made certain changes about him, Susan recognized many familiar mannerisms, such as the way he tilted his head when he talked to her, the rumbling baritone of his voice that managed to touch an inner spark every time she heard it and the way his eyes flashed with good humor. When he grinned she was instantly reminded of the boy in the back seat, who shared the same wide smile. How could she ever have forgotten?

By the end of the day she grudgingly had to admit that Tony had his full share of charisma. Steve was totally enthralled, and if she were honest, she had to admit he'd woven something of a spell around her as well.

They stopped for hamburgers and shakes before going home. Two of the places they'd seen had caught Tony's imagination and he began to ply Susan with questions as to her choice between the two. She refused to give him a definitive answer. Instead, she agreed with him when he pointed out their good qualities and possible drawbacks.

By the time they returned home, Steve needed no prodding to get ready for bed. Out of politeness Susan invited Tony in, hoping he'd say no. He didn't.

"Would you like something to drink?" she asked as she stood in the middle of the living room.

"No, thanks." He came toward her in a steady stride. "Thank you for today, Susan. It meant a great deal to me." He stopped in front of her.

She tried to control her reaction to his closeness by refusing to step back from him. "Steve had a great time, as I'm sure you could tell."

Tony slipped his hand under Susan's chin, raising it slightly. "And how about Steve's mother? Did she have a great time, too?"

It wasn't fair that he should have such an effect on her. Her heart fluttered like a bird's wings in her chest, and she was having trouble with her breathing. Susan tried to find her voice. "I, uh, enjoyed today, too, Tony. Thank you." She glanced up at him, then wished she hadn't. The smoldering message in his eyes did nothing to help her pulse rate.

His arms slid around her waist and he lowered his lips to hers. There had been many women in his arms during the past eleven years, so why did it feel so natural and right to have Susan there once more? Tony took possession of her as though she'd always been his. His mouth began a gentle exploration and he felt the tenseness leave her body.

She didn't want to feel anything for him, but she could no longer deny that she had a strong attraction to this man. Susan relaxed in his arms, her mouth responding to his, her body conscious of his as she leaned into him.

"Uh, Mom, could I have some ice cream before I go to bed?"

Susan and Tony sprang apart as though they'd received an electric shock. Steve stood before them in his pajamas, his hands resting lightly on his hips. Although his face was flushed, his eyes danced with amusement. "I think maybe you guys need a chaperon or something."

Tony burst out laughing. Susan was mortified. She had not dated since Michael's death, so Steve had never seen her with another man. How could he seem so unconcerned? Surely he should be jealous, or at the very least resentful. On the contrary, he appeared delighted.

With commendable composure under the circumstances, Susan nodded. "I guess a small bowl won't hurt. We can't have you dying of starvation before morning."

When Steve disappeared into the kitchen, Tony chuckled. "It doesn't look like we shocked Steve by necking in the living room, does it?"

Susan could feel the color flush her cheeks and attempted to change the subject. "I really need to get some sleep as well. It's been a rather long day."

He grinned. "Yes, hasn't it? However, it's good to see some color in your face. If nothing else, the day did that for you."

If you only knew, she thought. "Yes, well, thank you again for inviting us."

"And here's your hat, don't let me rush you off,"

he added. She followed him to the door. He turned the knob, then glanced down at her. "I don't know what else Michael taught you, Susan, but he certainly managed to teach you to kiss!" The door opened and he left, closing it gently behind him.

"Ooohhhhh!" How dare he! Susan stormed down the hallway to her bedroom, wishing she had something to throw.

As Tony drove away, his thoughts were on the two people he'd just left. He'd been kidding himself when he'd decided he had no feelings for Susan. She'd been so much a part of his life that unbeknownst to him, he'd carried her with him in his heart all these years. Not that he intended to admit that to her. He could see that as far as she was concerned, her present life was all she needed or wanted. She had her home, her career, and her son. What more could she want?

Tony knew he would have to take it one step at a time. Steve was so lovable, it hadn't taken him long to wrap himself around Tony's heartstrings, right there next to his mother. She and Michael had done a fine job with him. He prayed to God he'd be given the opportunity to pick up where Michael had been forced to leave off.

"If you can hear me, Michael, I want you to know that I'll love them, and be there for them, if I'm given the chance."

Once again he saw the picture of the three of them on the mantel, and he saw the gently smiling gray eyes gazing at him. Michael had loved them, too. *Will I be given that chance?*

Chapter 4

The inviting aroma of freshly brewed coffee wafted its way into Susan's restful sleep. She stretched and slowly opened her eyes. The kitten calendar hanging next to the bed caught her attention. The tiny feline star of the month warily eyed a young turkey, which was just as warily returning the stare.

November. Tony had been back a month. She rolled over and buried her head under her pillow. Nothing had been the same since he exploded into their lives.

Steve was already growing used to having him around. He still talked about the hiking trip and the fun they'd had—and how excited everyone had been to have Tony join them. Susan had had to smile and appear pleased with each telling. Damn the man anyway! She had done her best to avoid him, and had been fairly successful, but she still had to listen to Steve rave on and on about him, ad nauseum.

A sudden thought occurred to her and she bolted upright in the bed. *I'm jealous! I'm actually jealous of the close relationship forming between the two of them!* She stared off into space, thinking furiously. *How humiliating!* She threw off her covers and got out of bed, then forced herself to look in the mirror. *Aren't you ashamed? Steve is happier than he's ever been, and you're petty enough to resent the fact it wasn't you who accomplished that fact.* She shook her head sadly. *I thought better of you. I really did.*

Another strong whiff of coffee caught her attention. *There's nothing like a cup of fresh coffee to console you when you're busy discovering your character defects,* she pointed out to herself. She picked up her hairbrush and vigorously ran it through her hair.

Since it was Saturday and she had nothing planned, Susan decided to be lazy, so she picked up her robe lying at the end of the bed and slipped her arms through its full, flowing sleeves. *Coffee first, then you can get dressed.*

After a quick stop in the bathroom to wash her face and try to get awake, she started down the hallway to the kitchen.

She heard Steve talking to Hannah and smiled. Another sign that her young son was growing up—he now let her sleep in on weekends. She could well remember the times when he'd be bouncing on her bed at dawn, reminding her the day had begun. *He's growing up so fast!* she lamented. *Where had the last ten years gone?*

When she reached the kitchen door Susan discovered it wasn't Hannah Steve was talking to with such animation. Tony sat at the small kitchen table, his long, muscular legs thrust out in a relaxed position, crossed at the ankles. He registered her shock at finding him in her kitchen and slowly smiled.

"Good morning," he said, his eyes twinkling.

The bright gold of his pullover sweater emphasized his broad shoulders and powerful arms. Susan was uncomfortably aware of how little she wore. She nervously tugged at the neck of her robe. "I'm sorry. I didn't know you were here," she muttered, and backed out of the kitchen.

Tony came to his feet in a graceful lunge. "Don't leave; you look fine. Coffee's made. Wouldn't you like a cup?"

How had he managed to reach her side so quickly? She could smell his aftershave, and was almost close enough to touch him. Her fingers trembled at the thought. *This is crazy! I used to act like this around him when we were teenagers! What's wrong with me?*

Tony took her hand and gently led her to the table, guiding her into the chair across from his, then reached for the coffeepot near his elbow. He poured her some and set it in front of her.

"Mom, Tony wants us to go with him this morning over to his new place. He just got the keys last night."

Susan freely admitted that mornings were not her best time, but this morning seemed to be breaking all records. She wasn't ready for Tony's presence at the moment. She admitted to herself she probably wouldn't have been ready at three in the afternoon, either, but at least she'd have had herself in some semblance of working order.

She sipped her coffee, trying to think rationally. She had agreed that Tony should get to know Steve, but she was certain she'd made it clear their plans were not to include her. So why was she being pushed into spending time with him?

Her gaze slowly focused on Tony. Was that sympathy she saw lurking in the black eyes staring at her so intently? She straightened her spine and frowned slightly. She certainly didn't need his sympathy, nor his blasted understanding.

Steve was too excited to sit still. He had been up and down from his chair several times since she'd walked into the room. Now he leaned against the table, watching her. The two sets of eyes staring at her, waiting for her response, were too much.

"I'm not going to be able to go, Steve," she muttered. "But I'm sure the two of you will have a good time."

"But Mom! You *have* to go. Tony and I don't know anything about kitchens and stuff like that. He said you'd be able to tell us what we need to buy."

She stared at the innocent face of the conniving man across from her. "Oh, did he?"

Unaware of the undercurrents, Steve agreed happily. "Yep. He said there were some things a man had to acknowledge that women knew better."

"How wise of Tony," Susan said through clenched teeth, then took another sip of her coffee.

It didn't help when Tony started to laugh. His laugh had always been one of the most attractive things about him. And it had always been impossible for Susan to ignore him in that mood. She took in the laugh lines that had formed around his eyes and the curves that accented the dimples in his cheeks. He had always hated those dimples, yet now they added to the character in his face.

"You need some breakfast, don't you?" she asked Steve.

His face broke into a grin that matched the one on the man across from her. "Oh, Mom. I ate hours ago. We've just been waiting for you to wake up so we can go."

"Well, you'll just have to wait for a while longer. I am not awake. It may take hours for me to reach that state of mind. In the meantime, I, for one, haven't had breakfast." She glanced at Tony. "How about you?"

"As a matter of fact, I ate before I came over."

She shrugged. She might as well give in as gracefully as possible. "All right. I'll eat, then I'll go get dressed so we can go."

Susan had forgotten how contagious Tony's exuberance was. By the end of the day she was wind-blown and tired, but exhilarated. She couldn't remember the last time she'd laughed so hard. It had almost been as though she'd forgotten how.

She stepped out of the shower that evening and caught a glimpse of herself in the oversize mirror in her bathroom. Gone was the composed, pale corporate attorney. In her place stood a flushed and admittedly glowing young woman with sparkling eyes. Tony had always had that effect on her. In that respect, nothing had changed.

Bright pictures of the day flashed through her mind—sitting in the small sports car next to Tony, with Steve curled into the poor excuse of a back seat; being aware of Tony's movements as he shifted gears, the muscles flexing in his thigh so close to her own; Tony making a game of inspecting the house and asking her advice.

They had spent the day as a family, and it had unnerved her. Tony's image was one of a confirmed bachelor. His romantic exploits had been as widely reported as his action on the diamond. Not that Susan had paid much attention, but it was hard to ignore it when his love life sometimes hit the sports segment of the six o'clock news. If Tony hadn't married by now, the obvious conclusion was he had no intention of marrying. Perhaps that was why he was so taken with Steve. He had found a son without the tedium of a marriage to produce him!

Susan blew her hair dry until it fell in disciplined

waves down her back. Tony had convinced her not to wear it up today, so it had taken a beating. She wished he didn't have quite so much influence over her, but it had been obvious right from the start of the day with their early morning encounter that there was little Tony Antonelli would suggest that she could refuse.

In fact, the day had taken her back to her childhood, with Steve taking Michael's place, the two of them following Tony's lead. She'd watched Steve as he'd unconsciously mimicked Tony's walk and gestures.

Oh, Steve. None of what happened was meant to deprive you of your father. But how can I tell you that the man you idolize walked away and didn't come back when I needed him the most?

Susan stepped into the bedroom and began looking through her closet. Tony had promised to take them out to eat at one of Steve's favorite restaurants overlooking the Pacific Ocean. Knowing the futility of trying to be excluded, Susan had only insisted she needed to get cleaned up and change clothes. She glanced at her watch. Steve was no doubt impatiently waiting for her.

He wasn't. When Susan walked into the living room, Tony was alone. "Where's Steve?"

Tony stared at her with obvious approval. Once again she'd left her hair down. "Oh," he answered in a casual tone, "he decided he was too tired to go out, so he fixed himself a sandwich and went on to bed.''

Susan stared at him in amazement. ''Steve is in bed? At seventy-thirty?''

Tony grinned at the tone of her voice. ''Yes. I was surprised myself. I reminded him that he was the one who had picked out the restaurant, but he said he'd go some other time.''

Susan spun on her heel and hurried down the hall. He was sick! When had it come on him? He'd seemed fine all day. She felt herself beginning to panic and sought a calm expression as she tapped on his door.

''Come in,'' came a sleepy voice.

She opened the door and found the room dark. Flipping on the bedside lamp, she sat down on Steve's bed. ''What's wrong, Steve?'' she asked softly, her hand automatically reaching for his forehead. It felt reassuringly cool.

''Nothing. I'm just tired,'' he muttered, his eyes refusing to meet hers.

''That's not like you to get so tired you can't eat!''

''I ate! I just decided I didn't want to go out to eat.'' His eyes glanced at her, then looked quickly away.

''All right. Then I'll explain to Tony that maybe we can make it some other time.''

''NO!'' Steve shot up off his pillow and stared at her in dismay. ''I mean, why don't you and Tony go ahead and have dinner together. Hannah's here if I need anything. I'll just get some rest tonight.''

She stared at her son, suddenly suspicious of his motives. "You want Tony and me to have dinner together?"

Relaxing back on his pillow, Steve gave her a smile that would melt anyone's heart. "Yeah, I thought you might like that."

"Why would you think that?"

He shrugged, a nonchalant gesture that caught her off guard with its sudden glimpse of the adult Steve would someday become. "Well, you guys are such good friends and everything. So I thought you might want to spend some time together. You know, catch up on old times and all."

"I see." Unfortunately, she certainly did see. "Tony and I have no reason to catch up on old times any more than we've already done. But it was a nice thought, Steve."

The disappointment on his face was almost her undoing. "You mean you won't go out with him?"

She shook her head gently. "I'm not interested in getting involved with anyone, Steve. You and I've talked about that before, remember?"

"But I thought Tony would be different."

"Why?"

"Because you've known him for so long."

"Which is exactly why I don't want to get involved with him. I've known him too long and too well. You know Tony has lots of women friends. I don't want to be one of them."

Those black eyes stared at her with hurt and disappointment, and she forced herself to return his gaze with calm resolution. Steve no doubt missed Michael, just as she did. He was obviously enthralled with having Tony suddenly appear in his life and show so much interest in him, but she refused to allow him to build up hopes that could never bear fruit.

"Are you still sleepy?" she asked with a soft smile.

He grinned sheepishly. "Not really. But now that I'm here I might as well go to sleep."

Susan started laughing and he reluctantly joined her. "A little extra sleep never hurt anybody, you know," she said. She leaned over and kissed him, then turned out the light and left the room, closing the door behind her.

As she walked back to the living room, she tried to decide what to tell Tony. It wouldn't do to admit that Steve was trying to play matchmaker. Nor would it do to admit how the thought had completely unnerved her.

Tony stood when she entered the room. "Is he all right?" The concern in his voice touched a response deep within her. His sincerity caused a twinge and she knew she couldn't lie.

"He's fine," she admitted. "I'm very much afraid he thought it was a good idea to give us some time alone together."

She wasn't prepared for the gust of laughter from Tony. "He must be a mind reader. Those have been my exact thoughts for the past hour or so." He strolled over to her. "I didn't get a chance to tell you how beautiful you look. Did you remember that peach was my favorite color on you?" His eyes were as bright as a starlit midnight sky.

She glanced down to look at what she was wearing. The soft, flowing dress had seemed to jump out at her when she'd gone through her closet. Had its choice been intentional? At this point she wasn't sure of anything except that Tony was standing entirely too close.

His arms slipped around her waist and pulled her unresisting body to him. "I think you've been outvoted, don't you? Doesn't the majority still rule?" he murmured, reminding her of their childhood agreement. Then all thought seemed to disappear when Tony lifted her chin with gentle fingers and brushed his lips softly against hers. As though savoring the taste, he touched her again, this time with more pressure, until her lips parted without volition.

She didn't remember sliding her arms around his neck, nor was she aware when he pulled her even closer to his body as their kiss deepened. His kisses had always had the ability to melt her, and age and experience had only added to his expertise.

He slackened his hold slightly, his lips charting a path, kiss by tiny kiss, from her mouth to the curve of her jaw. "Oh, God, Susan, if you only knew the many nights I dreamed you were in my arms, only to wake up and remember that you were no longer mine."

His words brought Susan out of the trance his kiss had placed her in. Abruptly she moved away from him. "You don't have to say things like that to me, Tony. I certainly don't believe that you've been pining away for me all these years."

"You're damn right I haven't. You taught me a lesson early in life. You were the only woman I ever wanted to marry, only I wasn't good enough for you. It was a hard lesson, but I learned it well."

"You still believe I preferred marriage to Michael, don't you? Even after what I told you?"

"You could have contacted me if you'd wanted to badly enough. And Michael was so convenient!"

The bitterness in his voice and the hurt in his eyes made her realize that Tony had not walked away unscathed from their relationship. She had never intended to discuss her marriage to Michael with anyone, particularly not Tony. But Michael was no longer there, and he had loved Tony enough not to want to see him in pain.

"You and Steve win, Tony. I'll go to dinner with you. I guess there are a few things I need to share with you, and I'll do it better after I've had a glass of wine." She smiled, hoping he would accept the peace offering.

Amazingly enough, he did. He slipped the stole she'd laid on the arm of a chair around her shoulders and escorted her out to the car.

Their table was next to a large window overlooking the beach. Spotlights highlighted the waves rolling in, creating an ever-changing, yet never-changing view of the Pacific. A candle surrounded by a pink globe cast a warm glow of color, enclosing the two of them in a private circle of shared memories.

Susan took another sip of her wine and waited for Tony to absorb the information she had just given him. It wasn't surprising that he was stunned. Nothing in his knowledge or experience would help him to understand the type of relationship she and Michael had shared.

The light was very flattering to Tony, with his dark coloring and flashing smile. Only he hadn't smiled much since they had sat down. Now she watched his profile as he gazed out the window abstractedly, his hand turning his wineglass in absentminded circles. He turned back to the glass, picked it up, then quickly swallowed the remaining liquid.

"I don't believe it," he finally said in a flat tone.

Whatever reaction she'd expected, that wasn't it. She wasn't used to being called a liar. How ironic. When she'd finally found the courage to share the intimate details of her marriage with someone, he didn't believe it. She shook her head wearily. Not that it mattered, really, what Tony believed.

"How could any man live with you for that many years and not make love to you, Susan?"

His agonized tone of voice surprised her. He almost sounded tortured. "Does it matter?"

"Of course it matters. I loved you. I thought you

loved me, but you married someone else. Now you tell me you lived with him but didn't share a bed with him?''

''Yes.''

''Why?''

She didn't want to answer his question, but she'd come this far—she really had no choice. ''Because I was in love with you and Michael knew it. Michael was the brother I never had. How could I let my brother make love to me?''

''Dammit, Susan, you can't be that naive. I'm sure Michael gave you time to adjust to marriage, but no man could live with you without wanting to make love to you.''

''Tony, that's what I've been trying to tell you. Michael was not attracted to me. I don't think he was ever sexually attracted to anyone.''

Tony stared at her, shocked. ''Are you trying to tell me that Michael was—''

''No. He wasn't interested in men, either, Tony. He just wasn't interested in a physical relationship of any kind. It was as though all his senses were caught up in making music. Didn't you ever notice that about him?''

The slight frown across his forehead was so familiar. That was the expression both he and Steve wore when they were concentrating on solving something. This time it was the mystery of Michael. Finally, he admitted, ''I guess maybe I did, but never gave it any thought.'' He reached over and took her hand. ''Were you ever able to talk to him about it?''

''Not at first. I was just grateful he seemed uninterested in me in that way. At first I was pregnant and upset. Then I got involved with school, had Steve, and continued with my schooling while Michael continued to be in his musical world.'' She glanced up and smiled. ''Not that he ignored us. He seemed to enjoy the diversion of a wife and son, but I knew that was all we were to him.'' She touched his hand lightly with her finger. ''Believe it or not, that was enough for me. I had had all I wanted of passion and turmoil. I relished the peaceful existence he gave us.''

Tony stared at the young woman across from him. The candlelight lent a soft flush to her pale face, her hair framing her features. She was serious. Somehow she'd managed to discard the warm, passionate creature he had known and loved. What had he and Michael done to the vibrant girl-child they had grown up with?

''For a woman who has discarded any feelings of passion, that was a rather good imitation you gave to the kiss we shared earlier.'' His statement was deliberately provocative and he was delighted to note the deepening flush on her cheeks. She wasn't quite as cold and calculating as she would like to believe, which certainly gave him hope.

From everything he had learned after meeting her again, he knew this woman was his. He'd made his claim on her eleven years ago. She had borne his son, and he now knew that she'd never been with another man. He was determined to win her love and her trust all over again, no matter how long it took him. Steve's reaction tonight gave him his greatest encouragement. Susan might not realize it, but from now on she was going to find herself subtly and deliberately led into the trap of his arms. Only this time he had every intention of tying her to him permanently.

Tony was quiet on their way home and Susan felt she understood why. She had probably made a mistake by revealing to him the nature of her relationship with Michael. But it was too late now to do anything about it.

She wasn't sure what to say when they arrived home. Should she invite him in or make her escape? *Where is all of your self-confidence when you need it?*

Tony gently removed the keys from her hand, opened her door, snapped on the hall light and held the door open for her. When she walked in she turned around and found him leaning against the closed front door.

"I, uh..." was as far as she got when he stepped forward and pulled her into his arms. The kiss he gave her was possessive, full of fire and passion. Susan gave herself up to the moment, no longer willing to be sane and sensible. This was Tony. When he finally loosened his hold, they both were having difficulty breathing. Tony reached behind him and opened the door, then gave her a mock salute.

"I'll be in touch," he said with a small smile. Then he was gone.

Susan stood there, staring at the closed door. What had all of that meant? What did she want it to mean? She wasn't sure, but she was very much afraid she was already more involved with him than she'd ever intended.

Chapter 5

The oncoming headlights were nearly blinding and Susan's headache seemed to worsen with each mile. Why had she ever agreed to allow Steve to spend the day with Tony? She shook her head wearily, knowing that after she reached Tony's beach home on the coast several miles north of Santa Barbara, she'd still have to face the long drive home.

Steve had been eager to spend the time with Tony, which wasn't surprising. Christmas holidays were nearing their end and he was bored. Of course, he still enjoyed being with Tony more than anything else.

A sharp twinge of jealousy hit her. *Stop it!* she warned herself. *You've had the past three months to get used to the idea that Tony is becoming a large part of your son's life. And it's been good for him.*

Susan was intelligent enough to recognize that she couldn't be all things to Steve, but she was honest enough to acknowledge that she had wanted to be. She hadn't wanted him to need anyone else. She had wanted him to be content with their life together.

Was this what happened between divorced parents—this pain of feeling inadequate, of wanting to be needed and appreciated, and loved best of all?

Tony had been good for Steve. She'd been amazed at how in tune the two of them seemed to be. She had already noticed, even before they'd spent much time together, how many of Steve's mannerisms were similar to Tony's. It was almost as though she had passed very little of her own traits on to her son.

Stop it! she repeated determinedly, and forcefully turned her thoughts to the meeting she had just left. One of the companies she represented had held their board of directors meeting at her firm and she had spent weeks preparing for it. The chairman had expected trouble and he hadn't been wrong, but he had never lost control of the situation. She had watched with silent admiration as he handled the dissenters with serenity and dispatch.

She enjoyed her work—the calm, disciplined, formal practice that went into being a corporate attorney. She had to be constantly on top of the rapidly changing tax laws in order to keep her clients fully informed and protected. It was exciting in its own way, but today had been exhausting.

Peering at the digital clock in the dashboard of her

car, she groaned. It couldn't be that late! She blinked and looked again. 10:54. Steve would be asleep by now, no doubt having given up on her. Tony would be irritated that she hadn't called to say she'd be late. To be honest, all she had thought about was getting away from the tense, highly charged arena of big business.

Susan slowed as she came to the turnoff leading to Tony's home. It was a beautiful place, but that wasn't surprising. Tony hadn't been concerned, evidently, about the amount he paid for the house, and his southern California home would answer anyone's dream of a modern palace, Susan mused.

The curving road continued to climb and she pictured the redwood and glass home perched on a cliff overlooking the ocean. She had purposely spent very little time there. How easy it would be to be lured into becoming a part of Tony's life once more, but it wasn't worth the pain.

Not that both Tony and Steve hadn't tried. They were always dreaming up some plan or activity that would include her. She had learned her lesson, though, when she discovered she wasn't immune to Tony's brand of charm. The best way to deal with it was not to deal with it, so she had been firm in refusing their many invitations to join them. *I am perfectly happy with my life now. I certainly don't need the complications of a man in it, especially Tony!*

She turned into the driveway, following its long, curving surface until it ended before a large garage.

A light mist coated the windshield and she realized the wind was growing stronger. She stepped out of her car, shoved the door closed and trotted up the long stairway to the front entrance.

The door opened at the top, soft light spilling out on the deck as a large shadow filled the doorway. She glanced up and saw Tony waiting for her, a gentle smile on his face.

"What are you doing out here? You're getting wet."

"So are you."

She laughed at his reasonable tone. "You're right."

He took her arm and escorted her into the house. "I have a fire waiting for you." He slipped her coat from her shoulders, his hands lingering slightly longer than necessary. "How about a drink?"

"That sounds great, but make it a small one. I seem to have skipped a couple of meals today, and I still have quite a drive ahead of me." She crossed over to the fireplace located in the conversation pit of the large room. Its west wall was made entirely of glass. Now that they were away from the hallway, Susan discovered the only light came from the fireplace and a couple of candles placed strategically by the sofa.

She raised her voice so that he could hear her from the kitchen. "Did I by chance interrupt something? This looks like a very romantic setting you have here." She glanced around when she heard his steps, then stared in surprise. He held a tray with a small glass of wine and a large bowl of what looked to be a mouthwatering Italian stew that his mother used to make. Several large slices of French bread were on the side, lightly toasted with melted butter, causing Susan's stomach to gurgle in anticipation.

He placed the tray on the small table in front of the sofa. "Have a seat and indulge yourself. I'm afraid Steve and I ate some time ago. I was about ready to send out the troops to look for you."

She could hear no accusation in his tone but she couldn't help feeling defensive. "I'm sorry I was so late getting here. The meeting ran on longer than anyone had anticipated." She picked up a slice of the bread and took a bite. It was delicious. "What troops?" she asked with interest.

"Boy Scout, what else?"

"Ah, yes. You're getting rather involved with that group, aren't you?"

"You might say that. Steve always seems to be volunteering me for something or other these days."

"And you love it."

"How'd you guess?" His dark eyes danced, and Susan felt the sharp jab of awareness that continued to keep pace with her whenever Tony was in the vicinity. "We had quite a bit to do today. You may recall we're trying to get his model race car finished before the next scout meeting, when we're to race them. We spent a large part of the afternoon and evening working on that in the garage." He grinned, a self-satisfied smile that reminded her painfully of Steve.

She hastily picked up the glass of wine and sipped, then determinedly started on the stew. It was every bit as good as Mama Angelina's. How she missed that lady. She realized that was another tie she and Tony shared that she had conveniently placed at the back of her mind.

"You never answered my question."

He looked at her, puzzled. "I'm sorry. I must not have heard it."

"I was just commenting on the romantic mood set in here and wondered if I interrupted anything." She glanced around the room as though expecting to see a scantily clad young woman draped on a piece of furniture.

Tony grinned at her expression. "Can't you tell? I was expecting you."

Well, of course he'd been expecting her to pick up Steve, but that wasn't what she meant. From his attitude the last three months, it was clear he saw her as a childhood friend—and as Steve's mother, of course. Since the night he'd teased her about her response to his kiss he'd been polite and friendly, but nothing more—which suited her just fine.

He'd spent a great deal of time with Steve, and in general had made his presence felt. Even Hannah had gotten into the habit of quoting Tony as though he were some kind of oracle. One day Susan had said with some disgust to her, "So what you're telling me is that the gospel according to Tony says we all have to watch what sort of food we put in our bodies...we are what we eat, is that right?''

Hannah had the grace to blush. ''I guess he's made a study of what good nutrition can do to help an athlete keep his body in top-notch condition. I found it very interesting.''

''That's okay, Hannah. I didn't mean to snap. It's just that when *both* you and Steve start quoting him, I feel a little outnumbered.''

For some reason she had the same feeling now, and Tony was the only other person in the room. Perhaps it was the intense way he was studying her. She continued to eat, avoiding his gaze.

''Where is Steve, by the way?''

''Asleep.''

''That's not surprising. Where?''

''I went ahead and put him to bed. Told him I'd try to talk you into staying over.''

His quiet words wreaked havoc within her. He made it sound so simple. She opened her mouth to protest and he held up his hands in the time-out signal. ''I know you won't be working tomorrow. Hannah will be gone for the weekend, and we still have quite a bit of work to do on the race car. We have much more room to work here in my garage, and it wouldn't hurt for you to relax and do nothing for a while, would it?''

''That isn't the point.''

''Then why don't you explain it to me?''

She paused, trying to marshal her arguments as well as calm her inner agitation before it showed. "We don't have any clothes here. There's no reason why I can't just bring him back tomorrow."

He grinned. "At the risk of being thought devious, I asked Hannah to pack some things for you. Your overnight case is in one of the *spare* bedrooms."

"You *are* devious, Tony, but tonight I'm too tired to care." Susan reached down and slipped off her shoes, then leaned her head back on the sofa. She closed her eyes, rubbing them distractedly.

"Are your eyes bothering you?"

"A bit. I managed to pick up a headache somewhere along the way today." It felt so good to relax, to know there would be no more demands made on her tonight.

"What did you think of supper? Steve and I made it."

"It was delicious. Mama Angelina would have been proud of you. You two make a great team."

"I think so."

She could think of nothing to say in reply. His voice had lost its teasing note, and the serious tone touched a chord deep within her. Finally, she sat up. "I believe I'll go on to bed after I've cleaned these up for you." She reached for the tray, but he stopped her.

"Leave them and go to bed, Susan. You're exhausted."

Mentally agreeing with his assessment of her condition, she wandered down the hallway, spotting her overnight case sitting at the end of the bed in one of the bedrooms. She found her nightshirt and made quick work of removing her makeup and brushing her teeth, then fell into bed.

She was unaware of Tony when he came in later to check on her. He stood near the bed, noting the circles under her eyes, her fragility, and wished he knew how to stop her from pushing herself so hard.

He'd gone slow with her over the past several weeks, getting her used to his being around. He'd made great strides with Steve, and had been the recipient of several confidences that convinced him more than ever that both of them needed him.

Tony's gaze traced the slight outline in bed and he sighed. God knew he needed both of them as well. The question was, how did he go about winning them over to his way of thinking? He retraced his steps, gently closing the door behind him. He wondered what Susan was trying to prove. Was her career so important to her, or was it what the career represented? She'd become a mother before she was little more than a child herself, accepting the responsibilities of adulthood. When would she learn that it was all right to relax and enjoy life a little? He hoped he could help her to do that. He had so much he wanted to give to her, to share with her, if she would only accept him.

Susan stirred, reluctant to give up the sleepy warmth that had enfolded her for the past several hours. She stretched, then went limp, her eyes refusing to open.

"Good morning." The husky baritone caused her lids to pop open in surprise. Susan had forgotten she had gone to bed at Tony's the night before. She certainly hadn't expected to be greeted by that voice first thing. It wasn't fair that he should look so good this early in the morning. His black curls were still damp from the shower and the beige pullover turtleneck sweater clung to his muscular chest almost indecently.

"Good morning," she parroted, not awake enough to think of anything more original to say.

"Breakfast is almost ready. Do you plan to join us?" His smile affected her as strongly as it always had. That smile had lured her into following him into several mischief-laden adventures. She would like to think she was immune to it. However, she had serious doubts about her resistance where Tony was concerned.

She sat up, the covers obligingly displaying her sleeping attire designed to look like a man's old-fashioned nightshirt, with vertical red and white stripes.

His smile widened into a grin. "It's hard for me to picture you as a sober, staid attorney in that outfit."

She glanced down, unconcerned. "That's all right. None of my clients ever see me this way."

"I should certainly hope not."

"Tony, as soon as you leave, I'll get up," she pointed out in a patient voice.

"Oh. I thought you'd let me see the rest of that dazzling piece of sleepwear."

"No."

"Too bad." He shrugged, then turned away. He looked over his shoulder when he reached the door. "Someday, maybe?" he said hopefully.

She shook her head firmly. The look of disappointment was very well done if he'd been able to control the dancing light in his eyes. "Good-bye, Tony," she insisted.

He laughed, closing the door behind him.

Susan stood up, glancing down at the brief length of her shirt. It modestly reached mid-thigh, but curved to her hips on each side. She entered the adjoining bathroom, slid the shirt over her head and stepped into the shower.

She wished she knew what Tony was up to by insisting they stay the night. She remembered the boy too well to believe the man could have changed that much. He was acting too innocent *not* to be up to something!

He'd followed her instructions very well, leaving her alone, focusing his time and energies on Steve. The change in Steve had been amazing. She hadn't been aware of how subdued he'd been until he'd become more outgoing and self-confident since meeting Tony. Steve had definitely blossomed. Even her mother noticed the difference. He was much more relaxed around his grandmother now, gently teasing her, causing a flush of pleasure to appear from time to time on her pale cheeks. If her mother only knew who had caused the change! For some reason Steve had adopted a protective attitude toward his relationship with Tony where his grandmother was concerned, similar to the one Susan had had when they were growing up, but for different reasons. Steve knew his grandmother's opinion of sports in general and grown men making a living playing boys' games in particular. Susan had been amused to watch him diplomatically sidestep any subject that would necessitate Tony's name entering the conversation.

For example, Steve was willing to discuss scouting without ever alluding to the assistance he was receiving on several of his projects. No doubt she should say something to him, explaining that omitting certain facts was tantamount to lying. Somehow, she hadn't been able to bring it up, feeling anything she said would be too hypocritical since he'd watched her deal with her mother in the same way for years.

She turned off the water, stepped out of the shower, quickly dried off and dressed. Not bothering with makeup, she ran a comb through her hair and padded back into the bedroom.

Steve was waiting for her. "Your breakfast is getting cold, Mom," he said with a touch of irritation.

"Sorry, Steve. Guess I'm moving at half speed this morning."

"Are you going to watch us build my racing car?"

"I hadn't given it much thought, why?"

"Just thought you'd want to see what we're doing," he said with elaborate unconcern.

"You bet I would. Wouldn't miss it for the world."

He grinned. "That's okay, Mom. I know you're really not into cars and things."

"It shows, huh?"

He nodded. "A little, but you do real well at the ball games."

"I try," she muttered, and walked over to him. She gave him a big hug.

He struggled to get out of her grip. "You don't have to get mushy, Mom. C'mon. Let's eat."

Tony was waiting for them in the kitchen. Her coffee was poured and waiting, as well as eggs, bacon and toast. She groaned. "I never eat that much for breakfast."

Tony stared at her with a stern look. "It shows. I'm going to put you on an athlete's training schedule, starting today."

Steve laughed. No one talked to his mom that way. He watched to see how she'd take it.

Susan sat down, surprised at the seriousness of Tony's command. Maybe she was pushing herself too hard and not eating correctly. She shrugged. It might be worth a try. Without a word she picked up her fork and started to eat.

Steve watched in amazement, then glanced at Tony, who winked at him. Obviously, this man had more influence over his mother than he'd given him credit for. It might be worth trying to pick up a few pointers.

Susan had long since wandered away from the intricate construction of Steve's race car when Tony finally called a halt. They sat back and admired it for a while, then Tony began to pick up his tools while Steve grabbed the broom to sweep up the sawdust.

Tony looked around, making sure everything had been put away, then walked over to Steve. "There's something I've wanted to discuss with you, Steve," he began in a hesitant tone.

Steve replaced the broom on its hook. "Yes, Tony?"

"I'm not sure if this is the right time, but there's something I think you should know." He stood there watching the young boy, wondering how to approach the sensitive subject.

Steve walked over and stood by Tony. "What is it?"

"I want you to know that I'm in love with your mother."

Steve went from acute concern to laughter in the beat of a moment, his infectious chuckle causing a red stain to cover Tony's cheeks. "Why don't you tell me something I don't know?" he asked when he finally managed to stop laughing.

Doggedly, Tony continued. "I want to marry her."

Steve stuck his hands into his back pockets and

rocked back and forth from his toes to his heels. "You got it really bad, huh?"

Tony nodded. "What would you think about my joining the family?"

Steve studied the serious expression on Tony's face. "You're really worried she won't marry you, aren't you?"

"That, and that you might be against the whole idea."

Steve grinned. "It isn't as if she doesn't know you, you know. You've known her longer than I have," he pointed out.

"That's true," Tony admitted carefully.

"She does seem to like you, I've noticed that," Steve added obligingly. "So when are you going to ask her?"

"That's what I thought I'd get your advice about. What do you suggest?"

"Well, how about tonight? Maybe after we eat I can go watch television in the den and you can build a fire...you know, kinda set the scene...then ask her."

"It sounds like you've given the matter some thought."

A suspicious flush appeared on Steve's cheeks. "Not exactly. That's the way they do it on all the mushy television shows." He crossed one foot over the other in an agitated movement. "That's usually when I go get something to eat," he confessed, making a face.

"Hmmm. That must be where I was, too. I didn't know that's how you went about it."

They started up the steps to the house. "Well, you can always try it and see if it works," Steve offered philosophically. "What have you got to lose?"

"What, indeed," Tony muttered to himself as they entered the house. Steve was right in one respect. There was no point in continuing to put it off. She must know how he felt about her; he'd never tried to hide his feelings where she was concerned. Instead, he'd tried to give her the space she seemed to need in order to adjust to his presence in her life.

It was a very thoughtful Tony who began to make plans for the evening. He hadn't been this nervous before the last game in the World Series! But he knew in his heart Susan was worth more to him than any pennant. He only hoped he could find the words to convince *her* of that.

Chapter 6

The chilly wind swooping along the deserted beach finally forced Susan to give up her solitary walk. Even wearing one of Tony's heavy jackets with a hood hadn't prevented her hands and feet from turning into blocks of ice. But the walk had been worth the chilled fingers and toes.

She couldn't remember a time when she'd felt such peace. Her brief solitude had fed a hitherto unknown need buried deep inside. When had she last taken time for herself? Whenever she wasn't working, she'd felt a compulsive need to be with Steve. Her life seemed to be a series of commitments to fulfill other people's needs and expectations. But what of her needs?

By the time she reached the beach entrance to Tony's home, her knees felt like spaghetti and she was huffing and puffing like the wolf in the story of the three little pigs. Steve had always enjoyed her exuberant rendition of that scene, she recalled with a grin.

She glanced down the long stairway she'd just climbed. She was really out of condition. Tony was right. She needed to start taking better care of herself.

Her walk had helped her come to terms with her feelings where Steve and Tony were concerned. Why had she expected to be all things for Steve? No one person could fulfill such a role. She recognized that their lives would have been different if Michael had lived, but he hadn't. Instead, Tony had come.

The rapport between the two would be noticeable to the most casual observer. They were good for each other, and if she sometimes felt left out of their magic circle, she had only herself to blame.

She tugged open the sliding glass door that led into the living room. The house was quiet. *They're probably still in the garage working on that car.* She shook her head in amazement at their persistence. *Where do they get their patience?*

Pleasantly tired from her sojourn on the beach, Susan wandered into the bedroom she'd used the night before. The soft bed looked so inviting. It was only a few minutes past one—plenty of time for a short nap before she and Steve needed to leave. She sank down onto the luxurious softness of the bed and pulled the bulky comforter over her. A short nap, that's all she needed.

However, the unaccustomed exercise and fresh air conspired with the warm cocoon of comforter and bed, and Susan fell into a deep, restful sleep.

The dark room confused her when she woke up hours later. She fumbled for the lamp by the bed. She couldn't believe the time—it was after six! She stumbled to the bathroom and splashed cool water on her face. *Why did I sleep so long?* she wondered. *Why didn't they wake me?*

She found them in the den, where Tony was showing Steve the strategies of backgammon. Their camaraderie touched her and for a moment she watched them—the unobserved observer.

Finally, she spoke. "Fine friends you guys are. You let me sleep away the entire afternoon!" She smiled to let them know she wasn't too concerned and strolled into the room, her hands in the back pockets of her jeans.

They both looked up at her in surprise, then Steve glanced at Tony uncertainly. "Were we supposed to wake you?" Tony inquired.

"Not really. I just prefer not to drive after dark, that's all, but it won't be the first time."

"But, Mom—" Steve's voice sounded anxious, but a glance from Tony caused him to be quiet.

Tony slowly came to his feet, stretching. Susan watched with fascination as his arms reached high over his head, his body sinuously easing the cramped muscles in his arms and shoulders. "I'm sorry," he said. "I assumed you knew you were invited to stay for the weekend. Dinner is almost ready—I would have called you before I let you sleep through our latest masterpiece.''

Spend the weekend! The suggestion set off tiny alarms within her and she wondered if they could hear the jangling. Up until now their encounters had been short and casual, but a whole weekend together?

Frantically, Susan searched her mind for an excuse—any excuse. Then she remembered her bulky briefcase with a feeling similar to the one a battered boxer had when he finally heard the bell ending a round.

''I have a large stack of work to catch up on before Monday,'' she explained ruefully. ''And since I was so busy all week preparing for the board meeting, I'm afraid I got behind with the rest of my work.'' She was pleased she'd thought of it. The work took on the qualities of an eleventh-hour reprieve—until Tony spoke.

''That's no problem. You can work in here all day tomorrow if you'd like.'' He gestured toward the walnut desk at one end of the room. ''You won't be disturbed.''

She stood there, staring at him helplessly. Now what? Steve's worried expression drew her attention. He really wanted to stay, that was obvious. What difference did it make where she worked? *Who are you kidding? Tony makes the difference. You aren't immune to him. Or have you forgotten?*

Tony waited for her answer, forcing himself to

show only polite interest in her decision. *Don't push her!* he warned himself. He spotted the wariness in her eyes and felt a definite sinking sensation somewhere deep within. His chances of getting a positive response to his marriage proposal seemed to shrink in number.

Then she smiled—her beautiful, who-cares, let's-go-for-it expression that used to precede their most exhilarating adventures together. That was the person he remembered and was hoping to find. Her smile at that time seemed to be a good omen.

"Sure, why not? I take it that's all right with you, Steve?"

Steve caught Tony's eye and gave them both a big grin. "You bet, Mom." He jumped up and gave her a fast hug, then turned crimson. "Uh, think I'll get washed up to eat."

Never had a meal tasted so good. Susan couldn't remember when she'd eaten so much. Not since Mama Angelina was cooking for all of them, she was certain. The wine Tony had chosen was perfect, and by the time dinner was over, Susan felt very relaxed and mellow.

"Mom, is it all right if I watch television now?"

Susan stared at Steve in surprise. Why would he want to watch television when Tony was around? "What were you planning to see?" She and Hannah carefully monitored what shows Steve watched.

The cherubic expression on Steve's face might

have warned her that his motives would not stand up to her scrutiny, but luckily for the plans he and Tony had made Susan was too relaxed to notice. "Jacques Cousteau has a special on."

She nodded. "If Tony doesn't mind, I don't."

Tony grinned. "No problem, Steve. You know where the television is—help yourself."

Susan had never seen Steve so eager to be gone. Perhaps the continual time spent in Tony's company was taking the edge off the hero worship, which was probably a good thing. A healthier, more realistic relationship could now develop.

"Why don't we go into the living room?" Tony suggested as he slid her chair away from the table. "We could sit in there and enjoy the fire and the quiet, if you'd like."

His hand rested lightly on her shoulder as they entered the room. The white foam of the waves was all that could be seen of the water, the muted roar of the incoming tide lending a pleasant rhythmic sound to the peaceful scene.

Tony flipped a switch and soft music filled the room. He motioned for her to sit down as he built up the fire until the flickering flames shot up once more in a mixture of bright colors. Susan became lost in the sight until Tony sat down beside her, placing two replenished wineglasses on the table in front of them.

"I rarely see you this relaxed," he murmured as he settled in next to her.

She smiled. "That's probably because I can't remember having been so relaxed in a long time.'' She glanced at him as she reached for her glass. ''Thank you. It sounds trite to say I needed a break, but it's true.'' She sipped from her glass, then sighed contentedly.

He leaned back, his arm falling carelessly along the back of the sofa behind her shoulders. ''I've enjoyed having both of you with me, but then, I'm sure you already realize that.''

Her head felt too heavy for her neck and she let it lean lazily against the warmth of his muscled arm and shoulder. ''You're being very polite, and I appreciate it. But I'm very much aware that the amount of time you're spending with Steve definitely cuts into your romantic life.''

''What makes you think so?''

''Because you're with him three or four times a week. I'm sure your female friends are wondering what you're up to.''

''Is that your subtle way of asking me if I'm seeing someone?''

Susan sat up straighter, realizing that was exactly what she was doing and resenting the fact that he saw right through her. ''I'm sorry. It's none of my business.''

Tony slowly tightened his arm around her shoulder, turning her to him. ''Would you like to make it your business?'' he whispered. Then before she had a chance to answer him, Tony leaned down and kissed her, if the soft, tentative touch of his lips on hers could be considered a kiss. It was more of a question, the slight hesitation giving the impression of unsureness. But that was ridiculous—this man unsure of himself? Whether on the diamond or off, Tony Antonelli always seemed to know exactly what he was doing.

Being in Tony's arms felt so natural, for that moment Susan felt she was where she belonged. That loosening of her reserve gave Tony all the encouragement he needed. With a soft moan he pulled her across his lap, nestling her in his arms and against his broad chest. His mouth captured hers, exploring, tasting, reacquainting them with the joys they had once shared.

Hesitantly, as though trying to find skills she had thought forgotten, Susan began to respond. Her hands slid tentatively across his chest, smoothing over the expanse of his soft sweater. Then they crept up around his neck and into his hair. She luxuriated in the feel of the curls that wrapped themselves tightly around her fingers.

Tony's kiss robbed her of all thought but him and his presence. As he reluctantly pulled away for air, Susan discovered that she, too, was out of breath. His hand trembled slightly as he stroked along her jaw. She rejoiced in knowing she affected him at least as much as he did her.

He kissed her once more, this time with a fiery passion that caught her unprepared. The possessiveness of the kiss caused such desire within her that she felt like a statue built of wax, melting from the heat. She responded with equal intensity and found herself being drawn down on the sofa, her body carefully aligned on top of his. His hands explored the contours of her spine, pausing and stroking across the gentle curve of her hips.

She could feel as well as hear the slight moan of pleasure he gave. Her sweater had long since pulled out of her slacks and she shivered when she felt his hand slide beneath her top, moving upward until it reached the clasp of her lacy bra.

The sudden feeling of her bare breasts as they rested against his chest seemed to bring Susan out of the daze she'd been in since dinner. What was she doing, necking on the couch while her son was in the next room? What was she thinking of? She stiffened as she acknowledged that was her problem. She hadn't been thinking at all—she'd been feeling—reacting—luxuriating in the closeness they shared, and had no business sharing. The past was over, and Tony Antonelli had no place in her future.

Tony felt her stiffen in his arms and he immediately paused. What was wrong? he wondered. She'd been with him every step of the way. What had changed her mind? He slowly eased his hand from beneath her sweater and began to caress her back in long, smooth strokes.

"What's wrong?" he finally asked.

Susan pushed herself up from her reclining position. Trying to hide the effect he'd had on her, Susan answered almost harshly. "Nothing's wrong. I'm a little old to be caught necking on the couch, that's all—particularly by my son."

Tony sat up, unconcerned that she could see how aroused he'd become. "I wouldn't do anything to embarrass you, Susan. I thought you knew that." He ran his hand through his already mussed curls. "In fact, I didn't intend any of this to happen."

She glanced around the dimly lit room, silently noting the fire, the soft music, and the beguiling view of the ocean from the wide expanse of glass. "Didn't you?" She forced herself to look back at him, then wished she hadn't. His nearness was shattering to her already shaky composure. "I would say you have set up an excellent seduction scene."

Tony stood up and began to pace restlessly. "As a matter of fact, seduction was the last thing I had on my mind. My thoughts were much more old-fashioned."

She stared up at him, puzzled. When he didn't say any more, she prodded. "Old-fashioned?"

He paused, staring at her intently. "Susan, is there some reason why you're driving yourself by putting in those long hours?"

Whatever she had expected, his seemingly abrupt change of subject wasn't it. "What does my working long hours have to do with your necking with me on the couch?" she asked in a reasonable tone.

"Nothing, dammit. Or everything, maybe. Are you content with your life now? Is this how you intend to spend the rest of your days?'' he demanded. ''Working until you're exhausted, squeezing in your extra time with Steve until you don't get enough rest? You don't eat right—you're entirely too thin. Is this what you want?''

His voice had grown steadily harsher as he talked, and Susan was bewildered. What had caused his change of mood? ''Tony, why don't you sit down and tell me why you're upset.''

''I'm not upset. I'm trying to find a way to ask you to marry me, but damn if I can come up with one. You've made it clear you don't need me, or anyone, in your life. You have everything you want—a well-established career, a nice home, a fantastic son. Why should you want a man around?''

If he hadn't been so irate, she would have laughed. It was the strangest marriage proposal she'd ever heard of. He had very clearly listed all the reasons why she wouldn't accept him. Unfortunately, he was right, but then he'd always seemed to understand her better than she understood herself.

Susan stood and walked over to him. ''Tony, you know you're very special to me. We shared a childhood together that I'll never forget. You gave me Steve, whom I love better than my life.'' She touched him gently, resting her fingertips along his cheek. ''I admire you tremendously for what you have done with your God-given talents. But our lifestyles are totally different. Can't you see that?''

Despite his strong intentions not to touch her,

Tony's arms clamped around her waist, pulling her close to him. "Doesn't it matter that we still love each other?"

She shook her head slowly. "You don't love me, Tony. I doubt that you ever did, really. I was a symbol to you, one you worked hard to earn. But you don't know me as a person. If it weren't for Steve, you would never have bothered to look me up—I know that. He's your son and it's natural that you would want to claim him, but you don't need to marry me to do that. I know you love him, it's very obvious. But we aren't a package deal."

Never had he felt such frustration. Her calm and objective analysis of their relationship was masterly described—and dead wrong.

She was a symbol, all right, a symbol of everything he'd ever wanted in a mate. It never mattered to him who she was or what part of town she was from—she'd been his from the first moment he'd seen her. He'd waited years for her, working hard to be able to prove to the world that he deserved her, only to have her marry someone else. He loved her as he'd never loved anyone, and he felt certain she loved him as well. Why was she denying it?

She stood in his arms watching him, wondering what thoughts were causing the painful expression on his face.

"Oh, my love. You are much more than a symbol to me." With his hand he pressed her hard against his body while his mouth seductively made claim to hers. She was his. He just needed a little more time to convince her. *Please God, grant me that time, and the patience it will take to win her.*

Once again Susan was lost in the feelings that only Tony seemed to be able to evoke within her. What would it be like to be married to him? To wake up each morning with him? And then she remembered. She wouldn't be with him. He would be on the road for months at a time, and she had her law practice. His romantic exploits were legendary. Why would he be willing to give them up? He wouldn't have to, of course, and she wouldn't be able to live with that knowledge. Yes, she loved him, but she knew she could never marry him. The pain of knowing he wanted her for Steve would always stand between them.

But for the moment, holding him and loving him was enough. It would have to be.

Tony abruptly stepped back, releasing her. He reached over and picked up his glass of wine. *Well, you certainly blew that one, sport.* He drank from the glass, wondering what he could do or say that would get through the wall Susan had so carefully built around herself.

"I'm glad you came back to Santa Barbara, Tony," she said softly, sinking down once more on the sofa. She, too, reached for her glass, as though it were her composure to be clutched and regained. "You've been very good for Steve."

He glanced at her in surprise. Hesitantly, he

stepped around the table in front of the sofa, and sat down facing her. "I'm glad to know you feel that way. Getting to know him has been the greatest thing that ever happened to me."

He reached over and took her hand, holding it loosely in his. "You know, there are nights when I lie awake, thinking back over all that happened, trying to picture our life together if I'd only known you needed me." He raised his hand, bringing her fingers to his lips and softly kissing them. "I'll never forget the day your mother told me you and Michael were engaged. I couldn't believe it. I kept thinking there had to be some mistake, and I had to get back and find out what was going on. When my roommate found me packing, he tried to talk me out of it, knowing I was throwing away my career if I walked out then. When reasoning didn't work, he tried to physically stop me and we got into one hell of a fight. The club fined us both. By then I was convinced you'd been stringing me along all that time, so we went out and got drunk, which cost another fine. It wasn't the greatest way to start my career. If it hadn't been for my roommate explaining what had happened, I'd probably have been shipped home." His gaze rose from her hand and found her eyes. "Maybe then I would have still had you."

"Tony, it's so pointless to keep dwelling on what might have been. I've been doing some of the same thing, and it's a waste of time. If only I'd tried to contact you, or allowed Michael to call. The words *if only* are the two most useless words in our language, and the saddest. Please don't dwell on the past."

"Dammit, I'm trying to work on our future. I want you, Susan. I want to marry you. I want to be a husband to you and a father to Steve. Why won't you give me that chance?"

The compelling intensity in his eyes shook her to her very soul. All of her carefully marshaled reasons seemed to flit from her mind like wisps of smoke dissipating in a breeze.

"Don't you understand? We're too different. We want different things from life. I want peace and tranquility; you crave excitement and the adulation of the crowd. I couldn't handle that."

"You've got to be kidding me. Is that the way you see me, as some sort of overgrown Boy Scout, still playing childish games of baseball, not wanting to grow up?"

Her silence was an answer. He sat there and stared at her for a moment, then drained his glass. "You know what your problem is? You're afraid to live. You're afraid to enjoy life, to jump in with both feet and learn, and make mistakes, and grow. Instead, you've manufactured a nice safe little world for yourself, where there's no waves—and very little life. Well, that may be all right for you, but I'll be damned if I'll let you pull Steve into that stifling little world." He stood up, staring down at her with contempt. "You're right. I don't know you at all. The woman I've loved for most of my life probably doesn't even exist." He started for the door. "I'm going to take a walk. I'll see you tomorrow."

Susan sat there staring at the fire long after he was gone. She had managed to convince him to her way of thinking. Why didn't she feel better about it? What was wrong with wanting a safe little world? Wasn't it better than pain and turmoil? Only with Tony had she been able to let go and experience the turbulent feelings of joy and ecstasy, and she'd paid dearly. She couldn't go through that another time. She didn't even want to try.

Tony jerked the cap from the pocket of his heavy jacket and jammed it onto his head. The wind had grown increasingly colder. It was no night for a stroll on the beach, but he had to get away.

What the hell was wrong with her? Couldn't she see they belonged together? How could a woman so obviously intelligent treat her emotions as negligible? She loved him, he knew it. Otherwise, she wouldn't respond to him the way she did every time he took her in his arms. He had watched the pulse at the base of her throat as it fluttered restlessly during their conversation. She was not unmoved by him. He didn't care what she told him or herself.

Somehow he had to break through that shell. He just had to, not only for his sake, but for her sake and Steve's as well.

The question was, how?

Chapter 7

January brought increasingly frigid weather and Susan found it did not improve her disposition in the least. *What happened to sunny southern California?* she wondered waspishly as she drove home one Friday evening.

If she were honest, she'd admit that she hadn't been in a very good frame of mind since the weekend she and Steve had spent at Tony's home.

Tony was definitely becoming a problem. Not that he had ever brought up their discussion again. That she could have dealt with. Instead, he seemed to have moved into her home. He went home at night, but he was always there when she got home, had dinner with them or insisted on taking them out to eat. Steve and Hannah doted on him. Susan was counting the days until he had to return to Florida for spring training!

It was almost as though he had given up all thought of marriage, except for one new wrinkle in his behavior—he seemed to take great pleasure in touching her whenever he had the chance. He had an annoying habit of dropping a kiss on the end of her nose, or her cheek, and occasionally her mouth whenever he happened to pass her. And that seemed to be frequently. He didn't even seem to care who saw him do it. Both Hannah and Steve took it in stride. Susan wished she could learn to do the same.

However, that morning he'd finally overreached himself. It was bad enough that she felt she was continually tripping over him in her home, but when she found him in her bedroom, that was too much!

She had taken her shower and hadn't bothered to put on anything but her lacy underwear to enter the bedroom. When she walked out of the bathroom she found Tony stretched out on her bed.

"What are you doing in here?" she demanded, grabbing her robe.

"Waiting to talk to you."

"Well, you can wait in the other room. How dare you come in here!"

He grinned and Susan fought a strong urge to throw something at him. "You know, it doesn't seem quite fair that you and I should have shared something so intimate in order to create Steve and yet I've never seen you without clothes." He relaxed on the bed as though waiting for the show with keen anticipation.

"Tony! Get out of my bedroom. Now!"

"Okay, if that's the way you want it. I had hoped to talk with you in private, though."

She stared at him with suspicion. "About what?"

"The race car competition coming up next week."

A look of disbelief flashed across Susan's face. "You came into my bedroom at seven in the morning in order to discuss the race car competition?"

"Um-hmm." How could a person look so innocent while his eyes were so full of devilish lights?

"I'll meet you for coffee in the kitchen in fifteen minutes, Tony. Take it or leave it." She marched over to her closet and began to sort through hangers, trying to concentrate on what she planned to wear for the day.

In one lithe move Tony was off the bed and beside her. "Oh, I definitely intend to take it," he murmured. His arms slipped around her waist and he leaned down to her, his mouth finding hers in a soft caress.

Susan felt the heat of his body through her thin robe, the hard, muscular planes of his chest pressing against her. She recognized the warm liquid feeling that flowed through her body at his touch and for a moment allowed herself the luxury of enjoying his nearness.

His mouth explored hers as though reacquainting itself with each surface, his tongue stroking hers, his lips reshaping hers to fit perfectly with his.

"Mom, do you know where my— Oh, hi, Tony. I didn't know you were here. Did you spend the night?" The bright tone of speculation and interest was as effective as a bucket of ice water thrown over her. Susan jerked out of Tony's arms, appalled at the nonchalant attitude of her son. Why would he think she'd allow Tony to spend the night!

Before she could gather her wits about her, Tony was casually explaining. "No, I stopped in early enough to follow your mom to the garage. She's having her car worked on today and I'm giving her a ride to the office."

"Oh," Steve responded. "I didn't know anything was wrong with it."

"Neither did I," Susan offered in an annoyed tone.

The expression on Tony's face turned serious. "Susan, I've been telling you for the last several weeks you needed new brakes, and you've kept agreeing with me, but you haven't done anything about it. So I made an appointment for them to be repaired today."

How dare he be so high-handed! She was trying to find the words to wither his arrogance and overbearing attitude when he dropped a hand on Steve's shoulder and guided him out the bedroom door. "What were you looking for, sport?"

"My new jacket I got for Christmas. I've looked everywhere for it."

"When did you see it last?"

"I wore it home from school yesterday. Don't you remember?"

"That's right, so you did. Well, let's retrace your

steps and see if you could have laid it down somewhere.''

The two of them disappeared down the hallway, chatting, while Susan sank down on the bed, her knees trembling.

Something would have to be done. She couldn't let things go on this way. He was taking over their lives, slowly but surely working his way into their daily existence. It was going to have to stop.

She reiterated that statement through clenched teeth as she neared home that evening. The car drove like a dream. When the mechanic had brought her the keys about midafternoon, he explained that since he had the car in and Mr. Antonelli had told him to check it over, he'd gone ahead and tuned it, greased it, and changed the oil and filters. When she asked for the bill he explained it had already been taken care of—by Mr. Antonelli. ''And he also gave me his autograph!'' he added with a big smile.

She had a few very choice things she intended to tell Mr. Antonelli when she saw him again, and if he followed his customary schedule, he'd be waiting for her when she got home.

But he wasn't. Steve met her at the door with a long face. ''Tony called and said he had to go out of town but he promised to be back by next Saturday for my race car competition.''

Susan wasn't prepared for the sudden sinking feeling she experienced when she heard that bit of news. Damn the man! How dare he keep her feelings on a yo-yo string, jerked first one way, then another. She'd spent weeks refusing to grow accustomed to his presence only to discover she'd done just that.

She was glad he'd left! It was a good lesson for her. In little over a month he'd be leaving again, to be gone for months. This would be what she would have gone through had she been foolish enough to have agreed to marry him. Only it would have been much worse, for then she would have grown used to sleeping with him, waking up in the morning with him, making love with him. Now she was glad she'd kept her head and not given in to her emotions. Life was much easier if she didn't depend on anyone but herself.

By Monday she was more than ready to go back to work. Susan had grown tired of trying to cheer up Steve over the weekend. He'd finally spent most of Saturday with one of his friends, but Sunday he was back home wondering where Tony had gone, and why, and when exactly she thought he might be back, until Susan was convinced she would go out of her mind.

Hannah hadn't been much help, either. She'd pointed out how much Tony enjoyed her beef Wellington the last time she'd made it and that it was too bad he wasn't there on Sunday. The office was going to be a marvelous escape from reminders of Tony.

Unfortunately for Susan's peace of mind, it didn't work out that way.

At eleven-thirty Donna stuck her head around

Susan's office door wearing a very peculiar expression on her face. "Susan, there's a delivery here for you."

Susan glanced up, surprised that Donna would interrupt her for such a common occurrence. Overnight deliveries in a law office were a customary procedure. "Can't you sign for it?" she asked, puzzled.

Donna's eyes grew larger. "Oh, sure, if you want me to." The obvious question in that last statement caused Susan to decide something strange was going on, so she got up and went out to Donna's office. A messenger stood there all right, but not from one of the regular services. He held a gigantic array of food. Upon closer inspection, Susan noted it was all health food, done up in various packages, sizes and shapes.

"Would you please sign here?" The man looked eager to be on his way. She couldn't blame him. He set the package down on Donna's desk and extended a receipt for her to sign. Susan recognized the name at the top of the receipt as a well-known health food restaurant.

After he left she and Donna eyed the food. "Here's a card," Donna volunteered. Just a corner peeked out from behind some freshly baked blueberry muffins, one of Susan's weaknesses.

Flipping the envelope open, Susan pulled out the card and read:

I don't want you falling off your eating just because I'm not there to keep an eye on you. You will receive a freshly prepared lunch each day until I get back. Make sure you eat it.

I love you,

Tony

P.S. And don't forget your vitamins!!

"I can't believe this," she muttered, sinking into the chair opposite Donna's desk.

"Who sent it?" her secretary asked.

"Who else? My health-nut friend, Tony."

"Tony Antonelli? Well, how very thoughtful of him. He obviously wants to see you put on some weight."

Susan studied the array of food before her with dismay. "Obviously."

"He must care a great deal about you to encourage you to eat right like that."

"You think so?"

Donna looked at her in disbelief. "Don't you?"

"At this point I don't know what I think, or if I think, or when I'm thinking. That man is driving me out of my mind."

Donna's face took on a dreamy expression as she rested her chin on the palm of her hand. "But what a way to go...." she said softly.

By Friday Susan was convinced beyond a shadow of a doubt that one of them had lost their mind, but she wasn't sure whether it was Tony or her.

The food arrived on Tuesday as promised, but so did an ornately wrapped square box tied with a mammoth red bow. She studied the box warily. There was no logo or name that told her where it came from, but she had a suspicion as to who sent it.

She tried to work, ignoring the box as much as possible, but when she realized she'd read the first page of the contract she was reviewing three times and still didn't know who the party of the first part was and what they were hoping to accomplish by the contract, it was time to face the inevitable. She wasn't going to be able to work until she knew what was in the box.

After making that decision it didn't take her long to remove the ribbon and paper, then open the top of the box, only to discover more tissue paper. When the last scrap was removed she found a baseball nestled inside a polished wood holder. It was ordinary enough, as baseballs go, except that every possible surface on it had been covered in a familiar handwriting. The words *I love you* were emblazoned all over it.

There was no card. The gift didn't need one.

On Wednesday Susan wasn't even surprised when Donna tapped on her door and with a big grin announced, "You have another delivery." She tossed her pen on the desk and prepared herself for whatever awaited her.

Five men walked into her office, each carrying an outsize bouquet of flowers. They paused, looking at her inquiringly. She waved her arm at the various tables and desk top, where they began to place them around the room. She solemnly signed for the deliveries and waited until the men left before her sense of humor got the best of her.

She sat down in her chair and started laughing. The flowers caused the office to shrink in size, but that wasn't what Susan found so amusing. All of the ornate decorations were the type found at funerals. What was he up to now?

After searching three of the arrangements, Susan found the card.

> It's better to be wed than dead. Don't bury those feelings. Admit you love me madly. Or at least a little. Please save me from my miserable single life. I need you desperately. (Would it help to remind you that I also love you to distraction?)
> Your
> Tony

Some comment and speculation had been expected when her hearty luncheons began to arrive each day, but the flowers brought everyone out of their offices to inspect and admire Susan's newly decorated office.

"Whoever he is, I admire his taste," Greg Bauerman admitted with a seductive smile. Greg was one of her partners who had spent considerable time attempting to console her after Michael's death. However, she had finally convinced him she didn't need his brand of consolation, and that perhaps his wife would better appreciate his thoughtfulness.

"Well, he certainly knows how to get your attention," admitted Jackie Lematta, one of the associates who worked in the corporate area with Susan.

"That he does, not to mention everyone else's in the office," Susan admitted.

When the furor died down and everyone went back to work, Susan recognized that for some reason she wasn't angry at Tony's flamboyant gesture. It was so in keeping with his personality, and his personality was one of the reasons she loved him so.

I really do love him, she finally admitted to herself with dismay. *I can no longer deny my feelings for him. But I am not going to marry him. It would be a disaster. My life is just the way I want it.*

Is it? a little voice in her head asked. Are you sure? Can you really walk away from what Tony is offering you?

Just what is he offering me, anyway? Okay, he says he loves me, and maybe he does, during his off season when he's bored and at loose ends. But what about the rest of the year when he's involved with baseball and traveling and the adoration of his fans, especially the female kind? What about while I'm sitting here in Santa Barbara practicing law and raising Steve? He's stayed away from us for eleven years with no problem. There's no reason to suppose he'll feel any differently when he gets back into his other world.

A very subdued Susan went home that evening.

By midafternoon on Thursday Susan was convinced that Tony's dramatic offerings had come to an end. Lunch had arrived on schedule but nothing else had been delivered. Susan realized she'd been mentally holding her breath every time Donna brought something to her, waiting for his next move, and forced herself to relax.

Her concentration began to improve and the stack on her desk rapidly dwindled. She'd even managed to push Tony to the back of her mind, hoping to keep him there, when she heard Donna burst into unrestrained laughter. She'd breathed that metaphorical sigh of relief too quickly. Now what?

When she stepped into Donna's office, she flinched. She couldn't help it. The room appeared to be full to overflowing—with multicolored balloons! Not the sort of small balloons you see children holding at carnivals and circuses. No, these balloons were large, helium-filled balloons with writing on them. The writing was identical on each one: TONY LOVES SUSAN.

"Oh...my...God," Susan uttered as she sank down on the corner of Donna's desk.

"I went ahead and signed for them before he started bringing them in," Donna volunteered cheerfully. "It took him several trips. Shall I help you move them into your office?"

The move into her office wasn't anything like the struggle to get all of the balloons into her car that evening. The most embarrassing aspect was the drive home, with the balloons that wouldn't fit inside merrily bobbing their colorful heads outside, their strings securely tied together. She attracted more attention than newlyweds with tin cans trailing from their car.

She almost didn't go to work on Friday. Enough was enough. When she finally convinced herself that the coward's way was not *her* way, she was almost an hour late for work.

That's when Donna informed her one of her clients called and asked if she could come to his plant that morning. Could she! She'd be delighted. Whatever happened, she wouldn't be there to face it.

She spent a productive morning with her client, ended up having lunch with several members of management and returned to her office with a bounce in her step and a smile on her lips.

She paused at Donna's desk to pick up her messages. Her secretary appeared to be busy transcribing a tape and glanced up distractedly, then continued typing. Obviously, nothing untoward had happened in her absence. However, to be on the safe side she opened her door carefully and peeked in. The flowers were still there, and she had of course taken home the balloons yesterday. There seemed to be nothing new to be found today. She breathed a sigh of relief and walked in—and found Tony sitting on her couch.

"Tony! When did you get back?"

Her heart seemed to be doing somersaults in her chest and the air supply to her lungs suddenly became dangerously low.

He stood, and Susan absently registered how good he looked in his dark brown slacks and well-tailored shirt. "A little over an hour ago. Donna said she wasn't sure when you'd be back, but was kind enough to allow me to wait for you in here."

Susan didn't remember moving toward him or his coming to her. All she knew was she was in his arms again, and she couldn't remember when they had felt so good to her.

Her hands found their way through his hair, and her mouth sought his, eager to quench the thirst that a week away from him had caused within her.

His reception was more than he had hoped for, but what he had longed and prayed for. Had he finally cut through her reserve? Was it time for him to push their relationship to its inevitable conclusion, the one that had been ordained years before when a lonely ten-year-old boy had looked into the clear blue eyes of a six-year-old girl, seeing the acceptance, feeling the rapport, yearning for the closeness of another human being?

His hands slid down her back and cupped her hips, pulling her closer against him. Her effect on him was almost instantaneous. He had spent the morning flight thinking of her, wondering if he dared go to her office, or if it would be better to wait and see her at her home. His final choice had been a selfish one—he didn't think he could wait the extra hours to see her.

He was glad he hadn't waited.

Their kiss was everything Susan had ever dreamed about—passionate, urgent and full of love. He was home. That was all that mattered—at the moment.

Chapter 8

"Look, Tony, they've got all our cars on display! Aren't they something?" Steve's excited voice carried over the noise of the milling people, causing several heads to turn.

Tony's arm was securely wrapped around Susan's waist, making it clear to everyone he was more than a casual friend.

She had dreaded today, even though she was careful not to let Steve know. It was his big day, the culmination of weeks and weeks of work. Today they would find out if his model race car was faster than all the rest. But for Susan it was a test of her ability to conceal her love for Tony.

Tony seemed to be as excited over the upcoming race as Steve. He visited with several of the fathers present, swapping stories of what they had done to make *their* race car different.

Tony glanced down at Susan and asked, "When are we supposed to eat, before or after the races?" His voice caused a ripple of awareness through her.

She glanced up and caught his warm gaze, and quickly looked away. "According to the posted schedule, they plan to have four heats before lunch, and the winners will compete after lunch—I packed something for us. Why, are you hungry?"

"A little. I skipped breakfast this morning."

Susan stopped walking and stared up at him in mock horror. "No! Not you, the man who insists breakfast is the most important meal of the day, the man who insists you are what you eat, the man—"

"All right, you've made your point. Let's just say that I overslept this morning and didn't have time to eat if I wanted to pick you two up by eight o'clock."

"You must have had a late night." She watched him with interest, curious to know what he had done after he left her house a little after ten.

A flush appeared on his cheeks. "It wasn't a late night, just a sleepless one." His gaze avoided hers.

"Oh, really? Now, why aren't you enjoying the restful sleep of the innocent?"

"You know damn good and well why not! After the good-night sendoff you gave me, promising so much, then backing off at the last possible moment, you actually wonder why I might have trouble sleeping? Even cold showers lose their effectiveness after the number of times I've been under one during the past few months.'' He glared at her. ''You know I'm not used to living like this!''

''Like what?'' she asked with wide-eyed innocence.

''Living without. And if you dare ask me 'Living without what?' with that sweet expression on your face, I may lose my reputation as a gentleman and show you right here and now.'' Since the last of that sentence had been muttered fiercely between clenched teeth, Susan decided she shouldn't continue to probe.

She certainly understood sleepless nights.

''C'mon, Tony. We're in the second heat. Let's go watch, okay?'' Steve tugged on Tony's hand, oblivious to the stares of recognition around them. Tony might be a star in every one else's eyes, but at the moment he was Steve's moral support.

Susan watched as they hurried away. It never occurred to Steve to ask her to join them, but then, why should it? The project had been theirs—she'd had nothing to do with it. So why should she feel left out now? Glancing around the room, she noted the number of women looking out of place and ill at ease and recognized she was not alone.

At the moment she was in a male-dominated world and she might as well make the best of it.

''Did Hannah fry the chicken?'' Tony asked, taking another bite from a crispy thigh.

''No, as a matter of fact, I did. Why?''

"You?" His eyes rounded with wonder. "Susan Spencer McCormick can cook? I'm shocked. Whatever would your mother say?"

She tossed a neatly cleaned chicken leg at him, where it bounced off his knee as they sat together at one end of the large room.

"Watch where you aim, lady," he scolded as he picked up the chicken leg and placed it with the scraps on his plate.

"It hit what I was aiming at," she explained. "Your knee."

"Right." He dusted off the crumbs from his thigh. "So when did you learn how to cook?"

She looked at him in surprise. "You're really serious, aren't you?"

"Sure I'm serious. Why would you ever bother? I know your mother never encouraged you to hang around the kitchen, and Hannah is certainly no slouch in that department."

Her mind traveled back over the years and the corners of her mouth rose softly. "I used to love to sit and watch Mama Angelina in the kitchen. She made cooking seem like a work of art. When she realized I was interested, she began to show me little things...how to chop vegetables, what to look for when buying fruit, the best cuts of meat to use for various dishes...and we went from there."

"You once mentioned that you used to take Steve over to see Mama. Did you ever tell her he was mine?"

"No, we never discussed it, but your mother always knew how I felt about you. When Michael and I suddenly married that summer I can remember seeing the pain in her eyes, but I was hurting, too, and couldn't talk to her about all that had happened. We were away at school when Steve was born, and by the time we returned you had bought her a home and she had moved. For the longest time I kept wanting to go see her, but I was afraid, until finally one day I couldn't stand it another moment. By that time Steve was about nine months old, crawling and full of energy. I bundled him up and went over there. I'll never forget it.

"I rang the doorbell and waited with Steve squirming in my arms. When she opened the door and saw us, her face lit up like a fireworks display. I threw my free arm around her neck and hugged her, then said, 'I brought Steve over to meet you, Mama Angelina. He needs you as much as I always have.' I pulled his little cap off and his curls fell across his forehead. He looked at her with those big black eyes of his and she gasped. She knew, Tony...oh, she knew. Her hands were shaking and she took him out of my arms and held him to her, crooning and crying, until he pulled away from her. All she said was 'Oh, Susan,' and she said that several times, shaking her head, tears pouring down her cheeks.

"But we never discussed it. She just asked me when I left that day when I was coming back and I told her I would come as often as she wanted me.

Tears filled her eyes and she shook her head impatiently and said, 'You come anytime you can. You know I love you like my own. And now I also have Stephen to love as well.'"

Susan was quiet for several minutes, the low murmur of the many voices in the room only a background for her memories. "When we weren't in school I spent a part of each day with her, so that she could get to know Steve, and he could learn to know her as well. She spent much of our time together teaching me how to prepare meals, even though we had Hannah. But I found it very soothing to work in the kitchen, and it made me feel closer to her, somehow."

When she looked at Tony she could see the pain etched on his face. "She never told me," he said in a low voice. "She never once mentioned you, or Steve, or what had happened." He ran his hand through his hair. "She must have blamed me."

"Why do you say that? She could just as well have blamed me."

He turned his gaze slowly until he was facing her. "Otherwise, she would have told me about his existence."

"I don't believe that was her motive. I think she figured if you didn't know about him it was because I hadn't told you, and she was going to stay out of it. I don't think your mother ever placed blame on people. I think she just accepted it, and loved us, don't you?"

"God, I hope so. I would hate to think she was hurt over what she must have seen as my irresponsibility. I had no business leaving you alone to face the situation by yourself. Believe me, I've paid for that poor judgment. I'm just wondering how much longer you're going to make me pay."

"What do you mean, I make you pay? I'm not blaming you for what happened. How many times do I have to say that?"

"Then if you aren't blaming me, why won't you marry me?"

"Tony! This is supposed to be a picnic lunch at a race car exhibition. Why are you bringing this up here?"

He shook his head, glancing around at the other people as though they had just materialized. "You're right. This isn't the time or the place, but the question is valid. I need an answer from you…and soon."

They cleared up their picnic remains, found Steve with one of his friends, and stayed the afternoon watching the rest of the races. Steve's car was eliminated on the second heat, but he'd had the thrill of winning the first one and seemed to be satisfied.

It was on the way home that Tony announced he had managed to get three tickets to see the Lakers play the following night. Steve was ecstatic. "That's great, Tony. How did you do it? I heard they've been sold out for weeks."

"Oh, I happen to know a fellow who owed me a favor. Anyway, we'll need to leave tomorrow afternoon to get there in time to find a place to park and eat before the game."

"Oh, Tony, I don't think I'd better go," Susan tried to say.

"Why not?" His tone was almost belligerent. "You don't care for basketball, either?"

"What do you mean, either?"

"I'm aware you don't approve of baseball, but I didn't realize your aversion covered all sports."

"That isn't true. I do like baseball."

"Funny, that's not the impression I get."

"Tony, did you guys have a fight or something? You sound awfully grouchy," Steve offered from the back seat.

"Sorry," Tony muttered, then in a voice too low for Steve to hear, he added, "That's what frustration does to you, among other things!"

Susan stared at him in the light from the passing cars. Steve was right. He sounded grouchy...he even looked grouchy. She reached over and patted his thigh, causing him to flinch, then glare at her. In her meekest voice Susan offered, "I'm sorry. I'd be happy to go to the game with you and Steve tomorrow."

Sunday turned out to be a beautiful day. The air seemed warmer to Susan, giving off hints of spring, even though it was barely February.

Steve was excited about seeing the Lakers play for the first time. She recognized another part of his education she had neglected, but it hadn't even occurred to her to try to take him to more sports events.

"How about lunch, sport? Think you can find room after the breakfast you managed to put away?" Tony ruffled Steve's curls and got a big grin for his efforts.

"Probably," Steve admitted.

They found a Mexican restaurant and Susan noticed that, like Steve, she wasn't having any trouble making a dent into the luncheon special she'd been served. Since Tony's arrival into their lives she had definitely put on weight. But she had to admit that she not only looked better, she felt much better. Notwithstanding the frustration of kissing him good night each evening and going to bed alone, she admitted to herself she was even sleeping better.

However, her dreams had definite erotic overtones to them.

"We'd better hurry, Tony," Steve insisted, "or we're going to miss the beginning of the game."

The coliseum was packed by the time they found their way to their seats, and Susan was glad to sit down. Tony had kept a tight hold on her hand as they wended their way through the crowd, and as soon as they sat down, his arm was around her shoulders.

It was not surprising to Susan that Tony had been recognized and stopped numerous times, accepting congratulations and listening to sports fans air their opinions on various rulings and calls. What surprised Susan was the way she seemed to be accepted as part of Tony's life. Tony made sure that both she and

Steve were not jostled away from him in the crowd, and she felt very protected.

By the time they got back to the car after the game was over, Susan couldn't wait to kick off her shoes and relax. They had a long drive home, but seeing Steve's excitement and enjoyment had been worth it. He didn't ask for much from anyone, and he had an innate ability to appreciate everything that was offered him.

She gave Steve a big hug before stepping back and letting him crawl into the minuscule back seat of Tony's sports car.

"What was *that* for?" Steve asked as he got in.

"Oh, I just felt like it. Isn't it all right for a mother to hug her son once in a while?" she answered, sitting down and closing the car door.

There was a thoughtful silence from the back of the car. Finally, a grudging voice admitted, "I suppose. Just don't make a habit of it."

She knew if she glanced at Tony, who was watching traffic, ready to pull out if he got a chance, she would burst into laughter. *That's part of the fun of sharing your child's antics with another person. No one, with the exception of the other parent, could possibly appreciate some of the comments and actions of your offspring. I'm glad Tony is here tonight.*

Steve was sound asleep by the time they hit the Ventura Freeway on the way home. Susan laid her head against the neck rest and found herself dozing.

"Susan?" Tony's low voice rumbled into the silence of the car. She rolled her head lazily toward him.

"Hmm?"

"I didn't know how to tell Steve, so I haven't. But I have to leave for Florida this week. I should have left this weekend, but I couldn't leave Steve before his race car was tested."

She'd known he was leaving. She'd known it was this month. So why did she have such an empty feeling in the pit of her stomach?

"Aren't you going to say anything?"

She stared at his profile, silhouetted by the lights on the dash. His jaw looked clenched, his face almost grim. "What do you want me to say?" she asked in a soft voice, aware of the boy asleep behind them.

"You could say *something,* like 'I'm going to miss you, Tony—' "

"I *am* going to miss you, but you already know that."

"Do I? How would I know? You continue to treat me as some casual neighbor, one of Steve's little friends come to play."

"Hardly *little,* Tony," she murmured with a sleepy smile.

"How about saying, 'I love you, and I've changed my mind about marrying you.' "

The silence after that remark became deafening as Susan refused to say what was in her heart, determined to stick to the decision she'd made.

After a while Tony sighed, a defeated sound that

pierced her. "All right, Susan, we'll play this game by your rules. But I think you're making a big mistake."

"Perhaps I am, but it *is* my decision."

"That may be true." He paused. "Obviously, it's true, but have you faced how your decision affects both me and Steve? I love him. I want to be with him. I want to be able to have him with me from time to time, show him the sights of some of the cities I've visited. I want you there with me, too. Doesn't that count for something?"

"Tony, please don't wake him up. Look. I understand how you must be feeling." She ignored his snort of disbelief. "But you have to look at it from my point of view. We have a quiet, stable existence here. It has been good for both of us to feel secure in who we are and what we are. Here we are our own persons. With you or around you we become part of Tony Antonelli's entourage."

"Is that what all of this is about? You're afraid you're going to lose your identity if you're married to me? C'mon, Susan, you're more secure than that!"

"What I'm saying is that life on the road is too unstable for either me or Steve, and staying in Santa Barbara while you're gone for months at a time won't work either."

"Why do you have to look at it as an either-or situation? Why can't we have the best of both worlds? You don't need to spend the entire season moving around with me, but you could fly and meet me whenever Steve had time off.'' He reached over and placed his hand over both of hers, lying clenched in her lap. ''Please don't push me out of your life again, love. I don't think I could stand it.''

They were both quiet the rest of the way home, each deeply buried in thought.

Steve managed to wake up enough to get out of the car and stumble up the walkway into the house. With Susan's help he stripped off his clothes and fell into bed. *He probably won't even remember coming home,* she thought with a soft smile as she tucked the covers around him and switched off the bedside lamp.

Tony was waiting for her in the living room, sipping on a drink as he sprawled at the end of one of the sofas. He waved at another glass of wine sitting on the table next to him. ''Come join me for one last drink together, then I've got to go. I've still got packing to do and my flight leaves at six in the morning.''

Her legs refused to support her weight and she plopped down beside him. ''You're leaving *tomorrow?* You said you had to leave sometime this week!'' Tony didn't miss the tone of accusation and dismay, but hid his feeling of satisfaction from her.

''Tomorrow is sometime this week, Susan. Most everyone else is down there today. I was given a twenty-four-hour extension. I can't abuse it.''

He set his glass on the table and turned to her. ''I'm a glutton for punishment, you know. I would very much like something to take with me over the next lonely months, a memory of you in my arms.'' He grinned, that heartstopping expression that caused her to melt. "Hell, I've grown so accustomed to those damn cold showers, I'd probably miss them if I didn't need them."

Why resist him when she didn't want to in the first place? In the second place, there were some memories she needed to store up as well.

His kiss made it clear he was hungry for her. His mouth was hot and passionate, turning her bones to liquid and her mind to putty. She tugged at his shirt until it came out of the snug waistband of his pants, then ran her hands along his muscled back, stroking over his shoulder blades and down his spine.

She heard his moan of appreciation and her heartbeat quickened. When his lips finally left hers she could see the hot desire in his eyes and at that moment she knew she would not deny Tony anything. She loved him. She'd always loved him. And he was leaving her tomorrow.

She still had tonight.

Susan made no move to stop him when he brushed her blouse from her shoulders, slipped off the straps of her teddy and slid his hands down her waist, leaving her bare.

"Dear God, Susan, you're beautiful."

For the first time since she could remember, she felt beautiful. She saw the love and desire he felt for her and she was complete, a woman wanted and needed. She unbuttoned his shirt and pushed it away, wanting to feel that wide, muscled expanse after all these months of denial. She explored the soft mat of dark hair covering his chest, her fingers lightly outlining his heavy shoulder muscles. She kissed him at the base of his throat, her tongue licking him lightly, and she felt his convulsive jerk at her touch.

This was what she wanted, what she'd waited for, and she no longer cared about anything, not even that Steve was in the next room. All she knew at the moment was that Tony was leaving, and that after tonight she would be alone.

He traced a line of kisses from her mouth, down the side of her neck, onto her collarbone, then paused. His hands cupped her breasts, their tautness reassuring him she wanted him as much as he wanted her. Once again his mouth moved lower, tentatively kissing her, his tongue touching her on her delicate curves until she thought she would cry out with wanting him.

She sighed with relief when his mouth found the crest of her breast, and while his tongue gently explored her, his hands caressed her body in long, inflammatory strokes. He wrapped his arms around her and they sank down onto the sofa. This was what she'd been missing all these years—the feel of Tony's body pressed urgently against her, the scent of him surrounding her, the warm taste of him against her lips.

Their kisses became deeper and more soul-stirring. She felt as though she'd been created to love this man and all she wanted at the moment was to please him.

His hands touched her with unbelievable delicacy,

gently exploring her innermost secrets. The feel of his aroused body shot flames of joy and unleashed desire through her. She loved him. Oh! How she loved him. And for tonight she could pretend they belonged together. Their remaining clothes disappeared as they both strove to get closer, ever closer, to each other.

Tony realized there would be no turning back. She was his for the taking. No longer an innocent child, she knew what she was doing. She wanted him every bit as much as he wanted her. Whether or not she admitted it to him, he knew she loved him, had known for weeks. Now she was giving herself openly and honestly. Again. *My God! It's happening all over again, just like eleven years ago.* He shook his head like a boxer who'd just received a blow to the head. *I can't go through that again!*

Susan had long since lost control of her thoughts. She only had the ability to feel, to react, to rejoice in their closeness. This was Tony, and she wanted him, desperately.

She felt his body stiffen, and she clutched him to her, trying to convey the message that it was all right. She wanted him to make love to her. She needed his love.

And then he was pulling away from her. With jerky movements accompanied by harsh breathing Tony reached down and grabbed his pants, stepped into them and stood up, pulling them up to his waist and fastening them.

"Tony?" Susan looked up at him, bewildered. He

glanced at her quickly, then away. He couldn't afford to look at her now or he couldn't do what he had to do. He had to make it clear to both of them that things were no longer the same. They had both changed. He couldn't take her, then leave her as he had before.

"What's wrong?" she whispered.

He searched for an explanation. He couldn't fight both of them on this. He needed her help. "I'm good enough to go to bed with, just not good enough to marry, is that it?" His voice sounded harsh, because his breathing was still so labored.

His comment had the desired effect. She stared at him as though he had slapped her. She sat up and looked around dazedly. Her clothes lay scattered around her. She found her slacks and slipped them on again. Her blouse was a wrinkled wad on the couch, but she grabbed it up anyway and with shaking fingers managed to button it.

Staring at the man standing only a few feet away from her but miles away in understanding, Susan said the only thing that came to mind. "I love you, Tony."

The contempt on his face made her cringe. "You have a strange way of showing it. You've deprived me of my son, but you're willing to take the chance of another pregnancy." He ran a hand through his hair. "Well, sorry, sweetheart, I haven't stooped to stud service yet. Okay, so you don't want to marry me. I guess I'll accept that. You don't give me any choice. But I'll be damned if I'll have an affair with you." He grabbed his jacket off the back of the chair and strode toward the door. "Tell Steve I'm sorry I didn't tell him good-bye, but I'll be calling him." He stopped and stared at her for a moment, memorizing her. She still stood by the couch, watching him helplessly. Her hair tumbled around her shoulders and down her back, her fuller figure curved enticingly, and he realized once again how much he was giving up by walking out the door. But he had his own self-respect to deal with. He loved her. He wanted to marry her, and he wasn't going to settle for anything less.

"Tony—" She held up a hand as though to beg him to stay, and he knew he couldn't wait any longer or even his self-respect would be thrown out the window.

"Good-bye, Susan. Hope you enjoy your safe little world. Maybe it will keep you warm nights."

She watched him open the door, step through, then gently close it. A slamming door would have been a much better punctuation to his statement. Somehow the gently closing door seemed so quietly final.

Tony was gone, just as she knew he would be. She had held out, knowing she was right in her decision. Her face felt wet and Susan realized that tears were streaming down her cheeks. How long had she been crying?

Tony was gone. Tony was gone. Tony was gone. She undressed to the rhythmic refrain, and for the next several weeks her life continued to the beat of those words.

Tony was gone.

Chapter 9

Susan stared out the window of her office at the sunshine. It was the second week in April and Tony had been gone two months. He'd left an empty hole in her life and her heart still throbbed with pain. She missed him terribly, and it didn't seem to be getting better.

He'd kept his word and stayed in touch with Steve. He called often, usually between the time Steve got home from school and Susan came home from work. It was obvious that he didn't want to speak with her. He was keeping the spirit as well as the letter of their agreement made last fall—he would stay close to Steve and out of her life.

That was the way she wanted it, wasn't it, the way she had insisted it must be? Only now she wasn't so sure and she was very much afraid it was too late to change it.

She wandered out to her secretary's desk. "Have I had any calls?"

Donna looked up in surprise. "No. Was I supposed to be holding them for you?"

"No, it just seemed so quiet around here, I thought I'd check."

Donna waved a hand at the window. "We're probably the only ones still inside on such a beautiful day. Everyone else is out somewhere enjoying the sunshine."

"I was thinking the same thing. Steve has a game after school tomorrow and I was hoping the nice weather would hold."

Donna watched her for a moment, puzzled. "Is there anything wrong?"

"No, of course not. Why do you ask?"

"Oh, I don't know. It's just that I've worked for you for over three years and this is the first time we've ever sat around and discussed the weather." She grinned. "So what did you think about Tony's interview on television last night?"

Susan refused to lie and say she hadn't seen it when in fact she, Steve and Hannah were glued to the set for a full hour before his appearance was scheduled to make sure they didn't miss it. "I thought it went quite well."

"Oh, so did I. Particularly when he refused to discuss the reason he's no longer vying for the title of Don Juan of the Diamond this year.''

Susan could feel the heat in her cheeks. ''Well, I guess I'd better get back to work,'' she said, trying to ignore Donna's knowing smile. She returned to her office only to end up standing in front of the window, staring out.

She had thought Tony looked tired and she wondered if he was getting enough rest. It had been so good to see him and she'd found herself studying him intently, looking for any changes, hoping he was all right.

She had to get him off her mind or she was going to go crazy. Just then the phone interrupted her thoughts and she eagerly went back to her desk to answer it.

''Susan McCormick.''

''Oh, Susan!'' Hannah's voice sounded distracted.

''What's wrong, Hannah?''

''Steve was about a block from home on his bike just now when some idiot made a corner too wide and went into the other lane—''

''Steve was hit by a car?'' She sank slowly into her chair.

''Yes. A neighbor came and got me and by the time I got there the ambulance was already on the scene. They told me to have you meet them at the hospital.''

''How bad is he?''

''They wouldn't say. All I know is that he was unconscious.''

Susan was already scrambling for her purse in the bottom drawer of her desk when she said, "I'll see you at the hospital."

As she ran through Donna's office, she said, "Call my dad and have him meet me at the hospital. Steve's been hurt."

Donna was already dialing before Susan had finished speaking.

Susan could scarcely recall later the drive to the hospital. She remembered being thankful it was only a few blocks from her office, and that traffic was so light. She remembered the orderly confusion of the hospital with the heavy traffic flow in the hallways near the emergency area and the quiet efficiency of the staff.

What she best recalled was Dr. Masters explaining what he'd found after examining Steve and allowing Susan to see him. "He regained consciousness while we were cleaning him up," he reassured her, "and he recognized me." He glanced down at the sleeping child. "His cuts and bruises look worse than they are. There should be no problem healing. What I'm concerned about is possible internal injury. I'm recommending that you give us permission to do some exploratory surgery. I don't like some of the vital signs. They point to some problems in the abdominal area."

She stared at him, wondering what he expected from her. If he thought surgery was necessary, how could she argue with him?

"Whatever you say, Doctor. You know what's best."

"I'll let you know as soon as I find out anything." He patted her shoulder reassuringly, then led her out into the hallway. Motioning to another door, he said, "Why don't you wait in there for now?" Then he disappeared behind the doors marked SURGERY. She found Hannah in the waiting room, calmly crocheting an afghan and for a flash Susan wished she had the patience for handwork of some sort. She sank into a chair and they began their vigil.

Hours later she was still waiting for news. Her mother and dad had joined them and she sat hunched over, her father's hand clenched between hers.

"Why don't we go get some coffee, Susan? I think it would help you to move about."

"I can't, Daddy. I don't want to miss Dr. Masters. Why is it taking so long? What are they doing?"

"Baby, exploratory surgery is just what it sounds like. They aren't sure what they're looking for, and it takes time. You don't want them to hurry and overlook something, do you?"

"No. I just want him to be all right."

"We all want that, love. Just be patient a little while longer." He stood up. "I'll go get some coffee for all of us."

Susan's mother sat across the room from them, alone in her grief. She had always insisted she could handle things without help and now was unable to either give or take comforting. But she was suffering.

Susan heard the slight whooshing sound as the door closed behind her father, and she felt as though she were held in some sort of suspended animation while she waited for his return.

When she heard the door again, she glanced up, but it wasn't her father.

"Tony!" Susan hadn't cried when she heard the news about Steve, nor when she'd gone through the routine of admitting him, waiting in the emergency area, nor when she learned he needed surgery. But seeing Tony seemed to knock all her composure from her. By the time she got to her feet he was there and she grabbed him, wrapping her arms tightly around his waist, her head burying itself in his chest. "Oh, Tony," she managed to say, "I'm so scared."

"I know, love, I know. How is he?"

"We don't know anything. He's been in surgery forever, it seems."

"Surgery? Why?"

"Internal injuries." She shuddered. "He also had several cuts and bruises around his face and arms, but the doctor said they aren't serious. There's a possible concussion." She clutched him closer. "Oh, Tony, he looked so terrible...and so small!"

"What are *you* doing here?" Marsha Spencer's voice sounded too loud in the otherwise quiet room. Of course she recognized him. He hadn't changed very much from the boisterous, troublesome child she had known. But this was the last place she ever expected to find him.

Before Tony had a chance to respond, Susan's dad walked through the door with the coffee. "I called him. He needed to be here, Marsha, and you might as well understand that now. Steve belongs to Tony as much as he does to Susan and he has as much right to be here as either of us does."

Stephen Spencer met the steady gaze of the man who held his daughter, then gave a slight nod of approval at his presence. He sat down by his wife. "The important thing at the moment, Marsha, is that a young life hangs in the balance in the other room. All of us love him, and he needs all the help and prayers he can get."

Marsha Spencer sat as still as a marble statue, her color resembling one also. She stared at the couple still standing in the middle of the room holding each other, as though she'd never seen either of them before in her life. "But Michael and Susan—"

"It was never Michael and Susan, my dear, except in your own mind. It was always Tony and Susan." Stephen Spencer's clear blue eyes gazed at his wife calmly. He took her cold hand between his two warm ones. "It will all come out all right, Marsha, don't worry. We don't need to make their decisions for them."

Marsha stared at the kind, loving face of her husband and sighed. Slowly she dropped her head on his shoulder and visibly relaxed.

Susan pulled back slightly from Tony. "Thank you for coming. I need you so much."

"I got here as soon as I could. I wanted to come. When the emergency call came in I left right away and chartered a jet to get here. I only wish I'd had enough sense to do something like that eleven years ago!"

"Don't, Tony. It no longer matters. What's important is that we're together now." Her voice caught on a sob, and she prayed she wasn't too late with her decision for the three of them.

It was almost as though Tony knew what she was thinking. "He's going to be all right, love. He's in good hands in there, and he's in God's hands as well. We'll make it together as a family yet."

Another hour went by before the door quietly opened once more. Dr. Masters stood before them in his surgical greens, his mask lying loose around his neck, a wide smile on his face. "He's going to be fine."

The response to his statement was audible and varied. All five people waiting had stood as soon as they saw him, and the "Thank Gods" and cries of joy prevented anyone from saying anything else for a few moments.

"What did you find, Doctor?" Tony finally asked.

"We found a few tears in his intestines, which is what took so long. It took time to find them, then suture them, and make sure we'd gotten everything. He's going to have to be in the hospital for a spell, waiting for them to heal, but he'll have an interesting scar to impress his friends. Hopefully, he'll feel it's an even trade.''

''When can we see him?'' was Susan's first coherent question.

He glanced at the clock on the wall. It was after ten. ''He won't be out of surgery for a little while yet. They're just finishing up. He'll probably be in the recovery room until morning.'' He glanced at the people gathered around him. ''Why don't you go home and get some rest?''

''But doctor—'' Susan's mother began, only to be quieted by her husband. He dropped his arm around her shoulders.

''He's right, my dear. We all need our rest. Let's go home now. It's been a rather hard day for you.''

They walked out the door together.

''C'mon, Susan,'' Tony said. ''I'll take you and Hannah home. You've had a pretty hard day yourself.''

Hannah looked up from her crocheting. ''That's all right, Tony. You take Susan on home. I've got my car whenever I decide to leave, but I think I'll stick around a while.'' She stared up at the doctor with a determined smile.

Dr. Masters laughed. ''You were always a stubborn woman, Hannah.''

''You should know,'' she retorted. ''You're the one who recommended me to take care of Steve when he first arrived.''

"I know, and I should have known better than to expect anything different now. You're worse than a mother hen with one chick."

"No I'm not, but I know I won't sleep anyway, so I might as well stay here for a while. Would it be possible for me to sit in his room?"

The doctor shrugged. "I certainly won't try to stop you. I'll leave word at the nurses' station that you're his private-duty nurse."

She smiled. "Thank you."

He shook his head and turned to Susan and Tony. "As though I had much of a choice."

"Are you sure I shouldn't stay, too?" Susan asked.

"Not you, too. You know there isn't a thing you can do for him tonight. You're going to need all the rest you can get for when he wakes up tomorrow. Trying to keep that young man flat on his back is going to take some doing."

"He's right, you know," Tony murmured. "Let me take you home."

The doctor followed them into the hallway. Tony turned and stuck out his hand. "Thank you for everything, Doctor."

Dr. Masters took his hand in a firm grip. "You've got a fine young man there, Tony. I know you must be very proud of him."

Tony's arm tightened around Susan's shoulders. "We are."

They watched as the doctor turned away. Then Tony and Susan began the long walk down the quiet hallway that led them to the world they'd known before the accident.

Susan stood before her bathroom mirror, slowly pulling the pins from her hair. Her head ached so, and it felt good to ease the tight pins out of the loop of hair at the nape of her neck.

"Here, drink this." Tony stood in the doorway of her bathroom, holding a brandy snifter out to her.

"I don't want anything to drink, Tony. I'm fine."

"I know. But drink it anyway. Why don't you hop in the shower while I look for something to eat? I'm sure Hannah has plenty in there." He turned around and headed out of the room. She heard her bedroom door close softly behind him.

By the time she walked into the kitchen Tony had reheated some homemade soup and had prepared a stack of sandwiches. "I realized I hadn't eaten for the last several meals and time zones, so I made enough for both of us." He looked up from stirring the soup and stopped talking. She looked like the young girl he had grown up with—her hair cascaded over her shoulders, her face was flushed from the hot steam of the shower and her bare toes peeked out from under her blue robe. "Where are your slippers?"

She looked around the room vaguely. "I don't know. I couldn't find them."

"Then put on some socks or something. There's no sense in your getting sick at a time like this, is there?"

She nodded obediently, and went in search of footwear. He shook his head. God, how he loved her, and if her reception of his presence was any indication, he hoped that eventually she was going to admit that she needed him as much as he loved and needed her. But not tonight. It was enough that she accepted his presence. He'd learned patience the hard way. He didn't intend to push for any declarations now.

"You aren't planning to drive out to your place tonight, are you?" she asked after she'd eaten. He was glad to see she still had a decent appetite. Not all of his winter's labors had been ignored.

"Sure, it's not all that far."

"But it's senseless to drive all that way when we need to be at the hospital early tomorrow." His heart bounced at the use of the word *we*, as though their going together were a foregone conclusion. "With both Hannah and Steve at the hospital, there are two extra beds."

"We'll see."

She looked at him imploringly. "Please stay, Tony. I don't want to be alone tonight, okay?"

His heart took two giant leaps, then settled sedately back in its proper place once more. When she looked at him like that, he'd promise her anything! "All right, if you insist."

She yawned, then gave him a sleepy smile. "I insist. I really *didn't* need that glass of brandy, Tony. I'm so relaxed, I'm about to fall out of this chair."

He stood up suddenly and scooped her up in his

arms. "We can take care of that problem right now. It's past your bedtime, woman." Her arms obligingly wrapped around his neck and he strode down the hallway toward her room. Placing her carefully on the bed, then pulling the covers back, he said, "I suppose you can get yourself ready from there," and began to back toward the door.

She looked up at him with sleepy dismay. "You aren't even going to kiss me good-night?"

He had only so much in the way of will power, and it was already being tested to the limits. "Not tonight, love. I'll see you in the morning." He turned away.

"Tony?"

He knew better than to turn back. Her soft voice had jolted through him like a series of electrical charges. He had never heard that particular entreaty in her tone before.

He stopped, turned slowly and leaned on the doorjamb for support. The soft lamp by the bed cast a halo around her. She stood by the turned-down bed, her robe a puddle of blue satin around her feet. The light behind her lovingly outlined her soft curves through the sheer fabric of her nightgown.

"What is it, love?" he finally managed to get out.

"Please stay with me tonight."

His tone was harsh with his effort at self-control. "I told you I would."

"I mean here." She gestured toward the bed. "With me." Before he could interrupt she said, "I need to know you're here, Tony. All I want you to do is hold me."

All she wanted! Her eyes melted any resistance he had left. He shrugged and started toward her, absently unbuttoning his shirt.

"You realize what you're saying, don't you?"

She nodded, her face solemn. "Yes. I love you, Tony. I always have…I always will. It's like a permanent condition within my body that nothing can seem to destroy." She could hardly speak for the lump in her throat, but she tried for lightness. "I was hoping your marriage proposal was still open for consideration…."

The look on his face caused her voice to fail. It was as though a light had flashed on deep within him. He glowed. There was no other word for it.

Then he was beside her. His hand trembled slightly as he placed it along her cheek. "Oh, Susan, love, I had almost given up hope of ever hearing you say that to me." His arms came around her in a tight clasp and the kiss he gave her expressed all the love—and the pain—he'd felt for so long. It was a possessive kiss, a kiss filled with commitment, and caring, and promises he vowed to keep.

He slid the straps of her nightgown from her shoulders and the soft material slithered down to rest lightly around her hips. His hands slipped to her firm breasts, caressing them with tenderness.

Susan could no longer resist touching him and she reached for his shirt, sliding it off his shoulders. Before he could slip his arms out of the sleeves, her hands were reaching for his belt.

Her eagerness spurred him on. How many nights had he dreamed of this? How many mornings had he awakened remembering her passionate presence in his dreams? But the reality was even more exciting.

They stood facing each other in the soft lamplight, luxuriating in the feeling of discovery and imminent exploration. The light accented Tony's magnificent build and Susan felt her body react to his.

He placed his hands on her waist, then slowly pressed downward until her gown found no more resistance and fell to her feet. Then he slowly leaned down and picked her up in his arms.

"I love you, Susan. But then, you already know that, don't you?"

She nodded, unable to speak. Her heart felt as though it were ready to burst with love for him, but she was unsure how to show it. Suddenly shy, she reached for the sheet when he laid her gingerly on the bed.

"Are you cold?" he asked, settling down beside her.

"Not really," she murmured.

He leaned up on his elbow and stared down at her. "Are you afraid of me?" he asked, gently pushing a curl behind her ear.

She shook her head. "I'm just not sure what to do. I want to show you my love, but I don't have any experience to fall back on."

He grinned. "That's all right. I'm sure we can find some time to help you gain some experience in this area." His hand slipped down to her breast and lightly stroked it.

She could feel the tension mount in her body. Although her breath seemed to be coming rapidly, her body felt heavy, as though she could hardly move.

He lowered his lips to hers, brushing them in a soft caress, then placed them on her breast. His soft curls brushed against her and she felt a tremor start deep within her, one she couldn't control.

Tony took his time initiating her into the art of making love. He wanted their time together to be perfect for her. He felt her body quicken beneath his loving hands and he patiently guided her into each successive step of intimacy. By the time he moved above her, there was no doubt in either of their minds that she was ready for his possession.

Once again he took his time, adjusting himself to her, kissing her with long, mind-drugging kisses, loving her with every kiss, touch and stroke. He carefully began the rhythmic motions of love. She belonged to him now, and neither of them was likely to forget it after this night.

Susan felt as though she were spiraling ever higher into a black void. She wound her arms tighter around his shoulders and clung, holding him convulsively as a sudden sparkle of showering stars exploded all around her, the brilliant incandescence blinding her to everything but Tony.

He recognized her fulfillment and let go of his fierce control. A final, powerful surge thrust him into the same fiery display of color, and for the first time in months Tony experienced the intense feeling of completion and relaxation that he had willingly given up, hoping to find it only with Susan.

It had been worth the wait.

He rolled to his side, pulling her onto his chest, where she fell into relaxed slumber for the first time in months. With a contented smile Tony joined her. For the first time in years they found peace in each other's arms.

Susan and Tony were at the hospital by six the next morning. They found Hannah asleep in a large chair in the room assigned to Steve, but Steve wasn't there yet.

Hannah woke up at the sound of the door opening and came to her feet, but when she saw who it was she relaxed.

"I thought you were Steve," she explained.

"Have you heard anything?" Susan asked.

"No." She glanced at her watch. "But he should be here within the hour."

"Why don't we go down to the cafeteria and get some breakfast," Tony suggested. "I'll leave word at the nurses' station to call us if they bring him down before we get back."

Neither woman felt like arguing with him and he

made sure both of them had full trays before they left the food line.

After her first cup of coffee Hannah studied the couple across the table from her. "Is it my imagination or do you two have some secret sleeping potion? You look much better than I feel this morning."

Tony glanced at Susan and saw a soft flush cover her cheeks. He reached over and took her hand, then smiled at Hannah. "I don't know about Susan, but I'm on top of the world this morning." He squeezed her hand gently. "Susan has agreed to marry me as soon as Steve is well enough to be at the wedding."

"Hallelujah!" Hannah exclaimed. "It's about time somebody woke up around here." Her smile radiated good will. "I couldn't be happier for you both."

"I don't know why I held out for so long," Susan admitted. "Everyone knows Tony's irresistible when he sets his mind on something."

Hannah grinned. "Actually, Steve and I had a bet going that you would be married before Tony left for spring training. I didn't think he'd talk you around quite so soon."

"You mean that's why Steve was so upset when Tony left? I thought it was because he'd left without telling him good-bye."

"That was part of it, of course. But he'd also made that bet...and he lost."

Tony leaned his arms on the table and with amused interest asked, "What was the bet?"

With a great deal of satisfaction Hannah explained,

"If he lost the bet, he had to keep his room clean, including vacuuming and scrubbing his bathtub every week without my having to remind him."

Tony and Susan started laughing. "And if he'd won?" Susan finally managed to ask.

Hannah shrugged. "Oh, then I had to make all of his favorite dishes at least once a week. It was a fair bet."

The page interrupted their conversation with, "Susan McCormick, please call Extension four two eight."

Susan was out of the chair before the end of the announcement. When she returned to the table, she was smiling. "That was the nurse on Steve's floor. Recovery just called and said they were bringing him down now."

The three of them left the cafeteria and went back upstairs. They were waiting in his room when he was wheeled in.

Even knowing what to expect, the sight of him was still a shock to Susan. There were several tubes running in and out of the covers. And he looked so still. His face was bruised and swollen, and the black stitches stood out in stark relief on his white face. "Oh, Steve," she whispered. Then she felt Tony's hand take hers and squeeze.

As they transferred Steve to the bed, his eyes fluttered open. "Mom?" His voice sounded sleepy and very weak.

"I'm right here, honey." She stepped over to the bed and picked up his limp hand.

"What happened?"

"What do you remember?"

"I'm not sure. I remember seeing Dr. Masters, and I remember hurting. What did I do?"

"You didn't do anything, darling, except try to get home from school. A car hit you, but you're going to be fine." She fought to keep the tears from filling her eyes.

"I'm very proud of you, Steve," Tony said, walking to the side of the bed by Susan.

Steve's eyes widened in sleepy wonder. "Tony?"

"That's right, son."

"How did you get here so quick?"

Tony's smile was tender. "I'll always be here, whenever you need me."

Steve's eyes drifted closed, then opened once more. He tried to smile, but the effort caused some pain and he gave a soft whimper. "I'm glad." His eyes closed once more.

Tony leaned over and kissed him on his forehead. "So am I, son. So am I."

Epilogue

"And here, ladies and gentlemen, to accept the award given by his teammates, coaching staff and the owners of the Atlanta Aces, for sixteen years of outstanding ballplaying, is Tony Antonelli!"

The master of ceremonies led the applause and cheering that reverberated through the huge ballroom of one of Atlanta's most prestigious hotels. Susan had a moment of quiet thankfulness that the traditional head table had been omitted for the evening, so that she didn't feel quite so much on display. She watched Tony thread his way around the large round dinner tables on his way to the podium. He was forced to stop repeatedly as various people patted his back and arms, or grabbed his hands.

Two-year-old Scott stirred in her arms, then relaxed

once again. Even if his daddy had caused all the commotion, the day had been too much for him, and he slept peacefully through the excitement. Susan stroked his dark curls away from his forehead with a smile. He looked so much like Tony, but then so did Steve, seated on the other side of four-year-old Tricia. At fifteen, Steve was an exact replica of his father at that age—large and well-built—and already catching the eye of the girls. Only Tricia had taken after her mother. Susan watched as Tricia sat up on her knees so she had a better view of Tony as he stepped up to the podium. Instead of dying down, the noise intensified and he stood there waiting, his famous smile lighting up the room—as well as Susan's heart.

She saw him glance over to their table and wink. Steve made the age-old gesture for "the champ" and they waited for the room to quiet.

Susan felt as though her body were too fragile to contain the burst of love and joy she felt for the man waiting patiently for the noise to subside. Because of his quiet determination and persistence, traits that had helped him forge his way to the top of his field, he had convinced her that they could make their marriage work despite separate careers, almost opposite personalities and circumstances that would have torn most couples apart.

He'd been right.

In the silence of the room Tony began to speak. Steve sat on the edge of his chair, hanging on to every word, his face radiating his pride.

Steve. How blessed they were to have him in good health. Although his recovery from his accident had been slow, he'd taken his recuperation period very well. Tony helped tremendously with that. She'd never forget the day Tony had had to fly back to Atlanta. He'd stayed for three days, making sure Steve was responding to treatment as expected. The pain had been predictable, but Susan would never forget how helpless she felt just sitting by his side and watching. But Tony seemed to know just what to do, what conversation to make, to keep Steve's mind off his discomfort as much as possible.

"By the way, Steve," Tony mentioned that day in a casual tone, "did your mom tell you she's agreed to marry me?"

"No kidding? Wow, Tony, that's great!" Then he looked over at his mother and frowned. "Why couldn't you've decided before he left, Mom? Then I wouldn't have to be working so hard on my room!"

Susan couldn't help it, she burst out laughing. "Oh, Steve, is that all it means to you?" she finally asked.

He had the grace to blush. "Well, no, not exactly." He looked at Tony very seriously and asked, "When are you going to get married?"

"Well, you've given me some pretty good advice in the past. What do you think?"

"I suppose you wanna marry her right away, huh?"

Tony's eyes danced as he took Susan's hand and

laid it against his cheek. "That sounds good to me. I've waited a long time for her, you know."

Steve studied the two of them in silence for a moment. "Yeah, I guess so. You probably want to marry her before you have to leave again, don't you?" His face held no expression, and Susan wasn't sure what that meant. But Tony obviously did.

"Oh, I don't mind waiting until you can be at the ceremony, if that's okay with you."

Steve's eyes lit up and his smile reminded Susan of summer sunshine—bright and sparkling. "Yeah, that'd be super."

"Then you'd better work hard at getting out of here, because I'm going to be counting the days."

Steve tried to straighten up in bed and Susan quickly pulled his pillow into a better position. "You bet, Tony. I can hardly wait. Then you'll be my *real* dad, right?"

Susan's heart lurched into an uncomfortable rhythm and she couldn't say a word.

"That's right, Steve," Tony said softly.

"And then I'll be Steve Antonelli, won't I?" he insisted, and Susan could no longer remain silent.

"It doesn't work that way, honey. My name will change, not yours."

"Oh." His crestfallen expression told Susan all she needed to know about Steve's feelings. But he wasn't the only one involved.

Later Tony told her to handle the situation however she felt best, but she understood how painful the reminder was to him. So she had gone to Michael's parents and had a long talk with them. They loved Steve, but they had long since recognized his resemblance to Tony. Michael's mother finally made the explanation that summed up how each of them felt.

"Michael loved Steve but he was never a father to him. He was too wrapped up in his music to really notice anyone else. Michael's music was his legacy to the world. But Steve—well, he's a very special legacy, and he belongs to Tony."

So Stephen Spencer McCormick became Stephen Spencer Antonelli as soon after the wedding as adoption papers could be processed.

The wedding. What a riot that had turned out to be! Their marriage took place in July, in the middle of baseball season. They made plans for a small family wedding in Santa Barbara, but it hadn't turned out quite that way.

The manager of Tony's team called Susan and asked them to consider getting married in Atlanta, otherwise his entire team intended to fly out for the wedding, baseball season and scheduled games notwithstanding! None of them intended to miss watching Tony's bachelor downfall.

A quick call to Tony confirmed the manager's concerns—everyone wanted to attend. So Susan spent the last few weeks before their wedding commuting between Atlanta, trying to take care of the arrangements for a large wedding, and Santa Barbara, trying to take care of her law practice. Air travel and the attendant jet-lag became part of her life. But it had been worth it. She'd been surprised to discover she enjoyed all of it—the teasing and confusion, the search for a church and the interviews with the pastor, and the anticipation of becoming, at long last, Mrs. Tony Antonelli.

Her parents flew to Atlanta for the wedding with Hannah and Steve, and Susan gladly yielded the burden of the final preparations to her mother, whose unflappable efficiency quickly dealt with the unexpected last-minute details. Once again, her mother had surprised her, accepting their marriage with quiet dignity.

The Spencers had taken Steve home with them while she and Tony had managed to spend three days completely alone.

As she forced her attention back to the banquet hall, Susan glanced at the sleeping Scott and fidgeting Tricia and ruefully acknowledged that their honeymoon seemed to have been their last time alone.

Tony had been so nervous! The wedding itself had been beautiful, partly because the weather had cooperated and partly because the service had been specially planned by them both. However, Tony had been so pale, Susan was convinced he was coming down with something and had visions of her new husband being fed antibiotics and fever-reducing medication during their entire honeymoon.

Susan had been too busy trying to get her work completed or turned over to other people to have much time to be nervous about the actual ceremony. But poor Tony had been the brunt of innumerable, and mostly unmentionable, practical jokes by his teammates. She wondered later how he had had the nerve to go through with the marriage! She remembered asking him about it when they were finally alone after the ceremony.

"You know I'm too stubborn to give in," he had muttered as he nuzzled her neck.

They were sitting in the living area of their luxurious hotel suite, Susan on Tony's lap on the overlong sofa. She noted that all the while he was making his explanations, his hand was smoothly sliding up and down her leg.

"Are we going to have any dinner?" she asked while he continued to nibble along her neck, his hand now resting on her knee and slowly moving upward.

"Dinner?" he repeated, then raised his head. "You're hungry?" His eyes showed pained disbelief.

In her most pedantic tones Susan explained, "It is very important to the body that it be fueled on a consistent basis. Studies have shown that three meals a day, taken at regular intervals—"

"What a little monster you are!" he exclaimed, grabbing her and sliding down on the sofa beside her. "You can't be hungry after all the food you put away at the reception!"

She feigned surprise. "Oh, I forgot about that. Will my body understand that was supposed to be my dinner?"

Once again his hand crept steadily up her thigh. "I fully intend to educate your body so it understands lots of things."

Her hands slipped through his hair. "I can hardly wait."

Susan was suddenly brought to the present by loud applause. She realized Tony had finished speaking and was returning to sit down beside her once more and she hadn't heard a word he'd said!

"Do you realize you made me lose my train of thought up there?" he whispered as he sat down and the master of ceremonies began speaking again.

"Me?" She looked at him in astonishment.

He grinned. "Who else? I glanced back here and you were staring at me with the most tantalizing smile on your face, the one you get in bed when—"

"Tony!" she gasped, then looked around quickly. Luckily, no one else was close enough to hear him.

"Are you ready to go? There's something about that particular expression on your face that turns my thoughts away from baseball, and everything else. Let's go home!"

As the banquet crowd began to stand and move around, Tony slipped Scott out of her arms, nestling him across his large chest. It was easy to explain that they needed to get home and put the children to bed. Yes, it might have been easier to get a sitter, Tony explained more than once, but he had wanted his entire family with him on the night he officially announced he was retiring from baseball.

It had been his last season and it had been another good one. Once again they'd made it into the World Series, and had won. Once again Tony had won the MVP award. He was proud of his honors, proud of his career, but made it clear to everyone that his family was the culmination of his greatest dreams.

He was waiting in bed for Susan when she walked out of the bathroom. She'd enjoyed the condominium in Atlanta but knew she wasn't going to miss it once it was sold. The beach house made a very nice full-time residence for them. Her gaze fell on Tony as he lay stretched out on the bed. The covers were already shoved to the bottom and his firmly muscled body lay there, unadorned, in all its glory.

She never grew tired of looking at him—at his wide shoulders and deep chest, his tapered waist and slender hips, his well-developed thighs and hardened calves. But most of all, what really affected her more than anything else was the love shining brightly from his dark eyes.

"Were you waiting for me?" she asked as she slipped off her robe and curled up against him.

"You could say that. I was just thinking about some of the things we used to plan when we were kids."

When they were kids. Steve never grew tired of listening to Tony's anecdotes about how his mother and father met, grew up together, and all the things they did. Even Tricia had a few favorite stories that she liked to hear at bedtime and Tony never seemed to tire of the retelling.

"What plans in particular were you thinking of?" The tip of her tongue teased his earlobe, causing him to shiver slightly.

"Uh, how can I think when you do that?" he muttered, leaning up on his elbow and staring down at her with a mock ferocious expression. She reached up and pulled his head down to hers, kissing him slowly but very thoroughly. When she finally let go of him, she smiled.

"Would you like me to repeat the question?"

"Question?"

"Um-hmm. What plans did we have as kids that you were thinking of?"

"Oh, yes." His mischievous grin made her realize she'd taken the bait—he hadn't forgotten for a moment. "Remember when we were first talking about getting married, and we agreed that someday we would have four children?" All the while he was talking he was slipping the sheer nightgown from Susan, effectively distracting her from the conversation.

"That was a long time ago, Tony."

"I know. You were just a baby then. Now you're a middle-aged matron," he whispered.

"What!" She sat up in bed, incensed.

"What I mean is, I'm sure you feel that three children are more than enough for your nerves, and you're ready to settle down and wait for your grandchildren, right?"

"Tony, for your information, I am only thirty-three years old. That is not middle-aged. That is not time to wait for grandchildren."

"Then what would you say to our having another child in say, oh, nine months or so?"

She leaned back on her pillow, fully aware of his strategy. She assumed a slightly worried frown. "But Tony, let's face it. You've already hit retirement age. Isn't that a little too much to ask of an old man like you?"

The ensuing struggle, amid baritone chuckles and soprano giggles, eventually came to a most satisfying conclusion, disproving all myths about retired baseball players and so-called middle-aged matrons.

If Tony's plans for a larger family didn't work out, it was certainly not from lack of trying and the total cooperation of both parties.

* * * * *

HAWK'S FLIGHT

This one is for you, Michelle—
for your loving support
when I needed it the most—with my love.

Chapter 1

Hawk waited.

When virtues were handed out, Hawk somehow missed out on patience. He didn't handle waiting around well, and today was no exception. He glanced at his watch.

What's keeping Dr. Winston? His office called almost an hour ago to charter a plane.

Hawk stood in the cramped office of Horizon Aviation Service, his elbow resting on the counter. The doctor, whom he'd never met, needed to fly to Flagstaff due to some family emergency. Hawk had been the only one available to take the flight, causing him to postpone his vacation plans for a few hours.

Oh, well. It wouldn't be the first time he'd had to

change his plans. Come to think of it, when had any of his plans *ever* worked out as he expected?

Not that he'd minded helping his friend Rick get the charter service going in El Paso, but it had brought him back to the States a year earlier than he'd intended. Now that Horizon Aviation was solidly established Hawk knew it was time for him to be making new plans.

He never stayed in one place too long. A restless nature and an inquisitive mind kept him on the move.

Hawk was ready for change—he definitely needed the vacation. Eighteen months of long hours and hard work had taken their toll. He pictured himself hiking into the mountains of Mexico's interior, enjoying the solitude and the tranquility of nature.

If the good doctor will get a move on, we'll be in Flagstaff in a few hours. With a good night's sleep, I can be flying south by sunup tomorrow.

Hawk caught a glimpse of a late-model car through the office door and he watched as it pulled in across the street. A young woman threw open the driver's door and leaped out, ignoring the wavering heat waves that rose from the sizzling asphalt of the airport's parking lot. Her rose-colored summer suit, although flattering to her petite figure, made her look overdressed for the hot Texas sun.

She hurried to the back of her car and opened the trunk lid. When she leaned over, Hawk admired the way her slim skirt clung to her curves. It also revealed a pair of very shapely legs. He slowly straightened from his leaning position at the counter. She was a good-looking woman, no doubt about it.

Grabbing a small bag out of the trunk, she slammed the lid and started across the pavement toward him, her high heels sinking slightly in the heat-softened surface. Hawk had to revise his original opinion of her as she came closer. The woman was more than good-looking—she was stunning!

He tried to understand his strong reaction to her. Maybe it was because she wore a look of fragility—she was small with delicate features. Maybe it was her fair complexion that gave her a porcelain-doll appearance. With her soft ivory coloring she was either a visitor to the dry desert air of El Paso or she spent all of her time indoors.

He caught a flash of fiery red in her dark brown hair where the sun picked out highlights. She wore it in a jaunty topknot, with wispy curls framing her face. Hawk wondered about the color of her eyes, hidden by sunglasses.

Her skin glowed and he could almost feel its silkiness as though he'd already experienced the sensation of running his hand along her cheek. His palm tingled.

What's happening to me? he wondered. He'd seen beautiful women before, and she wasn't even his type. Women who looked like she did were notoriously spoiled, and that was a breed he was careful to avoid. *The heat must be getting to me.*

He wondered what she was doing there. He glanced at Rick, who was taking flight charter information over the phone. *Maybe he's got himself a new girl and didn't want me to know. I'll have to tease him about being afraid I'd try to cut in on his territory.*

They both knew that would never happen. Hawk had a standard attitude toward women—he could take 'em or leave 'em. He generally left them—before they decided to discuss a more permanent arrangement.

His gaze returned to the woman rapidly approaching the door. She was different from the women he'd known in a way he couldn't define, and it made him uneasy. He could feel a tightening deep within him, as though warning him to prepare to do battle with his reactions to her.

Hawk deliberately straightened and turned away from the door. He leaned both elbows on the counter. *That's enough ogling for one day,* he reminded himself. *I wish to hell the good doctor would get here if he's got such an all-fired emergency!*

Paige swung open the heavy glass door to the air charter service and stepped inside the refreshingly cool room, pausing to remove her sunglasses and to adjust her eyes after the white glare of the July sun. She looked around the tiny office, wondering if she'd made the right decision. When her receptionist managed to charter a plane for her, she was so grateful she hadn't questioned her further.

Paige glanced around the room with dismay, beginning to have second thoughts. Large maps, posters and calendars cluttered the walls. A battered desk and two nondescript chairs waited for occupants on the public side of the counter, while another desk and miscellaneous office equipment sat in a crowded jumble behind it.

Two men occupied the office. One was standing in front of the waist-high counter, and the other was talking on the phone in the office section.

She wondered how long the man at the counter had been waiting. She glanced at her watch, then determinedly walked over to the counter, hoping the man on the phone would glance up. She needed to be on her way—now.

"Were you looking for someone?"

Paige stared up at the man beside her. Seen up close, he looked almost intimidating. He appeared to be at least six feet tall, but it was his build she found most disquieting.

He was broad-shouldered, with muscled arms emphasized by the khaki shirt he wore, the sleeves rolled up halfway between his shoulder and elbow. Thick, black hair fell across his forehead, and his face had the high cheekbones and rich skin tones that generally denoted some Indian blood, which wasn't an unusual sight in the southwest. His voice had a full-bodied, rich sound that created a slight tingling within her. She forced herself to meet his black eyes. The man looked tough as well as formidable. Whatever he was thinking, he gave nothing away.

Paige decided she didn't have time to waste, and perhaps he could help her. "Actually, I'm here to charter a plane," she explained.

He stiffened, staring at her with suspicion. "Your name is—"

"Paige Winston."

"*Doctor* Winston?" A note of disbelief crept into his voice.

"That's right." She glanced at the man on the phone, who had yet to acknowledge her presence. "Do you know how much longer he'll be?"

The man shrugged. "It doesn't matter—I'm your pilot. I'm ready to go whenever you are."

"*You're* my pilot?" she asked in surprise.

"Yes. I understand you need to get to Flagstaff right away."

The slight doubt in his tone brought her to her senses. She didn't care who was flying her, so long as she got there as soon as possible. "Yes. Yes, I do. My father's been vacationing near Flagstaff and had a heart attack." She brushed her fingers distractedly through the curls that clung to her forehead. "He's in the hospital there now."

He nodded, then reached over and picked up the

small bag resting at her feet. Motioning her to a door she hadn't noticed, he said, "This way."

The blinding sun hit Paige like a furnace blast of heat and glare and she quickly fumbled for her sunglasses. When she got them on she discovered the pilot was halfway to a small plane sitting on the edge of the runway.

Her heart pounded in her chest. She was expected to fly in *that*? It was so small! She glanced around nervously, but saw nothing bigger. The pilot turned around and stared at her, frowning slightly. He, too, had placed sunglasses over his eyes, but his were mirrored and Paige saw only her own reflection as she hurried up to him, breathless from the heat and her fear of the small plane.

He held out his hand, and when Paige placed hers uncertainly into it, he lifted her to the wing of the plane, motioning for her to crawl into the tiny door that was before her.

Paige discovered her suit was not the most practical choice of apparel for the trip, but then, she hadn't given it a thought when she'd rushed home and thrown a few things in a bag. All she could think about was her father.

How serious was his heart attack? What condition would he be in when she arrived? He had to be all right. He *had* to be. Not only was he her parent, but he was her business partner and best friend as well. She couldn't survive without him!

Paige scrambled inside, tugging at her skirt as she slid into the seat next to the pilot's position. She glanced around, bewildered at the gauges and switches that covered the dash. A small steering mechanism was in front of her, and she fervently prayed she wasn't expected to know anything about it.

Hawk followed her into the plane, made sure her seat belt was properly fastened, then settled into the seat next to her, checking that he had all the necessary maps and papers for the flight. He'd already gone through the preflight checklist before she arrived, knowing that saving time was important, but he ran an experienced glance over everything one more time.

He picked up the mike and contacted the control tower, requesting takeoff instructions. Within minutes they were airborne.

Paige watched the brown baked surface of El Paso fall away below their plane as they climbed. Mount Franklin continued to perform its centuries-old sentinel duty overlooking the sprawling city.

"You okay?"

Paige gave a nervous jerk when the pilot spoke. What was there about the man that caused her to overreact to him? He was polite enough, so that wasn't it. It had something to do with the sound of his voice—as though somehow she should recognize it. Yet she knew she'd never seen him before in her life.

Paige glanced at him and nodded. "I'm fine." She

cleared her throat. "When do you expect to reach Flagstaff?"

He studied the instruments in front of him for a moment, a slight frown creasing his brow. Then he smiled at her. His teeth flashed white against his bronzed complexion. "We're due in by seven, barring complications."

"What sort of complications?" she asked nervously.

"There's a storm moving in from the north that I'm hoping to avoid. That may mean flying due west, then north. It could mean a longer flight, but it will be a much more comfortable ride."

She shuddered. She'd never cared for flying, even in large commercial planes. This small one made her feel she was barely balanced in the air.

Trying to sound calm, Paige said, "I'm so glad I was able to charter a plane on such short notice." She knew she was chattering, but she needed to get her mind off her thoughts.

"An hour later and you'd been out of luck."

"You mean you'd have been gone on another charter?"

The corner of his mouth turned up in a slight smile. "No, ma'am. I'd have been gone on my vacation."

"Oh!" Paige wondered if he'd been upset about having to take her. She couldn't tell. "I'm sorry," she offered.

"No problem. I intend to spend the night in Flagstaff and leave for Mexico in the morning."

"Do you have family in Mexico?"

"No. A friend of mine has a large hacienda down in the interior. It's got a landing strip I intend to use. I plan to backpack into the mountains and do some fishing."

"By yourself?"

He looked at her in surprise. "Sure."

She couldn't imagine spending a vacation alone. For that matter, she couldn't imagine spending a vacation camping. The Great Outdoors was a total mystery to her and she'd never had any desire to get better acquainted.

"I'm glad I didn't ruin your plans for you."

"Don't worry. You didn't."

"Have you been flying long?" she heard herself blurt out. She hadn't meant to sound so apprehensive, but it was too late to rephrase her question.

He grinned again and her heart tripled its already rapid beat. He had a beautiful smile, one that stirred up all sorts of butterflies within her that had nothing to do with her nervousness.

"About twenty years."

"Twenty!" She stared at him in disbelief. He couldn't be much older than her thirty years.

"I've been flying since I was sixteen."

"Wasn't that a little young to start?"

"I suppose, but I'd been on my own since I was

fourteen. I made friends with a pilot and was underfoot so much of the time he finally hired me to work around his aviation service. I think he finally started teaching me how to fly to stop all my pestering questions."

His comments created all sorts of questions in her mind. Where was his family during that time? Why had he left home? It occurred to her that she didn't even know his name.

"I'm afraid you have me at a disadvantage. You know my name but I don't know yours."

"Hawk."

"Hawk?"

"That's right."

She wondered if that were a nickname but didn't want to press. Instead she stared out the window, trying not to think about how far off the ground they were.

"What made you decide to become a doctor?"

His deep voice interrupted her nervous thoughts, although his question didn't particularly surprise her. She'd spent most of her life answering that question in one form or another.

"Several reasons, actually," she admitted. "My father is a doctor—a pediatrician. I can't remember a time when I didn't want to be a doctor as well. And I love children. I've never been sorry for following in my father's footsteps. We have a clinic in El Paso."

"How long have you been a doctor?"

"Four years."

"You must have started rather young yourself. You barely look old enough to vote," he stated with a slow smile.

"I've been old enough to vote for several years now."

He smiled at her prim tone, then picked up the mike and spoke into it. When a disembodied voice responded, he asked for an update of the storm moving in, then listened intently as the voice rattled off what to Paige was incomprehensible data about clouds, winds and air currents.

She knew there was no reason for her to worry about the weather. He was obviously staying on top of things. She just wished she could get her queasy stomach to understand that, not to mention her racing pulse.

"Have you flown much?" His question was a welcome diversion.

"Uh, no, I haven't."

His smile was very reassuring. "Why don't you just relax, lay your head back and close your eyes. You'd be surprised how that helps."

Paige nodded, knowing it would be ridiculous to deny her nervousness. A perfectly good tissue lay shredded in her lap. He probably wouldn't believe an explanation that shredding tissues was a new hobby of hers.

She closed her eyes with a quiet determination, but her father immediately came to mind and they flashed open once more. *Your worrying won't contribute to his recovery,* she reminded herself.

Paige glanced over at Hawk, covertly studying his profile. She found him intriguing—he was different from anyone she'd ever met. He seemed to have forgotten her as he donned earphones. She could no longer hear the radio.

Slowly and imperceptibly, Paige began to relax. The work load at the clinic had been heavy since her father had gone and she knew she'd been overdoing it. *Oh, Dad, please be all right.* Her loving message winged its way to him. She hoped he knew of her concern. *I'll be with you in a few short hours. Please hang on.*

Her long lashes dropped one last time, then stayed down. Paige slept.

It was some time later when Hawk spared a glance in her direction. She really must have been tired to be sleeping through the increasingly rough gusts of wind that grabbed the plane and shook it—like a giant hand wanting to play.

He didn't care for the approaching storm or the way the oil pressure gauge was acting. He'd spent the entire morning working on that oil line and had been convinced he'd discovered and repaired the problem. *So what the hell's wrong with the gauge?*

Paige was jolted awake by a thundering crash. She

glanced out the window of the plane and recoiled in horror. Black rolling clouds seemed to engulf them. She looked at Hawk and noted his grim expression as he wrestled the plane through the swirling wind currents.

"It looks like the storm you mentioned earlier found us," she said, trying to mask her concern.

Without looking at her, he nodded. "Right now the storm is the least of our worries."

"What do you mean?"

"I've got to put this baby down in the first available space. We're losing oil pressure."

She looked down, but could see nothing but angry dark clouds. What had happened to the sunlight?

"Where are we?"

"Eastern Arizona," he said in a terse tone.

She tried to remember her geography. What was in eastern Arizona? Hopefully it was desert and saguaro cactus. Or was that the Phoenix area?

Hawk continued to bring the plane down to a lower elevation, praying to break free of the clouds shortly, giving him some visual idea of where they could land.

His prayer was answered almost immediately. The dark clouds began to thin out and patches of green appeared. So far, so good. He glanced back at the oil pressure gauge. It was still dropping.

Paige saw the land and felt her heart leap in her chest. Mountains. Green-covered mountains. Would he find a place flat enough to land?

Once again she stared at the man who held their lives in his hands. He'd removed his glasses, and, except for the slight frown line between his brows, his expression was impassive. She wondered if Indians were taught that look or whether it came to them naturally. She was certain her fear was written in large block letters across her face.

It was too late to ask herself if she trusted the man. Much too late. After all, it was his life as much as it was hers. But she knew nothing about his skills or his background, and she recognized how foolish she'd been not to find out more about him before taking off in the plane.

But would it have made any difference? Her receptionist had tried to find other ways to get to Flagstaff. Chartering the plane had been the quickest, at least it had seemed so at the time.

Paige glanced down again, then wished she hadn't. The ground was coming up closer at an alarming rate. She took a quick breath of relief when Hawk leveled off, skimming the tops of the large ponderosa pine trees that dotted the land. Paige could see no place where he could safely land the plane.

Hawk shared her thought but refused to panic. He'd been in tight spots before. He forced himself to remember landings he'd made in southeast Asia, in Central and South America, when he'd been able to put his plane down in very little space. But those times had been different—his plane had been in good working order.

He checked the oil pressure once again and was heartened to see it was holding for the moment. There was obviously a leak, but maybe it wasn't as bad as he feared.

If he could get the plane down without damaging it, he had enough tools to make some repairs. He mentally inventoried what he had stowed in back—his camping equipment, his AM-FM radio, and the food supplies he'd planned to take to Mexico. It could be worse. All he needed to do was find a place to land.

There it was. He sent up a prayer of thanks. He'd spotted a meadow, lightly dotted with aspen, but relatively clear of the larger pines that would put a quick end to a forced landing. Then he glanced at the oil pressure gauge. Once again it was dropping.

He no longer had a choice. He had to put it down.

"This is it. We're going in."

His deep voice echoed in the small compartment. How could he sound so calm? Paige wondered if this was the time her life should be rapidly flashing across her mind. If so, her thoughts weren't cooperating. All she could think about was her father. Was he still alive? How was she going to reach him? What would the shock of her not arriving do to him? If only she knew his condition.

Her last conscious thought was: *There was so much I still wanted to do in life...*

Chapter 2

Paige groaned.

Icy water trickled down her face. She shifted, and a sharp pain shot through her head. *Is this what a hangover feels like?* she wondered fuzzily. *But I don't even drink.*

Other sensations seeped into her consciousness. She was moving, but not under her own power. The steady thudding that accompanied the pain in her head was coming from the hard wall pressed firmly against her right ear. Steel bands were strapped around her shoulders and knees. She tried to raise her head, but blackness engulfed her once again.

Minutes later, or maybe hours, Paige felt as though she were being held captive by miniature natives, only inches tall. Several held her head while their friends took turns beating on it with their minuscule hammers. Why wouldn't they leave her alone?

She attempted to raise her hand to her head, only to find it firmly tucked under a cover. At least they hadn't tied her down. If she could only free her hand, she could fight them back. One arm swing should swat them away like flies. But they certainly carried a mean wallop to be so small.

"You need to lie still, Paige. You're going to be all right...try to rest."

Where had she heard that voice before? The deep, warm tones comforted her. They were much deeper than her father's voice. Her father.

"Dad!" She tried to sit up. Where was he? He'd needed her for something. What was it?

"It's all right, honey. We'll get you to your father yet." The voice held a quiet authority that soothed her. Who was it?

An arm slipped under her shoulders and brought her forward. The movement caused the sadistic natives to double their efforts. "Please stop," she murmured, wondering if they spoke English.

"I'm sorry, but you'll be more comfortable without these wet clothes."

She wanted to explain that she wasn't talking to the quiet voice murmuring in her ear. It was those blasted natives practicing their construction skills on her defenseless head. But it took too much effort to explain.

A cool wet cloth gently touched her forehead, and she sighed with pleasure. Never had anything felt so good. Soothing strokes bathed her face and a gentle hand pushed her thick hair from her face.

"You have a slight concussion, Dr. Winston, but I don't think it's too bad. I'm sure you'll feel better by morning."

I hope, Hawk silently added.

He sounded so confident that Paige drifted into a natural sleep, content to wait for relief. Maybe the natives had been scattered when she sat up. Serve them right. They were insufferably rude.

Paige shifted in her sleep. At least she attempted to shift, but couldn't move. What was wrong with her? She opened her eyes and decided she had finally flipped over the edge of sanity into a surrealistic existence.

Nothing made sense. Her head rested on a hard, bronzed surface that moved gently. Her body rested comfortably against something large and warm. A canvas surface seemed to surround her, but it was hard to tell in the gloom. Was it night or day?

She attempted to raise her head, relieved to discover her tiny torturers must have given up and gone home, leaving her head with a dull ache. Her pillow shifted, and she focused fuzzily on a pair of black eyes a few inches away staring at her with concern.

What beautiful eyes, she thought dreamily.

"How do you feel?" the man asked, his voice rumbling in his chest. She realized her head had been resting on his shoulder.

"Like I should never have had that first drink," she admitted, and wondered why he chuckled.

Paige discovered she was lying entwined with a man with gorgeous black eyes. *So this is what my subconscious is up to when my back is turned. It has me in bed with a beautiful specimen of virile manhood the minute I slip over the edge. Interesting.* She wondered how long she would be in this condition, but decided she might as well enjoy it while she was there.

Paige discovered her hand draped across his bare chest and she tentatively moved her fingers. They worked. She could feel the warmth of his skin under the sensitive pads of her fingertips. She brushed her hand over his chest and smiled. *Not bad. Not bad at all.*

Other sensations began to impinge on her. She was cozily curled along the man's side, both of his arms wrapped around her. One of her legs was neatly tucked between his, her thigh nestling intimately against him. A warm tide of embarrassment swept through her. Never had one of her dreams been so vivid. Not only could she feel the steady beat of his heart beneath her palm, his soft breath felt like a feather rhythmically brushing against her forehead.

Paige knew that all she needed to do was roll over and look at her clock to come out of it, but she couldn't resist the temptation to enjoy the dream for another few moments.

She absently noted that the only thing each of them had on were their briefs, and yet she was quite warm. The covers fit snugly around them. She raised her head slightly and discovered they were in a sleeping bag.

A sleeping bag? Now where did her subconscious come up with that one? She'd never been camping in her life. The outdoors was a total mystery to her and, as far as she was concerned, would remain that way.

Oh well, a dream was a dream, and she obviously had no control over what was put in it. But a sleeping bag, of all things!

The man shifted slightly, and her thoughts flew back to him. Had his breathing changed? Had his arm tightened around her? His heartbeat had definitely increased.

Then she realized what was happening and jerked her leg away from him. *Okay, time to wake up now. We know what kind of dream this could turn into.* Paige tried to sit up, but was hampered by the man and the covers.

She blinked her eyes, trying to focus on the clock sitting on the nightstand beside her bed. She couldn't even find the nightstand. When she forced herself into a sitting position, the top of her head brushed against canvas.

An ominous feeling suddenly gripped her—a very ominous feeling.

She wasn't dreaming. She was definitely awake, but nothing made sense.

Paige tried to recall the reason why she was there, and the dull throbbing in her head increased its rhythm. She felt along her temple and discovered a large bump just below her hairline.

Panic began to course through her. She searched her memory for her name. Paige Winston. Her age? Thirty. Her occupation? Pediatrician. Her address? Thirteen-twenty-eight La Donna Drive, El Paso, Texas.

So far, so good. *Just take it easy. You've suffered a blow to your head and you're obviously disoriented.* Her medical training was striving to take over and be objective, but she could feel her heart slamming against her chest and she was breathing in short, panting breaths.

Now, then. The next step is to figure out where you are. She gazed around the small area enclosed by canvas, searching for clues. Nothing looked familiar.

Slowly she turned around and stared at the man still lying next to her. She was positive she'd never seen him before in her life. "Do I know you?" she asked politely, a tentative smile hovering on her face.

Hawk blinked in surprise. After only a few hours of sleep, his brain felt sluggish and he wasn't prepared for his passenger's unexpected question. He leaned up on his elbow, his muscled arm flexing painfully where her head had rested for the past several hours.

"Don't you remember?"

That question had to rank as one of the most stupid ones of all times, she decided in disgust. Why else would she have asked? "Didn't anyone ever tell you it's impolite to answer a question with a question?" Paige grumbled. She studied his face for a moment. She did not know this man. Of course she didn't. In which case, she needed to understand why they were in a sleeping bag together under some sort of canvas cover.

She rubbed her aching head, vaguely remembering the constant pounding from the night before. She wondered if this were what a hangover felt like. If so, she knew she'd made the right decision years ago when she decided not to drink.

Hawk watched her in concern. Her concussion must be worse than he'd first thought. He slipped his forefinger under her chin and slowly turned her head until he could see her eyes. Yes, they were definitely dilated. At least the right one was, which wasn't surprising considering the large knot on her temple.

Now what? He had done the best he could last night after they landed. He'd found makeshift shelter for her under the trees until he could unload the plane, set up the tent, and spread out the bedroll. His fear for her had galvanized his actions. He'd never forget the relief he felt when she had come to, even if it had only been for a few minutes.

"Do you remember anything about last night?" he asked, noting her puzzled expression with concern. "Do you remember the plane going down?"

She stared at him in bewilderment. A plane? He was asking about a plane going down.

Paige recalled watching a television news report of a jumbo jet crashing at the end of a runway, going up in smoke and flames. When had she seen that?

Paige rubbed her head thoughtfully. "I don't think so," she finally admitted softly.

Now what? Hawk wondered. Was there any reason to feed her fears by admitting that although they had made it down safely, the plane was in no condition to fly out under its own power?

"It doesn't matter." He edged away from her in the confined bed. "I've got to look for some dry wood to get a fire going. Are you going to be all right if I leave you for a few moments?"

His anxious gaze confused her. What was the matter with her brain? Her thoughts seemed to be sloshing around in some kind of gooey liquid, refusing to form any reasonable shape or make any kind of sense. She couldn't understand what she was doing here when she should be waking up in her own bed, in her own home, and getting ready to go to the clinic.

Hawk couldn't help it. Her anxious frown as she sat in the curve of his arm, the covers modestly tucked around her breasts, leaving her silky-soft back open to his appreciative view, was too much for him to ignore. He pulled her back down to him with some vague idea of trying to comfort her. "It's going to be all right, honey. Please don't worry. I won't let anything happen to you." He leaned over and touched his lips gently to hers.

As kisses go, his was far from demanding. It was almost soothing, and she relaxed in his arms, enjoying the sensation of being held and comforted.

She *had* to be dreaming. There was no other explanation. Maybe it was a dream within a dream, but she'd never dreamed of anyone who looked like him before. His kiss took her breath away.

Hawk pulled away from her slightly, surprised at his actions. He'd only meant to console her, and he found her warm response unexpected.

He forgot who they were and why they were there as, once again, he leaned down and kissed her. Her mouth parted slightly, unconsciously inviting his intimacy. She tasted so sweet, so warm and loving. Hawk soon lost himself in exploration.

What is happening to me? Paige wondered. Never had she felt this way before. Never had a man affected her so.

Who was he?

Paige stiffened and pulled away from him while she studied his features for a clue to his identity. She saw thick black hair that fell across his broad forehead; high cheekbones and rich skin tones; and magnificent black eyes that mesmerized her.

But who was he? And what were they doing in a sleeping bag together? They certainly weren't strangers to each other!

Maybe the bump on her head had been worse than she thought. What if she were more than just disoriented? What if she were suffering from some form of amnesia?

Paige closed her eyes and tried to blot out her surroundings. *Relax. Stay calm. Everything's going to be all right. Don't panic. Try not to panic your companion. He doesn't need to know how little you can remember. Maybe it will all come back to you in a few minutes.*

She opened her eyes and found herself staring deeply into his. "Were we in a plane crash?"

His well-shaped lips formed a small smile. "Not exactly. I was forced to land in a meadow last night."

"Oh." She continued to study him. He was so close she could see her reflection in his eyes. At least she'd learned something about him. He was a pilot. "Where are we?"

He shifted restlessly, moving slightly away from her. "Somewhere in eastern Arizona."

Arizona! What in the world are we doing in Arizona?

None of this made sense. How much of her life had she forgotten?

Paige rubbed her forehead. The pain made her feel as though her head were expanding with each heart beat. She tried to swallow, and her throat felt as though it had experienced a six-month drought. "May I have a drink of water, please?"

Hawk stared at her. Surely, as a doctor she should know a person with a concussion shouldn't have liquids. That was basic medical knowledge. *But she's not a doctor at the moment,* he reminded himself. *She's more of a patient. You can't expect her to diagnose and treat herself.*

He ran his hand down the side of her head, brushing the hair away so that it fell in long waves down her back. "I'm afraid I can't give you anything to drink, Paige." She stared at him in bewilderment. "I think you have a concussion. You mustn't drink anything."

Of course not, she thought. *I know that. I've treated several children with mild to severe concussions. But I had no idea what one felt like.*

I've got to get out of here, Hawk prodded himself. He didn't know what he'd been thinking of, kissing her like that. If only she hadn't looked so bewildered and vulnerable. A strange feeling had swept over him—a need to protect her. *If I don't watch it, the only protection she'll need is from me!* He threw back the cover and reached for his Levi's.

The tent was too small for him to stand up. He wriggled the pants over his long legs, then threw the tent flap open and crawled out. It was still raining.

Swell.

That was all they needed. The storm from the night before appeared to be a forerunner of more to come. He glanced around as he slowly stood up. The sky was heavily overcast, and he wondered how he was going to get word where they were to anyone.

He had flown off course yesterday, trying to get away from the worst of the storm. No one would be looking for them in this area. There had been no response to his repeated calls on the radio. All he'd gotten was static. Somehow he had to get them some help. But how and from where?

He watched the rain beat a monotonous rhythm around him. He was going to have a hell of a time finding wood dry enough to burn.

While he uncovered small limbs and peeled bark from larger ones, Hawk organized his thoughts and sought solutions.

He and the doctor were fortunate in one respect—they had plenty of food and camping equipment, enough to survive for a few weeks at least. He glanced back at the tent, nestled along the edge of a sheer cliff towering above the meadow. It looked as though he and his attractive passenger might be camping there for a few days.

He didn't see how she would be able to reach her father anytime soon. Now that he thought about it, he realized that she hadn't even mentioned her father this morning, which was surprising. Could it be possible she didn't remember why they were flying to Flagstaff? Or did she even remember where they'd been going?

Hawk had seen more head wounds over the years than he wished, and he knew they caused unpredictable consequences. Paige appeared confused and disoriented, and apparently suffered from some form of memory loss. He could think of nothing that he could do for her in that respect. He knew very little about her.

Glancing around the meadow, Hawk was somewhat reassured about their situation. If they had to be marooned somewhere, he'd at least found a location that offered comfortable accommodations.

Uncertain about the possibility of flooding, Hawk had set up camp on the hillside overlooking the meadow and stream that cut through its center. The tent was almost hidden among the boulders and trees, but spotters could see his plane if they flew over.

He winced at the thought of his plane. The damage had been considerable, but any forced landing that could be walked away from was considered an unqualified success.

Only, Paige hadn't walked away. Once again he saw her as she'd been last night. She'd been wearing her hair in some sort of topknot on her head, but it had come down, its mahogany-colored length falling around her shoulders and down her back. Her delicate features and fair complexion emphasized her vulnerability, and he could still taste the fear that had threatened to engulf him when he'd discovered her unconscious. Never had he seen a more beautiful sight than when her eyes slowly opened to reveal their navy-blue color.

Hawk faced the situation head-on. He'd been strongly attracted to her from the first moment he saw her. How else could he explain his insane impulse to kiss her? She'd looked so bewildered—so beautiful—and he'd spent the night holding her in his arms, praying she would be all right. But he would have to ignore his reaction to her. What he had to do was take care of her and get them out of there.

He stared up at the sky. There was a real possibility they wouldn't be spotted anytime soon, in which case their only choice would be to wait until Paige regained her strength, then consider their options. They might have to hike out of the mountains.

In the meantime he might as well try to relax and enjoy their forced camping trip. They certainly weren't in a life-threatening situation as long as Paige continued to show signs of improvement.

The fire finally caught, and Hawk relaxed a little.

He would have to make certain he didn't let it go out, after all the trouble he'd had getting it started. He straightened and went over to his box of provisions. At last he could make some coffee.

Hawk heard a movement behind him and turned around in time to watch Paige crawl hesitantly out of the tent. She wore the tailored suit and high-heeled shoes she'd had on the day before.

She stood in front of the tent staring around the clearing with bewilderment. Hawk realized she was swaying, and he dashed over to her.

"Paige, honey, you shouldn't be out of bed." He coaxed her back into the tent. "You need to lie quietly and give your head a chance to heal." She docilely sat back down on the sleeping bag. "The last thing we need is for you to get chilled." Hawk knelt beside her and hurriedly unbuttoned her blouse. "Your clothes are still damp," he explained as he unzipped her skirt and slid it down her legs. Her shoes came off last, leaving her in a lacy half slip and bra. He knew she'd be more comfortable without the constriction across her chest but didn't want to upset her by removing anything more. Hawk tucked her into the bedroll once more.

"Please stay in bed today, all right?"

She nodded her head, looking up at him like a trusting child. He found the cloth he'd used the night before and moistened it with water from his canteen. Gently he placed it on her forehead.

"What's your name?"

Her dark blue eyes continued to watch him. He felt his heart make a convulsive leap in his chest. So she still didn't remember him. Not a good sign. She didn't appear to be upset, just confused. The important thing for him to keep in mind was that she mustn't get upset. Perhaps it was just as well she couldn't recall much at the moment. As long as she didn't remember her father's illness on her own, he saw no reason to upset her with the news under the present circumstances.

He brushed his knuckles across her cheek. "My name is Hawk."

"Hawk?"

"That's right."

"So you're a hawk. I've wondered where a hawk lives. Now I know." Her voice had a little-girl quality, nothing like her normal husky tone. "He lives high in the mountains, in a rainy glen, hidden away from the troubles of the world." Her eyes drifted closed. "I'm glad I'm a hawk, too."

He sat there by her side most of the day, only leaving for short periods of time—to try the radio in the plane again, to make something to eat for himself. He made sure she didn't sleep too long at a time and listened for any sound that might mean someone was looking for them.

The hours passed slowly while he made his rounds

between the fire, the plane and the tent. Toward evening the rain stopped and he hoped the clearing skies would bring help, but by nightfall there was no sign of rescue.

Chapter 3

Paige dreamed of soaring in the sky, dipping and swooping down through mountains and valleys and over bubbling springs. Sometimes she was alone. Other times a beautiful hawk flew next to her. A hawk with luminous black eyes.

She was hot. Paige pushed against the covers, but they wouldn't move. She tried to sit up and couldn't. Her eyes reluctantly opened, but it was too dark to see anything.

Where am I? she wondered in confusion. Mental pictures flashed across her mind of a man—a campfire—rain dripping from the trees—a tent.

That was it. She was in a tent. She tried to move again and recognized the hard surface at her back was warm, and breathing. She was curled up with a man.

She didn't know any men on that basis. So what was she doing there?

Her head hurt, but nothing like it had been hurting. She rubbed along her temple and felt the large bump there. That's right. She'd got hit on the head. But how? And when?

A large, muscular arm rested across her waist, keeping her snug against the man who shared her bed. *This is a sleeping bag...I remember now. I'm camping with this man. What did he say his name was?*

She couldn't remember. While she concentrated on remembering—she knew it was imperative that she recall his name—Paige fell asleep once more.

Sunlight filtered through the open flap of the tent when Paige opened her eyes again. She was alone. Raising up on her elbow, she looked outside and saw sunshine. She also could see a man moving around a campfire and smell coffee brewing. It smelled wonderful.

When she sat up, Paige discovered that the horrible pounding in her head she'd experienced the day before was gone. Thank God.

Who was the man who had looked after her? She could remember him coming into the tent, stroking her hair, placing a damp cloth on her forehead, speaking to her, but it all seemed like something she'd dreamed.

Now, however, she had to face the fact that she was not dreaming. For some reason she was alone with a man she could swear she'd never seen before.

Not only did they seem to be camping together, they were sleeping together. Why? She could think of only one explanation—she must be married to him.

Paige tried to concentrate, tried to find some memory regarding a wedding. The only thing she got for her efforts was increased pain. If only she felt better, she was certain she'd be able to clear the confusion in her mind.

He had mentioned a plane. She rubbed her forehead distractedly. She remembered nothing about a plane.

Could it be possible she was married? She recalled the intimate way they'd spent the last two nights. She could think of no other explanation. Perhaps if she explained her lack of memory to him, he'd be willing to fill in the gaps for her.

Paige stretched, pleased to discover how much better she felt now that she had some course of action. Surely her memory loss was temporary. She glanced at the man by the fire once more. *It would help if I could remember his name.*

The tent was almost stifling when Paige crawled out of the bedroll. She looked around for her clothes, but all she saw was a backpack in the corner of the tent.

When she opened it, she found men's clothing. Shrugging at the inexplicable details of the trip, Paige dug around until she found a bright red-and-black-plaid shirt. It was much too large for her, but better than nothing. She rolled the sleeve up until she found her hand hidden in the folds, repeated the process with the other sleeve, then hesitantly stepped out of the tent.

"Where are my clothes?"

Hawk spun around at the sound of her voice. His jaw dropped. Paige stood in front of the tent with one of his shirts on. The shirttail hung halfway to her knees in front, but the sides came up high on her thighs. He caught his breath. Her long, well-shaped legs could be the envy of a Las Vegas showgirl. His gaze wandered to her trim ankles and bare feet before he forced himself to meet her eyes. He really hadn't needed a visual reminder of what he'd held in his arms for the past two nights.

She looked as if she felt better and he needed to say something—anything—to let her know he was glad. His tongue, however, seemed to have disappeared.

He strode over to the stack of bags and provisions covered by canvas and partially sheltered by a tree. He picked up her small bag and returned to her side.

"Here you are," he said quietly.

Paige felt shy around him for some reason. She accepted her bag with a nod and disappeared once again inside the tent.

Kneeling beside her suitcase, she threw open the lid, only to stare at its contents with dismay. There were a couple of changes of underwear, one pair of slacks and a few skirts and blouses. A pair of low-heeled shoes were tossed in on top. Outside of her small bag of toiletries, that was all she'd packed.

Paige threw open the flap to ask where the rest of her clothes were and remembered she didn't know her husband's name. The situation was ridiculous and getting worse by the minute.

"Where are the rest of my things?" she asked when he turned around.

Hawk walked over to the tent, concerned. "You only brought the one bag, Paige," he answered with a slight frown.

She nodded, determined not to get upset. Glancing over at the fire, she said, "That coffee smells delicious. I guess it's being out-of-doors or something, but I'm starved."

He lifted her chin and looked into her eyes. They were much clearer this morning. Surely it would be all right for her to eat something. "I'll pour you some coffee while you get dressed. Breakfast shouldn't take long."

When she stepped out of the tent, Hawk smiled reassuringly. Paige's navy-blue slacks and long-sleeved pink blouse looked more appropriate to their present environment than her suit, and the low-heeled shoes were much more practical than high heels.

Paige gave him a hesitant smile and Hawk impulsively walked over and held out his hand to her, much as he would have to a shy child. She brushed her thick hair behind her shoulder and slowly reached for his proffered support. They walked back to the fire together.

Hawk was relieved to have the rain gone, although

everything was still soaked. He threw a piece of canvas over a large rock and motioned for Paige to sit down.

She was weaker than she'd realized. Just the small amount of exertion she'd gone through made her head swim. Perhaps she'd take it easy today—maybe take a nap after she ate.

Hawk poured their coffee in silence while he tried to figure out a way to find out how she was feeling and what she could remember.

Paige accepted her cup and took a sip. *Ah, did that ever taste good!* She looked up and caught Hawk staring at her. It was no use. She couldn't remember anything about him and she might as well be honest before anything further developed between them!

"I might as well admit to you that I seem to have a problem." She glanced at him, then abruptly dropped her gaze to her cup of coffee. "I'm afraid the blow to my head knocked out a few rather important memories." She forced her gaze to meet his and was encouraged by the warm look in his eyes. "I not only don't remember your name, but I don't remember anything about our marriage."

Marriage! Alarms began to jangle in Hawk's head.

She nodded, determined to be completely open with him. "I don't even know what I did with my ring," she confessed, holding up her slender hand and revealing its bare condition.

Hawk stared at her, speechless. Where the hell did she get the idea they were married?

Then he recalled sharing the sleeping bag with her during the past two nights. At the time, it had seemed like a sensible idea. The first night she'd been in shock and he needed to get her warm. Body heat was the quickest way under the circumstances, and he'd stripped them both down and hurriedly placed her in the warm cocoon consisting of the two of them wrapped in a down-filled bed.

But what about the second night? Why don't you explain to her that you aren't married but that she's expected to share the only sleeping bag until you're rescued!

"Hawk," he finally managed to say.

She stared at him uncertainly.

"My name is Hawk."

"Hawk? Is that your last name, your first name, or a nickname?"

Her question surprised him. Few people asked, but then, few people cared. If she was somehow under the impression they were married, he supposed the question was understandable.

"My mother named me Black Hawk, but I took my father's name later. My legal papers state my name as Hawk Cameron, but I seldom use anything but Hawk."

She was quiet for several minutes, trying to assimilate the information he'd just given her. "Black Hawk is an unusual name."

He shrugged. "I suppose to most people. But to

my mother, who was a Jicarilla Apache, it was a fine name, very honorable."

"How did your father feel about your name?"

"He never heard it. According to my mother, my father never stayed in one place very long. He'd been gone several months before I showed up." He stated the facts surrounding his birth without expression.

She sat there trying to dredge up a mental picture of his mother, but drew a blank. "Hawk," she experimented. *Hawk Cameron. Mrs. Hawk Cameron. Paige Cameron. Paige Winston Cameron.* Why didn't it seem more familiar? For that matter, why didn't *he* seem more familiar?

Paige could feel the slight pressure in her head once more, and she recalled her dream of the miniature natives practicing their skills on her head. "Not again," she murmured distractedly.

"What's wrong?"

"It's my head," she muttered. "It feels like hammers are being pounded on it from all sides."

Hawk stood up suddenly. "Why don't you go lie down again and I'll try to find something light for you to eat. You still aren't recovered."

Paige rubbed her hand across her temple. "Yes, I'm sure I'll feel better once I rest for a while." He followed her into the tent and helped her take off her blouse and slacks with brisk efficiency. It was only when he brushed his hand through her hair, tenderly tucking a lock behind her ear, that Paige experienced an inexplicable feeling of unease. "We *are* married, aren't we?"

He gazed into her troubled eyes. *She needs to rest, and she doesn't need to worry about anything.* Those were the priorities of the moment.

Hawk kissed her gently on the forehead, then straightened, pulling the covers to her chin. Making a sudden decision, he responded, "Yes, Paige, we're married. Try to rest now."

She smiled and closed her eyes. Hawk left the tent and went back to the food cooking over the open fire. *Okay, smart guy, you've got all the answers. What do you intend to do now?*

Hours later he still hadn't come up with a solution. When he crawled inside the tent to check on her he discovered her gaze following his cramped movements. "There isn't much room in here, is there?" she asked softly.

"No," he agreed. "When I bought it I hadn't intended to share the tent with anyone."

"Have you had it long?"

He smiled. "For more years than I can remember."

"You must enjoy being out-of-doors."

"Yes, very much."

"I don't think I've ever been camping," she said uncertainly. "Or did you already know that?"

"No. But I had already guessed as much."

She shifted restlessly and he picked up her hand, letting it lie palm upward in his larger one. "Are you hungry?"

Paige couldn't get used to her reaction to him. Her skin tingled wherever he touched her. His warm gaze seemed to draw her closer to him somehow, and she had the strangest desire to wrap her arms around him—to be held in his arms.

She gave him a tentative smile. "A little."

"I'll bring you something to eat," he promised. "You just relax and I'll be right back." Hawk abruptly left the confined area.

What is she doing to me? he wondered in dismay. Her eyes seemed to haunt him. They were so expressive of her pain and bewilderment—and her wariness of him. *And why not? How can she be expected to remember a marriage that doesn't exist?*

As soon as she was stronger he'd tell her the truth. If they weren't found in the next few days they could make plans to hike out of the mountains. She'd be better able to handle the news about her father when she was stronger.

In the meantime, he saw no harm in fostering the idea that their trip was in the nature of a vacation. If it made her more comfortable to believe they were married, he'd allow her that fantasy. He'd just have to keep in mind their true status.

For some reason it was important to Hawk that Paige think well of him. Surely she'd understand the reason for his innocent deception once she remembered the reason for their flight.

Paige was asleep when Hawk returned to the tent with her meal. He decided to wait for her to wake up and stretched out beside her, enjoying the opportunity to leisurely study her.

He couldn't understand why all of his protective instincts were aroused by this woman. But she was like no other he'd ever known. Her clear, melodious voice seemed to gently flow through him, and he'd often caught himself absorbing its sound like the parched earth soaked up life-giving rain.

How ironic she thought they were married. No two people could be more different. She was well educated and obviously successful in her field. He, on the other hand, had learned about life the hard way.

Because of his inquisitive nature he'd picked up a considerable amount of knowledge during his travels—and he'd spent time over the years reading about subjects that fascinated him. But he knew he was far from the polished male that Paige was accustomed to.

"Why are you frowning?" Her voice startled him from his thoughts.

"I was just thinking."

Her lips curved into a gentle smile. "Ferocious thoughts, apparently."

He grinned. "Something like that. I'm afraid your meal is cold, but I thought you needed your rest."

She turned onto her side. "I feel as though all I've done is sleep. I haven't been very good company."

"I'm not complaining." He resisted the urge to lean over and kiss her. "I'll be right back with some hot food."

When he returned she was sitting up, pulling a

brush through her tangled hair. He handed her a plate, then set a steaming cup down beside her. Once again he left, this time returning with another plate and cup.

They ate in companionable silence. Hawk was glad to see that Paige had a good appetite. Even her color seemed to be improved. Hopefully the worst was over.

"Hawk?"

"Hmm?"

"Could you try to help me fill in some of the blanks in my memory?"

He tensed. "Are you sure you're ready to start probing? There isn't any real hurry, is there?"

She sighed. "I suppose not. I just feel so stupid at the moment."

"It seems to me that's a very understandable reaction. I'm sure anyone would feel the same way." He took their plates and stacked them on the ground near the opening of the tent. "Why don't you rest for a while longer? I'm sure everything will come back to you in time—just don't push it."

"Thank you for taking such good care of me, Hawk."

He glanced over his shoulder and grinned. "My pleasure." His smile caused a distinct disruption to her normally steady heartbeat.

He crawled out of the tent, then paused. "Try to look at this as a well-earned vacation. Relax and enjoy it." He picked up their dishes and walked away.

Of course, he was right. There was very little that

could be done. Either her memory would return or it wouldn't.

Paige couldn't help but wonder how long they'd been married. She found him very attractive and from a certain look she'd noticed she could tell that he felt the same way about her.

She smiled to herself as she curled up once again. *Not a bad reaction for a married couple to have toward each other. I must admit I've got darned good taste for picking a husband.*

Chapter 4

Hawk disgustedly climbed out of the plane a few hours later. Nothing. He could get absolutely nothing on the radio. He had even tried his portable, battery operated AM-FM radio and got nothing but static.

He jumped down off the wing of the plane and looked up at the mountains surrounding them. He wasn't surprised at the lack of reception.

Walking around to the front of the plane, Hawk winced at the damage. He'd hit a partially concealed rock after they'd touched ground, causing the left wheel to crumple. The plane had gone over on its nose, effectively demolishing the propeller and damaging the left wing. That was probably when Paige hit her head.

At least he hadn't ruptured the fuel line, so they

hadn't faced the added danger of fire. He just wished he knew what had gone wrong with the oil pressure.

At least they had been lucky in some respects. The camping equipment had come through relatively unharmed and it was making their forced stay much more pleasant. Paige was as comfortable as possible under the circumstances.

Paige. His thoughts kept coming back to her. He had checked on her several more times since they'd eaten. She'd been peacefully asleep with a slight smile on her lips every time he'd looked in on her.

Why did she have to be so beautiful? Not to mention lovable. He'd quickly discovered she wasn't the typically spoiled beautiful woman. In fact, she seemed unaware of her looks. Where had she been all these years not to know the impact she had on a man?

He hated to be the one to break the news to her that her father was gravely ill—and that at the present time there seemed no way to get her to him. He could only hope she would regain her memory on her own.

Hawk started back toward their campsite. He could hear the small stream as he approached it. He knew that all mountain streams flowed toward larger streams that eventually became rivers. If he were to follow it, the stream would lead him to people who had settled near the rivers. People meant telephones and rescue, but he didn't know how long it would take. He didn't dare try such a venture with Paige until she was fully recovered.

It was time to go check on her, time to plan something to eat again, time to decide what to tell her about their sleeping arrangements. He could feel his body's instinctive reaction to the idea. He wished he didn't find her so damned attractive. Now that she was feeling better, he had no excuse to continue to share the sleeping bag.

The alternative was to be a gentleman and use the extra blanket he'd brought along at the last minute. At this altitude the nights were never warm.

He had to face it—his mother had not raised a gentleman. So where did that leave them?

"Hawk?"

His head jerked up, and he saw her standing by the dying fire. She looked adorable, standing there with his plaid shirt serving as a jacket. She had brushed her hair until it fell in rippling waves onto her shoulders and down her back.

Seeing her standing there looking so young and vulnerable affected him strangely. He wanted to hold her close and protect her from harm. He also had to fight a strong urge to make passionate love to her. Hawk could understand the second urge, but he couldn't understand his fierce desire to protect her.

He took his time walking over to her, trying to get a grip on his emotions. "How do you feel?" he asked, lightly brushing his hand across her cheek.

She smiled. "Much better, thank you." She had trouble meeting his eyes. "Hawk, do you know where my hairpins are? I can't find any of them."

He grinned. "There's no telling. They're probably

strewn between here and the plane. But you don't need them."

She looked up at him in dismay. "Of course I do. I can't go around with my hair hanging in my face."

"You could always braid it."

She stared at him for a moment, then slowly smiled. "I suppose I could. Why didn't I think of that?"

He gathered her hair into both his hands, smoothing it, stroking the glossy waves. "I'll do it, if you'd like." She nodded and stood quietly while he plaited her hair into one long braid, tying it with a small piece of twine and letting it fall to her waist.

"You have beautiful hair," he said gruffly, stepping back from her. She turned around to thank him, the words dying on her lips when she saw the look in his eyes. They were blazing with intense heat.

She watched his mouth slowly lower to hers.

His lips felt surprisingly soft as they hesitantly touched hers, and Paige felt a ripple of feeling run through her body. His arms stole around her as though they had a will of their own and knew where they belonged. She felt a stirring deep inside her, a gentle awakening of sensations that she couldn't remember ever having experienced.

Hawk's kiss deepened and the intensity of his searching mouth seduced her into relaxing in his arms. Without a conscious decision Paige discovered she wanted to feel his mouth on hers, his warm, muscular body pressed intimately against her. She slipped her hands around his neck, bringing her even closer to him. Perhaps her mind had blotted out all memory of him, but her body reacted to him with sudden warmth and welcome.

His lips explored her face with gentle, loving touches. He seemed to be memorizing the surface of her face with his mouth—her eyes, the curve of her cheeks, the sensitive length of her neck. When Paige felt certain her knees would no longer support her he returned his mouth to her lips, seemingly starved for the taste of them.

As they kissed, Hawk loosened his hold on her, gently stroking her spine with his hands, learning the contours of her back and increasing the pressure until she felt almost a part of him.

Paige became aware of his body's reaction to her and knew what he expected—what he had a right to expect—and her heart seemed to stop beating in her chest.

No! Not yet! I don't know him. At least I don't remember. It's too soon. I'm not ready.

She turned her head from his seeking mouth and buried her face in his warm neck. "Hawk, please. We need to talk."

The sound of her breathless voice brought him back to his surroundings and what he was doing. Shocked at his intense reaction to her, he abruptly dropped his arms and stepped away from her.

"I'm sorry." His voice was a hoarse whisper.

She stared up at him, her eyes almost purple in their

darkened state. "It isn't your fault, Hawk. It's mine. I'm so sorry our trip turned out this way." She backed away from him, watching his face as he stared at her, confused.

Paige tried to joke about it. "It must be tough to look forward to a vacation only to discover your wife suddenly doesn't know you."

"Don't..."

"I'm sure this is only temporary, but you see, I guess I'm still a little shy with you. I'm just not ready to..."

"You don't have to explain to me, Paige. I'm sorry I got carried away just now. You have nothing to feel guilty about."

His eyes glowed intensely, and she couldn't resist resting her palm along his cheek. "I wish we could pretend we just met and get acquainted all over again."

His breath caught in his chest. She looked so wistful, and so very vulnerable. Actually, her suggestion had considerable merit. They had to do something while they waited and he needed to keep in mind not to touch her. He could handle that. He'd better be able to handle that.

Hawk stepped back from Paige and grinned. "Good idea. Why don't we get something going to eat before dark and we'll trade the stories of our lives." He paused, uncertain. "Or do you remember any of the past?"

She gave him a puzzled smile. "It's strange, because I seem to remember who I am and what I am, but I can't remember who you are or what we're doing here together."

Hawk dug through the food supplies and found a package that could be easily cooked in a pot over the grill. Paige sat down on a nearby boulder to watch. She knew she needed to learn more about how to survive in the wilderness.

When he didn't say anything, she finally said, "I've managed to figure out that we are camping, but I don't understand why. Did I dream it, or did you mention something about a plane?"

He glanced up from his meal preparation. "We were in a plane that I had to land during a storm." He stared out over the meadow. "You can't see it from here. I'll take you down there tomorrow, if you're feeling up to it. Maybe you'll recognize something."

"Where were we going?"

Damn. I was afraid you'd ask that question!

The silence lengthened between them. Finally Hawk looked up at her. "Well, I had in mind a camping trip, but not exactly here."

She laughed. "No, I can understand that. So you were flying the plane. Is that a hobby of yours?"

"No. That's how I make my living."

"Oh." In a musing tone, Paige continued, "You know, it's hard for me to think of you as my husband." Embarrassed at the admission, she dropped her gaze to the fire. Finally she forced herself to look at him. "Have we been married long?"

Hawk shook his head but kept his eyes on the stew he was stirring.

"I didn't think so. Otherwise, I don't think I could have forgotten you so completely." She studied the lean build of the man kneeling before her. He looked tough, but surprisingly graceful as he prepared their meal with economical movements. She shook her head ruefully. "I'm having to eat a lot of my words. I always said I would never get married."

That statement brought his gaze up to fasten intently on her. She noticed his surprised expression and blushed. She could actually feel the warmth spread over her neck and face. It was a rather absurd remark to make to her husband.

She knew he needed an explanation. "You see, I grew up watching how unhappy my mother was, married to a doctor. My father was rarely available to take her places. She could never count on his being home at a regular time for meals. Mother ended up having to make a life of her own, independent of my dad. They loved each other, there was never any question of that, but the life of a dedicated doctor precludes a normal married life." She paused, studying him. "Surely I told you all that when you first proposed, didn't I?"

She looked like a young girl sitting curled up on the rock with her braid draped across her shoulder. He straightened slowly and walked over to her. His eyes were on her level and he leaned toward her, kissing her gently on her nose. "No, we never did get around to discussing why you were still single when we met."

Paige was having trouble with her breathing, a condition that seemed to occur whenever Hawk was anywhere near. "Oh. Well, then I was extremely unfair to you not to have mentioned it."

Studying the man in front of her, Paige had a hunch she knew why she'd never mentioned it. Perhaps she hadn't wanted to discourage him. There was something elemental about him that spoke to her. In some respects she felt as though she'd always known him and been a part of his life.

She realized she was sitting there, holding her breath, hoping he would kiss her again. Paige acknowledged to herself that she wanted his arms around her, wanted to feel his strong body against hers. All of her senses pressed to convince her mind that she must love this man very much to have married him. Why fight her reaction to him?

Hawk's hands came up to rest lightly on Paige's waist. His mouth hovered inches from hers. "Are you ready to eat?" he asked softly.

Her obvious disappointment at his prosaic words would have been laughable if Hawk had been in the right frame of mind. He recognized her reaction to him and it didn't help him at all—it only made his strong response to her harder to control. One of them needed to stay in control of the situation, and she had enough to contend with trying to recover from her injury. Hawk couldn't hold her responsible for the misunderstanding of their relationship. He could only try to keep the situation within reasonable bounds.

While they ate they watched the sunlight slowly creep up the eastern cliff overlooking the meadow and disappear.

Evening approached. Hawk became lost in his thoughts of what tomorrow might bring. Search planes should have found them today. Since he'd seen or heard nothing, he had to accept the fact that there was a good possibility they would have to come to their own rescue.

"Are you based in El Paso?" Paige's question startled Hawk from his reverie.

"Yes."

"How long have you lived there?"

"A little over a year."

"You said you were a pilot. Do you have your own business?"

"No. I have a friend in the air charter business, and I've been helping him get it started."

"It sounds like fascinating work."

"I enjoy it."

"I have a feeling we don't have much time to spend together when we're both working." She glanced out over the peaceful scene. "Is that why we decided to go camping? To have more time together?"

He didn't want to lie anymore, but Hawk didn't

know what to say. Paige was taking their situation in stride, quickly adapting to the change in circumstances and her loss of memory. He could understand her need for answers, but he hated to continue the deception for any longer than was necessary.

"Paige, I know you're concerned about your memory, but don't push it. Most of your questions will be answered for you when you're feeling better." He stood up. "Why don't you try to get some sleep?" He picked up their dishes and began to clean them.

Paige knew he was right. She was still very wobbly, and the least amount of exertion seemed to tire her. She was surprised to discover how eager she was to learn more about this man. She had gone against a lifetime of strongly held principles in order to marry him. He had to be a very special person.

"Thank you, Hawk."

He looked up from building the fire for the night. "For what?"

"For taking care of me. For being so patient. I know all of this has been a strain on you."

He slowly came to his feet. They stood facing each other, the flickering fire between them. "You're very easy to care for, Paige."

She had an impulsive desire to fling herself into his arms and hold on to him, not a particularly sensible action if she was determined to keep some distance between them.

"I'm sure to feel more like my old self tomorrow."

"I agree. All you need is more rest." He looked

down toward the meadow. "I think I'll try the radio again. Who knows? Maybe this time I'll get lucky." Hawk took a couple of steps away, then paused. When he turned around, his face bore signs of strain. "Don't worry about my disturbing you, Paige. I've got a spare blanket. I think I'll sleep out here by the fire."

She tried to see the expression in his eyes, but the light from the fire wasn't bright enough. "Don't you want to sleep with me?"

"That's not the point. You need to get your rest, and—"

"I slept very well with you for the past two nights. Why should I be disturbed tonight?"

"Well, I, uh, you don't know me and—"

"I don't *remember* you, Hawk, there's a difference. You've made it clear you don't intend to push me. Believe me, I appreciate that very much, but there's no reason for you to sleep out here in the cold when we can continue to share the sleeping bag. Is there?"

Good question. Is there? Can you continue to fight the attraction and your reaction to her? Hawk ran his hand distractedly through his hair. *What can I say to her?*

"If anyone's going to sleep with the blanket," she said, "it will be me. I see no reason for you to be uncomfortable because I don't seem to have my head on straight."

They stood there staring at each other, two strong-willed people whom circumstances had thrown together in a bizarre situation.

Hawk sighed. "All right, Paige. We'll continue to share the sleeping bag, if that's the way you want it."

She could feel a bubbly sensation within her which she tried to cover with a formal nod of her head. "That's the way I want it."

She watched him walk away from her, disappearing in the darkness. The dancing arc of his flashlight helped her track his progress down the hill until even the light went out of sight.

Paige shivered, realizing that she was alone. Hurriedly she turned to the tent, glad to have the light from the fire to help her find her way. Her thoughts kept returning to the man who'd just left.

I love him, she told herself. *I must love him or I wouldn't be married to him.* Paige found one of Hawk's T-shirts in his backpack and decided to use it as a nightshirt. She sat down and pulled off her shoes.

He was an easy man to love. She thought of his quiet manner, his knowledge of the outdoors, his kindness to her. She thought of his magnificent build, of his voice that made her feel as though a soft brush had been smoothed across her body whenever he spoke to her. Most of all, she thought of how he made her feel every time he took her in his arms. She was pleased with her choice of a husband. If only she could remember making it!

When she curled up into the sleeping bag, Paige

hoped that when she woke up the next day, she would remember everything between them.

Hawk heartily hoped the same. On his way to the plane, he knelt beside the stream and stuck his hand into the icy water racing across the rocks. He tried not to think about the night and the enforced intimacy of their sleeping arrangements.

He'd tried. He'd even surprised himself. Paige was evoking too many unfamiliar emotions within him, and he didn't know how to deal with them. How else could he explain his chivalrous impulse? What had shocked him was the sincerity of his offer. He didn't want her to be uncomfortable around him. What he wanted was for her to accept him. Why? What in the hell difference did it make?

The tent was quiet when Hawk eventually crawled inside. Until now his camping gear had been perfectly adequate for the demands he made on it, but now he found himself wishing he'd gone for extra sleeping bags and a larger tent.

He shone his flashlight briefly around the area, careful not to send the full rays toward Paige. She was sound asleep. Good. She needed her rest, just as he needed his. He sighed, thinking about trying to sleep with her. The last two nights had been difficult. He was afraid tonight was going to be impossible, but he had to try.

She'd been through his things, he noticed. Not that it mattered, but he wondered what she'd been looking for. Was it possible she was trying to find out more about him? He looked at his clothes, tightly packed. Of course not. They would tell her nothing.

He sat down and pulled off his boots, pants and shirt. He carefully lifted the edge of the sleeping bag and smiled. She was wearing one of his undershirts, no doubt as an attempt at modesty. He wondered if she knew how fetching she looked in the soft shirt, her breasts impudently teasing him through the thin material with their provocative tilt.

He flipped off the flashlight, took several deep breaths, then eased his way down alongside her. The only way the two of them fit in the bag was for him to pull her into the curve of his arm and he reluctantly did so. She cuddled next to him as though they'd spent most of their lives sleeping together in that position.

Hawk sighed. It was going to be a long night. He tried to concentrate on the next day. He had to think of anything but the warm, tempting body lying so trustingly against him.

She stirred and murmured, "Good night, love."

His heart pounded in his chest. Was she even aware of what she'd called him? What would it be like to know he was this woman's love?

She said nothing more, and Hawk realized she was asleep. Yet even in her sleep she'd been aware of him, just as he was aware of her. His hand slowly stroked her shoulder, then down her side, where it slid into the indentation between her ribs and hips. She was so small—so delicate—and so precious. He pulled her closer to his side, then determinedly closed his eyes.

Chapter 5

Sparkling sunlight warmed the meadow in early-morning splendor. Tiny droplets of water clung to the tall blades of grass and multileafed bushes and trees. A young doe grazed by the stream, pausing to look around the glen for any sign of alien life. She noted only the natural inhabitants—a family of rabbits, a couple of noisy squirrels and a busy racoon, already about their day's business. A blue jay scolded a venturesome chipmunk, and a mockingbird mimicked the lecture.

After three days the natural inhabitants of the meadow had come to accept the unusual presence of the ungainly birdlike structure lying drunkenly in their midst.

Hawk stood on the knoll near the tent, absorbing

the scene before him. The place had everything he had intended to find in Mexico, with one addition—the beautiful woman he'd left asleep inside his tent.

He rubbed the back of his neck ruefully. The sleeping arrangements may have become acceptable to Paige, but the forced intimacy was playing havoc with Hawk. Celibacy had never been one of his virtues, particularly when he was continually reminded of the condition by the constant presence of an attractive and intelligent woman. No one who knew him would believe his behavior these past few days. He had trouble believing it himself.

He would have to stay away from her—keep himself busy exploring and fishing. Under ordinary circumstances, that should be all that was necessary. He raised his arms high above his head and stretched, trying to get the kinks out of his back. Unfortunately, these weren't ordinary circumstances.

Hawk strode down the hill. He might as well start making plans to get them out of there as soon as Paige could travel. Glancing around at the cliffs, he decided the first thing to do would be to get up where he could see the surrounding area. Maybe he would spot something—some sign of civilization. If so, he could probably leave Paige alone for a few hours while he went for help.

With a definite plan of action in mind, Hawk felt more in control of the situation. *Someday I'll look back on this episode and laugh. I'll remember it as my closest encounter with matrimony.*

* * *

Paige reached for Hawk, her eyes opening when she couldn't find him. Confused, she sat up. The tent gave mute testimony that she was alone. Slowly Paige settled back into the covers.

She barely remembered his coming to bed last night, yet she knew he'd been there. At one point she'd awakened to find herself curled on his chest, her face buried in his neck. She smiled at the memory.

What a set of new experiences she'd encountered in the past few days. She'd never before spent a night out-of-doors, never cooked on an open fire, and never tried to stay clean with the help of water dancing merrily along in a small stream. She was surprised to discover how much she'd enjoyed it. Maybe the bump on her head had changed her entire perspective. She couldn't remember ever feeling so lighthearted, so eager to involve herself in something besides her profession.

Paige had a fleeting thought of her father. She hoped her being away wouldn't create too much work on the rest of them, although her father was always nagging her to take some time off. He believed in periodic vacations as a means of resting the mind as well as the body.

Vacation. What was it about the thought of a vacation that bothered her so? Not her vacation—her father's.

He'd been planning to go to Flagstaff, to do some fishing. Had he gone? Paige rubbed her head uneasily.

The pain was never far away, it seemed, and it got worse when she thought of her father. How strange.

She closed her eyes and tried to relax. *Don't push it. Each day you're better than the day before. Relax. Think of something soothing and pleasant.*

Her thoughts drifted, eventually settling on a pleasing subject. Hawk. The name fit him. He seemed to be a part of the outdoors, in tune with nature.

She found him fascinating. Hawk didn't need to call attention to himself—he'd be noticeable in any group. His strength seemed to be an innate part of him, something he took for granted. She found herself watching him whenever he was in sight. He moved with the flowing grace of a large cat. His worn Levi's and multiwashed shirts emphasized his muscular frame, and yet he seemed unconscious of his appearance. He also seemed unconscious of her, treating her more as an acquaintance than as his wife.

Paige sighed, then brightened slightly as she remembered the night before. Hawk might be cool toward her during the day, but at night he held her as though she were part of him.

Was it possible they had quarreled? Perhaps the trip had been planned to draw them closer together. From knowledge of her own nature, Paige had a hunch the problem stemmed from her obsession with her work.

If only she could remember. Because if that were true, she'd need to use their time together to mend the breach between them.

Now that she was awake, she might as well get up.

Throwing back the covers, Paige reached for her pants with a frown. They were so hot during the day, but what else did she have to wear?

Digging into her small case, she came up with one of her straight skirts. With a little ingenuity, she could alter the skirt into a pair of shorts, which would provide some welcome relief from the warm, sunny days.

Paige found her emergency sewing kit in her handbag, then sat down crosslegged on the sleeping bag and started ripping out stitches in the skirt. Her small scissors gave her the most trouble, but she finally managed to cut off some of the length of the skirt.

It was almost an hour later when she stepped out of the tent. Her newly-made shorts hugged the curve of her hips, ending high on her thighs. She wore a thin, jade-green blouse with the top two buttons open, the tail tied in a knot under her breasts.

Too bad Hawk isn't here, she thought with a grin. *I could announce to him that he's Tarzan, me Jane.*

The sun was already high in the sky, but Paige saw no sign of Hawk. Should she wait or go ahead and eat without him? She wandered down to the stream and washed her face and hands. Oh, what she wouldn't give for a hot bath, or even a shower. Camping certainly left out a few of the basic amenities she'd always taken for granted.

A shadow fell over her and she glanced up, startled. Hawk stood between her and the sun—and her stomach flipped over. The only thing he wore was a pair of Levi's, hung low on his lean hips, and a scuffed pair of moccasins. He could have posed for one of Remington's paintings.

His chest was wide and muscled, and her fingers twitched with the remembered sensations of touching him there. The muscles in his arms rippled when he rested his hands lightly on his hips. His skin glistened in the sun, and for a moment she thought it was from perspiration, but when she slowly came to her feet she realized he was soaking wet, water forming tiny rivulets through his hair and coursing down his neck and shoulders.

Her mouth felt dry, and she had to swallow before she could speak. Searching frantically for a light tone, she asked, "What happened, did you fall in?"

Hawk noticed with dismay Paige's new outfit, and he knew without a shadow of a doubt his willpower was being tested to its limits. Once again she had her hair in a single braid, and the thin blouse did nothing to hide the jaunty tilt of her breasts. The sleek shorts she wore merely emphasized the beautiful shape of her legs.

What had she just said? He shook his head, and the tiny droplets flew over them both. She backed away with a laugh, her hands trying to shield her face.

"I'd love to have a shower, Hawk, but that wasn't exactly what I had in mind."

She glanced up at him, her eyes sparkling, her skin glowing, her smile causing his heart to pound in his chest, and his feelings for her exploded within him. It was at that moment that he knew he loved her.

Hawk had never experienced the emotion before; he had never even come close, and he had no idea what to do about it. He just recognized that what he was feeling for the laughing woman before him was love, and it was slowly driving him out of his mind.

"Are you serious about wanting to take a shower?"

The sun was still in her eyes and she couldn't see Hawk's face clearly, but his voice sounded strained.

"Oh, yes. I'd love to be able to really scrub down and feel clean."

He glanced at the towel and washcloth she carried, items she'd found in his bag along with a bar of soap. "There's a waterfall not far from here where you can shower and bathe. Do you want to go now, or wait until after we eat? The water will be a little warmer then."

She glanced around the meadow, already cherishing the area. Why hadn't she known of the joys of outdoor living, especially if they included a shower? She grabbed his hand. "Let's eat first. I'll show you how much I've learned about cooking over an open fire." She ran ahead of him, pulling him laughingly behind her. Then she made a ceremony of brushing off a place for him to sit down so that he could watch her preparations.

"How's your head?" He studied her face and wondered if she knew about the five freckles that artistically decorated her dainty nose. Only the bruise near her temple marred the delicate softness of her skin.

Paige looked up from stirring the biscuit mixture she intended to bake in the iron skillet. "It's fine. Really."

"Have you remembered anything more?"

She glanced down at the bowl she held, then forced her gaze to meet his. "No. I'm sorry."

"You don't have to apologize. It's not your fault."

"Well, maybe not, but it certainly has put a crimp in our vacation together."

"Uh, Paige, I want to talk to you about that..."

"Good, because I want to talk to *you* about it as well!"

She placed the biscuits in the skillet, covering them as she'd seen him do, then started mixing the dehydrated eggs with canned milk. She learned quickly, he had to give her that.

"All right," he said quietly. "What did you want to say?"

Now that she had his undivided attention, she was unsure of herself. She'd been rehearsing what she would say, but it was different with him sitting there, half dressed, watching her so intently. "Well...I've been having some uneasy feelings about us." She paused, but couldn't bring herself to look at him.

He didn't respond.

"You mentioned that we hadn't been married long. From what I can tell, you're a very independent person." She glanced up at him and was surprised to see a slight smile hovering on his lips.

"That's very true."

She nodded. "So am I. I'm also opinionated and hardheaded." She waited, but he didn't comment. Their argument must have been worse than she thought! "What I'm trying to say is I feel there's something wrong between us. Did we have a fight about something?"

"No, Paige. That isn't it at all."

Okay. Now is the time to tell her the truth, painful though it might be for her. With calm deliberation, Hawk began. "I met you when you came to the air charter service and chartered a plane."

She looked puzzled. "Why ever would I do a thing like that? I don't even like to fly."

"You said you wanted to fly to Flagstaff to see your father." He watched her and waited for her reaction.

A sudden pain shot through her head. Paige absently rubbed her temple. Her father. Flagstaff. He had planned to go to Flagstaff on his vacation. Had he already gone? He must have. Why else would she be joining him? But why?

"If my father were in Flagstaff, I don't understand why I would go as well. We would be very shorthanded at the clinic." She shook her head, bewildered. "It doesn't make sense. Nothing makes sense." She caught Hawk watching her intently.

"Hawk, how long have we known each other?"

Hawk answered her in a firm, deliberate tone. "We just met."

She stared at him with a mixture of horror and dismay on her face. Hawk waited for her to reach the natural conclusion. Only she didn't.

"I can't believe it. I eloped with someone I barely knew!" She stared at him in shock, but she was in no greater shock than he. That was not the conclusion he'd expected her to reach. It was not the conclusion that was going to help him out of the situation he was in. What the hell was he supposed to say to her now?

She sank down beside the fire and abstractedly stirred their breakfast. Almost talking to herself, she muttered, "I must have been under a tremendous strain. My years of constantly pushing myself must have been too much for me." She glanced up at him. "Was I by any chance running screaming down the streets when you first saw me?"

He started laughing, then shook his head.

"Will you be honest with me? I mean, give me a straight answer if I ask you something?" She came over and knelt in front of him.

At last, here it comes, and the charade will be over. Not before its time, he thought.

She stared at him in solemn concentration. "Did I ask you to marry me?"

Bewildered by her intense expression and the tension he could feel radiating from her body, he slowly shook his head no.

"Oh, thank God!" she said, and threw her arms around him in an expression of relief. Breakfast was forgotten for the moment. Hawk found himself flat on his back, with Paige staring down at him from her position on his chest. "Oh, Hawk, you had me so worried. I've never been interested in dating, or getting involved with anyone. I never had the time or inclination for flirtations or affairs. And for a moment I thought you were going to tell me I'd engineered our whole relationship." She stared into his dark eyes, seeing herself mirrored there. "I'm so glad you were crazy enough to propose to someone you barely knew—and so glad I was crazy enough to say yes!"

With those last words her mouth settled contentedly on Hawk's, proving once again she was a fast learner. She traced his lower lip with her tongue, her lips moving lightly over the surface of his firm mouth, while her hands gently explored the wide expanse of his chest.

Hawk's arms came around her. Somewhere in his deepest conscience alarms were going off, but he was obeying instincts older than his conscience. He held her to him, her body resting lightly on top of his, her breasts lying trustingly open to his view. His hand slid into the opening of her blouse, gently touching her. Her body quivered like an arrow finding its mark. He could feel his self-imposed restraints slipping away from him. She felt so good in his arms, just as though that's where she belonged.

Hawk smelled something burning.

He rolled, laying her on the ground, and leaped to his feet. Their breakfast was smoldering on the fire. He managed to rescue the pans, but the ingredients were past saving.

"Lesson number one, young lady. A cook never leaves the kitchen while preparing meals."

Paige lay on her back, breathless, and watched Hawk as he found more food and began to prepare another meal. While she caught her breath she tried to deal with the new information she'd just received. Staid, stodgy Dr. Paige Winston, the dedicated spinster of the pediatrics ward, had so fallen out of character as to meet a tall, dashing stranger and elope with him.

She wondered if her father knew about it. Exactly how long had they been married? Could it be possible they were on their honeymoon? Hawk would have some more questions to answer—but not quite yet. She needed time to think things through. Every new bit of information unnerved her. Paige wasn't sure she was ready to face what their relationship would do to her settled way of life.

I suppose Hawk didn't know how to tell me we had just gotten married. That's why being married seemed so strange to me at first. We've probably never even made love. The thought of the two of them making love seemed to set all her nerve endings tingling.

She watched the sun glisten on Hawk's bronzed back. *It will be up to me to change the situation. He's made it clear he doesn't intend to touch me.* She smiled at the thought that he was willing to wait for her memory to return before initiating lovemaking. How could she let him know that she'd built up enough memories about him since they'd been there?

Paige trusted her own judgment. Whatever her reasons that had convinced her to marry him in the first place were good enough for her now.

Hawk turned to call her over to eat and found Paige staring at him with warm tenderness. He realized she was still under the impression they were married. Their situation was becoming increasingly explosive. The safest course for them both was for him to tell her about her father and the truth about them, and ask her to forgive him his deception.

I'll tell her right after we eat.

Chapter 6

Only he didn't. Instead, Paige convinced him she felt well enough to go exploring.

"Do I have to put on my long pants?" She glanced down at her bare legs.

"Aren't you afraid you'll burn?" Hawk resolutely kept his eyes on her face.

Paige stared up at the sun for a moment, then shrugged. "I'd rather risk it than put on those hot slacks again." With a warm smile she added, "Perhaps we can stay in the shade."

When she smiled at him Hawk had trouble remembering his train of thought. "We won't leave the meadow, so you probably will be all right."

Paige looked out over the pastoral scene. "How big is the meadow?"

Hawk checked the fire, then started down toward the water. "I'd guess it's about a mile long, maybe a half-mile wide." He pointed downstream. "Not too far in that direction the area narrows into a canyon."

"Have you been that far?"

"Yes. I also climbed the ridge behind us, hoping I'd see some sign of civilization. But no luck."

They crossed the stream, and Paige walked over to the plane. It was the first time she'd been up close to it. She studied it thoughtfully. It didn't look at all familiar. She tried to picture herself in it, but couldn't. Flying wasn't one of her favorite things to do. It was ironic she'd married a pilot.

Paige found the view from the valley very appealing—so peaceful and untouched. She felt as though she and Hawk were the only two people on earth.

A sudden thought occurred to her. "There must be a radio in the plane. Have you been trying it?"

Hawk nodded. "I've been trying it for days, but can't pick up anything."

"Do you think anyone will find us?"

"I'm beginning to have my doubts. They would have located us by now, I'm afraid."

"What if nobody finds us?"

"We'll have to hike out of here."

"When?"

He looked up in the sky as though waiting for divine guidance. "I'm not sure. If I were alone I'd leave today, but I don't think you're ready to try it."

"Why not?"

"Because you're still not recovered from that knock on your head." He glanced down at her shoes. "And I'm concerned that you don't have the proper shoes or clothes to take the strain of a trip like that. From what I could see, the going won't be easy."

"So we sit and wait."

"For a while, yes."

"I don't mind. I'm really enjoying the vacation. I just feel guilty being away from the clinic. But it's too late to worry about it. I must have made some sort of arrangements before I left."

Hawk was silent. He didn't know what to do about her continued loss of memory. On the one hand, so long as she thought they were married and this was only a slight alteration of their original plans, Paige was relaxed. Getting upset would be the worst thing for her.

Learning that her father had suffered a heart attack would be a tremendous shock to her, he knew. It was obvious the two of them were very close. She would be frantic to get out of there.

He glanced toward the end of the meadow and wondered how long it would take them to find help. She might be able to take a day's hike, if they took it easy. But what if it took several days, even a week? He hated to take the risk.

"How about my showing you that waterfall I told you about?" Hawk waited for her to join him by the stream before he added, "Would you like to take a shower now?"

"Would I? Just lead the way."

They returned to the tent and gathered up towels, soap and Paige's shampoo, then started down the hill once more.

Hawk led the way, Paige content to follow and enjoy the scenery. A slight path showed through the grass along the stream, and Paige realized Hawk had been along there enough to leave a faint trail. It wound along beside the water, skirting boulders and trees, but always returned to follow the stream wherever possible.

Paige heard the sound of rushing water before she saw it. A large overhang, part of the hillside that appeared to have been eroded by the elements, jutted out over the stream, hiding the waterfall from sight.

Hawk took Paige's hand and helped her over the rocks and dirt that had formed a blockade of sorts to their passage. They paused when they reached the top.

"Oh, Hawk, this is beautiful."

From their viewpoint the waterfall still towered above them at almost a right angle to the previous course of the stream. The abrupt turn had formed a pool where the water eddied and circled before finding its way downhill once more. The sunlight caught the water in flashes of brilliant crystal. Paige could hardly wait to get into it.

She looked at Hawk uncertainly. She just couldn't go in while he was standing there watching her.

He glanced down at her and smiled. "I think I'm going to go a little farther upstream for a while. Why don't you stay here and bathe? I should be back in about a half hour or so."

Bless you for being so understanding, she thought. She nodded shyly and began the descent to the water while Hawk turned his back and started up the higher incline that created the waterfall.

The area near the stream was strewn with rocks of various sizes. Paige found one that was flat enough so she could sit down. She pulled off her shoes, regarding them with concern. The soft leather was scratched and scuffed. They'd certainly taken a beating during the past few days.

She slipped her shorts and shirt off, folded them neatly, then laid them in a stack. Standing up, she glanced around self-consciously before she stepped out of her briefs. Hastily removing her bra, Paige stepped gingerly into the water. The summer sun had taken some of the icy chill away, and it felt good.

Moving carefully, Paige waded toward the waterfall, eager to feel its freshness beating upon her. The bottom suddenly disappeared and she let out a yelp as she plunged in deeper. The sun hadn't had a chance to warm the depths, and the cold water caused shivers to dance across her skin.

Paige determinedly swam across the pool until the spray from above started falling around her. She felt for bottom and eventually found it. The water was up to her shoulders.

Since her hair was already wet, Paige went back for her shampoo and vigorously scrubbed her head.

Never before had she appreciated the feeling of clean hair quite so much.

After thoroughly rinsing her hair, Paige swam over to the edge of the pool where it was shallow enough for her to stand and soap herself. Now that she was used to the water temperature she found it invigorating. *All the comforts of home.*

Aware of time passing, bringing Hawk's return near, Paige quickly finished and swam to the deeper water. She felt so good. Perhaps she could talk Hawk into taking her on up the trail. She waded back to the side of the pool where her clothes lay. Once again she glanced around shyly before grabbing her towel and briskly drying off. Within minutes she was dressed.

There was still no sign of Hawk, and Paige relaxed by stretching out on the large flat rock and turning her face up to the sun. She lay there with her eyes closed, listening to the sounds of the glade—the twittering of the birds in the trees, the slight rustling of the leaves as a playful breeze flirted among them—and slowly drifted off to sleep.

Hawk watched Paige from his position high on the cliff near where the water fell to the rocks below. He had given her plenty of time to bathe and get dressed—or so he had thought. But when he'd paused at the edge of the drop before following the trail downward, he'd discovered that Paige was at that moment stepping out of the water.

The shock of seeing her nude stopped him in his

tracks. He'd undressed her in the dark the night they were forced down. His only concern at that time had been to care for her and to bring her body temperature up.

Now he could see her in the sparkling sunlight, her hair streaming down her back, her shoulders narrowing to a tiny waistline, her hips swelling in a gentle curve that he found utterly enticing.

She was already dressed and stretched out on the rock before he realized he'd been standing there watching her like some sort of Peeping Tom. *Is this what you're reduced to?* he asked himself in disgust. Thank God she hadn't seen him lurking up there as though hoping to catch her. He shook his head, trying to clear it, and started down the steep slope.

A cloud passed across the sun, or so it felt to Paige, and she opened her eyes. Hawk stood there, his shadow across her. She smiled, a sleepy, contented smile, and stretched. "That was marvelous, Hawk. Thank you for bringing me up here."

"No problem," he responded in a gruff voice. "Are you ready to go back?"

She sat up. "Not really. I managed to rest while I was waiting for you." She stood up. "Would you mind if we go up the trail a little farther?"

How could he deny her anything when she looked at him like that? Maybe it would help him to exercise some of his frustrations out of his system.

He held out his hand. "We'll go if you'll promise not to overdo it."

She took his hand and held her other one up in a pledge position. "I promise," she vowed.

Paige was enthralled with the variety of plants, birds and animals they saw as well as Hawk's knowledge of them all. He knew their names, and he knew what plants could be used for medicinal purposes. He seemed to be at home in that environment, and Paige found herself envying him his freedom.

Now that you're married to him, it can be your environment too, she reminded herself. She sighed in contentment.

The climb was more strenuous than Paige had anticipated, and by the time they reached the ridge overlooking the meadow her head felt as though the little natives were back, hammering ferociously.

Hawk took one look at her white face and swore. "I knew better than to let you come this far. Your headache's back, isn't it?"

"A little," she admitted. "I just need to rest for a moment. I'll be okay." She sank down on a rock and tried to let the view soothe her.

Hawk sat down beside her and gathered her into his arms. "I'm so sorry, honey."

She rested her head against his chest. His heart seemed to be racing. "It's not your fault, Hawk."

"I'm responsible for you, and I haven't done a very good job of looking after you."

"You've done an excellent job of looking after me. How do you think I would survive in the wilderness alone?"

"But that's the point. We shouldn't have to be camping at all."

She pulled her head back and gazed at him. "You never intended to take me camping, did you?"

"No."

At least that explained why she didn't have the proper clothes for camping. "You were taking me to Flagstaff to leave me with my father, weren't you?"

"Yes."

What could have happened to their relationship in a few short days that she would have run to her father and he would have made plans to go off camping without her?

She knows most of it now, Hawk thought. *Let her think we've had a fight, at least until I can get her to her father.*

"Do you think you feel up to starting back?" He deliberately lightened his tone. "It's always easier going downhill."

All she wanted to do was lie down, but first she had to make it back to camp. Paige stood up and swayed.

Without a word Hawk lifted her into his arms. She fastened her hands behind his neck, laid her head on his chest with a soft sigh, and closed her eyes. She felt tired, so very tired.

Hawk took his time making sure each step he took was firmly placed. Thankfully he found a more circuitous route back to the campsite that wasn't as steep as the way they had come.

He felt Paige relax in his arms and realized she'd fallen asleep. He pulled her closer to him. She looked like a child being carried to bed, and he felt his heart expand with love for her.

How could he regret their time together—regret the chance to get to know Paige? He glanced down at her once again. She still had mauve smudges under her eyes. Why had he allowed her to coax him into ignoring his better judgment?

Because you become melted butter whenever she looks at you with those wide, pansy-colored eyes.

They reached camp at dusk. Paige had not awakened. Hawk carefully laid her on the bedroll, then returned to the fire and made plans for a meal. Thank God they had sufficient provisions. They could stay there for weeks if necessary. Only Hawk knew he couldn't last that long around Paige without cracking under the strain of wanting to make love to her. His whole body ached, and only part of the pain could be blamed on the hike he'd made that afternoon with Paige in his arms.

Night had drawn its anonymous cloak around them when Paige joined Hawk by the fire. "I'm sorry to conk out on you like that."

Hawk smiled. "No problem. Feeling better now?"

Paige nodded. "I don't understand why the pain gets so bad at times. Whenever I try to concentrate—to remember—my head feels like it's going to explode."

He handed her a plate and a steaming cup. "The

answer is obvious, doctor. Don't think. Don't concentrate. Let it come in its own time."

"That's easy for you to say. You don't have any missing gaps in your memory."

"What I'm trying to say is that worrying about it not only isn't helping you, it's actually causing more harm."

She was silent while she thought about what he said. She began to eat. He was right—as usual. They ate in companionable silence while they watched the fire flicker and dance before them.

"Have we ever made love?" Paige inquired abruptly, ending the silence.

Unfortunately Hawk had just taken a swallow of coffee. He choked. In a strangled voice he finally managed to get out, "What on earth made you ask that?"

"I've been thinking about everything you've said. You avoid discussion of our marriage as though it were a mistake. You've admitted we haven't known each other long, so we obviously haven't been married long, and for some reason you don't seem to want to discuss it."

Hawk stood up. "That's right. I don't. Have you finished eating?"

Paige looked down at her plate, surprised to see it empty. "I guess I have."

He took her dishes, then brought her cup back to her full of coffee. Sitting down beside her, Hawk took her hand in his.

"Paige, please drop the subject of our marriage. Forget it. It isn't important at the moment. What is important is for you to relax, quit probing and get well. We're going to be faced with hiking out of here one of these days, I'm afraid. You've got to be ready for that." He turned her hand palm upward and slowly traced her life line with his index finger. "I care for you very much and I promise that I won't ever do anything to hurt you. You're going to have to trust me."

"I do. I've already trusted you with my life. I just don't understand what went wrong between us."

"Nothing went wrong between us. Won't you accept that?"

"I suppose I have to."

"It would help." He stood up, pulling her up with him. "Go to bed now and try to get some more rest. Will you do that, please?"

Paige's gaze searched his face. He looked grim, almost in pain. She wanted to wipe away the look of strain, to hold him close and convince him that whatever their problems, they could work them out together.

"All right, Hawk. Whatever you say." She went up on tiptoe and brushed her lips gently against his. "Good night, love."

He watched her disappear inside the tent. Hawk picked up his coffee cup and for the first time since he'd been forced to land wished for something stronger to drink.

Hawk sat in front of the fire staring into the flames for several hours. Maybe he couldn't control loving her, but he could damned well control what he did about it.

He intended to do nothing. Nothing at all.

Chapter 7

"After I left the Middle East, I was in Southeast Asia for about three years." Hawk sorted through his fishing gear as he talked. He and Paige were by a pool formed by a turn in the stream that ran through the meadow. Hawk was leaning on his elbow as he picked up weights and lures, then carefully separated them into the tiny compartments of his fishing tackle box.

Paige lay flat on her back a couple of feet away. She was enjoying the quiet sounds of the meadow, the shade of the aspen where they had decided to rest, but most of all, she was enjoying Hawk telling her about his life. "Were you ever in the military?"

He shook his head. "No, I did some work for our armed forces, but on a civilian basis."

She watched the leafy shadows form patterns of light and shadow across him. Once again Hawk had dispensed with a shirt, and Paige stared at his tanned chest with unconscious yearning. "Haven't you ever had a place you called home, Hawk?"

He stared off in the distance for a moment, sorting through his memories. "I was born on the reservation near Dulce, New Mexico. For the first fourteen years of my life, I lived with my mother. I enjoyed those years...took them for granted." He gave his head a tiny shake. "But my mother got pneumonia one winter, and died." His fist clenched, the only sign of emotion she saw. "There was no excuse for losing her. I don't think she cared if she lived or not. She felt she'd raised me, I suppose, and wasn't needed." The quiet ripple of the water was the only sound. "She was wrong...but I never had a chance to tell her differently," he finally said in a low tone.

"So you left," Paige guessed. "And you decided you didn't need anyone."

He glanced at her in surprise. "Why do you say that?"

"Because I've seen children react in that manner when they've lost someone close to them. It's a fear of allowing someone else to get close and perhaps losing them as well." She picked up a twig and traced the blade of grass in front of her. "It's hard to lose someone when you're so young. I was eighteen when Mother died of cancer."

"But you had your father," he reminded her.

She smiled. "Yes. He was there for me, and I'll always be grateful for that. He helped me through the healing process that follows grief." Paige was silent for a few moments, then added, "I'd like to think we helped each other." She glanced up at him. "Have you met my dad?"

Hawk shook his head.

"I think you'll like him." Her eyes sparkled as she took in his indolent pose beside her. "I *know* he'll like you." She wrinkled her nose at him. "You're just what the doctor ordered."

Paige rolled to her side and leaned up on her elbow. Hawk had finished with his tackle box and had sat it behind him. Now she lay inches away from him. He could smell the light fragrance she wore, the heat of the summer day enhancing it, mingled with the soft, evocative smell that was her. He took a deep breath, trying to ignore the messages his senses were giving him. "What do you mean?"

"You have to understand that even as a little girl I was always seriously determined to grow up to be a doctor. With that type of dedication, I refused to allow anything to distract me." She ran her finger down his nose. "Even boys."

"You mean you never dated?"

"Some. I went to all the school activities and dances, that sort of thing, but I just wasn't interested in involvement. I wanted to hurry and grow up—to get on with life."

"It looks like you succeeded."

"Too much, according to Dad. He says I haven't taken time to stop and enjoy myself along the way." She gazed out across the meadow. "I'm beginning to understand what he meant."

Her sigh of contentment reminded Hawk that he needed to do something about their situation. He studied Paige, lying so close beside him. Did she have the stamina to hike out?

Their time during the past few days had been well spent. Paige no longer seemed to be suffering from headaches and her energy level was steadily increasing. He wished he had some idea how far they'd have to hike to find help. He'd be better prepared to make a decision.

"Paige?"

"Hmm?"

"Do you think you'd be up to hiking out of here?"

She looked at him in surprise. "I guess so. Are you getting bored?"

He laughed. "No, as a matter of fact, I'm not."

She smiled, and his heart seemed to melt in his chest. "I'm glad. Neither am I."

"What I'm saying is...I don't think anyone is going to find us, so we might better start seeing about rescuing ourselves."

She stretched, raising her arm high over her head. When she brought it down, it landed lightly on his shoulder. She began to draw small circles on his bare flesh. "Are you sorry you ended up having to camp with me?"

Hawk could feel his body tensing at her touch. Dear God, how he wished she would remember the truth. *Do you, really?* an inner voice whispered to him. *Aren't you enjoying your time with her more than you've ever enjoyed anything in your life?*

He sat up. "Not really."

Paige grinned. "I'm glad." She sat up too, and rested her head on his shoulder. "Next camping trip I'll make sure to pack the right kind of clothes."

"Paige..."

"Hawk..." They spoke at the same time.

"What were you going to say?" he asked.

"Nothing important, really. I just wondered if you'd like to go swimming."

"Swimming?"

"Uh-huh. It's really warm today. You know where that waterfall is—where we've been showering. It's deep enough to swim, if you'd like to."

If I'd like to!

Paige jumped to her feet. "Come on. Let's try it—you might even like it." She laughed, a light, happy sound that was Hawk's undoing. He wanted this woman to be happy. He wanted to spend the rest of his life making her happy, but he didn't have the slightest idea how to do that.

She grabbed his hand and pulled him to his feet, leading the way while they followed the stream to the waterfall. The splashing water made a merry sound in the quiet of the warm day.

Paige immediately sat down and took off her shoes.

It occurred to Hawk that swimming wasn't a good idea, but he couldn't seem to find his voice to explain why before she took off her blouse and shorts.

The tiny wisps of clothing she now wore hid nothing from view. Her skin turned a rosy hue as she determinedly met his startled gaze. "I don't know why I'm so bashful with you. After all, we *are* married." With a hint of defiance she unsnapped her bra, then stepped out of her tiny briefs.

The past few days had begun to tan her arms and legs, and her tan emphasized the ivory sheen of the rest of her. Hawk could only stare.

His gaze caused her blush to burn deeper, and Paige hurriedly lowered herself into the water. *How brazen can you get,* she admonished herself. *He's been a perfect gentleman, considerate of your condition, and you're flaunting yourself like some sex-starved wanton.*

But she wanted to let him know that her loss of memory didn't have to prevent them from enjoying their idyllic time together. His aloof attitude was no longer necessary, but she didn't know how to tell him. Hopefully he would understand that she was showing him.

She heard a splash behind her and knew that Hawk had joined her, but she didn't quite have the courage to turn around and face him. Instead, she swam to the side of the pool where they had left the soap and shampoo. She began to unbraid her hair, impatiently tugging at the strands. When her hair was free, she vigorously shampooed it, working up a lather, then stood under the waterfall to rinse it.

After diving under the water to make sure all the soap was gone, Paige came up face first, squeezing the water from her hair. Hawk stood a few feet away, watching her with such a tender, yearning expression her heart felt as though it would burst within her.

The water barely covered his hips. He'd followed her example and left his clothes on the large rock beside the stream. The sun on the water shot sparks of light all around him. The water glistened on his shoulders and chest, and Paige knew he was the most beautiful thing she'd ever seen—handsomely rugged, symmetrically formed, his face reflecting his love for her. *Of course he loves me, just as I love him. That's the best reason for marriage I know.*

She moved over to him, watching his eyes dilate as she approached. The water was much deeper on her, it stopped just below her breasts, so that they seemed to be floating. She didn't stop until she was touching him, her breasts lightly rubbing his chest.

"Do you know what I think?" she asked in a husky voice.

It was all he could do to keep his hands off her. He could feel the trembling throughout his body, and he knew that she was close enough to feel his reaction to her.

"No." He had trouble getting the short syllable past his dry lips.

"I think the reason I wasn't interested in anyone,

and didn't want to get involved, was because I was waiting for you. Somehow I knew you were out there somewhere and that I'd know you when I saw you." She placed her arms around his neck, pulling her body against his. "I'm so glad I waited."

Hawk's strong self-discipline broke and his arms wrapped around her, pulling her even closer to him. His mouth found hers in a yearning kiss that held all the pent-up emotion he'd been fighting for days. "Oh, Paige, I love you so much," he muttered when he finally paused to take a breath.

She was having trouble breathing. "I love you too, Hawk. I feel that I've loved you all of my life."

The soft call of a bird sounded in a nearby tree, and an errant breeze whispered softly through the leaves. Hawk found her mouth once more and took possession, recognizing that it was time to quit fighting what was between them—knowing this was what he needed, what they both needed—and wanted. The world was light years away. They were in their own special paradise, just the two of them, and they were in love.

He could feel the flutter of her pulse under his hand where it rested lightly across her collarbone. His heart felt as though it would crack the wall of his chest with its heavy thudding. He could no longer resist touching her after all the many nights he'd lain awake, holding her, wanting her, determined to resist. Now his resistance was gone.

Paige felt his light touch shimmer down her body,

tracing the curve of her waist and hips. She had never been touched like that and had no idea how much she would welcome it. Perhaps it was only his touch that could make her feel so loved and wanted.

Hawk became aware they were still standing in the small pool. He swung Paige up in his arms and slowly walked to the edge of the stream, his kiss possessing her. When he climbed out of the water he knelt on the grass that covered the flat area nearby, placing her gently on the ground.

His hand rested lightly on her ribs and slowly smoothed across her stomach, her abdomen, then lower. He paused. She was so delicate, so beautiful.

Hawk stretched out beside Paige, determined not to rush her. He leaned over her, his hair brushing against her shoulder while his lips traced a line across the soft swell of her breast. His mouth settled briefly on the darkened tip, then carefully caressed its mate.

A languorous feeling flowed through Paige, her thoughts seeming to float away like the soft wisp of cloud overhead. She could only feel. She felt the touch of his mouth so intimately pressed to her body; she felt his hand gently stroke across her thigh and hip. The moist heat of his body radiated his special scent and she found it heady.

Her tentative fingers tried to imitate what he was doing. He'd been her teacher all week. It was time for a new lesson—this time in the art of loving.

Her hand brushed down his chest and she felt the muscles of his stomach and abdomen. Her fingers lightly brushed against his arousal, and his whole body jerked.

"I'm sorry," she whispered.

"Don't be. It's just that I'm not sure of my control where you're concerned. You've tested it to its limits, I'm afraid."

She looked deep into his eyes and saw the love and desire within them. Her voice shook as she said, "You don't need to have control with me, Hawk. Just love me."

"I do. Very much."

Hawk began to show her how to express her love in physical terms, and Paige responded like a flower bud opening to the sun in full maturity. She had waited for years for this man and it scared her to think she might not have recognized him when they first met. But she had. She hadn't let convention, different life-styles, or different backgrounds sway her.

Now he was hers.

Hawk carefully lowered his body over hers. She was so small and he didn't want to hurt her. His mouth claimed hers once again and his hand gently brushed across her upper thighs. He pulled back slightly to see her face, to watch her reaction as he took her for the first time, but he hoped fervently, not for the last.

She lifted drowsy eyelids to gaze dreamily at him, and Hawk felt as though a giant hand grabbed his heart and squeezed. How could he make love to her while she believed they were married? How could he take advantage of what she felt for him without telling her the truth?

He cupped her face between his hands, his weight still on his elbows. "Paige, darling, listen to me..."

Her smile was heartstopping. "I'm listening. Is this where you tell me you're a virgin?"

He choked, a chuckle almost strangling him. "No, I'm afraid not."

"I figured as much. Most thirty-six-year-old adventurers I've met have the same problem."

How could she joke when everything was so serious? *But she has no idea what I have to tell her.*

"How many thirty-six-year-old adventurers have you known?" he murmured, unable to resist the temptation to kiss her once more. He tried to ignore how well their bodies fit together. He was so close to taking her, so very close.

She kissed him back. In a breathless voice she managed to say, "Oh, dozens I'm sure. I just can't recall their names at the moment."

"That's good. Oh, baby, you feel so good, and I want you so much."

"But you're afraid it's going to hurt me, aren't you? Please don't worry. If I'm willing, you shouldn't mind."

"Paige. There's something I have to tell you. I can't make love to you without your knowing."

His grim tone caught her attention. Then she realized how still he was, how full of tension. The lazy seductiveness of a few moments ago was gone. "What is it?"

"Paige, the day of the crash you hired me to fly you to Flagstaff because you'd heard your father was...ill. The plane went down a few hours later."

He could feel her stiffen beneath him, and he rolled away from her, coming up on his side to stare down at her. He watched the myriad emotions flashing across her face and he wished he could protect her from them. But it was too late.

Somewhere deep inside her Paige could feel the pain starting. Confused emotions darted at her from several different directions at once. Hawk was telling her they didn't know each other. He was telling her he was only a man hired to fly her to her father. He was telling her...

Paige sprang to her feet, frantically searching for her clothes. She spun around, hastily pulling them on, refusing to face the man who still lay where she'd left him, seemingly unconscious of his nudity.

When she was dressed she spoke without looking at him. "So this whole scene has been a complete farce. Not only am I not married to you, I don't even *know* you."

"That's not true, Paige. We may not have known each other when you hired me, but we've had several days together, and I think we've learned a great deal about each other. I know I've told you more about myself than I've ever told another living soul."

She finally forced herself to look at him, then

flinched. He was making no effort to cover himself, a reminder of what had so nearly happened.

"Would you please put on some clothes?" Her tone was icy and his heart sank. She was taking it as badly as he'd imagined. But then, what could he have expected?

"Paige, I think we need to talk about this."

"About what? About the fool I've made of myself? That really isn't necessary. I'm well aware of it. The frustrated spinster finds the man of her dreams and decides she's married to him. That makes all those fantasies acceptable, doesn't it? I'm sure you've had a hard time not laughing in my face!"

"I haven't been laughing, Paige. I've been falling in love with you."

"Stop it! You don't need to continue the charade now. I understand. The only other thing I need to know is why I was flying to see my father. Surely you can tell me that. You said he was ill. My father is never ill."

By this time Hawk had pulled on his Levi's and stepped into his moccasins. He combed his hair back with his hands. When he walked over to where Paige stood, she backed away from him. He stopped, resting his hands on his hips.

"You told me that your father had a heart attack. That was why you were in a hurry to get there."

Paige felt faint and she sank down on the large rock where she'd had her clothes. The news was fresh to her, and the shock was every bit as severe as the first time she'd heard it. "A heart attack..."

"Yes."

"And you've kept me here all this time when I needed to be in Flagstaff!" Her voice rose in agitation.

He waved his arm. "Well, as you can see, I don't have a magic carpet that will whisk you away. Otherwise, I would have sent you right on."

"But why haven't we hiked out?"

"Because I thought you needed to recover. I didn't know if you had the strength and the stamina for what will probably be a very grueling trip." He dropped his hands. "I kept hoping someone would find us."

Distraught, Paige looked around the peaceful meadow. "You're an Indian. Why haven't you sent up smoke signals?"

"Very funny."

"I'm not *trying* to be funny. I'm trying to get out of this place."

"What do you think *I've* been doing?" he demanded.

"Seducing me."

They stared at each other in anger, in hurt, and in despair. Their paradise had disappeared, along with any dreams of a possible future.

Hawk stared at her for a long time, his face grim. Finally he spoke. "If I'd been trying to seduce you, Paige, we wouldn't be having this conversation. I would have gone ahead and made love to you." His mouth turned up in a sardonic smile. "You certainly weren't doing anything to stop me."

He disappeared upstream, heading away from their camp.

Chapter 8

Paige didn't remember returning to the camp, but she found herself sitting in front of the tent. Their tent. They had spent several nights together, nights wrapped in each other's arms, nights when she'd wondered why he didn't make love to her.

Now she knew.

The pain had grown and blossomed within her until it seemed to consume her. Her whole body ached and she shook so hard it was almost as if she was undergoing a chill.

Shock. I'm in shock. My dad is ill. My marriage is nonexistent.

There was no Hawk in her life. There never had been—there never would be. Hawk was a mirage that had lingered longer than most.

He didn't make love to you. He could have. He knew it—you knew it. But he didn't. A sob escaped her.

How can I face him again? How can I pretend that nothing has changed? Everything has changed. Nothing will ever be the same. I can't face him. I just can't.

Paige glanced around the meadow. She remembered all she had learned from Hawk during the week. He'd pointed the way downstream that would be the best direction to go if they had to walk out. She hadn't cared. She hadn't wanted to leave. She hadn't known about her dad.

Oh, Dad, please don't die. I need you so much. Never more than I do now.

A growing determination seemed to grab her, forcing her out of her misery. She had to get to her father and she had to get away from Hawk. Standing up, she looked toward the stream. She didn't know where he'd gone and didn't care. He knew she wanted to leave here. She glanced around at the tent. There was no way she could stay there another night.

Once her mind was made up, Paige wasted no time gathering some supplies, taking the extra blanket and changing into her heaviest clothes. She wrapped everything she'd gathered in the blanket, then folded it as small as she could and tied it around her waist with some of Hawk's twine. It was bulky, but it left her hands free.

She stared up at the sun, trying to figure the time.

She had no idea, but it seemed to be early afternoon. There must be several hours of daylight left. Perhaps she could find someone before dusk. It was better than sitting there waiting to face Hawk.

Hours later Paige wondered if she'd made a mistake. She was hot, tired and hungry, and the terrain had become increasingly rugged. The stream had left the pretty meadow and dropped at an alarming rate through giant boulders and tumbling rocks. She could no longer follow the waterway and was forced to fight through the underbrush, hoping not to lose track of the stream, the only guide she had.

Paige was glad she'd taken the time to rebraid her hair. It had snagged on an overhanging limb, but would have been so much worse loose. As it was, she felt as though a giant had tried to pull her hair out by the roots.

The soft mauve of twilight was touching the mountains around her when Paige slipped and fell, rolling down a rough incline until she landed in a heap at the bottom. Luckily she'd been deposited once again by the stream that had grown into an energetic river since leaving the meadow. She lay there, too sore to know if she were truly hurt or not.

Eventually Paige forced herself into a sitting position. Her clothes had saved her from abrasions but they'd paid the price with several rips and tears. She gingerly tested each ankle. They seemed to be all right, and she breathed a quiet prayer of thanks.

She looked around and discovered that she was sitting on a slight overhang above the river—not a bad place to camp for the night. She wasn't too far from the water, but far enough not to be bothered by any of the forest inhabitants who might want a drink. She hoped. Hawk had described some of the animals that lived in the area, most of which she'd only seen in a zoo. She would just as soon leave it that way.

If she were going to spend the night there, she needed to gather wood for a fire. With fresh determination, Paige limped into the underbrush, dragging out dead limbs. She didn't have anything to chop them up, but she had matches and she'd watched Hawk start a fire by peeling off the dry bark of the dead limbs.

He'd taught her a lot.

She sat back on her heels and thought about him. The hard physical exercise she'd experienced during the past several hours had taken away some of her emotional pain. In fact, she'd been able to identify part of the pain—pride and anger at being fooled. After all, he *had* lied to her. She had specifically asked him if they were married, and he had said yes.

She wondered why. What had he gained out of the charade? If he'd made love to her that first night, or any night afterward, she could better understand the lie. She shook her head. None of it made sense.

Once Paige had the fire going, she quickly pulled out the packets of food she'd brought, glad she'd decided to bring the small pot despite its bulk. She dumped the food in the pan, adding water, then watched it come to a boil. Never had she been so hungry. Never had she been so alone.

Alone. Paige had never really thought about what that meant before. She'd always been so busy with her life, snatching moments for herself to catch up on reading or writing, taking her solitary life for granted.

What if she were lost? What if she never found another person in all of this wilderness? What had made her think she could blithely take off and find her way out of there when Hawk had been hesitant to try?

She was a fool. Her pride and hurt feelings had compounded the problem, and now she'd taken an action she couldn't change. She wasn't even sure she could find her way back to the meadow, even if she tried. And she was too tired to try. Her head was throbbing for the first time in days, and she knew she'd overdone it.

Hawk had been right. She wasn't strong enough, and she didn't have the stamina—but she had to keep going.

Tomorrow. She would get a good night's rest and start out again tomorrow, and the next day, and the next. She had food. She would stay close to the river so she'd have water. She had a bed of sorts. She would make it because she had no choice.

Hawk knew he had to return to camp and face Paige sooner or later, but he wasn't looking forward to it. The strenuous hike upstream had done him good. It had helped to clear his brain of the fever Paige created within him whenever he was around her.

He hadn't realized how isolated he'd been from people until Paige appeared in his life. Since his mother's death, he'd never formed a close relationship with anyone. He'd never had any responsibilities to anyone else; he'd never concerned himself over another person; he'd never felt protective toward another person—until Paige.

Of course she was upset. He'd spent the afternoon thinking about how he would have felt in her place and knew he'd have been mad as hell at the deception. He hadn't really faced until now how hurt she'd be—or maybe he'd been so wrapped up in what he was feeling that he hadn't given a thought to her feelings.

He'd hurt her, and she was the one person whom he wouldn't have hurt for the world. He'd spent the afternoon trying to figure out a way to ask her forgiveness, to explain his reasoning for allowing her to think they were married.

He'd also come to grips with the problem that had been eating at him for days. They had no future together. He'd allowed himself to live in the world created by Paige's misunderstanding of their relationship. He should have known better. She had her life, had even explained to him the heavy demands made on a doctor and why she never expected to marry.

He knew marriage was not part of his plans, just like they'd never been a part of his father's. It was bred into him; he was too restless to stay in one place for long.

So where did they go from there? What could he say to Paige? *I love you, but you wouldn't fit into my life-style, so it's just as well we aren't actually married?*

It was late afternoon when a grim-faced Hawk returned to their camp, determined to face Paige and be as honest as possible with her, only to find her gone.

He had no trouble reading the signs of her activity, and noted with unconscious approval what she'd chosen to take with her. Then the realization of what she had done hit him. She was going to try to make it out of the mountains alone!

"Paige!" His bellow echoed around the meadow, startling the small animals and birds. Of course, she couldn't hear him. He tried to determine how long she'd been gone. She must have left hours ago. He glanced up at the sun. He had to find her. He had deliberately omitted some of the stories that might have frightened her—that frightened him just thinking about her being on her own. Not all the animals in the mountains were friendly. There were pumas and other wildlife that were aggressive predators.

Hawk broke camp in his usual, thorough manner, packing the tent and sleeping bag in their small cases and stowing them on his backpack. He gave only fleeting thought to his plane, wondering if he'd ever find it again. Right now he had more immediate concerns.

He started downstream at a slow trot, following her trail.

Hawk found himself cursing under his breath, the first sound he'd made during the past several miles. From her tracks he could tell she was tired. Of course she was tired. There was no trail to follow and the rugged area where the stream fell to the lower slopes of the mountain range was treacherous.

Daylight was fading and he still hadn't caught up with her. The sensible thing to do was wait for daylight, then pick up her trail again. Not that he needed to track her. She was staying as close to the stream as she could. She must have remembered what he'd told her.

Would she remember that he'd also told her he loved her?

He knelt by the water and drank, trying to decide what to do. He'd gained on her; her tracks weren't but a couple of hours old. But could he keep going without possible injury to himself?

I can't sit here and wait, he decided. He dug into his pack for a small flashlight and started down the incline. It was going to be a long night.

Hawk lost track of time. He didn't seem to be making much progress, and having to watch where he was going by the small light was even more time-consuming. Then his luck began to turn.

The moon appeared over the rim of the surrounding hills. Thank God for a full moon. Within minutes the landscape was touched by a ghostly hue. He still had to be careful. The light could be deceptive, and he didn't need to step into a hole that he'd mistaken for a shadow.

He paused at the top of a long slope and spotted her fire. He hadn't realized how frightened he'd been for her until he saw the light and her small shape huddled nearby. Then his knees almost buckled with relief.

She was all right. He took his time coming down, taking care to place each foot on firm ground. He was over halfway down when he came to the place where she had fallen. The rocks and brush showed that she had rolled. His heart leaped, then settled painfully back in his chest. She had to be all right. Otherwise, she couldn't have set up camp. He could see that she had chosen well. Despite everything, he was proud of her.

Paige kept waking up, then dozing back off. She had built a large fire, not only for warmth but to keep any animals away. Hawk had assured her that most of the wildlife was more afraid of her than she was of them, but she didn't want to take any chances.

She lay there remembering how well she'd slept with Hawk. Already she missed him so much. Her wounded pride and bouts of self-pity were small comfort to her now. She wondered what he was doing. She pictured him sitting beside the fire in the meadow, watching the moon come up. It was beautiful tonight. Would he miss her? He was probably relieved to have her gone.

Paige cringed at some of her memories; she'd behaved like a wife in love with her handsome husband. Hawk had handled her so well. He hadn't encouraged her, but he had been careful not to hurt her feelings. He'd also told her he loved her.

She had a feeling he didn't admit that to many people. From what he'd told her about himself, he let very few people get close to him. But he'd been gentle with her, teaching her how to camp, how to read trail signs, how to fish. He'd been so patient with her lack of knowledge about his world. Would she ever see him again?

"Paige?"

She bolted upright, wondering if she were dreaming that he'd called to her. Glancing at the fire, she saw Hawk standing at the edge of its light. Or was it her imagination? She blinked her eyes, and when she opened them again he was striding across the clearing toward her.

"Hawk!" Forgotten were the hurts of the day, both physical and emotional. Paige was aware of only one overwhelming thought. She loved Hawk as she had loved no one before in her life. It no longer mattered that he had lied to her. The important thing was that he'd followed and found her. Paige flew across the small space that separated them and into Hawk's arms.

She feels so good in my arms.

I'm so glad he's here.

I wasn't sure I'd ever see her again.

I was afraid I'd never see him again.

Dear God, how I love this woman.

How can I hide my love for this man?

"You okay?" Hawk rasped past a tightened throat.

Her head was buried in his chest, but she nodded vigorously. "I'm fine, now that you're here."

He smiled, holding her close. "You know, all you would have had to do was tell me you were bored. We could have hiked out together."

She laughed, her voice shaking slightly. "Now why didn't I think of that? It *was* a rather lonely hike."

He let go of her reluctantly, then swung the heavy pack off his shoulders. "I brought you your bed. Thought it might be a little more comfortable."

"I haven't really been cold. The fire was nice."

"You did a good job of building it. I'm proud of you."

She tried to see his eyes in the flickering light from the fire. "Are you?"

He nodded. "More than you can possibly imagine."

"I'm glad."

A strong current flowed between them and their minds seemed to touch, to recall another place, another time, when their love and their need to express that love had almost overwhelmed them.

Hawk broke the tension between them by turning away. "Let me get the tent up and you can have the sleeping bag. I'll sleep by the fire." He became very busy as he continued to explain. "We can take off at daylight. It shouldn't be much farther to some sign of civilization." His matter-of-fact words were given away by the gruffness in his voice.

Paige silently helped to spread the canvas, the two of them working together in unspoken harmony. Within minutes a new camp was ready.

"Have you eaten?" she asked, breaking the silence at last. The unspoken communication was tearing at her emotions.

"I had some jerky and leftover sourdough bread," he admitted. "I didn't want to stop and heat up something."

"Do you want anything now?"

The multiple meaning hung in the air between them, daring him to give her an honest answer.

"No, I'll wait until morning. I need to get some rest." He sat down near her blanket and began to tug off his boots.

Paige watched him uncertainly. What did she expect from him? She realized that whatever she wanted, she would have to let him know. He was not the kind of man to take advantage of a situation, no matter what she'd accused him of earlier in the day.

What did she want? She crawled into the tent and found the sleeping bag open and waiting for her. She slid out of her shirt and slacks, glad to have the privacy of the tent and the freedom away from the constricting clothes. Then she stretched out in the bag and sighed. Its padding was heavenly after the hard surface she'd been lying on—that Hawk was now lying on. She sat up, wondering if he were already asleep.

She lifted the flap. He was stretched out on the blanket, his hands behind his head, staring at the fire. The movement from the tent caught his attention and he glanced over at her.

"You okay?"

She smiled. That was a familiar question with him. Was she okay? She wasn't sure. She wasn't sure about anything. All she knew was that she loved him and she wanted to be with him.

"Why don't you sleep in here?" she asked.

His slow smile disarmed her. "Don't tempt me. I'm afraid I'm fresh out of willpower this evening."

She swallowed, trying to dislodge the lump in her throat. "I'm inviting you to share the sleeping bag with me, Hawk. I'm not insisting your willpower accompany you."

Surprised, he stared at her across the intervening space. There was no way he could misinterpret her suggestion.

Like a sleepwalker Hawk came slowly to his feet. He leaned over and methodically picked up his boots and blanket, then padded softly over to her.

Paige scooted back from the door, giving him room to crawl in. The only light inside the tent was the reflection of the brightly burning fire through the canvas. She crawled inside the bag and waited.

For a moment, Hawk made no movement. Then he slowly began to undress. She heard the rustle of his clothes, and her heart kept up its steady thumping to the harsh sounds of his breathing. She felt him reach for the cover, and she raised it, guiding his hand inside. She heard his breath catch, and then he was lying beside her.

Never had the sleeping bag seemed so small. They had only been able to share it because she'd slept practically on top of him. It took only a moment for her to find the position she'd grown used to—her head on his shoulder, her body snuggled against him, her leg tucked between his. But the tension between them now was almost unbearable.

Hawk tried to control his breathing and his heartbeat. He tried to think of every unpleasant chore he'd ever had to do. He tried to forget the woman in his arms. Then she shifted, and he was lost.

"Hawk?" she whispered.

"Hmm?"

"Teach me how to love you." She felt the heavy thudding of his heart beneath the palm of her hand. Paige raised her head slightly until her lips rested softly against his.

Hawk tightened his arms around her and deepened the kiss. He had waited a lifetime for this woman, and for whatever reason she was now in his arms. He had tried to resist her, but could no longer fight what they both wanted to happen.

Paige had learned a great deal about making love that afternoon by the waterfall. For the first time she'd discovered her sensuous nature and learned something about Hawk's. She wanted to give him pleasure, to express her love for him in every way she could.

Paige was only a shadowy figure in the darkened tent, but Hawk's memory of the afternoon told him how she looked as she lay in his arms tenderly kissing him along his jawline. He could feel the slight perspiration on his forehead, caused by the restraints he'd placed on himself. He didn't want to hurt her by rushing their lovemaking, but his pent-up emotions were taking their toll.

Slowly he turned her over, then carefully lowered himself to her. Her arms snaked around his neck in an eager embrace, reassuring him of her lack of fear. Hawk slid his hands under her hips, carefully positioning her. Then his mouth found hers once more. This woman was his; he knew that in some deep, fundamental way. He found her waiting for him, and he took her with warm tenderness and loving patience.

Paige trembled with the force of her feelings. *I belong to him now,* she thought with a sense of rightness. She felt surrounded and consumed by him, swept up in the wonder of his possession—and in the tingling of desire that raced through her when he began the gentle rocking movement deep within her.

She held him closer, ever closer, learning to meet his rhythm, to join it, to experience the inexplicable joy of physical union between two people who have already merged their emotions.

She could feel the hard muscles of his back beneath her fingertips; his hands caressing her sides, then sliding to her breasts; his mouth as it memorized the contours of her face. Most of all, she could feel a tension inside of her, as though a spring was being wound, tighter and tighter, and she gasped as it suddenly seemed to project her straight up into the moonlit sky, a cascade of stars spreading its brilliance around her.

Hawk made one final lunge, then held her in a grip so tight she could scarcely breathe. He rolled over, still holding her, and gasped for air. Resting on his chest was like trying to float on a tidal wave, and Paige chuckled.

Hawk growled, "That is not a proper response to my lovemaking, I'll have you know. I think my heart is going to quit on me any minute, and all you can do is laugh!"

She stroked his jaw. "Not at you, love. Never at you. I was just thinking about what an active pillow I've found to rest my head on."

She could feel his grin against her palm. He shifted so that she could lie by his side and he sat up, reaching for his backpack.

"What are you doing?" she asked with relaxed interest.

"Getting a towel. I feel like I've been in the shower."

"You mean making love to me is like taking a shower?"

"Hardly." He relaxed back beside her, pulling her close. "Did I hurt you?"

"If you did, I wasn't aware of it." She leaned up to try to see his face, but it was too dark. "Hawk? Is it always like that?"

"I have no idea. It's never been like that for me before."

"I just wondered. Because if it was, I've got many years to regret. I had no idea making love could be so beautiful."

"Neither did I. You see, that's the first time I've ever made *love*." He sighed. "I may never recover."

Paige placed her head on his shoulder with a contented smile. If she had her way, he never would.

Chapter 9

Paige's dream was delightful—full of light and color and happiness. She and Hawk were together, loving each other, on their honeymoon—honeymoon? Her eyes flew open, and it was as though her dream continued.

She was curled against Hawk's chest, her head resting against the soft movement of his breathing, her hand resting over his heart. Her body was tucked neatly by his side, her thigh intimately nestled between his. Overhead a bright sun beat down on the canvas so that she felt as though they were gingerbread people baking in an oven.

Hawk stirred beneath her, pulling her closer against him. There was a satisfying familiarity about the scene that Paige found reassuring. It was the slight differences that caused her heart to race.

This morning there were no clothes to separate them, and the slight soreness Paige experienced was new. Hawk's hold on her was much more possessive. His hand covered her breast as though for protection.

She glanced up at his face. He looked tired. She realized she'd never seen him asleep. In the past, he'd already been gone by the time she woke up. Now she studied him with a newfound possessiveness.

She studied the thick line of his brows that almost touched across his nose and noted the way his skin glistened in the warmth of the tent. Dark lashes rested against high cheekbones that gave him an autocratic, almost arrogant appearance. Her finger lightly touched his wide, strong chin, then traced the firm jawline to his ear.

He jerked his head suddenly and captured the tip of her finger between his teeth. She yelped.

"Is that any way to treat your tired old Indian guide when he's trying to catch up on his sleep?" he complained in a husky voice.

She leaned over him, watching him with suspicion. His eyes remained closed. "Why is it my fault you're tired?" she asked with interest.

His hand slid around the back of her neck and coaxed her mouth to within a couple of inches of his. "Honey, if you can't remember that, you've got a bigger problem with your memory than we guessed." His mouth captured hers in a lazy kiss that effectively ended their teasing.

Of course she remembered. She remembered waking up during the night to Hawk's erotic touch as he gave a strong impression of a man determined to memorize every inch of her body. How could she forget?

His lovemaking had been slow and very thorough. She felt that she could spend the rest of her life in his arms and never grow bored.

"Shouldn't we be leaving?" she managed to whisper when his kiss finally ended.

"We should have left several hours ago," he admitted ruefully.

She started to shift her leg and his thighs clamped down on her like a vise, effectively holding her prisoner—a very willing prisoner. From that position she could tell the effect she had on him. Even as inexperienced as she was, she'd had the ability to respond to him, to satisfy him—and to keep him still wanting her. Paige sighed with fervent pleasure.

He pulled her over on top of him. She grinned. "Is this what is considered the view from the top?"

"Could be. What do you think?"

"I think I could become addictive."

His mouth found the soft spot at the base of her neck where her pulse quivered. His tongue explored the area until she shivered, then he pressed his lips along a trail to her chin, tipping her head down until he found her mouth.

Time no longer mattered. They were lost in the pleasure of learning more about each other. Hawk introduced her to new sensations, new intimacies, that carried Paige to a dimension where she could share the intense love she felt for Hawk by expressing it in arousing and exhilarating ways.

This morning Paige set the rhythm for their love-making. From her position on top of Hawk she discovered how to tease and torment him until his greater strength finally forced her to accept his hard length within her, a most satisfactory conclusion for both of them to her teasing. She slowly built the spiraling emotional structure that led them to the top, where they soared together on a mindless plane of sensation and pleasure, slowly circling back to earth, wrapped in each other's arms. Then, limp from her exertions, Paige lay quietly on Hawk's chest, content to rest.

Because her ear was pressed against his chest, she heard the rumble of his voice as the words left his lips. "We need to be moving, love."

She raised her head and stared at him in bewilderment. "I thought we were."

His smile lit up the small tent. "I mean we need to get down the trail...what there is of it, anyway."

"Oh." She dropped her head and thought about her father. She and Hawk had been together for almost a week. That meant he'd had his heart attack seven days ago. Seven days. If he'd survived the initial attack, he would have passed the crisis stage by now. Had he made it?

She sat up, sliding off Hawk in one graceful movement. He pretended overwhelming relief that he could now breathe again, but she ignored him. She also ignored her lack of clothing when she threw the flap of the tent open and stepped out of the tent. It was another beautiful day.

She glanced down at her shoulder and discovered a long scratch, no doubt picked up on her travels the day before. Walking over to the edge of the swollen stream, she knelt down to wash off the scratch and rinse her face.

Paige only had a moment's warning before hands grasped her around the waist and she was propelled into the river, securely held against a large, warm body.

They hit the water with a resounding splash. Her squeal of shock was due as much to the unexpected push as it was to the temperature of the water. She came up sputtering, discovering she was little more than waist-deep in the clear running river. Hawk was sitting so that the water came almost to his neck.

"That was rude!" she declared in her most haughty, well-bred tones.

"Was it?" His look of repentance needed a little work to be convincing.

"I could have drowned."

"Not while I was holding you."

His infectious grin totally destroyed her efforts to solemnly discuss the deficiencies of his deportment as reflected by his recent behavior. She resolved the matter by splashing water in his face and an olympic-sized water fight ensued, scaring the wildlife around their campsite.

Paige couldn't remember when she'd ever acted so childish—certainly not as a child nor as an earnest adolescent. When they discovered, to no one's surprise, that Hawk could outmaneuver, outswim and outguess Paige, she conceded defeat and proceeded to bathe herself, as though getting into the water had been entirely her own idea.

By the time she crawled out of the river to dry her hair in the sun, Hawk had their meal prepared. Paige was surprised to discover how unself-conscious she was with him. She grabbed his shirt to put on after drying herself, and ate unconcernedly, oblivious to the side glances she received from Hawk. She was modestly covered. It wasn't her fault that he was aware of what she didn't have on underneath that shirt.

"I never thought I'd ever be envious of a piece of my clothing," he said after finishing his cup of coffee. He stood up, staring down at the cleavage revealed by the loose shirt.

In the carefully modulated tone of a professional doctor, she inquired, "Tell me, sir, how long have you noticed having this insatiable sexual appetite?"

He leaned over and picked up her empty dishes and shrugged. "Only since being around you, doctor."

"I see. Then the cure is obvious." She stood up and headed toward the tent.

"Is it?" His gaze followed her graceful body as she walked away from him.

She stopped and looked back over her shoulder. "Of course. Remove the source, and you remove the problem." She disappeared inside the tent.

He washed up their dishes and deftly packed them away. "Isn't that a rather drastic solution?" He raised his voice so that she would hear him.

A few minutes later she stepped out, chastely covered in her own rather bedraggled clothes, a little worse for the wear they'd had the day before. "Drastic, perhaps, but certainly effective."

They pulled the tent down in companionable silence. When he had everything back in his knapsack, giving Paige a smaller pack to carry, Hawk finally admitted, "I'd prefer a less effective cure, if you could arrange it."

Following the river, Hawk started off and Paige fell in step behind him. She admired the width of his shoulders and the seemingly weightless way he carried the pack that she knew must weigh at least sixty pounds. "Well, it might take some experimenting, trying various concepts, to find a suitable cure."

Without turning around, he answered, "Whatever you say, doc. I know I'm in good hands, so you have my permission to experiment to your heart's content."

My heart will be content only when you're around, she decided, but thought it more politic not to mention it.

Hawk set a steady pace that seemed to eat up the miles. He was an expert at picking the easiest path, Paige discovered, and wished she'd managed to control her feelings enough not to have struck out on her own the day before.

When the way was rough, Hawk helped her, and Paige discovered her most exhilarating feeling came with his silent look of admiration when she determinedly stayed up with him.

It was midafternoon when their good luck seemed to run out. The river disappeared underground through a hole in the canyon wall.

Hawk stood there, his hands on his hips, and studied the rugged terrain around them. They were in some type of canyon and there didn't seem to be a way out. "Why don't we stop here? It's a good place to eat and get some rest," he finally said.

Paige sank down gratefully. Her body had been protesting the unusual treatment for the past two hours, but she'd been determined not to ask Hawk to stop. They were hiking out because she'd insisted. She refused to admit it was too much for her.

Hawk was right. There was shade here, and the water was still sparkling clear. With some stiffness Paige knelt by the river and scooped it up in her hands to drink. Then she splashed it on her face to cool off. Was it only that morning that they had played in the water? It seemed years ago.

Their entire time together seemed to have lasted forever. She could scarcely remember her life before

Hawk and she refused to think about what it would be like when they returned to their daily routines. All she had was here and now. It was enough, because it had to be enough.

Hawk handed her a large piece of sourdough bread and a piece of jerky. A cup of cold water was in his other hand.

"Thank you," she murmured, seating herself cross-legged under a shade tree a short distance away.

Hawk stared at her, concerned. Had he pushed her too hard? She sounded different—as though they were barely acquainted, as though they knew nothing about each other, or as though she cared nothing for him.

That was the difference. From the time she was aware of him after their forced landing, she had been warm to him. Wary, perhaps, but she'd projected a strong vibration of caring. Now it was almost as though she'd erected a shield between them. He wondered if it were to protect herself or him. He sat down next to her, biting into the bread and staring into the distance.

Perhaps she was trying to protect him. She'd had time to come to terms with their new relationship, or rather, their lack of a formal one. Yet she had given herself to him—totally, without reservation. What did it mean?

Had she finally found a man who could arouse her and she'd decided to further her education? What did he mean to her? What could he mean? She was a career woman—he was a maverick.

Hawk finished eating, then stretched out in the shade and closed his eyes. He refused to worry about it. He had nothing to offer her and they both knew it. He'd learned at an early age to take what life offered and not question it. As a philosophy, it wasn't a bad way to survive. The secret was not to want something you could never have.

Paige studied Hawk's relaxed position and envied him his ability to fall asleep immediately, to wake up alert, and to be in control of his emotions at all times. Her problem was that he had stirred up emotions within her she'd never known existed. Now that they were alive and well and clamoring to be used, she didn't know what to do with them.

Trying to deal with emotions on an intellectual basis was impossible. Emotions were like errant children, bounding out of control at the least provocation. No matter how much time she spent reasoning with them, they proceeded to go their merry way, ignoring the consequences.

What she had to keep in mind was the importance of getting to Flagstaff. Up until now, her father and her profession had been her entire life. She could only pray that her father was all right.

She mentally listed all the positive items in his favor—his relative youth, the fact that he did take care of himself, and that he knew the importance of good health. Paige had to leave him in God's hands, but she prayed that God in his mercy would grant her a few more years with him.

For the first time in her life, Paige faced how much she'd taken her father for granted. Although she'd loved her mother, her thinking processes had been more like her father's and she'd had trouble relating to her maternal parent. She understood her mother's pain at being on the outskirts of her father's life, but she couldn't relate to it, because she had made herself a part of his life as soon as she could.

Instead of sitting around wishing for something, I've always gone after what I wanted, she realized in surprise. The sudden insight into her own character surprised her. Paige had never been one to spend much time in self-analysis.

"We need to go, Paige..." Hawk's deep voice brought her out of a surprisingly deep sleep. She hadn't meant to sleep, only to rest her eyes. Hawk stood over her with one hand outstretched. She grasped it and pulled herself up. He increased her momentum so that she fell against him. With calm deliberation he found her mouth with his and gave her a leisurely, but very thorough, kiss.

Damn him! Her new resolution to hold herself aloof from him disappeared, and she could feel her body melt against him. *It just isn't fair.* She returned his kiss with fervor, until he pulled away from her, his expression strained.

"I'd like to get out of this area before nightfall. Hopefully it levels out down a little lower. There's a possibility the river will return to the surface and we can find it."

Once again Hawk led the way, and Paige followed. She couldn't help but wonder what would have happened to them if she'd had another kind of pilot, one who didn't know how to survive in the wilderness. She shook her head impatiently. *Don't think about it. Just be thankful for Hawk.*

She had reason to reiterate that thought several times as the rugged miles continued to unroll beneath their feet. The river no longer guided them. They scrambled up one side of a hill, then down the other. Paige wondered how Hawk knew which way to go. She was turned around in her directions. She was also exhausted.

Twilight was beginning to place its mystical touch around them when Hawk finally halted. "We'll camp here."

Paige wearily looked around. The place looked no different than many other places they'd passed, but she asked no questions at all. Instead she helped Hawk put up the tent, spread the sleeping bag, gather wood and prepare a simple meal.

They were both too tired for conversation. They spent little time in front of the fire after eating. Instead they both stripped down and crawled into the sleeping bag, immediately falling asleep.

It was light outside, but the sun wasn't up when Hawk gently shook Paige awake. She groaned, trying to find her comforting pillow. "We need to get started, love," he said in a low voice that brought her out of her dream-filled sleep.

Paige sat up groggily, feeling aches and pains in places she'd never known existed. She'd thought she was in good physical condition, but this little outing was rapidly convincing her otherwise.

Hawk felt as though a hand was tightening around his heart as he watched her painful movements. He'd been amazed at her stamina and the valiant effort she'd been making. But they couldn't afford to waste time now. They were away from water, and their food supply was dwindling. He had to do everything he could to find a settlement of some sort that day.

Paige reluctantly pulled on her clothes, vowing to burn them as soon as she found a place to buy more. She was sick of them, sick of walking, sick of trying to keep up with the robot she was with who never seemed to get tired, or hungry, or thirsty. She glared up at him and froze. The tender look in his eyes caused tears to form in her eyes.

She slipped her arms around his neck. "Oh, Hawk, I love you so much. I'm sorry to be such a tenderfoot."

His arms came around her in a fierce hug. "I love you, too. And you're doing fine, just fine. We should be out of here today."

She pulled back from him in surprise. "You think so?"

He nodded, unwilling to make a more emphatic statement on such an uncertainty.

She hugged him back. "Won't that be great? Just think how it will feel to have a hot bath for a change, and eat something besides jerky and dried fruit, and sleep in a nice, comfortable bed, and ..."

"But madam, you paid an incredible amount of money for this special safari into the wilds of eastern Arizona. I thought you wanted to get your money's worth." His fake British accent was very well done.

"That's true, young man, very true. However, you didn't mention the exercise program in your brochure, or I might have had second thoughts."

He scratched his head thoughtfully. "Perhaps we should revise the brochure, do you think?"

"Definitely. But don't expect an overwhelming amount of people to sign up."

He drew himself up to his full height. "But madam, we only cater to the most elite clientele. Surely you recognized that."

She looked at their clothes, white with dust, ragged and torn, and at the battered camping supplies that had kept them going, and she laughed. "I'm glad to hear it. I want nothing but the best. I thought that was understood." Her gaze turned back to him. "I'm so glad I got it."

She was irresistible in that mood, and he didn't even try to resist. Instead he gathered her into his arms and kissed her with all the fervency he possessed.

A few minutes later he let her down with a sigh. "We still need to leave."

"I know."

"I could stay here all day and make love to you, you know that, don't you?"

"I'm glad," she whispered, in awe of the miracle that had brought them together and caused such similar strong feelings to occur in each of them for the other.

Hawk firmly set her aside and left the tent, and Paige hurriedly repacked what they had taken out of the backpack the night before, then efficiently rolled up the sleeping bag. She was getting almost as good at packing as Hawk. Almost.

A little hero worship never hurt anyone, she decided. Wearily she crawled out of the tent to begin a new day.

Chapter 10

The river reappeared about midmorning but was nothing like the one they'd been following. This one seemed out of control, raging along in a rolling frenzy.

Hawk found a small pocket of shallow water that had already been heated by the sun and suggested they take time to bathe. Paige hadn't realized what a luxury water could be. It felt so good to feel clean again. She took her hair down and washed it, luxuriating in the cool water.

It's amazing how different your outlook is when you're clean and well fed, Paige decided, looking for Hawk to share her bit of philosophy. But when she spotted him, all previous thoughts flew from her head. He stood under a rocky overhang where part of the river gushed over the side, taking a vigorous shower.

She could only stare at his unconscious male beauty. His bronzed skin glistened in the sunlight and water, and she visually traced a path from his broad chest to his waist and hips, down to his thighs and well-developed calves. Only his feet were hidden in the swirling water.

Paige slicked her wet hair back from her face, then started swimming toward him, ignoring the pull of the current. The bubbling water broke over her head several times, but her gaze never left the man ahead of her.

Hawk had turned his back to her, his face raised to the hard-driving water, and didn't hear her approach. She waded out of the deeper water until he was close enough to touch. He couldn't have heard her with the rushing water all around him; he could only have sensed her presence. But he turned as though knowing she were there.

The message in her eyes was unmistakable, and it fanned a flame within him that had never gone out since the first time he saw her.

Without a word he scooped her up in his arms and strode out of the water. Their things were packed, but he spotted the blanket she had made into a small pack for her, and without breaking stride he reached for it, shook it out and lowered her on one side of it. She watched as he flicked the other half open.

Still without speaking, Hawk reached for her, his need obvious. Their communication was more basic than words, and when she flowed into his arms an explosion of desire swept over them.

There was no gentleness between them. Instead theirs was a fierce enactment of possession. They belonged together—they belonged to each other—and they used the act of love to reinforce that statement. Hawk took her in a powerful, surging drive and she was with him all the way. Her arms locked around his neck and her legs wrapped around him, encouraging the savage swirl of emotions that gripped them.

You're mine, you're mine, you belong to me, only to me—his rhythm matched the litany of phrases running through his head. She responded to him as though she had heard the refrain and affirmed it.

Paige found herself once again in that other world of pleasurable sensation, her body flexing convulsively as she toppled over the edge of the sky. Hawk's harsh breathing filled her world when he made his final plunge, then collapsed in her arms, his chest heaving.

I feel that every part of me has melted and remolded itself around him. She enjoyed the weight of his body pressing against her; knew that he'd lost control this time, and she was reassured. He hadn't been able to completely hide from her what he was feeling.

They lay there, bodies intertwined, as the world began to impinge once more on their consciousness. Hawk shifted, rolling free of her and sat up. His folded arms rested against his raised knees and his head dropped against his arms.

"I'm sorry."

Paige felt too limp to move, but she forced herself into a sitting position. "For what?"

"For being so rough."

"It's obvious I'm beyond redemption, then. I enjoyed it. Thoroughly."

He raised his head and stared at her smiling face. Then he rested his forehead against hers. "Oh, Paige, you're a constant surprise. You never say what I expect. You're not like anyone I've ever known." He sighed. "What am I going to do with you?"

She tried to sound light and cheerful. "Love me?"

His black eyes glistened with emotion. "Is that enough?"

She stared at him, feeling his uncertainty as though it were her own. And perhaps it was. "It will have to be."

Midafternoon found them facing a dilemma. They needed to cross the river, but the rushing water had widened to a dangerous degree. There were no fordable spots that Hawk could find.

He toyed with the alternative. They could stay on this side of the river in the hope it would continue toward civilization. But crossing was the quickest way to get to help. He had spotted their first sign of the twentieth century over the last rise—a towering antenna standing tall on the next ridge over from them. That antenna had to have a power station nearby, which meant there was a road to follow. It was time to leave their guide, the river. But first they had to cross it.

Hawk planned carefully. He made them stop and eat first. Then he built a small raft to carry their provisions. They stripped down to essentials, so that the heavy drag of water wouldn't catch in their clothes. He was thankful the bedroll and tent were in waterproof containers.

The care he took in making the crossing would have placed them safely on the other side, except for one unforeseen detail, and that detail made a mockery of all his precautions.

They laughed when all of their provisions and clothes were neatly strapped to the small raft. "Do you realize that if we lose that raft, we'll never dare come out of hiding?" Paige stood there in her brief shorts and blouse tied under her breasts. Hawk had dispensed with everything but his briefs.

"Now's a lousy time to ask, but how good of a swimmer are you?" he asked with a slight smile. The smile didn't reach his concerned eyes.

"Better than average," she assured him. "I haven't won any gold medals or anything, but I can stay afloat."

He glanced over at the water that was moving swiftly past. "It's hard to tell how deep it is along here, but there's no way to cross either upstream or downstream from here, so this place wins by default.'' A limb came floating by, then disappeared in the suction of the water. ''The rains up in the mountains must have caused this heavy flow. Normally by July the mountain streams are quiet and subdued.''

''I guess somebody forgot to point out the date to this one.''

''A definite oversight, but it can't be helped.'' He stepped off the bank into water up to his knees. Dragging the small raft alongside him, he motioned to her. ''I'm not going to hang on to you. It would be more of a hindrance than a help.'' He pointed to the other bank about 150 yards downstream. ''That's where we'll end up, hopefully. When the current catches you, keep swimming as straight as you can.'' He watched as she slid into the water beside him.

Just one more adventure to tell my grandkids, she decided with characteristic resolution.

Hawk gave her a head start, wanting to keep her in his line of vision. He pulled the raft along beside him, keeping it upstream of him so that he would have better control—which is why he didn't see the tree stump suddenly churn up to the surface right beside him.

He didn't have time to evade it. The long roots caught the raft, flipping it high into the air, and the tree trunk slammed into Hawk, carrying him down the river in its curling grasp.

Paige was concentrating on putting as much power into each stroke as she had. She was wondering how long she could keep it up when she heard a loud, crashing sound behind her. She jerked her head around in time to see the raft go tumbling and Hawk disappear beneath the tree stump.

"Hawk!"

Water sloshed into her mouth and she sputtered. She fought to keep her head out of the water and began to swim furiously after the twisting, turning stump. The swirling water kept washing over her, and she couldn't keep up with the stump.

She had to find Hawk. He had to be all right. She closed her eyes for a split second, frightened at the thought that he might not be all right. Not Hawk. He was too strong. He'd been through too many things and survived. He was tough. He'd make it. She knew he'd make it.

At first she thought her foot had caught on something in the river. Then she realized she'd found bottom. With her last remaining strength Paige pulled herself through the dragging water until she reached dry land and collapsed in a heap. She lay there, gasping for air, praying for strength. She had to get up and find Hawk—he needed her.

When Paige opened her eyes she knew too much time had passed. The sun had moved into the west. Shaking, she got to her feet and looked around. The ridge where the antenna stood was no longer visible. She wasn't even sure which direction to look. She only knew it was somewhere on this side of the river.

The river continued to rush by, but there was no sign of Hawk. She felt a burning and looked down at her legs, absently noting they were raw with scrapes. She ignored them.

Hawk had gone downstream. Therefore, she had to go downstream. It was a fundamental decision, one that took no effort at all. She couldn't afford to waste her energy—she had to find Hawk.

Paige stumbled along the river, but saw no sign of anyone. It was as though she were completely alone in this strange world. *Maybe Hawk found the tree stump provided faster transportation.* She forced her shoulders straight and continued walking.

It was only when she spotted their raft, innocently floating along the edge of the river, that she cried. She cried all the while she tugged it from the water and spread their clothes and provisions out to dry. She wasn't even sure why. So much had gotten wet, maybe that was it. Or maybe it was because Hawk had taken so much care to protect her and their belongings, but had not taken enough care of himself.

I'm not going to let you leave me, damn you, or our things. I'll find you, if it takes all night.

It didn't take all night.

The sun had set, casting its last scarlet rays into the sky, when Paige saw something lying in the water. She couldn't run; the pack she carried weighted her so that she was forced to place each foot carefully in order to keep her balance. She wasn't even sure she wanted to find out what it was.

Hawk was draped over a large rock protruding near the center of the river. When the stump sweeping him along downstream had connected with the rock, the stump had catapulted into the air, freeing him. But by that time he was barely conscious.

He'd hung on to the rock until he found the strength to crawl up on it, but didn't have the strength to make it to shore.

Paige dropped the pack and stared at him. He looked so pale and still, but he was breathing. One side of his face was bloodied and bruised, but he was alive. His side looked as though he'd been kicked by an angry bull.

If she could just get to him.

Then she remembered the raft. How far back was it? She couldn't remember, but it didn't matter. She had to find it. Paige dropped the backpack and hurried back along the way she'd come, fear lending speed to her failing body.

The light was rapidly fading by the time she returned. Hawk hadn't moved.

They would need a fire, but she didn't want to take the time to build one until she could get him to dry land. At least the large rock he had found was big enough to take his full length, so he hadn't been subjected to the continual pounding of the water.

She slipped into the water, surprised at how much colder it felt, and pushed the raft ahead of her. The current wasn't too bad on this side of the large rock, and she only had to go a small distance where her feet wouldn't touch bottom.

"Hawk?" she pulled herself up beside him, struggling not to lose her grip on the raft. "Hawk, please answer me." She dipped her hand in the water, then brushed it across his face.

He groaned.

"We need to get you out of here, Hawk. Can you help me?"

His eyelids fluttered, then were still. She didn't have time to waste. By gently shoving on his unhurt side she managed to shift him until he began to slide into the water. Paige quickly grabbed the raft and maneuvered it under his head. If she could just keep them afloat, they would make it.

Paige never remembered the details of that nightmare journey back to shore, or how she managed to get him out of the water. But she did it. She rolled him onto the blanket and then dragged him next to the fire she managed to build. Once again Hawk's precautions had helped—the matches had stayed dry in their waterproof pouch.

Her next priority was to examine his wounds. From the flickering light of the campfire she could see that one side of his face was bruised, swollen and scratched, although most of the bleeding had stopped. His side was scraped raw from his armpit to his hip.

His pulse was strong and steady—a reassuring sign—but he had an angry welt across his forehead, which could explain his unconscious state. *This seems to be our trip for head wounds. I wonder if you'll know who I am when you wake up.*

She needed to get him warm. She warmed the blanket by the fire, making sure it was dry before wrapping him up in it once more.

When his eyes opened, she could have wept with relief. Instead she stroked his cheek and asked, "How do you feel?"

He stared up at her, his eyes dulled with pain. Then they seemed to focus on her face and brighten. "I'm not sure," he whispered. "Kinda like I've been in a barroom brawl." He touched the side of his face and winced.

"As a matter of fact—" she tried to keep her voice steady and unconcerned "—that's what you look like." She brushed his hair back. "How does your side feel?"

Hawk drew a breath, then abruptly stopped, pain obvious on his face. "Like hell."

"I can't be certain without X rays, but you may have a cracked rib or two. You took quite a jolt."

"What happened?"

"What do you remember?"

A gleam appeared in his eyes that could have been amusement at their reversed positions. "I remember swimming across the river and something hitting me. What was it?"

"A tree stump. You got caught in the roots and were dragged downstream."

He lay there, staring at her. "I could have drowned."

"Yes."

"How did you find me?"

She forced a smile. "Easy. You were sunning yourself on a rock in the middle of the river when I came along."

He frowned. "I remember that—I remember trying to hang on so I wouldn't be swept back into the water."

"You did a great job of hanging on. When I found you, you'd crawled up on top of it."

He looked at her, disbelief plain on his face. "You found me on the rock?"

"Uh-huh."

"How the hell did you get me off it?"

"I used the raft. You should be pleased with your construction skills. It took quite a beating today, but it's still intact."

She placed her hand on his forehead. He felt warm. Too warm.

Paige nonchalantly came to her feet. "I think I'll put the tent up now. I'm very glad to report the waterproof cover kept the sleeping bag from getting soaked. You could write all kinds of endorsements for your camping gear after this trip."

Hawk tried to respond with a smile, but the pain and swelling in his jaw stopped him. Paige tucked the blanket tighter around him, then left his side. Within moments he was asleep.

The tent was much tougher to put up by herself, but Paige managed. The sleeping bag was warm from being spread in front of the fire by the time she arranged it inside the tent.

Hawk was still asleep when she returned to his side. "Hawk? Can you walk to the tent? Your bed is ready."

He roused himself, staring around the area as though trying to get his bearings. With Paige's help he made it to bed, then dutifully drank the hot soup she brought him.

Paige could see his pain, and fear clutched at her. He wasn't going to be able to go any farther—not on his own.

What were they going to do?

Afraid that she would hurt him if she shared the sleeping bag with him, Paige wrapped up in the blanket and stretched out by his side. Never had she felt so helpless to care for someone.

She checked on him several times during the night. He was restless and feverish, but never awakened. Paige made sure he stayed covered, fearing complications due to exposure. It was almost dawn when she dozed off, and later she thought she was dreaming because she heard voices. They were speaking in a language she didn't recognize. Paige woke up with a start, realizing that someone was outside.

She jerked open the flap and crawled out of the tent. Two men stood there, staring at her as though a Martian had landed in front of them demanding to find their leader. She felt the same way. They were dressed in Levi's and plaid Western shirts, but their hair was long and tied at the nape of their necks. Their

Western hats shaded bronzed faces. Unsmiling bronzed faces.

"Did you know you're on posted property here, lady?" one of them finally asked.

She burst out laughing, almost hysterical with relief. "Are we? Well, you see, we really aren't camping, even though it looks like it. Our plane was forced down up there... She waved her arm over her shoulder and they looked up at the mountain range behind her, then back at her with twin expressions of disbelief. "My...uh, friend was hurt yesterday when we crossed the river. Is there any way we can get him to a doctor?"

She knew better than to explain that she was a doctor. She could tell she'd stretched her credibility with them to the outer limits.

One of them stepped inside of the tent. When he came out he spoke to his companion, but not in English. His friend nodded and disappeared through the trees.

"Where's he going?" she asked in alarm. Didn't they care that Hawk was hurt?

The remaining man answered, "He's gone to bring a truck up here. It's too far to carry him."

"Oh."

"He's Apache, isn't he?"

Surprised, she said, "I believe so. Why do you ask?"

The man grinned, changing his austere expression

into a friendly one. "Are you aware you're on the Apache Reservation?"

She shook her head.

"I don't recognize him. Is he from around here?"

"He said he's originally from Dulce, New Mexico."

"Ahhh. A Jicarilla." He nodded, seemingly satisfied.

Paige looked around. "How long will it take your friend to get here?"

"He should make it in about an hour."

She went over to their supplies and found the coffeepot. "I thought I'd make some coffee, then try to get Hawk to drink some water."

"Your friend's name is Hawk?"

"That's right."

"You don't hear those names much anymore. My name is John Anthony. My friend is Roger Thomas."

"Oh." Why did she feel as though she'd stumbled into an Alice in Wonderland scene?

They'd made it. They'd found their way out of the wilderness and down to civilization. She glanced at the man hunched over, feeding the fire. Yes. Civilization. *Oh, Hawk, if you could only enjoy this with me. We made it, thanks to you. Please get well for me.*

Paige sat back from the bed, pleased to see Hawk resting naturally. They'd been brought to a mobile home by their rescuers, who'd explained they were almost a day's drive from the closest town. They'd put Hawk to bed and she'd begun to bathe him with cold water, trying to get his temperature down.

His fever had finally broken. She'd been afraid of pneumonia, but she was beginning to hope the worst was over. After two days of vigil by his bedside, Paige felt limp with exhaustion.

Deciding that it was safe to leave him, she walked down the short hall to the kitchen. A young woman was stirring something that smelled delicious in a large pot. She smiled when Paige paused in the doorway.

"Hi. I'm sorry I wasn't here when you and your husband first arrived. I'm Alicia, John Anthony's daughter."

She was the picture of youthful freshness, Paige thought with a smile. Her tight faded jeans emphasized the shapely length of her legs in knee-high leather boots. A red T-shirt enhanced her dark skin, and her short haircut accented her large black eyes. A real beauty. She looked to be in her late teens.

First things first. "He isn't my husband. My name is Paige Winston. Hawk Cameron was flying me to Flagstaff last week when we had to make an emergency landing."

"Oh." Alicia's eyes lit up. "I went back to introduce myself when I got home, but you'd fallen asleep in the chair. Hawk looks like he's been in a fight."

"He was. With a tree stump. If you think *he* looks

bad, you oughta see the other guy,'' she said with an exaggerated drawl.

They both laughed. Alicia's eyes sparkled. ''He's very handsome, isn't he?'' she asked shyly.

Paige could feel her reaction to Alicia's innocent words somewhere deep inside. ''Yes, he is.''

''Have you known him long?''

''No. Just since our mishap.''

''So you don't know if he's married.''

''I think it's a safe bet to guess he isn't.''

Alicia's smile became even brighter. ''Well, if there's anything I can do to help, please let me know.''

''As a matter of fact, there is. Your father told me you didn't have a phone. Can you tell me where I might find one?''

Alicia thought for a moment. ''The nearest one is about twenty-five miles from here.'' She grinned. ''Twenty-five long miles—it takes hours to get there. I'm sure my father would be willing to give you a ride, though.''

Paige sat down at the small kitchen table. Her brain seemed to be as sluggish as molasses.

Alicia dished up a steaming bowl of stew. ''Here, have something to eat. After that why don't you take a nice, relaxing shower and get some sleep.'' She sat down across from Paige and looked at her with concern. ''You look exhausted. If Hawk needs anything, I can either take care of him or call you.'' She reached over and softly patted Paige's hand. "You can sleep in my room if you'd like."

Paige could feel tears prickling at the back of her eyes and knew she'd been pushing herself too hard if a young girl's thoughtfulness could make her feel weepy.

"Thank you, Alicia. You and your dad have been great, taking us in like this."

Alicia's smile lit up the kitchen. "We've enjoyed having you. I'm just sorry we can't help out with a phone—your families must be frantic for some sort of word. You both were tremendously lucky."

"I know. Hawk made most of our luck. I wouldn't have made it without him."

Alicia's smile was very understanding. "He's really special, isn't he?"

"Yes," Paige murmured, "he really is."

When Hawk woke up the next morning he was surprised to see a young Indian girl sitting by his bed.

"Good morning," she offered shyly.

He tried to smile, but one side of his face felt like it was made of plaster of Paris. He felt along his cheekbone and discovered bandages covered half his face.

"Where am I?" He heard himself and almost groaned aloud. Not the most original question, but dammit, he seemed to have misplaced a few things—like a river, a raft and a companion. Before she could answer, he interrupted with, "Where's Paige?"

"Oh, she's asleep. She sat up with you until quite late last night. I told her I'd check on you if she wanted to go on to bed."

He mentally digested that, feeling better to know that Paige wasn't far away.

"This is my father's home," the young girl explained. "I'm Alicia Anthony. My father and a friend found you and Dr. Winston camping near the river day before yesterday, so they brought you here." She gave him a very sympathetic smile. "Dr. Winston said you were running a temperature."

He took a few minutes to consider the information Alicia gave him. So they'd been here for two days. He only had vague memories of warm hands caring for him and a soft voice. Paige. He smiled. It had been her turn to look after an invalid.

Hawk felt a tightness on his forehead and touched it lightly. A large bump sat above his right eye. "I must have really gotten a blow to my head to make a knot that big." He looked at the young girl who was watching him so intently. "I'm pretty hard-headed."

"Dr. Winston was quite concerned," she admitted. "You were very lucky to have a doctor with you."

"You know, I never thought of it that way. I guess you're right." He grinned, a lopsided grin to ease the tightness of his swollen jaw and face.

Alicia stared at him for a moment, her gaze admiring. Then, blushing, she rushed into speech to cover her confusion. "Dr. Winston was also trying to find out how she could get to Flagstaff. She seems most anxious to leave."

Of course. He'd forgotten about her father. They needed to leave right away.

"She explained that you were her pilot and she didn't want to leave you until she was sure you were going to be all right."

Her pilot. She doesn't want to leave...until I'm all right. He stared at the young girl. *Of course. Now we're in the real world and we revert back to our former roles. She's Dr. Winston and I'm just the pilot.*

Hawk tried to sit up, and a pain shot through his chest.

"Oh, Hawk, you shouldn't be moving around. Dr. Winston said she's almost certain a couple of your ribs are broken." She leaned over and pulled his pillow higher. "Why don't you lie back and I'll bring you something to eat? I bet you're starved!"

He glanced up into her glowing eyes, full of admiration. He ignored the pain in his side, and in his head. He ignored the pain of knowing that whatever he and Paige had shared was over. That was yesterday. He had to live with today. He smiled at the girl hovering anxiously beside him. "That sounds fine, just fine."

He would deal with his pain later, as he always did—alone.

Chapter 11

The sound of Alicia's light, tinkling laugh settled like a feather in Paige's sleep, tickling at her consciousness, taunting her with its subtle sensuality.

When Paige had finally fallen asleep, she had succumbed to the deep, healing rest of the exhausted. Hawk's fever was down; she'd managed to tape up his ribs and to clean up the contusions and abrasions on his face and head. He was going to be all right.

She'd left him sleeping peacefully, but from the sounds in the other room he was not only awake but enjoying company. She heard the deep rumble of his voice, then Alicia's clear, delighted laughter.

Paige tried to ignore the twinge of pain that shot through her. He wasn't her personal property, after all. There hadn't even been the most rudimentary of commitments made. *Hadn't there?* she asked herself. *Perhaps not on his part, but you know very well you would never give yourself to a man if you hadn't made a commitment of love to him.*

She dug through her small supply of clothes and decided to try one of the skirts and blouses. They were sadly wrinkled but she took them into the small bathroom with her and hung them while she showered, hoping the wrinkles would disappear in the steam.

Has he asked for your commitment? Has he asked anything of you? Her inner voice continued to probe. She reviewed their time together, all of their conversations, and his lovemaking. He'd convinced her he'd never before experienced the feelings he'd shared with her. *That was something, wasn't it?* Perhaps, but what? Where did she stand with him now? Where did they go from here?

Paige had never before been faced with her own vulnerability, and she was afraid of what the future might bring.

After her shower, Paige dressed and did her hair carefully in the topknot she generally wore in the summer. Feeling much more like her old self, she went down the hall to see Hawk.

She found him sitting up in bed sipping a cup of coffee. A tray of empty dishes on the table nearby attested to the fact he had eaten, and well.

Alicia was seated by the bed, but hopped up when

Paige walked in. "Your patient is doing much better this morning, doctor," she announced brightly.

Paige smiled at Hawk. "I'm certainly glad to hear it."

He did not return her smile. In fact, his glance was one he might have given a casual acquaintance. "I'm surprised to still find you here, Dr. Winston. I figured you'd be on your way to Flagstaff by now."

Dr. Winston? Then Paige glanced at Alicia's interested expression. *He wants to keep up appearances, does he? I wonder why?*

Suddenly shy, Paige walked over to the side of the bed and reached for his forehead. "Any fever this morning?"

He flinched away from her hand. "Of course not. There's nothing wrong with me but a few scrapes and bruises." His voice was brusque.

"And a couple of broken ribs," she added.

"You don't know that for sure," he insisted.

"True. Without X rays, I can't be positive. But there's every indication."

He shrugged, then winced. "Maybe so. But they'll heal."

She grinned. "And you're tough, right?"

He stared at her, his expression giving nothing of his thoughts away. "Tough enough."

Tension grew in the room, and even Alicia became aware of it. She picked up the tray and said, "Well, I'll go wash these up." She paused at the door and gave Hawk a dazzling smile. "You behave now."

For the first time since Paige had walked into the room Hawk's face relaxed into a soul-wrenching smile. "I don't have the strength to do anything else." His smile widened to a grin when she laughed.

"Why aren't you gone?" Hawk asked Paige in a careless tone after Alicia disappeared down the hall.

"Because I didn't want to go off and leave you," she explained patiently.

He shifted restlessly in the bed. "There's no reason for you to stick around here. I'm sure Alicia's dad will give you a ride into the nearest town and you can find some kind of transportation to Flagstaff."

"Do you intend to go to Flagstaff?"

His eyes suddenly veered away from her and he looked out the window as though intently studying the scenery. "I might, later. There's no rush for me. I've got to figure out if we can salvage the plane. That might be quite a project."

She sat down by the bed and placed her hand over his. She could feel him tense. "Hawk, what's wrong?"

He rolled his head slowly on the pillow so that he was facing her. Without expression he said, "You are the one who just told me."

"You know that's not what I'm talking about."

A nerve began to jump in his cheek, and she realized his teeth were tightly clamped. He shrugged.

"I guess I'm having trouble knowing how to thank you for saving my life...then telling you goodbye."

His gaze dropped and he studied her hand still lying on top of his.

"Oh, Hawk, is that what this is all about? Can't your macho self-esteem accept a little help from a tenderfoot female?" she teased.

He grinned, and it was close to his natural, humorous expression. "Oh, my macho image might have been knocked around a bit, but I think it's going to survive."

She cocked her head to one side and asked, "Why do we have to say goodbye?" She hoped he couldn't hear her heart pounding in her chest. The answer to that question held all the hopes for their future.

Once more his gaze met hers and the sadness in his eyes caused her throat to tighten in despair. *No!* she protested silently. *Don't say it!*

But he did. "No matter how we got here, and who saved whom, the fact remains that my job is over. I'm sure the insurance will cover all your costs. I'm sorry I didn't get you to Flagstaff."

"But what about us, Hawk?"

He jerked his hand away from under hers. "There is no *us*, Paige. What did you expect? I'm not some tame lapdog that you can come home to each evening. I'm too restless to stay in one place, anyway. But even if I could, I wouldn't want to live on the fringe of your life. I'd want all of you, not just the leftovers when you were through with your work each day."

He was putting into words what Paige had known all along. So why did it hurt so much to know that he recognized the futility of trying to prolong their relationship as much as she did?

Because I wanted to believe in happy ever after and love overcoming all obstacles and that love will find a way. She could feel the tears sliding down her cheeks but refused to try to hide them. "I love you, Hawk."

His impassive expression threatened to completely break her composure. *Damn his stoic Indian heritage!*

"What we shared was very special," he finally said in a low voice. "Nothing can ever change that."

"But I want more than just a week with you, Hawk," she pleaded.

A lopsided smile appeared on his face. "You've always existed in an environment where you got whatever you wanted, Paige, but life isn't always like that for everyone. You and I live in two different worlds. We've always known that."

They both heard the sound of a vehicle on gravel drive up and stop outside the trailer.

"That's probably Alicia's dad. She said he was going to come back to take you into town." His eyes were level and without expression when he added, "You'd better go with him."

She nodded, defeated by his polite, calm attitude. There was nothing for her to say—he'd said it all.

Paige paused at the door to the bedroom and turned. For a moment she thought she saw anguish on his face, but it was gone and he continued to meet her gaze without flinching. "Goodbye, Hawk. Take care of yourself."

"You too."

She was thankful she didn't see anyone as she hastened back to the room she'd shared with Alicia. She gathered up the few things that had survived the past week and walked out to meet John.

Paige felt as though she'd been bouncing in the front seat of the pickup truck for years. Sooner or later she was bound to reach Flagstaff.

John had taken her to a little settlement where she found a pay phone and called the hospital. The news was good. She'd even been able to speak to her father and to explain that she was on her way to see him. He'd sounded fine—much better than she felt, as a matter of fact. *Just remember, Paige old girl, nobody's died of a broken heart.*

John had taken her to his brother's house and explained that his brother was going into Flagstaff that day and could give her a ride. She thankfully accepted their help and began her lonely journey back to her old life. She tried to plan what she would do when she reached Flagstaff—find a motel; go shopping; try to forget Hawk; take a hot, soaking bath; try to forget Hawk; go see her father; eat dinner; try to forget Hawk.

Paige rested her head against the back of the seat and closed her eyes.

Try to forget Hawk. That would be the hardest thing to do. There was so much to remember...

"How would you like to learn how to fish?" Hawk had asked Paige the second day they were together.

"Are you sure fishing is part of the curriculum?" she managed to answer. Her head was still sore and she hadn't felt like doing much.

"Wellll..." He ran his hand through his already rumpled hair. "It's the least strenuous thing I can think of for you to do, under the circumstances." He lightly touched the side of her head.

"Good point. I hope I'm not being graded on my performance as a camping mate. Otherwise, I'd have flunked by now."

Hawk laughed. His eyes were so beautiful—they sparkled when he laughed. She loved to say things to amuse him. "You're in luck. You aren't being graded this week. You've been put on the sick list and relieved of all duties."

She gave an exaggerated sigh of relief. "In that case, let's get on with this serious business of fishing."

By the end of the afternoon, they realized she had a long way to go to get the hang of it. Paige had managed to snag a bush, a limb, two rocks, and made a rat's nest of the line before admitting defeat.

"You're giving up?" Hawk asked with simulated surprise.

"Before you fire me. Yes, I am."

"You mean you don't like to fish?"

"How would I know? I haven't had a hook in the water yet. Is there a chance there *are* fish somewhere besides the water?"

"'Fraid not."

"Then we cannot consider that I have been fishing."

Hawk found some shade by the stream and suggested they rest after their strenuous afternoon. Paige was more than ready to comply. The least bit of exercise and her head tended to swim.

He pulled her head into his lap and softly stroked her hair from her face. "Have you ever been deep-sea fishing?"

"Uh-uh. Can you imagine what I'd do with one of *those* lines?" She relaxed, soothed by his gentle touch.

"Oh, you probably wouldn't have any problem at all. They have everything rigged up for you on the boat so that all you do is cast out, then sit and wait for a strike." He smiled at his memories. "Boy, can that be exciting."

"Do you go often?"

"Whenever the mood strikes me."

"It must be nice to do whatever you want, whenever you want."

"It has its advantages...and its disadvantages. It can get a little lonely."

"Not anymore. Or have you already forgotten you now have a wife that will tag along?"

* * *

He'd changed the subject, Paige remembered now, pointing out a bird, then suggesting she go to sleep to rest her head. He'd had several opportunities to tell her the truth, but Paige reluctantly faced that they were during the time when she was still suffering from her concussion.

He hadn't wanted to upset her. Instead he'd allowed her to believe they were married, giving her time to fall in love with him.

The pickup slowed, then turned onto the highway. The relief from the jouncing was tremendous. Paige rubbed her head. She no longer had pain of any kind, but she'd never remembered her lost hours.

From what Hawk told her, she'd only forgotten the call about her father, and the plane ride. If only she hadn't assumed she was married. What had made her assume such a thing?

Because you would never have shared a man's bed without being married, her inner voice pointed out implacably.

Oh, that.

Yes, that.

But I ended up making love to him, anyway, she pointed out.

Only after you recognized how deeply you were in love with him. The need to express that love was stronger than thirty years of inhibitions.

Paige could find no answer to that.

* * *

It was dark when they reached Flagstaff. Paige had John's brother drop her off at the mall so that she could find something decent to wear to the hospital. He refused payment for the ride, explaining it hadn't been out of his way.

By the time she found what she needed, it was after nine o'clock. She checked into a small motel near the hospital, called to find out the latest news regarding her father, and decided to wait until morning to visit him. The trip into town had taken more out of her than she'd expected. Paige wondered how long it would take her to recover from her experiences during the past week.

Eight weeks later she was still asking herself the same question.

Her father was more to the point. "What are you trying to do to yourself, Paige, have a coronary by the time you're thirty-five?"

Paige had stopped off to see Phillip Winston at his home. At fifty-four, Phillip looked ten years younger, though his russet-colored hair was freely frosted with silver.

"Dad, please don't fuss. We've been over this before. I am *not*, repeat *not*, working too hard. I am eating enough, I am sleeping enough, there is nothing wrong with me. I'm working the same hours I've always worked." She leaned over and kissed him as he sat in the shade out on his patio. "Besides, I stopped by today to check on *your* health, not to discuss mine.''

''You never want to discuss yours,'' he grumbled.

''That's because there's nothing to discuss.''

''If you say so.''

''Good. I'm glad to have that out of the way.'' She settled comfortably in the chaise lounge next to his and sipped from the tall, frosted glass of iced tea that Sarah, Phillip's indomitable housekeeper, had brought out to them. ''Your problem, dear doctor, is that you're bored, so you're letting your imagination have a field day.''

''I *know* I'm bored, Paige. Why the hell wouldn't I be? I could have been back to work two weeks ago.''

''Of course you could have,'' she agreed smoothly, ''and been back in the hospital the week afterward.''

''I am not an invalid and I'm tired of being treated like one.''

Paige couldn't conceal the amusement in her eyes. ''Oh, I don't think Sarah and I treat you like an invalid. I think we treat you more as a child having periodic temper tantrums. That's because that's the way you've been behaving.'' She enjoyed another swallow of her refreshing beverage while she watched that thrust hit home.

Phillip stared at her, startled. The Paige he was used to wouldn't have been quite so caustic, but he ruefully acknowledged to himself she might have some cause.

"Have I really been that bad?"

"Let me put it this way—I've got patients in the hospital right now who are handling their convalescence with more maturity than you've been showing."

"Temper tantrums, huh?"

"Close."

Phillip sighed. "Okay. I'll behave."

"Oh, we don't expect miracles, love, just a little more effort on your part. Believe it or not, we all want to see you back at the clinic just as badly as you want to be there."

He reached over and patted her hand. "Yes, little mother hen, but please don't patronize me."

Paige's eyes glistened with pain. "Dad, I don't mean to sound patronizing, but you scared all of us with that heart attack. We don't want it recurring."

"Amen to that."

"Look, I've got to run. There's a young patient I want to check on. He went home three days ago, and I promised to visit him."

"Aren't you staying for lunch?"

She glanced at her watch. "Not today. I'll grab something later—and I'll be back to see you tomorrow." She stood up. "Would you like me to bring you a coloring book and some crayons?" He threw a small pillow at her as she opened the sliding-glass door into the house. "That's strange. All my other patients are generally delighted with the suggestion."

With a fond smile, Phillip watched her leave. He

was inordinately proud of his daughter and didn't care who knew it. He'd always felt they had a good, close relationship—until recently.

Something was definitely bothering her. Her excuse that she was busy at the clinic made sense, but she'd always stayed busy and had seemed to thrive on the hectic pace. That was no longer true.

He could tell she wasn't sleeping well, and she'd lost weight. Paige had always been slender, burning up calories relentlessly as soon as she consumed them, but now her appetite was practically nonexistent.

Phillip had a strong hunch all of her behavior could be traced back to her week in the wilderness. Whenever he tried to discuss it with her, she changed the subject.

He didn't like to see himself as a nosy parent. In fact, Phillip took pride in the fact that he'd always allowed Paige the freedom to make her own decisions without his influence. So why was he feeling the need to confront her with her recent behavior and demand some answers, like the father of a recalcitrant teenager?

He was worried about her—not only because she was his daughter, but because she was his partner and his friend. Phillip suddenly recognized that had one of his other partners or associates been behaving in a similar manner he would not have hesitated to sit down with them and try to find out what was wrong. That's what friends were for.

The next time Paige came over, he'd approach her as a friend rather than a father to see if he could get her to open up to him.

It was plain that she needed someone, but he had a sneaking hunch it wasn't her father!

The late-August sun continued to beat down on the city of El Paso. Wisps of hair stuck to Paige's forehead and she decided to stop and have lunch somewhere quiet and air-conditioned rather than drive through a fast-food place.

Her young patient was doing nicely and she was glad she'd taken the time to check on him. His corrective surgery was healing satisfactorily, and she was pleased with his progress.

She took the next exit off the freeway and saw a Luby's Cafeteria sign. Just what she needed. With her lack of appetite these days, a delicious array of attractive choices would encourage her to eat.

She remembered the meals she'd shared with Hawk. Hawk. Sooner or later her thoughts always returned to him and to their time together. Paige wondered if he ever thought of her. Oh, how she wished she could quit thinking about him!

It was unfortunate for Paige's peace of mind that she'd no sooner found a small table and begun to eat than Hawk walked into the cafeteria with three other men.

They were all dressed in colorful coveralls, and she

realized the cafeteria wasn't too far from the airport. Why had she picked this particular place to eat today?

She watched him hungrily, making a mockery of all of her determined efforts to forget him. The four of them were all laughing and joking with each other and the people behind the counter. It was obvious they were regular customers.

He looked marvelous. *At least you know he hasn't been pining away for you.*

The men took their loaded trays to a table across the large room. She discovered she'd been holding her breath, waiting for him to notice her. He didn't. He sat in profile to her and she had an opportunity to prove or to disprove her theories. For weeks she'd tried to convince herself he had only seemed attractive to her because of the environment they'd shared. Paige had to concede that she found him devastatingly attractive regardless of his environment.

Two women walked by the table occupied by the men and stopped. Paige watched Hawk glance up at them and smile—the warm, sensuous smile that accelerated her pulse rate.

Hastily finishing her glass of iced tea, Paige stood up abruptly. Whatever interest he'd shown in her before, he had none now, and she was making herself needlessly miserable by dwelling on what they had shared.

Ignoring the temptation to go over to him and say hello, she made herself walk out of the cafeteria without a backward glance. They had already said all there was to say to each other.

Hawk glanced toward the door and watched a woman leave the cafeteria. She reminded him of Paige, but that wasn't unusual. Everywhere he went these days, he was reminded of Paige.

He couldn't forget her.

It had taken him several weeks to recover from his injuries, including the ribs. Paige had been right about them. It had taken him several more weeks to get his plane out of that meadow.

He'd also found out why no one had found him and Paige. The control tower had lost track of him in the storm and he was nowhere near where he was supposed to be when they were forced down. They could have stayed there for six months and probably not been spotted.

A tiny curve appeared on his lips at the thought. *That might not have been so bad. Maybe I could have gotten her out of my system in that length of time.*

Who was he kidding? He'd already discovered how difficult it was to forget her. He would welcome a nice case of total amnesia about now. He could remember everything she had said to him, everything they had done together, and at night he dreamed he was making love to her. His memories were driving him out of his mind.

Now he thought he saw her everywhere he went. He shook his head.

"Where've you been, Hawk? I've asked you to hand me the salt three times. You tryin' to save me from sodium poisoning or something?" His friend grinned at him.

"Sorry. I was thinking."

"Yeah, we noticed. Our conversation must be too boring for you, right?"

"You got it."

They finished their meal heckling each other, and once again Hawk tried to put Paige out of his mind.

A few days later he decided that the best thing for him to do would be to look her up—go see her—maybe take her to dinner. No doubt his imagination was building her up too much. If he saw her in her natural environment, he'd be reminded of why they had no future together.

He found her number listed in the telephone book, but when he called he discovered he'd reached her answering service. An answering service. What other woman of his acquaintance had a damned answering service? He refused the offer to have Paige return his call, but he couldn't get her out of his mind.

When Hawk saw the mention in the local paper of a hospital benefit being held he thought about attending. It would give him a chance to see her, maybe speak to her—find out if she was all right. He could treat it as a casual meeting between acquaintances. If he could see her one more time, he was sure he'd be better able to deal with his feelings.

Ten days later he realized how big a fool he'd been.

Hawk leaned against the marble pillar of the mammoth hotel convention room, watching the cream of the city's society dancing by, decked out in all their finery. The glittering decorations had turned the room into a magical fairyland. Unfortunately Hawk had never believed in fairy tales. He felt ridiculous in his rented formal wear, unaware of the admiring glances he was receiving from several of the women in the room. Why had he ever thought going there was a good idea?

What if Paige didn't come? Why had he thought she would? Were doctors obligated to attend these affairs?

Hawk slowly straightened as he spotted her at the entrance to the ballroom. Paige wore an ivory gown that flowed around her petite form with flattering attention to her feminine shape. She wore her hair loose around her shoulders, and Hawk suffered a sharp pain as memories assailed him.

Her hand rested lightly on the sleeve of the distinguished man who stood by her side, tall and slim. The resemblance was strong. Paige's father. Hawk felt a slight easing of tension. At least her father was all right—one question answered. He watched them circulate around the room, greeting the dignitaries, making conversation, and the gulf between them had never been more apparent to him.

She was like a fairy-tale princess holding court. Several men stood around her, vying for her attention. Why had she made her life sound so lacking in social contact? She appeared comfortable and at ease, totally in her element.

He'd seen enough. More than enough. He recognized that more than the room separated them. He'd never be comfortable in her environment. He wouldn't want to try.

Paige accepted the lighthearted teasing regarding her appearance with a smile.

"How come you never dress like that when you're at the hospital?" Rob Hartman asked.

She glanced down at her gown. "Because I'd probably trip over my skirt halfway through making rounds."

"No. I mean wear your hair down like that."

Paige knew why she'd worn her hair loose. She'd been thinking of Hawk, remembering how he'd enjoyed running his hands through it. Her father had noticed the new style when he came to pick her up and commented on how attractive she looked.

"Sorry, Rob. It isn't practical to wear it loose during the day." She smiled and absently glanced around the room. A tall, attractive man in superbly tailored clothes strode toward the exit. *He looks like Hawk,* she thought. With a small gasp Paige realized it *was* Hawk—and he was leaving.

"Excuse me for a moment, will you?" she murmured. Without waiting for a response, she hurried across the floor.

Of course it was Hawk. No one else had that indefinable air of authority and arrogance he carried—nor walked with the lithe grace of a jungle cat.

People stopped her repeatedly while she tried to catch up with him. By the time she reached the door he was no longer in sight.

Why had he come? To see her? If so, why hadn't he spoken to her? She could make no sense of his behavior, but long after the evening had been forgotten by others, Paige remembered Hawk's presence at the gala event.

She could think of only one reason why he'd attended—to see her.

Twelve

Paige shook her head at the proffered plate of food. "I can't eat another bite, Dad. I'm stuffed."

Phillip glanced at the plate in front of his daughter. She had only taken a few spoonfuls of food on it, and he shook his head. "Paige, you aren't eating enough to keep a bird alive."

She laughed. "Remember when you used to tease me about eating like a bird—a vulture?"

He grinned. "So you did, as a teenager. But you burned it off before it turned into fat. Now you're burning calories you can't afford to lose." He bit off his next thought, determined to choose a better time to discuss his concerns with her.

Sarah came into the dining room with a pot of coffee and poured them each another cup.

"Sarah, your meal was delicious, as always," Paige told her.

The older woman smiled. "I'm glad you enjoyed it."

Phillip stood up. "Why don't we have our coffee in the den, Paige, so we can stretch out and get comfortable."

Paige had fallen into the habit of spending Friday evenings with her father years ago. Nothing had broken that routine. It gave them a chance to catch up on personal news as well as professional problems they might have. Paige had long since discovered that although they worked in the same clinic, they rarely had time to see each other, except while passing in the hall.

Paige settled back in one of her dad's recliners with a sigh. She couldn't remember when she'd felt so tired. A fleeting image of hiking through rugged mountains flashed before her, but she determinedly shoved it away. That happened in another lifetime—to someone else.

"Paige?"

"Hmm?"

"I'm worried about you."

She glanced up at her father in surprise. He was stretched out in another recliner, looking well and rested. He had been given permission to work in the clinic on a part-time, consulting basis for the next few weeks, cheering him up considerably.

"What do you mean?"

"You've lost weight—you aren't eating—I don't think you're getting enough rest—and it bothers me. I thought you and I were friends."

She stared at him. "We *are* friends."

"But not close enough to share our troubles?"

Puzzled by his serious tone, Paige replied, "Dad, I don't know what you're talking about."

He shrugged. He couldn't force her to talk, not if she didn't want to, but he could read the signs. She needed to talk to someone. Desperately. His eyes were filled with love and concern when he said, "Paige, have you thought about getting professional counseling?"

Was she that bad? she wondered with dismay. Was it so obvious that she was suffering? She'd made every effort to forget Hawk and their time together. She'd managed to put him out of her mind for large blocks of time during the day, but he invariably showed up in her dreams at night until she thought she was losing her mind.

Maybe she was.

She sat up in her chair so that she faced Phillip. Maybe it would help to talk about it.

"Do you remember when you had your heart attack and I flew to Flagstaff...or at least I tried to fly?"

He nodded, unwilling to interrupt now that she seemed to have started.

"Being marooned with another person for a week gives you a chance to know him better than if you'd known him for years." She searched for words to explain what happened between her and Hawk. She wasn't even sure that she herself understood.

"I'm sure it would," Phillip murmured.

"I've never known anyone like Hawk Cameron. He's as different as any alien that might have landed from another planet." She looked up and met his quiet gaze. "I found him fascinating."

She waited for his comment, but he made none. He seemed to be waiting for her to continue.

"Hawk is a loner. He's been on his own since he was fourteen...traveled and worked all over the world...and is content to continue his wanderings. I doubt that he'll ever settle in one place."

Phillip was beginning to understand, more by what Paige wasn't saying than her actual statements. "You fell in love with him," he stated quietly.

Her head jerked up from studying her fingers twisting together in her lap. She stared at him in confusion. "I don't know what I feel anymore. I can't seem to forget him. I can recall every conversation we ever had, everything we ever did together..." Her slight blush gave Phillip enough information to draw his own conclusions. "He taught me so much about how to survive in a wilderness, how to rely on myself and nature's provisions, even though he'd brought enough equipment to keep us in comfort." She shook her head. "I don't understand why I miss him so much."

Her dad smiled. "It certainly sounds like love to me."

"How do you get over it?"

"Why should you want to?"

She shrugged. "I don't have much choice. He made it clear we come from two different worlds."

"You already knew that."

"Yes."

"But it doesn't make any difference to you."

Her eyes slowly filled with tears until Phillip was only a blur. "No. It doesn't."

"So what do you intend to do about it?"

"Not a thing. It takes more than one person loving to make a relationship work."

"Ohhhh," Phillip drew out. "Now I understand. Although you fell in love with him, he showed no interest in you."

Paige could feel the heat in her body at the memory of the amount of interest Hawk had shown toward her. In a low voice that Phillip could scarcely hear, she murmured, "He said he loved me."

"Maybe he does."

"But not enough."

"Now I'm not sure I understand what *you* mean. What sort of measuring stick are you using?"

"He told me he wasn't some sort of tame lapdog to wait around until I had some time to give to him." Her hurt and pain echoed through the words.

It was unfortunate that Phillip laughed. Her eyes widened with pain at the sound.

"Paige, honey, you wouldn't be interested in a tame lapdog that sat around and waited for your attention. Why does that comment upset you?"

She thought about his question for a long while. "I guess because I felt he was criticizing my dedication to my profession. I had already told him I didn't have time for a personal relationship in my life."

"Then I don't blame him for his remark. You had already made it clear you weren't willing to change anything in your life to accommodate a relationship with him."

Surprised at his insight, Paige stared at her father with dismay. "That's right, I did."

"So what did you expect him to do...or say? If he's half the man you've described to me, he would want more than bits and pieces of your life."

"That's true, but that's all I have to give."

"Is it?"

"You're a doctor. You know how demanding a profession it is."

"Yes, and I know that I made some serious mistakes in choosing to let it take over my life."

She'd never heard her father talk that way, and when she saw the pain in his face she realized he had some painful memories of his own.

"I loved your mother more than you could possibly imagine, Paige. She was everything I'd ever wanted in a wife...or a lover. And wonder of wonders, she felt the same way about me. Those kinds of shared feelings are very rare and should be appreciated and treasured. They should never be taken for granted." Phillip paused and swallowed, as though his throat had been constricted.

"In my arrogance I took our love for each other for granted. I was young and ambitious—" he gave a rueful shrug "—and very shortsighted. I assumed we had forever together, but in the meantime I had a practice to build, a living to make, demands on my time to fulfill..."

He faced Paige, the pain in his eyes almost more than she could bear. "Then it was too late to change the habits I'd set up. Too late to arrange my schedule so that I could stay home with your mother." He shook his head. "She never complained, although I knew she felt that she came second in my life. But she was wrong. So wrong. I just assumed that we'd have time together later...always later...at some mystical point in life. I didn't realize that I needed to realign my priorities at the very beginning, because some of us aren't given enough time for all we want to do."

Tears ran down Paige's face as she listened to her father. She had memories of her own that confirmed what he was saying. She remembered her mother's joy when her dad came home early and spent any time with them. Her mother counted the days to his vacation when they were off together, away from the heavy demands of his profession.

Paige had always known how much her mother had loved her dad. She'd never understood until now how much her father had loved her mother.

He had given Paige a great deal to think about.

* * *

Paige stared up at the ceiling above her bed late that night, thinking of all she'd learned. Life was full of choices—almost too many. Sometimes one choice wiped out many equally fulfilling ones.

Is that what she'd done by choosing medicine as a career? She'd never cared before. Her dedication was all-encompassing and satisfying. She'd never needed anything more to make her life complete—until now.

She needed Hawk. She needed his calm, level-headed attitude toward life that seemed to keep things in perspective. She needed his love and affection, his teasing, his enjoyment of his surroundings—and his steady warmth in her bed each night.

But how did he feel? He'd made it clear he didn't want to be tied down, hadn't he? He enjoyed his present life-style—free to come and go as he pleased.

What if he didn't want her?

She recalled the day they'd found the river again and saw him once again standing under the hard-driving water pouring over the lip of the falls. She saw the look on his face, the love and desire shining in his eyes when he had turned around and had seen her standing there before him.

She remembered the urgency of his lovemaking, the fierce possession, his loss of control with her. He had wanted her then. Was there any way she could make him want her now? Even if he wanted her, would he be willing to share her life?

A sudden thought struck her. A thought so foreign that she was shaken. Was she willing to share *his* life?

Paige spent many days and sleepless nights facing that thought-provoking question.

The late-September sun beat down on the metal hangar where Hawk was working on the engine of his plane. He could feel the perspiration trickling down his back, underneath his mechanic's coveralls.

He rapped his knuckle against one of the parts deep inside the engine and colored the air with a few pungent statements regarding the engine, the plane and El Paso's hot weather.

Straightening, Hawk rubbed his back, tired from the bent-over position he'd held for so long, and glanced out the hangar door. The blue Texas sky looked like a backdrop to Mount Franklin, sitting there like a crouching cat overlooking the city. He walked over to the water fountain and took a long, reviving drink.

Hawk knew he was in bad shape, but he wasn't sure what the hell to do about it. Not that he hadn't tried—he'd almost killed himself trying.

He still couldn't forget Paige. Seeing her at the formal benefit had convinced him they could never make a relationship work, but it hadn't helped him to forget her. That was the first night Hawk had gone out and deliberately drunk himself into oblivion. Unfortunately it hadn't been the last.

He'd tried to replace her memory with other women. He knew several in El Paso and he began to call them. Only, they seemed different to him somehow. Their conversations were boring. Had he ever bothered sitting around talking with them before? Probably not. He decided he probably wouldn't find anyone like Paige to talk to, but he could certainly replace her in bed.

After the third attempt, he'd quit trying. The damn woman had turned him into a eunuch. Embarrassed, he'd had to explain to his dates that he'd had too much to drink. After he'd left them he'd made damn sure that was the case before he finally went to bed.

Damn her.

Rick walked into the hangar just as Hawk picked up a small wrench.

"Uh, Hawk..." Rick was never sure how to approach Hawk anymore. He was worse than a grizzly with a thorn in its paw. Rick didn't think Hawk would be any too pleased with the news he had for him.

"Yeah?" Hawk was already reaching for the troubled insides of the engine.

"There's somebody here to see you."

Hawk raised his head in surprise. No one ever came out to the airport to see him. "Who is it?" The frown he wore wasn't encouraging.

"Well, I only saw her once, but I think it's the same woman who chartered the plane last summer to go to Flagstaff." He shuffled his feet. "I didn't ask her for her name."

Hawk felt like Rick had just picked up a sledgehammer and swung into his midsection. He could scarcely breathe, and the pain in his chest made him realize his lungs had quit working.

"Paige?" he said faintly.

"Yeah, I think that's her name. Dr. Winston, isn't it?"

"Paige is here?"

Rick nodded, surprised at the stunned expression on Hawk's face. He had no way of knowing that Hawk was certain his mind had finally managed to conjure her up in the flesh since he'd been thinking of her for so long.

"What's she want?" he asked gruffly, staring down at the forgotten tool in his hand.

Rick scratched his head. "Well, she said something about wanting to charter a plane or something...said she only wanted you for the pilot."

What the hell? She needed a plane so she'd looked up her old pal, the half-breed pilot? What kind of game was she playing?

"Tell her I'm busy."

"I did."

"So?"

"So, she said she'd wait."

Once again the air was full of Hawk's invective as he discussed the vagaries of certain women who could take off in the middle of the day and wait around indefinitely to see someone.

Rick waited. "What do you want me to tell her?"

Hawk stared at his friend. He and Rick had met in southeast Asia more years ago than either cared to admit. They knew each other too well for him to try to fool Rick now.

He groaned, knowing he was going to have to see her one more time. "Send her out here."

Rick looked around the large hangar in surprise. "Out here? She'll get dirty around all these greasy parts."

"That's just too damned bad, isn't it? If she wants to see me, she can come out here. I'm not going to get cleaned up to talk to some society dame."

Rick backed away. "Okay, no need to take your bad mood out on me, Hawk. Just back off, will you?"

Hawk stared at his friend in alarm. "I'm sorry, Rick. I didn't mean to come across so strong."

Rick waved his hand. "No problem. The trouble with you is lack of a good love life." He laughed as he walked away.

If only Rick knew just how accurate his teasing comment had been. Hawk didn't need Paige's presence to remind him that he hadn't been with a woman since he'd been with her.

Hawk grabbed a rag and began to wipe the grease off his hands. He stood there, facing the door where she would enter, bracing himself to deal with her one more time. At least he'd make sure this would be the last time.

The door hesitantly opened and Paige peeked around, then walked into the hangar. She wore a sleeveless dress made of some type of sheer material, the skirt swirling around her knees. The style drew attention to her beautifully shaped legs and highlighted her slim ankles. Sandles with high heels accented the delicate arch of her small feet. Hawk felt his body react to her.

Just what he needed—visible evidence that she still had a strong effect on him.

She walked toward him as though unsure of her welcome. As she drew closer he realized she'd lost weight. Her air of fragility was even more enhanced. He stood where he was, forcing her to come to him.

When Paige opened the door to the hangar she was shaking so hard she was certain she'd be unable to walk through it. Then her attention was drawn to the foreign-looking garage area of the charter service. She'd never seen anything like it. The building was huge, sheltering three planes and several engines, all partially broken down.

At first she didn't see Hawk—until he moved. He wore greasy coveralls, bright red, and a grease smear across his cheek. The force of her heartbeat seemed to shake her entire body when she spotted him. He stood there watching her, unsmiling.

Paige had thought about this meeting for weeks. She and her father had discussed the possible outcomes and how she might deal with them. What if he refused her? How could she survive without him? It didn't bear thinking about.

She reminded herself that she'd never been one to sit and wait for something to happen, and she couldn't wait any longer for Hawk. She had to face him once and for all. As she neared where he stood she suddenly wished she'd waited a while longer. She wasn't ready for this!

"Hello, Hawk."

"Why aren't you at the clinic?" were his first words.

"I have Wednesday afternoons off."

"Oh."

He looked down at the rag he held, then continued to clean his hands as though removing the grease from his fingers was the most important thing in his life at the moment.

"How have you been? Are your ribs all right?"

"Fine. I'm just fine. How about you?"

She smiled. How honest dared she be? *I'm miserable, Hawk. I haven't had a decent night's sleep since I last slept in your arms. I haven't enjoyed a meal since the last one we cooked out on an open fire.* "Okay, I guess."

He stared at her, waiting, but when she didn't say any more he impatiently asked, "What brought you out here?"

She tensed at his abrupt question. Being close to him, she caught the slight scent of his after-shave—the scent that had haunted so many of her dreams. What she wanted to do was throw herself into his arms, but he made it obvious she wouldn't be welcomed.

Maybe she should leave. She'd already received

her answer, in his tone, his speech, and his body language. She meant nothing to him.

Or he's hiding his feelings. Remember—he's good at that. You always had trouble trying to figure out what he was thinking.

Paige took a deep breath and then slowly exhaled. "I wanted to charter a plane to go camping...and I was hoping you'd be willing to pilot me."

Go camping! Was she out of her mind? Hawk's glance fell, and he noticed her hands. They were systematically shredding a tissue. A slight smile formed on his lips, then was quickly gone. *She's nervous. I wonder why?*

He shook his head. "Sorry, Paige, but I'm not available to fly you anywhere. Didn't Rick tell you I'm leaving El Paso?"

Paige couldn't have been more shocked at his words than if he'd slapped her across her face. In all of her fantasies the one constant was that Hawk would somehow be nearby.

"Where are you going?" Her lips were so stiff she could barely move them.

"A Peruvian landowner I met a few years ago called and asked if I'd be interested in coming to work for him. He's got extensive landholdings and decided having a plane and a full-time pilot on hand would make his life much simpler."

"When will you be leaving?"

Her words hung between them, slowly dissipating in the continued silence. Finally he shrugged, then motioned to the plane behind him. "Whenever I can get this thing running again. It hasn't acted right since I cracked up in that meadow in Arizona."

Paige looked closer at the plane behind him. "You mean this is the plane we were in?"

"Yes. It's the only one I have, but I'm thinking of selling it and buying another one before I go to South America. I'm not sure I really trust this one anymore."

He leaned against the wing and patted the side of the plane. It was an affectionate pat, effectively negating his words.

"How did you get it back here?"

"It wasn't easy. I flew a helicopter in and worked on it. Finally had to get some help to get it out of there, but we managed."

"Hawk?" She couldn't hide the trembling in her voice.

His eyes met hers in a calm stare. "Yes?"

"Would you like to come over to my place tonight for dinner?"

His expression never changed. "Why?"

"Because I want to see you again...and talk to you."

"What about?"

She fought to keep from saying *us*, because she knew the answer to that. He refused to accept there was a chance for the two of them. But she was ready to fight for the love they shared. A couple of times since she'd entered the hangar Paige had seen past the stoic facade he wore. He'd missed her. Just as she'd missed him. Somehow she had to convince him to give them a chance, but she needed more time to plan. His intention to leave El Paso threw all of her thoughts out of kilter.

"Do we have to have a reason to spend an evening together?" she finally asked.

"Not really. I just don't see the point myself."

"Please, Hawk. For me."

When she looks at me with those waiflike blue eyes pleading, I'm lost. All of my willpower deserts me. This has to be the dumbest thing I've ever done. I must get some sort of pleasure out of making myself miserable. There's a name for people who enjoy being miserable.

"What time?"

Her smile made him flinch—it was so beautiful. If he hadn't still been holding the grease rag he would probably have dragged her into his arms and kissed her silly, but he managed to restrain himself.

"Why don't you come at seven." She fished around in her purse and found a pad and pencil. She wrote something down and tore off the sheet, handing it to him. "Here's my address." She seemed to be memorizing his features. "I'll let you get back to your plane. I'm sorry to have interrupted you." She backed up from him. "I'll see you tonight at seven." Paige left quickly, before he could change his mind.

Hawk continued to stand there, staring at the door she'd closed behind her. He was going to have dinner with her. He was going to her home to see where and how she lived. In other words, he was going to collect more memories of her to try to forget.

"I've got to be out of my ever-loving mind," he muttered in a gruff voice, turning back to the engine.

Chapter 13

Paige hurried to the door when she heard the bell. She didn't care if Hawk knew she was eager to see him. She had rushed home from the airport and industriously planned a menu to dazzle him, then realized what she was doing and laughed. They were so very far past that stage in their relationship. Yet he'd never been in her home. For that matter, she had no idea where he lived, either. None of that was important, she thought as she swung open the front door.

Hawk stood there waiting. He looked wonderful to her, wearing tailored chocolate-brown slacks, a creamy beige shirt that emphasized his dark good looks and a look in his eyes that was the most encouragement Paige had received from him all day!

"Come in," she said with a smile, and stepped back from the door.

Hawk stared at her in confusion. Gone was the doctor image he'd tried to focus on all afternoon. In its place stood a gorgeous woman in a caftan of swirling autumn colors. Bright earrings dangled from her pierced ears, peeking through the riotous curls that surrounded her face and shoulders.

Not fair. Not fair at all, Hawk decided. She ushered him into the living room, where he found more surprises. The place was nothing like what he had pictured. Her home was small, tucked within one of the many subdivisions in El Paso. Her living room looked comfortable and well used—nothing like the picture-perfect place he'd conjured up in his mind. Scatter pillows dotted the room with color and candles scented the air with the subtle smell of spices.

"I'm so glad you came over," Paige said breathlessly. He glanced down at her so close by his side. "I've missed you—very much."

Once again his body betrayed him as it responded to the woman only inches away from him. He turned slowly to her, gently stroking her hair behind her ear. "I've missed you too," he finally admitted to them both.

She slid her arms around his neck, going up on tiptoe to reach him. Hawk needed no more encouragement. His arms snaked around her waist and he pulled her tightly against him. His mouth found hers and his kiss left no doubt that he was hungry for her.

For the first time in months Paige felt as though

she had found her rightful place. Her home would always be in Hawk's arms.

Hawk's reaction to Paige made a mockery of all his fine intentions. He'd spent the afternoon steeling himself for the evening, determined not to give away any of his feelings for her. He'd decided to show them both that he could spend one last evening with her and they could part as friends.

As a matter of fact, he was feeling quite friendly toward her. Any friendlier and he would explode! Hawk reluctantly placed his hands at Paige's tiny waist and gently pushed her away from him.

Just as reluctantly Paige dropped her arms from around his neck. It felt so good to be near Hawk once more. She had felt his arousal and was reassured even more that her evening might have a happy ending. He certainly couldn't pretend to be indifferent to her.

"Are you hungry?" she asked, then realized how that sounded. Her face flushed.

Hawk started laughing. He hadn't laughed in months, but the release of his feelings felt great—wonderful. What was the use of denying it? He loved this woman to distraction. He might as well enjoy the little time he had with her.

"As a matter of fact..." he drawled, his eyes dancing.

Paige unconsciously placed her hands on her cheeks to cool them, then discovered what she'd done and dropped them to her side. He rubbed the back of his hand against her cheek. "It's good to see you with some color."

"Yes, well, uh, why don't we go into the dining room?" she asked nervously, and turned away.

The table was beautifully arranged with long tapered candles casting a glow to the room. A delicate bouquet of flowers added color.

"I'll go get the wine," she explained, and disappeared into the kitchen. She took a few minutes to force herself to relax, then found the wine in the refrigerator and returned to the other room. "Would you mind pouring?"

"Not at all." He took the bottle and the corkscrew from her. Paige returned to the kitchen and began to bring out their meal.

By the time they were through eating, both of them were more relaxed. They had quickly fallen into their former easy camaraderie. Paige asked him many questions; she wanted to know everything that had happened to him since she'd left him.

"I'm sure Alicia was upset when you left," she finally offered over the rim of her wineglass.

At least he has the grace to squirm at the reminder, she thought, watching him.

"Alicia was a nice kid. Very helpful."

"I can imagine."

"But she was just a kid. Hell, I'm old enough to be her father!"

"A very precocious father, but I suppose that's true."

"Speaking of fathers, you haven't mentioned how your dad is doing."

Paige sensed a deliberate change of subject. "He's doing great. Chomping at the bit to get back to a full-time routine."

"I suppose you've been pretty busy too."

"Yes, the clinic has been going through some major upheavals."

"How's that?"

"Well, we've hired three more doctors, and I've been cutting back considerably on my hours."

He stared at her in disbelief. "Why would you do that?"

She smiled. "Because that's what I want to do."

A sudden suspicion grabbed him, causing him to tense. "Are you pregnant?"

The look of worry and concern on his face almost decided Paige to put him out of his misery at once, but she couldn't quite resist stringing him along for a moment. "Funny you should ask."

He leaned across the table, studying her intently. "You are, aren't you? You've been sick, haven't you? That's why you're so thin."

"And if I am?" she asked with interest, folding her fingers together and resting her chin lightly on them.

Hawk stood up abruptly and began to pace the room. He'd never given it a thought. Not once. All the women he'd ever known had been experienced and knew how to look after themselves. But Paige hadn't been experienced. He'd recognized that immediately. And he'd done nothing to protect her.

What a bastard you are, he told himself. *In every sense of the word. You were going to go off to another country without even finding out—without even discovering if a child was on the way. Just like your father did.*

Paige stood up and began to clear the table. She'd taken all their dishes to the kitchen before Hawk followed her.

"We're going to get married," he stated firmly as soon as he walked through the kitchen door.

Paige turned around from the sink and stared at him. Never had she seen him so serious. "Why?"

He wasn't prepared for her question. The reason was obvious enough, wasn't it?

"Are you saying that you'd be willing to marry me because I might be pregnant?" she asked.

"Of course."

"But what about our different life-styles, our different worlds?"

A very stubborn expression appeared on his face. "Then we'll have to work something out between us...some sort of compromise. I know I'm not the type of person you'd ever marry, but I'm not going to let a child of mine come into this world not knowing its father."

Paige walked over to where Hawk stood in the middle of the kitchen floor and gently stroked his jaw. "Hawk, you're the only type of person I could ever imagine marrying. I spent almost a week thinking I was married to you, and I've never been happier." She leaned up and kissed him on the cheek. "I willingly accept your most romantic proposal," she whispered.

Fierce joy flooded Hawk at her words. She was going to marry him. He couldn't believe it. They were going to be married! Forgotten were all his plans to spend his life alone. Forgotten were all of his vows not to get involved. Dammit all, he *was* involved! He became involved the first time he made love to Paige.

"When is the baby due?" he asked.

Paige took him by the hand and led him back into the living room. She gently pushed him until he sat down on the sofa, then she draped herself across his lap, her arms curled around his neck.

"Hawk, do you love me?" she asked, staring straight into his eyes.

He'd lost the battle—with himself and with her—but for some reason he felt as though he'd won all the jackpots ever offered. He nuzzled her neck, tasting her, smelling her soft flowerlike scent. "Very much."

"That's good, because when we get married I'm all you'll get...at least for a while."

He raised his head and stared at her, bemused.

"I'm not pregnant, Hawk," she whispered.

"But you said...?"

"No, *you* said, and I let you think it." She settled more comfortably into his lap with a little wriggle that created havoc with Hawk's concentration. "You see,

I've spent the past several weeks trying to figure out a way to convince you that we could have a fine life together."

He opened his mouth to speak, and she placed her fingertips gently across his lips.

"I discovered that you were the most important thing in my life. More important than my career, even though I enjoy it very much. And I couldn't figure out a way to convince you." She dropped her head to his shoulder so that she no longer had to face him. "I'm ashamed to admit that when I discovered I wasn't pregnant I cried for hours. I had so wanted your baby, Hawk. I was even despicable enough to consider using a pregnancy in the hope you'd be swayed into giving us a chance together."

She kissed him lightly in front of his ear, then followed the strong jawline to his chin, her soft kisses creating chills along his spine.

"I love you, Hawk, and I want to marry you. But I'm not pregnant."

When she glanced up at him she couldn't speak. His eyes glistened with moisture, the tenderness and love in them causing her to catch her breath.

"Paige, love, how can I resist you?"

"I was hoping you couldn't."

He dropped his head on the back of the sofa. "So what now? I suppose I need to call the landowner in Peru and tell him I'm not coming..." he said, as though thinking aloud.

"Not necessarily. Why don't you call him and ask

if he could use a medical doctor anywhere on his staff."

Hawk's head snapped forward. "Are you serious?"

"I've never been more serious in my life. What is that old saying? Whither thou goest?" She smiled softly. "I don't want you to change, Hawk. I fell in love with the man you are. All I want to do is become a part of your life. Is that so hard to understand?"

Hawk couldn't believe what he was hearing. "But you're a doctor. You're already established here. Why would you want to move?"

"That's simple—to be with you. Hawk, I'll always be a doctor. Nothing can change that—it's a basic part of me. But there are sick people everywhere. If you're too restless to stay in one place, fine. We'll both move on."

"I think you've lost your mind."

"No, just my heart."

"I can't let you do it."

"Does that mean you're withdrawing your proposal?"

"No, but—I mean, maybe we need to think about this for a while..."

"That's all I've thought about for months. I have to be honest with you and admit it took me a while to work out all of my priorities. But I have them in order now. That is, if you want me."

"Want you! You've haunted me for months. I tried everything I knew to erase you from my mind." He bitterly recalled some of his more resounding failures. "I just want you to be sure."

"I love you, Hawk."

"Oh, dear God, Paige, I love you too. I just hope we're doing the right thing," he said in a husky voice. He kissed her, and Paige knew it was going to be all right. Love really would find a way.

Her thoughts scattered as Hawk deepened his possession of her mouth, his hands sliding down to the hem of her caftan, then slowly climbing once again. Everything was going to be just fine.

Three years later Paige was still convinced. Everything was just fine.

She turned over in their roomy, double sleeping bag and studied the sleeping man beside her with deep-seated love. She'd discovered a fascinating phenomenon—the longer she was with Hawk the more she loved him. Her love seemed to grow like a prolific plant that had been pampered and fed with the finest nutrients.

She watched him quietly, not wanting to wake him. He looked so tired. He'd been working too hard, which was the reason for their vacation.

Only, this time she'd known what to pack for a couple of weeks in the great outdoors. When they'd arrived back in the States last week, Hawk had borrowed a helicopter from Rick and explained they wanted to go camping—in eastern Arizona.

They'd found a lake fed by underground streams

and decided to stay for a few days. During their exploring Hawk had even found them a waterfall.

Peru had been an education Paige wouldn't have wanted to miss. She had grown to love the people in the village near their small home, and fortunately they had come to accept her. She'd been able to teach them how to care for their young ones, and found the experience very satisfying and fulfilling.

Hawk turned over, effectively pinning her into place by throwing an arm and a leg over her. "Move over, you big ox. You don't have to take up all the room," she complained, chuckling.

"Who's a big ox?"

"You are," she muttered.

"Is that any way for you to talk to your dearly beloved?"

"It is when your dearly beloved weighs almost two hundred pounds."

"I see. Does this mean that the honeymoon is over?"

"Of course not. We've only been married three years. Honeymoons are supposed to last up to twenty-five years. After that, we'll be on our own."

He tried to hide his smile, but was unsuccessful. "Are you warm enough?"

"Yes. This new camping gear is great, and so roomy."

Hawk stared up at the ceiling of their tent. It was a six-man tent, large enough so they could move around comfortably. He would never try to do any backpacking with it, but then, he didn't need to.

"Do you want to go fishing?"

She looked at him with suspicion. "I thought you said you weren't going to fish with me anymore when I caught more yesterday than you did."

He smiled innocently. "I changed my mind."

She digested his remark. "Why?"

"Because I love to watch you make all those faces when you bait your hook."

"Oh, Hawk, don't make fun of me."

"But darling, I love to make fun of you, and to love you, and to laugh with you. I love to do everything with you." His actions soon followed the example of his words.

With easy familiarity he touched her in all those places that fanned the flame of her desire, and she was soon lost to everything but him. The years had also taught Paige how to love Hawk, and she delighted in causing him to lose his iron control.

"Oh, honey, you feel so good," he whispered some time later. The only peace Hawk had found in the world was there in her arms. He lay there, trying to catch his breath, while she stroked her fingers through his hair.

"Hawk?"

"Hmm."

"Is it definite we're moving to Alaska after our vacation?"

He lifted his head, then dropped it on her breast

once more. "Uh-huh. The letter was waiting for me in El Paso, confirming the date we're due up there. I forgot to show it to you."

"So now we're officially partners. We'll be flying supplies and medical attention to people who are isolated."

"Uh-huh."

"Hawk?"

"Hmm?"

"I have a confession to make."

He raised his head. "You talk too much?" he offered with a straight face.

"That too. But it may have more serious consequences."

He shifted slightly, so that he was lying beside her. "What's wrong?"

"Maybe nothing, but then again..."

"Paige..." he said in a warning voice.

She stared at him uncertainly, then decided to come right out with it. "I forgot to pack my birth-control pills for our vacation." She waited, watching his face apprehensively.

His impassive expression fell into place. *Damn*, Paige thought with vexation. *He can still hide what he's thinking and feeling from me when he wants to!*

"I find it interesting that you've waited almost a week to inform me of that little bit of vital information."

"I know. I'm ashamed. I really am."

"But not enough to have said anything about it before now."

"No, because...well, because I didn't get pregnant the other time we were camping and we didn't take any precautions then either."

He studied her anxious expression for a moment, then grinned. "I take it you're ready to start our family, even if it means in Alaska."

She nodded her head. "Oh, Hawk, it wasn't a conscious decision, but I'll admit that when I discovered I didn't have them, I wasn't sorry."

"You are a sneaky, scheming woman, you know that, don't you?"

She nodded slowly.

"Because if you weren't a sneaky, scheming woman, I would be doing all of this traveling on my own, with no one to keep me warm and keep me company and keep me well taken care of." His tone of voice finally convinced her he was teasing. "So why should I expect the choice of when to become a parent to be left in my hands? Now I know how it feels to be henpecked."

"You henpecked? Hah!" Paige sat up, then discovered her legs were still entwined with Hawk's.

"And I love it," he murmured, rolling over onto his back and pulling her down onto his chest. He pulled her face down to his. "I hope you *are* pregnant," he said in a fierce undertone close to her ear. "In fact, if you aren't, I'm most willing to spend whatever time necessary to see that you do become pregnant as soon as possible."

She sighed, relaxing her head on his chest. "It's that sort of devotion to duty that makes me love you so much," Paige said, closing her eyes with complete contentment.

* * * * *

Desire

MAN OF THE MONTH

July 2000
BACHELOR DOCTOR
#1303 by Barbara Boswell

August 2000
THE RETURN OF ADAMS CADE
#1309 by BJ James
Men of Belle Terre

September 2000
SLOW WALTZ ACROSS TEXAS
#1315 by Peggy Moreland
Texas Grooms

October 2000
THE DAKOTA MAN
#1321 by Joan Hohl

November 2000
HER PERFECT MAN
#1328 by Mary Lynn Baxter

December 2000
IRRESISTIBLE YOU
#1333 by Barbara Boswell

MAN OF THE MONTH

For twenty years Silhouette has been giving you the ultimate in romantic reads. Come join some of your favorite authors in helping us to celebrate our anniversary with the most rugged, sexy and lovable heroes ever!

Available at your favorite retail outlet.

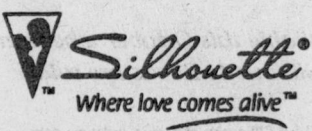

Silhouette®
Where love comes alive™

Visit Silhouette at www.eHarlequin.com

SDMOM00-3

"Who writes the best romance fiction today?
No doubt it's Jayne Ann Krentz."
—Affaire de Coeur

JAYNE ANN KRENTZ

writes compelling stories that keep her fans demanding more!

Be sure to look for these other stories originally written as

STEPHANIE JAMES

NIGHTWALKER
FABULOUS BEAST
NIGHT OF THE MAGICIAN
THE SILVER SNARE
THE DEVIL TO PAY
TO TAME THE HUNTER

Available this October wherever Silhouette Books are sold.

Visit Silhouette at www.eHarlequin.com **PSJAMES**

You're not going to believe this offer!

In October and November 2000, buy any two Harlequin or Silhouette books and save $10.00 off future purchases, or buy any three and save $20.00 off future purchases!

Just fill out this form and attach 2 proofs of purchase (cash register receipts) from October and November 2000 books and Harlequin will send you a coupon booklet worth a total savings of $10.00 off future purchases of Harlequin and Silhouette books in 2001. Send us 3 proofs of purchase and we will send you a coupon booklet worth a total savings of $20.00 off future purchases.

Saving money has never been this easy.

I accept your offer! Please send me a coupon booklet:

Name: ______________________________

Address: ____________________ City: ______________

State/Prov.: ____________________ Zip/Postal Code: __________

Optional Survey!

In a typical month, how many Harlequin or Silhouette books would you buy new at retail stores?

☐ Less than 1 ☐ 1 ☐ 2 ☐ 3 to 4 ☐ 5+

Which of the following statements best describes how you buy Harlequin or Silhouette books? Choose one answer only that best describes you.

☐ I am a regular buyer and reader
☐ I am a regular reader but buy only occasionally
☐ I only buy and read for specific times of the year, e.g. vacations
☐ I subscribe through Reader Service but also buy at retail stores
☐ I mainly borrow and buy only occasionally
☐ I am an occasional buyer and reader

Which of the following statements best describes how you choose the Harlequin and Silhouette series books you buy new at retail stores? By "series," we mean books within a particular line, such as *Harlequin PRESENTS* or *Silhouette SPECIAL EDITION*. Choose one answer only that best describes you.

☐ I only buy books from my favorite series
☐ I generally buy books from my favorite series but also buy books from other series on occasion
☐ I buy some books from my favorite series but also buy from many other series regularly
☐ I buy all types of books depending on my mood and what I find interesting and have no favorite series

Please send this form, along with your cash register receipts as proofs of purchase, to:
In the U.S.: Harlequin Books, P.O. Box 9057, Buffalo, NY 14269
In Canada: Harlequin Books, P.O. Box 622, Fort Erie, Ontario L2A 5X3
(Allow 4-6 weeks for delivery) Offer expires December 31, 2000.

PHQ4002

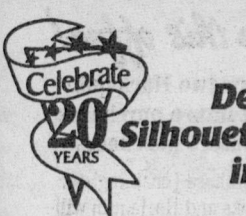

Desire celebrates Silhouette's 20th anniversary in grand style!

Don't miss:

- ***The Dakota Man* by Joan Hohl**
Another unforgettable MAN OF THE MONTH
On sale October 2000

- ***Marriage Prey* by Annette Broadrick**
Her special anniversary title!
On sale November 2000

- ***Slow Fever* by Cait London**
Part of her new miniseries FREEDOM VALLEY
On sale December 2000

Plus:

FORTUNE'S CHILDREN: THE GROOMS
On sale August through December 2000
Exciting new titles from Leanne Banks, Kathryn Jensen, Shawna Delacorte, Caroline Cross and Peggy Moreland

Every woman wants to be loved…
BODY & SOUL
Desire's highly sensuous new promotion features stories from Jennifer Greene, Anne Marie Winston and Dixie Browning!

Available at your favorite retail outlet.

Celebrate 20 YEARS

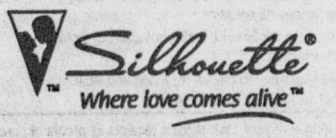

Silhouette®
Where love comes alive™

Visit Silhouette at www.eHarlequin.com

PS20SD

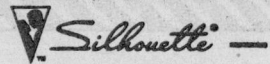

Silhouette® —

where love comes alive—online...

eHARLEQUIN.com

your romantic books

- Shop online! Visit Shop eHarlequin and discover a wide selection of new releases and classic favorites at great discounted prices.
- Read our daily and weekly Internet exclusive serials, and participate in our interactive novel in the reading room.
- Ever dreamed of being a writer? Enter your chapter for a chance to become a featured author in our Writing Round Robin novel.

your romantic life

- Check out our feature articles on dating, flirting and other important romance topics and get your daily love dose with tips on how to keep the romance alive every day.

your community

- Have a Heart-to-Heart with other members about the latest books and meet your favorite authors.
- Discuss your romantic dilemma in the Tales from the Heart message board.

your romantic escapes

- Learn what the stars have in store for you with our daily Passionscopes and weekly Eroticscopes.
- Get the latest scoop on your favorite royals in Royal Romance.

SINTA1

If you enjoyed what you just read, then we've got an offer you can't resist!

Take 2 bestselling novels FREE! Plus get a FREE surprise gift!

Clip this page and mail it to The Best of the Best™

IN U.S.A.	**IN CANADA**
3010 Walden Ave.	P.O. Box 609
P.O. Box 1867	Fort Erie, Ontario
Buffalo, N.Y. 14240-1867	L2A 5X3

YES! Please send me 2 free Best of the Best™ novels and my free surprise gift. Then send me 4 brand-new novels every month, which I will receive before they're available in stores. In the U.S.A., bill me at the bargain price of $4.24 plus 25¢ delivery per book and applicable sales tax, if any*. In Canada, bill me at the bargain price of $4.74 plus 25¢ delivery per book and applicable taxes**. That's the complete price and a savings of over 15% off the cover prices—what a great deal! I understand that accepting the 2 free books and gift places me under no obligation ever to buy any books. I can always return a shipment and cancel at any time. Even if I never buy another book from The Best of the Best™, the 2 free books and gift are mine to keep forever. So why not take us up on our invitation. You'll be glad you did!

185 MEN C229
385 MEN C23A

Name (PLEASE PRINT)

Address Apt.#

City State/Prov. Zip/Postal Code

* Terms and prices subject to change without notice. Sales tax applicable in N.Y.
** Canadian residents will be charged applicable provincial taxes and GST.
All orders subject to approval. Offer limited to one per household.
® are registered trademarks of Harlequin Enterprises Limited.

BOB00 ©1998 Harlequin Enterprises Limited

USA Today Bestselling Author

SHARON SALA

has won readers' hearts with thrilling tales of romantic suspense. Now Silhouette Books is proud to present five passionate stories from this beloved author.

Available in August 2000:

ALWAYS A LADY

A beauty queen whose dreams have been dashed in a tragic twist of fate seeks shelter for her wounded spirit in the arms of a rough-edged cowboy....

Available in September 2000:

GENTLE PERSUASION

A brooding detective risks everything to protect the woman he once let walk away from him....

Available in October 2000:

SARA'S ANGEL

A woman on the run searches desperately for a reclusive Native American secret agent—the only man who can save her from the danger that stalks her!

Available in November 2000:

HONOR'S PROMISE

A struggling waitress discovers she is really a rich heiress—and must enter a powerful new world of wealth and privilege on the arm of a handsome stranger....

Available in December 2000:

KING'S RANSOM

A lone woman returns home to the ranch where she was raised, and discovers danger—as well as the man she once loved with all her heart....

Visit Silhouette at www.eHarlequin.com PSSALA

#1 *New York Times* bestselling author

NORA ROBERTS

introduces the loyal and loving, tempestuous and tantalizing Stanislaski family.

Coming in November 2000:

The Stanislaski Brothers

Mikhail and Alex

Their immigrant roots and warm, supportive home had made Mikhail and Alex Stanislaski both strong and passionate. And their charm makes them irresistible....

In February 2001, watch for

THE STANISLASKI SISTERS: *Natasha and Rachel*

And a brand-new Stanislaski story from Silhouette Special Edition,

CONSIDERING KATE

Available at your favorite retail outlet.

Silhouette®

Where love comes alive™

Visit Silhouette at www.eHarlequin.com PSSTANBR2